PENGUIN BOOKS

Cemetery Girl

David Bell is currently an assistant professor of English at Western Kentucky University in Bowling Green, Kentucky. He received an MA in creative writing from Miami University in Oxford, Ohio, and a PhD in American literature and creative writing from the University of Cincinnati. He has been nominated for the Pushcart Prize twice. He is also the author of *The Hiding Place*.

D1512965

Cemetery Girl

DAVID BELL

PENGUIN BOOKS

PENGUIN BOOKS

UK | USA | Canada | Ireland | Australia
India | New Zealand | South Africa

Penguin Books is part of the Penguin Random House group of companies
whose addresses can be found at global.penguinrandomhouse.com.

First published in the United States of America by New American Library,
a division of Penguin Group (USA) Inc. 2011
Published in Great Britain in Penguin Books 2015

001

Copyright © David J. Bell, 2011

The moral right of the author has been asserted

Set in 12.5/14.75pt Garamond MT Std
Typeset by Jouve (UK), Milton Keynes
Printed in Great Britain by Clays Ltd, St Ives plc

A CIP catalogue record for this book is available from the British Library

ISBN: 978-1-405-93195-3

www.greenpenguin.co.uk

In memory of my dad,
Herbert Henry Bell (1932–2011)

Prologue

Let me tell you something about my daughter.

My daughter disappeared, and there were times I wondered if she was somehow responsible.

Caitlin wasn't like most kids – she wasn't immature or childish. She wasn't ignorant. In fact, she possessed a preternatural understanding of how the world worked, how *humans* worked. And she used that knowledge to deceive me more than once, which is why sometimes – I am ashamed to admit – I questioned her role in what happened.

Caitlin disappeared four years ago – when she was twelve. But the first time I became aware of her ability to deceive she was only six, and the two of us were spending a Saturday together. There were many days like that one with Caitlin, and I always remember them as some of the happiest. Quiet. Simple. As easy and effortless as floating in a pool of water.

On that particular day, Caitlin was playing with a group of kids from the neighborhood. Back then, a number of families with small children lived on our street, and the kids were all about the same age. They ran around together in the yards, playing on swing sets and jumping in leaves. No matter where the kids went, a set of adult eyes watched them. We liked the neighborhood for that reason.

Unfortunately, shortly after we moved in, and not long after Caitlin was born, the city widened the boulevard that sat perpendicular to our street in the hope of accommodating more traffic. This brought more cars to our neighborhood. Every parent on the block felt the same degree of concern, and some talked about moving away. But we wanted to stay, so we made a rule for Caitlin: do not ever cross the street without one of us watching. Not ever.

Anyway, on that Saturday – although it was only later that it would become *that Saturday* – with my wife, Abby, out of the house for the evening, I cooked hamburgers in a skillet, managing, as always, to splatter the stove top with a liberal amount of grease. I also baked frozen premade french fries in the oven; it was exactly the kind of meal a dad makes when he's left in charge of his daughter.

At dinnertime, I stepped into our front yard, expecting to see Caitlin nearby with the other kids, or at the very least I expected to hear their voices. But I didn't. I stood in the late-afternoon shade of the big maple in front of our house, and I looked one way, then the other, hoping to catch sight of Caitlin and her little posse. I was just about to call her name when I finally saw her.

She was standing at the far end of the street, where they had widened the thoroughfare a few years earlier. I knew it was Caitlin, even from that distance, because she had left the house that afternoon wearing a bright pink top, and that electric burst of color stood out against the muted browns and oranges of the fall. I started toward her, lifting my hand and getting ready to wave, when Caitlin made a quick move toward the street.

I'll never know if she saw the car.

It turned onto our street, moving faster than it should

have, and its grille filled my vision, looming behind Caitlin like a ravenous silver mouth.

My heart jumped.

I froze, and for a long moment, time ceased.

Then the driver slammed on his brakes and stopped a couple of feet from my child.

Inches from crushing her.

But Caitlin didn't hesitate. She took one quick glance at the car, but despite its proximity to her body, she kept on walking across the street, into a yard, and around the back of the house, acting as though nothing out of the ordinary had happened. I remained rooted to my spot, as dumb and still as stone, my mouth frozen in the process of forming the shout that never came.

After a brief pause, the car moved forward again. It came down the street slowly, right past me. A couple about my age occupied the front seats; the man was driving. His wife or girlfriend waved her arms frantically, her face angry, no doubt chastising him for his carelessness. And the man held his right hand in a placating gesture as though asking for calm, for time to explain. They didn't even notice me.

What should I have done? Flagged them down and chewed them out? Pulled the man out of the car and pummeled him with my fists? The truth was that Caitlin had darted in front of them, and if she had been hit or run over, I couldn't have blamed them for the accident. My daughter was careless, extremely careless and – more importantly – disobedient. And, yes, I had been careless, too. I had let her go too easily, too thoughtlessly. I deserved my share of the blame as a parent.

I went back inside the house, where the smell of fried hamburger hung thick in the air, and waited for Caitlin to enter the front door.

You might think I grew more and more angry as I waited, that I paced and stewed and contemplated the appropriate punishment for a child who blatantly disobeyed me and almost ended up dead as a result. But I didn't. Abby and I agreed we would never raise our voices to Caitlin, and we would certainly never lay hands on her in anger.

About thirty minutes later, Caitlin came bustling through the front door. She strolled into the kitchen and bounded up onto a chair.

I set the table with paper plates and napkins. Caitlin sniffled and carefully wiped her nose with a tissue. She looked at me, her face cheery and full of expectation.

'Can we eat?' she asked.

'Not yet,' I said. 'Caitlin, honey, I want to ask you something.'

'What?'

I took a deep breath. 'Did you cross the street while you were out? Did you cross the street without permission?'

She didn't flush or blink or swallow. 'No, Dad.'

'Are you sure, honey? Are you sure I didn't see you crossing the street?'

Her voice remained calm. 'I'm sure, Dad. I didn't.'

I held a paper napkin and twined it between my fingers. I released it, letting it drop to the table. Caitlin, for her part, didn't seem to notice. She stared back at me, eyes wide and innocent. They were completely free of guile.

I said, 'Are you telling me you didn't cross the street and almost get hit by a car? I saw you, honey. I was in the yard watching you.'

Her face flushed a little. A tint of red appeared in her cheeks, and while Caitlin wasn't a crier, I thought she might break down after being caught in such a blatant lie. But she didn't crack. She remained composed, a little six-year-old poker player.

'I didn't, Dad,' she said. 'No.'

I didn't lose my temper or send her to her room or give her a patented fatherly lecture on the importance of telling the truth. I didn't do anything except stand up from the table, go to the stove, and make her a plate of food. I brought back the food and put it in front of her. The two of us sat there, as the sunlight slanted through the kitchen window, eating our burgers and fries like an all-American father and daughter. We chewed our food and talked about her friends and what time we thought her mom would be home. We never again spoke about crossing the street or her near fatal run-in with the car.

And I never told Abby about it.

At some point, all parents realize their children have layers that may remain forever unexplored. Maybe I learned it sooner than most. For whatever reason, Caitlin's uncharted depths formed a black hole at the center of my being, and when she disappeared six years later, I thought of that moment often.

PART ONE

Chapter One

Somehow, the dog knew he wasn't coming back.

I picked up Frosty's leash and jiggled it while walking to the door, but he didn't follow. Ordinarily, that sound made him jump and run, his nails clacking against our hardwood floors, but this time he slinked away, head down, eyes averted. I called his name, but he ignored me. So I went to him.

Frosty was a big dog, a yellow Lab, gentle and friendly and smart enough to recognize something unusual in my voice, something that told him this wasn't going to be a normal walk.

I made a grab for his collar. Frosty tucked his head down against his shoulder so I couldn't attach the leash. Up close, I smelled the rich scent of his fur, felt his hot breath against my hand.

'Frosty, no.'

My frustration grew, and I gritted my teeth, felt the molars grind against one another in the back of my mouth. Frosty ducked even more. Without thinking, I brought my free hand up and gave him a little swat on the snout. He surprised me by yelping, and I immediately felt like a jerk, an indefensible son of a bitch. I'd never hit him before, not even during training.

He cowered even more, but when I reached out again,

he lifted his head, allowing me to attach the leash to his collar.

I straightened up, took a deep breath. I felt utterly ineffectual.

'What's going on?'

I turned. Abby stood in the kitchen doorway. Her hair was pulled back in a ponytail and her eyes were wide as she considered me. Even though it was Saturday, she wore a black skirt and striped blouse. Her feet were bare. She used to dress down on weekends, but now she dressed the same every day, as though she were about to rush off to church because she probably was.

'Nothing,' I said.

'I thought I heard the dog squeal.'

'He did. I hit him.'

Her eyes narrowed.

'I'm getting rid of him,' I said. 'Taking him to the pound.'

'Oh,' she said. She raised her hand and placed it against her chest.

'Isn't that what you want? You've been after me to do it for almost a year.'

'Yes, I do want that,' she said. 'I thought you didn't.'

Frosty sat at my feet, head down. Defeated. The refrigerator cycled, made a low humming noise and then shut off. I shrugged.

'You keep saying we have to move on with our lives. Right? Turn the page?'

She nodded, a little uncertain. Over the past couple of years, Abby's face had rarely shown uncertainty. Her involvement with the church made her seem certain all the time, as though nothing were ever in doubt. Except for me. I knew she harbored doubts about me. As a last resort, I was sacrificing the dog. A show of good faith on my part. But I didn't think she'd let me go through with it. I thought once she saw Frosty on his leash, ready to be led out the door and to the pound, she'd stop me.

Tears stood in her eyes, and she took a deep breath.

'I think we do need to do that, Tom.' She sighed. 'With the memorial service coming up, I think we can move on.' She sighed again, and it sounded more like a hiccup, almost a cry. 'I used to love Frosty, but every time I look at him now, I think of Caitlin. And I can't. I don't want to do it anymore.'

'You're sure, Abby? Really? He's such a good dog.'

She shook her head, tapped her foot against the floor. 'I'm sure, Tom.'

'Fine.' I tugged the leash, harder than I needed to, and Frosty jerked to his feet. His paws clattered against the floor, slow and methodical. Dead dog walking. 'Will you be here when I get back?'

'I have a meeting at church.'

I nodded, my hand on the doorknob of the back door.

'It's funny,' I said.

'What is, Tom? What's funny?'

'You say you can't stand to see Frosty because he reminds you of Caitlin. I love having Frosty around for the same reason.'

'Tom. Don't.'

'I won't.' I opened the door and stepped outside, leading the only known witness to my daughter's abduction to his demise.

*

11

I didn't go straight to the pound. My guilt got the better of me – guilt over Frosty's impending doom, guilt over the slap on the nose, guilt over who knows how many things – so I drove a short distance and stopped at the park. When I pulled into the lot, Frosty perked up. His ears rose, his tail thumped against the backseat, and he started panting, filling the enclosed car with his musky dog breath. I found a spot in the shade and climbed out, then opened the back door for Frosty. He jumped down, nose to the ground, sniffing every square inch he came across, stopping only to pee against a small tree. I took that opportunity to attach the leash again and let Frosty lead me through the park.

Since it was a Saturday and late summer, the park was full of activity. At the baseball diamond near the road, a boys team practiced, their aluminum bats pinging with every contact. Joggers and speed walkers traced the running track, and I followed along in their wakes, letting Frosty pull me off to the side every ten feet while he inspected a fallen branch or a curious scent. I tried to tell myself I was there for the dog, that he deserved to spend his final moments on this earth doing the things he loved the most: romping through the park, chasing butterflies, or charging after squirrels. But it was a lie. Caitlin had disappeared from that park four years ago, while walking Frosty, and I found myself returning there, alone, again and again.

The park occupied nearly two hundred acres just two blocks from our house. To the east and south, new subdivisions with streets named after variations on deer – Running Fawn, Leaping Hart – dotted the landscape. The bricks of the houses were new and gleaming, the streets smooth and unstained. As we walked, Frosty continued to huff at the end of his leash, his tail bobbing like a metronome. Forgiveness came quickly to him. My earlier transgression was apparently forgotten, and I didn't have time to think about it anyway. I knew that Frosty was leading me toward the edge of the park where it bordered Oak Ridge, the oldest operational cemetery inside the town's limits and the site of Caitlin's upcoming memorial service and 'burial', which was scheduled for later in the week.

The neat rows of headstones and cleanly cropped grass came into view. I must have slowed, because Frosty turned his head back to look at me, one eyebrow cocked. I hadn't been to the park or the cemetery in the weeks since Abby decided to hold the memorial service and place a headstone in Caitlin's honor. She had been receiving 'counseling' from the pastor of her church – Pastor Chris – and he apparently felt that four years was enough time to grieve for a lost child. He'd managed to convince Abby it was time to move on.

I used to take some measure of comfort from cemeteries, even after Caitlin disappeared. They assured me that even death could be beautiful, that even after we are gone, some memory, some monument to our lives could still exist and endure.

My cell phone buzzed in my pocket.

I jumped a little when the vibration started. Frosty turned his head around, his tongue hanging out of his mouth.

I dug the phone out of my pocket, expecting it to be Abby checking in. I might have ignored it if it had been her, but the caller ID told a different story. It was my brother. Actually, my half brother, Buster. His given name is William, but he acquired his nickname as a child when he managed to break everything he touched.

I answered just before voice mail kicked in.

'What's up, boss?' he asked.

His voice possessed its usual hail-fellow-well-met cheer. Talking to him on the phone was like conversing with a particularly convincing telemarketer, one who could almost make you believe your ship had come in and you'd be a fool to pass up the current offer. Buster maintained this tone even though we hadn't spoken to each other in close to six months. He'd moved an hour away the year before, and our communication, which had always been sporadic, slowed to a drip. We shared a mother – dead five years earlier – but had different fathers. My dad died when I was four. My mom remarried and had Buster.

I told him I was walking the dog.

'Good, good.' He cleared his throat. I heard someone talk in the background on his end of the line. It sounded like a woman. 'I wanted to tell you I'm coming to town this week.'

'What for?'

'For the funeral,' he said. 'Or whatever the hell it is that Abby's doing. I know you didn't invite me, and you might not even want me to come, but Abby called. She said she wanted all of the family there, and since you don't have much – I mean, I'm pretty much it these days. Right?'

'It's not that I didn't want you to come,' I said. Frosty and I stood alongside the cemetery and I could see the area where Caitlin's marker would go up in a few days. 'I just thought you wouldn't want to come because —'

'Because it's so fucked-up.'

I hesitated. 'Yeah, because of that.'

'What's she going to do, bury an empty coffin? How do you have a funeral for someone who might not be dead?'

'We didn't buy a coffin.'

'But you bought a plot and a headstone?'

Frosty tugged on the leash, indicating he wanted to move on.

'Yeah,' I said.

'Jesus. Is this because of that wackadoodle church she belongs to? What's it called?'

I regretted ever answering the phone. 'Christ's Community Church.'

'That's original,' he said. 'Aren't they all Christ's churches? Remember when people belonged to actual churches? You know, Baptists, Methodists, Presbyterians. I hate hearing about these anything-goes religions, you know? Just put up a warehouse and a coffee bar and let them come in and feel good about themselves.'

'I didn't know you were so easily offended.'

'Stupidity pisses me off. That herd mentality. How much is it costing you to buy this cenotaph and plot? A couple thousand bucks?'

Frosty pulled against the leash again, and I tugged back, trying to keep him still.

'Buy what?' I asked.

'A cenotaph. That's what they call it when you put up a marker and there's no body under it. A cenotaph. You're not the only one who knows the big words, professor.'

'Look, I have to go. The dog's done his business.'

'I'll call you when I get to town. Okay?'

'Sure. But don't feel obligated —'

'I do feel obligated,' he said. His voice dripped with sincerity, and I wanted to believe him. I really did. 'For you, anything. Just let me know. I'll be by your side.'

Frosty and I faced the choice of going around the track again, something we almost never did, or getting in the car and completing my mission. Frosty pulled a little in the direction of the car, but I pulled harder, and we entered the cemetery together.

I knew they didn't want pets in there, digging up flowers and shitting and pissing on the graves. But Frosty's tank was pretty well emptied, and I preferred to face the prospect of an accident in the cemetery over delivering him to the pound.

We walked down the road that cut through the center of the cemetery, then turned right and headed toward the back. I recognized the names on the larger headstones, the same names that adorned the buildings and parks throughout town. Potter. Hardcastle. Greenwood. Cooper. They didn't skimp on death, these founding families and innovative educators, these city councilmen and spiritual leaders. Not only did they have elaborate headstones, beautifully engraved and clean as the day they were cut, but they paid for life-sized guardians to watch over the graves. Vigilant Virgin Marys and winged angels, Christ with his eyes cast to heaven as though begging for intercession. While the stone we'd picked out for Caitlin didn't approach those lofty heights, it wasn't cheap either. Buster was right – we'd spent too much money.

I read the signs posted at knee level and found section B; then I worked my way up until I came to the number. Despite the presence of the sleeping and buried dead, it was a beautiful day. The temperature climbed toward eighty, and only a few high, puffy clouds disrupted the blue of the sky. In the distance, somewhere, a lawn mower engine churned, but I couldn't see where it was, and when I looked around the cemetery, I found myself alone. The walkers and joggers kept up their work in the park, so I just listened to Frosty's panting breath and rattling collar.

'It's just a little detour, boy.'

Most of the cemetery was full, the stones nestled close together so that it didn't appear there was any room left for new burials. I kept my eyes peeled for a small open place, a last remaining plot that we purchased only to – hopefully – never fill. My eyes wandered over husbands buried with their wives, the headstones a monument to eternal love and union. I saw children buried near their parents. Veterans of wars, their stones decorated with small, fluttering flags. And then I thought I saw Caitlin's name.

It was a brief glimpse, something caught out of the corner of my eye, and I just as quickly dismissed it, assuming that my eyes and mind, in their haste to find a closer connection to my daughter, simply imagined her name. But as I came closer, I saw it again, chiseled into a large rectangular headstone. It was really there. CAITLIN ANN STUART. DAUGHTER. FRIEND. ANGEL. 1992–2004.

The stone didn't belong there.

Abby had told me it wouldn't be placed until days after the service, that when we stood at the grave on Wednesday for the memorial, we'd just be facing a small area of green grass. No earth would be churned, no stone in place. And I took comfort in that scenario because it seemed less permanent somehow, less final than what Abby had intended. I convinced myself that the ceremony would bear no real relation to my daughter, that we were there remembering some other kid or maybe even some person I never knew. A stranger, the faceless, nameless victim of a distant tragedy.

I stared at the slab. Frosty walked away, pulling the leash taut, and sniffed at a nearby stone while a chorus of cicadas rose and fell in the trees above, their chittering eventually winding down like a worn-out clock. I often tried to imagine what had happened to Caitlin. Try as I might, a coherent, sensible narrative concerning the events that had taken place just yards from where I stood in the cemetery never formed in my mind. But I did hear the soundtrack in my head. Often.

I lay in my bed at night, the lights from passing cars dancing on the ceiling and walls, and I heard Caitlin's screams, the sound of her voice rising in terror and growing hoarse. Did she cry? Was her face soaked with tears and snot? Did she suffer? How long did she call for me?

I pounded the mattress in frustration, buried my face in the pillows until it felt like my head would explode.

I knew the statistics. After forty-eight hours, the odds of a child being found alive were next to none. But I managed to ignore the numbers and pretend they didn't apply to me. Not then. Not ever. I still stopped at the front door every night, flipped on the porch light, and made sure the spare key – the one Caitlin occasionally used to let herself in after school – lay under the same flowerpot, right where she could find it.

But it was difficult to argue with a headstone.

Frosty came back and nudged at my calf with his snout. I could tell he was growing impatient and wanted to move on. He didn't like to stand still when there were sticks to fetch and trees to mark. I shooed him away, lost in my own thoughts. I resented Abby for the ease with which she chose to move on, to accept that our lives would go forward without any hope of seeing our daughter again. I'd crusaded on behalf of my daughter's memory, and for what? To find out that life progressed without me as well as Caitlin?

'Frosty. Come here.'

He wandered back, happy, tail wagging. I crouched in the grass and placed my hands on either side of his head. He opened his eyes wide but didn't resist, perhaps remembering the swat he'd received earlier. I felt his hot, stinking breath in my face, saw the stains on his long teeth. I asked the dog a question I had asked him several times before, ever since that day he came home from the park trailing his leash with Caitlin nowhere in sight.

'Frosty? What did you see that day? What happened?'

He stared back at me, his panting increasing. He didn't like the way I was holding him, and he squirmed.

'What did you see?'

He started to slip away, so I pulled him back. He shook

his head as though trying to knock the feeling of my hands off his body. I stood up.

'Fuck you,' I said. 'Fuck you for not being able to talk.'

I looked at the headstone once more, letting the image of my daughter's name and possible – *likely* – date of death burn into my brain, before giving the leash another tug.

'Come on, Frosty,' I said. 'We've got someplace to go.'

Chapter Two

Buster came to the memorial service late.

I'd assumed he wasn't coming at all. He liked to promise to do something – come hell or high water – and then not follow through. His appearance surprised me, but not his tardiness.

As I stood in the back of the church, feeling constrained by my coat and tie, a whirl of emotions stewed within me. Every person who passed by, every hand I shook or hug I received, brought me closer to tears and bitterness. I associated a memory, a fleeting glimpse of Caitlin, in so many of the faces I saw. A girl who'd gone to school with Caitlin, for example, looked grown-up and every one of her sixteen years. Did Caitlin reach that age somewhere in the world away from us? Did she ever become a young woman? When I saw a former neighbor, an elderly woman who used to babysit for us when Caitlin was a child, I wondered: Why was she allowed to live, approaching eighty, while Caitlin might be dead?

My throat felt full of cotton, and I choked back against the crying and the anger until my jaw ached. I did this not because I didn't feel the tears or anger were heartfelt, but because I feared that giving in to them would validate the entire ceremony, making real what I still refused to accept.

By the time Buster came in – late and apologizing – my feelings toward him shifted a little, and I welcomed the distraction his appearance provided. Most everyone else was seated, and all that remained was for us – the funeral party – to walk down the aisle.

'I'm sorry,' Buster said. 'My car. And then the traffic . . .'

To his credit, he wore a suit. It looked like he'd borrowed it from a midget, but still, it was a suit. The pant legs rode up above the tops of his shoes, revealing white socks, and I doubt he could have buttoned the jacket. He wore a pair of cheap sunglasses that hung loose on his face and kept sliding down the bridge of his nose. He pushed them up with the knuckle of his right index finger every few seconds.

No one said anything for a long moment. We – Abby, Buster, Pastor Chris, and I – stood in an awkward little circle, waiting for someone to speak.

Finally, Pastor Chris smiled and said, 'We're glad you're here.'

Abby remembered her manners before I did. 'This is Tom's stepbrother —'

'*Half* brother,' Buster said.

'Half brother, William,' Abby said.

Buster shook hands with Pastor Chris, then leaned in and gave Abby an awkward peck on the cheek. She averted her eyes like a child receiving an inoculation. She'd never liked Buster, which is why I was so surprised that she'd gone to the trouble of inviting him. She'd meant it as a gesture of goodwill, something she was willing to sacrifice for me, I'm sure. So I clung to whatever faint hope remained for us – between Frosty's departure and the memorial service, she and I might be able to dig our way back toward common ground. I never imagined Caitlin's homecoming without imagining the three of us reuniting as a family. I couldn't think of it any other way, even though I knew there had been cracks in our marriage even before Caitlin disappeared.

'Quite a church,' Buster said.

And it was. A former warehouse purchased by Christ's Church eight years earlier and converted. It sat two thousand people and included a workout center and coffee bar in the back. Plans were in the works to buy a large video projection system so that Pastor Chris could be seen up close and personal by everyone. More than once, Abby mentioned donating money toward that cause.

'We should begin,' Pastor Chris said, looking at his watch and then the settling crowd. 'Is that okay with all of you?'

Abby nodded silently, and so did I. She reached out and took my hand. The gesture surprised me. Her hand felt unfamiliar in mine, the hand of a stranger, but the good kind of strangeness that comes when two people have just met and are beginning to get to know each other. My heart sped up a little; I squeezed her hand in mine and she squeezed back. Like two scared children, we followed Pastor Chris down the aisle to the front of the church with Buster trailing behind.

Pastor Chris was like a celebrity at the altar. His straight white teeth gleamed, and despite his slightly thinning, slightly graying hair, he still looked youthful and vibrant. At forty-five, a couple of years older than Abby and me, he ran obsessively, even competed in the occasional marathon, and his body was trim and sleek under his perfectly fitted suit. He believed that God rewarded those who maintained their bodies and that exercise kept the spirit sharp, so it was no surprise that the addition of the workout facility to the church complex had been his idea.

Buster and I grew up Catholic, trundled off to Mass every Sunday morning by my overbearing stepfather, who believed that to miss one Sunday was a sin of the worst kind. While I no longer practiced or believed much of anything, I found it difficult to attend a new church, especially one that seemed so different from the religion I knew. Christ's Community Church felt too touchy-feely, too positive for me. Pastor Chris offered nothing but encouragement to his congregation, as well as the sense that heaven could be attained through the application of a series of steps found in a self-help book. I expected my spiritual leaders to be removed and slightly dogmatic, wrapped in their colorful vestments and staring down at me, and I didn't respond well when one of them wanted to be my friend. I also couldn't fully understand the nature of Abby's relationship with Pastor Chris. I understood the spiritual side of it – Abby was looking for guidance and community and found it in the church. But in recent months she'd grown even closer to Pastor Chris, going out to lunch with him on weekdays and referring to him as her 'best friend'. Never in the eighteen years of our marriage had I suspected Abby of infidelity, but the 'friendship' with Pastor Chris – as well as the perilous state of our own marriage – made me wonder.

Abby and I continued to hold hands through the beginning of the service as Pastor Chris led the congregation through a series of prayers and readings from scripture, including the one in which Jesus raises Lazarus from the dead. Buster sat to my right, holding his sunglasses in his left hand and bouncing them against his thigh. He seemed older. The crow's-feet at the corners of his eyes looked more permanent, the gray in his hair more visible. But he appeared to be paying attention, his eyes focused on the altar, and my initial instinct turned out to be wrong: I was glad to have him there. My brother. My closest blood relation.

Pastor Chris started his sermon – which I still thought of as a homily – by thanking all the friends and community members in attendance. But they were Abby's friends and people from the church. Her family was a small one. Her father had died when Caitlin was little, and her mother had retired to Florida. She and Abby had not been close over the years, and while Abby had extended an invitation to the service, her mother had apparently chosen not to come. For my part, I didn't invite any of my colleagues from the university to attend. It was a sabbatical year for me, one I'd reluctantly decided to take in an effort to complete another book, and I knew my colleagues would not mix well with the evangelical crowd.

Pastor Chris continued, his voice a little high and reedy, almost like an adolescent's on the brink of changing. 'While we're here as the result of a tragedy, the loss of a young life, we are also here to support one another as well as to take comfort from Christ's eternal pledge to us. And what is that pledge? The pledge is that those who die having been redeemed by Christ's eternal love shall not die, but rather have eternal life in Christ's glory.'

Voices through the church muttered 'Amen', including

Abby's. I studied her face in profile. Somewhere in there, I told myself, a vestige of the person I fell in love with nearly twenty years ago still remained. It must. But it was increasingly difficult for me to find it, to see her, and as I watched her mutter 'Amens' under her breath and stare at Pastor Chris like he himself incarnated the Second Coming, I wondered if what I knew of her, or thought I knew of her, was gone forever, just like Caitlin.

'I was blessed to speak with Tom and Abby last night.' At the sound of my name, I turned back to Pastor Chris. It took me a moment to process his words. He said he'd spoken to us – to *me* the night before – but he hadn't. I hadn't seen the man. 'And while they are understandably devastated by the loss of their dear Caitlin, they both told me, Tom as well as Abby, that they took comfort from the fact that Caitlin is now in heaven, reunited with Christ and basking in his divine love.'

I looked at Abby again, but she still stared forward, muttering her 'Amens'. Buster leaned in to me on the other side. His breath smelled like cough drops.

'You were really shoveling it last night.'

'I didn't say that,' I whispered.

I removed my hand from Abby's. She didn't seem to notice.

After the last prayer and the final song, we filed out. Abby, Buster, and I went first with Pastor Chris; then we stood around at the back of the church while people headed to their cars. Abby and I stood side by side, still not touching.

'I'm going to ride with Buster,' I said.

'You don't want to ride with us?' Abby asked.

'Buster doesn't know his way.'

'It's a procession,' she said. 'He can ride with us.'

'I need to talk to him,' I said, breaking off eye contact with her. 'It's fine.'

'But you're going to the cemetery, right, Tom? You'll be there?'

I didn't answer. I put my hand on Buster's arm and guided him toward the parking lot.

We stopped in Shaggy's, a bar near campus. Students occupied most of the tables. Guys were trying hard to impress the girls, and the girls sat back, absorbing the boys' attentions, encouraging more. We ordered sandwiches and then Buster asked for a pitcher of beer. When the waitress left, I asked him if he was drinking again.

'Just beer,' he said as nonchalantly as a man waiting for a bus. He'd been in rehab twice and then was arrested for drinking and driving. He'd also been arrested for indecent exposure, a fact that had caught the attention of the detectives investigating Caitlin's disappearance. Buster claimed he'd been drunk and lost his clothes, but at some point he'd run past a group of children in a park and was initially charged with the more serious crime of child enticement and lewd and lascivious behavior. He'd spent two days in jail and served a thousand hours of community service. 'You sure you don't want to go to the boneyard? We can still make it.'

I shook my head. 'Forget it.'

'Abby's going to be pissed.'

I shrugged. He was right, of course. But when I heard Pastor Chris ascribing beliefs to me, actual words even, that clearly weren't mine, something gave way. I tried to go along, to appease, but I'd reached my limit. Someone – maybe Pastor Chris, maybe Abby – decided to lie, to misrepresent my beliefs in public. I couldn't stand being part of it, being lumped in with the flock of blind sheep.

The beer came and Buster poured it into the disposable plastic cups they provided. One of the drawbacks of living in a college town – restaurants and bars don't invest in glassware. I took a sip and it felt good. And then another. That was all it took to start a buzz at the base of my skull.

My phone buzzed in my pocket. A text.

Need to see you. Four p.m.

'What's that about?' Buster asked. 'Abby?'

'No. Liann Stipes.'

'Who?'

'She's a lawyer here in town. She handles the everyday stuff – mortgages, wills. Small-time criminal cases.'

'What does she want with you?' Buster asked. 'You making a will?'

'Her daughter was murdered about ten years ago. She was just sixteen. They caught the guy and convicted him.'

'They fry him?' Buster asked.

'Life in prison. No parole. Are you sure you didn't meet Liann right after Caitlin disappeared? She was at our house a lot.'

'I wasn't around much then,' he said.

I studied his face for a moment. He took a long drink of his beer and ignored my interest. 'Anyway,' I said, 'she really tried to help us out. She's become something of a crusader and an advocate on behalf of missing or murdered children and their families. She likes to see that the

28

bad guys get punished. She doesn't handle the prosecutions, of course, but she advises the families, sort of an informal legal counselor. That's what she's been doing for us. She tries her best to help victims' families sort through all the mess of their cases. Dealing with the cops, dealing with the media. She tries to keep our spirits up. And she believes in justice.'

'A lawyer.' Buster made a gagging face.

'She's not really a lawyer to me. She's more of a friend. Like I said, an advocate.'

He kept making the face, so I ignored him. I wrote back and asked where she wanted to meet.

The Fantasy Club.

'Hmm.' I stared at the screen. 'She wants to meet me in a strip joint.'

'Interesting place to meet a missing-children's advocate.'

'Who knows? She meets a lot of interesting people in these cases. She gets to know the victims and their families pretty well. She seems to know everything and everybody. I just wish I knew what she wanted to tell me. She can be so fucking secretive sometimes, like she's in the CIA. Jesus.'

'Drink up. It'll help pass the time.' Buster drained half his cup on the first try, then polished off the rest and poured more. He nodded, encouraging me. 'Tell me why we're bailing on the graveside service.'

'I didn't say any of that stuff at the church, that stuff about heaven. That idiot, Pastor Chris, made it up. Or Abby did. But it's not just the stuff from church,' I said.

'Yeah?'

The beer tasted good. Real good. I felt myself reaching

my limit. My stepfather — Buster's father — drank. He drank and he raged at us and he usually passed out on the couch. I never acquired the habit, but Buster did.

'I knew Abby was going to buy the headstone,' I said. 'Hell, I knew how much it cost. But she promised me it wouldn't be up yet. She promised me. And it was there the other day when I went to the cemetery, the day I talked to you on the phone while I was walking Frosty.' Just saying his name caused a spasm of guilt in my chest. Where was Frosty? In an abusive home? Sitting in his own filth, waiting for the gas chamber? 'The headstone has her name on it. My little girl. And it says she died four years ago. It's a big fucking thing, too. You can't miss it. Can you believe that?'

'Which part?'

'Any of it.'

Someone put coins in the jukebox, and a country song came on too loud. The steel guitar whined and someone else shouted in protest. The bartender bent down behind the bar and, mercifully, the volume dropped.

Buster put down his cup and steepled his fingers in front of his face. He looked thoughtful, sincere. 'Have you ever thought —? And I'm only saying this because I do care about you. I really do. I mean, I know I can be a royal screwup. I know Abby can't stand me and all that. Hell, maybe you can't stand me either. I wouldn't blame you.'

'I can stand you. Most of the time.'

He smiled. 'Thanks.'

'And I think I know where you're going with this . . .'

'You know the odds,' Buster said. 'But it's probably true.

There was never a ransom demand. She probably did die that day. There's been no evidence to the contrary.'

I closed my eyes. Even in the noisy bar, I could imagine the screams. Caitlin's voice. High. Cracking. Stretched to its limit. *Daddy!*

'I don't like to think we lost her that day,' I said.

'That's fine. I understand. What are the cops saying?' He reached behind him, to an empty table, and grabbed a bowl of peanuts.

'Very little. When we do hear from them, it's the same stuff. They have one detective on it. The feds have pulled out. They call it an active case, but what does that mean? I know they have other things. Newer cases.'

'They still think she ran away?'

'It makes it easier on them, right? If she ran away, there's no crime. She'd be sixteen now . . .' I paused.

'We can drop it if you want,' Buster said.

I nodded.

Our food came. Buster salted his fries and started eating. I stared at my plate, my appetite uncertain.

'I stopped by your house on the way to that crazy church,' he said. 'I thought I might catch you. I knocked and knocked, but nothing.'

'We were at the church already.'

'I know that. But Frosty didn't bark.'

I shook my head. 'He's gone.'

'But you were just walking him the other day. He died? What happened?'

I shrugged. 'I took him to the shelter. He's an older dog, set in his ways. They said there's a chance someone will adopt him, but if not, well, they euthanize the dogs eventually.'

'Did he get sick?'

I shook my head.

Recognition spread across his face. 'Abby wanted him gone?'

I didn't respond. I picked up a french fry and popped it in my mouth.

'And you did it? You took him to the pound?'

'I did it for Abby. And for me. He was Caitlin's dog. He was a reminder of what we lost. If it helps us to turn the page . . .'

'Jesus. That's cold.'

'The dog who knew too much. Except how to tell us what he knew.' I emptied my cup and poured more beer for Buster and myself.

'How are things with you and Abby?'

I started eating my lukewarm food. 'The same.'

'That good?'

'We're fine.'

'Let me ask you something, and if I'm crossing a line here, just let me know.'

I laughed. 'Would that stop you?'

'No.' He signaled the waitress for another pitcher. 'But I'm just wondering . . . do you two still do it? I mean, do you sleep in the same bed? Do you fuck?'

The pitcher came. 'Put that on my brother's tab,' I said.

'You can put it all on my tab. My treat.' He winked at me. 'I guess I owe you a few.' He didn't refill his cup. 'Well?'

'I know you're trying to provoke me now. It always ends up this way with you.'

'You don't fuck? Ever?' He shook his head. 'I don't know how anyone could live that way. I just have to get something, you know? I can't live without it.' He kept shaking his head. 'See, I'm really just trying to find out why you stay married to someone who you don't have anything going on with. She's at that freaky church; you're a college professor. She wants to do this whole funeral thing. You don't. She thinks Caitlin's dead . . .'

'She hasn't worked for a long time. She gave up teaching when Caitlin was born.'

'So?'

'Our lives are intertwined. It's not as easy as you make it sound.'

'Isn't it?' He pushed away his plate and drank more. He let out a hissing burp. 'I think it is easy. Easy for me to see anyway. The dog's gone. The headstone's been laid. People are moving on. Remember when Dad died? My dad? Remember how you cried at the funeral?'

'I didn't cry.'

'You did.'

'Not for him, I didn't.'

Buster sighed. 'He raised you.'

'If you want to call it that.'

Buster leaned back. He brought his hand up and scratched his jaw. I could tell he was angry. Whenever we talked about my stepfather, one or both of us ended up full of anger. But Buster managed to swallow his this time. When he spoke again, his voice was even.

'Here's my point – it wasn't long after the old man died that you went off to grad school. You started a new life, a new career. You met Abby. You had a baby. It was like his

33

death liberated you in a way. You know, they say we don't fully become ourselves until our parents die. Maybe that's why I'm something of a late bloomer.' He spoke the last sentence without a trace of irony. 'Maybe you have the chance for a new life here. Now. If you just . . . accept things . . .'

I stared at him across our dirty, cluttered table. I thought about walking out – hell, I thought about punching him. But instead, I just signaled for the waitress, who brought the check.

'Give it to him,' I said. 'We're finished here.'

Chapter Three

'Do you mind making a stop?'

'Where?' Buster asked.

When Buster saw the animal shelter, he sighed. 'You're kidding, right? He's dead.'

'Just give me a minute.'

In the lobby, I smelled the accumulated odors of hundreds of caged animals. Their fur, their waste, their food. Their fear and desperation. The door at the back, the one that led to the cages, muffled the sounds, but I could still hear a faint chorus of barks and yelps. I asked the woman working at the counter about Frosty, and she seemed immediately confused by my request.

'He's your dog?' she asked.

'Yes.'

'And he was lost?'

'No, I brought him here. He's a yellow Lab. Frosty's his name. I wanted to get rid of him, but now I want him back.'

She pursed her lips like the nuns from my grade school.

'Well, I'll see,' she said. 'But this doesn't happen often.' She stopped at the door to the cages and looked back at me. 'You'll have to pay the adoption donation even if he is your dog.'

I nodded my assent. While she was gone, I looked around the lobby. The faces of dogs and cats in need of homes stared back at me from one bulletin board, and next to that another one held flyers advertising missing pets. We didn't make a new flyer for Caitlin this year. The police created an age progression image, one showing Caitlin at age fifteen, and it was so warped and distorted – the eyes too large, the hair artificial – I couldn't bear to look at it. I thought it belonged in a mortician's textbook, an example of what not to do to preserve the image of a loved one. But the police distributed it anyway, and from time to time I came across a faded, wrinkling copy in the corner of a coffee shop or stuck to a community bulletin board downtown.

The woman reappeared so quickly I knew she bore bad news.

'He's gone,' she said matter-of-factly, as though talking about a housefly.

'I thought you kept them for a week —'

'He's been adopted,' she said. 'Someone got him yesterday.'

'Okay, can you just tell me who it is? I need him back.'

She shook her head, the lips pursed again. 'We can't do that, sir.'

'But he's my dog.'

'You brought him in here. You gave him away.'

'It was a mistake. A misunderstanding.' I leaned against the counter, letting it support most of my weight. I felt drained by the day. And guilty. I'd hoped having Frosty back would lift me.

'We can't give out that information. It's private.'

'I know, but —'

'We can't just have people coming in here and getting personal information about our clients.'

'Okay, okay. I get it.'

'We have plenty of other dogs here,' she said. 'Good dogs.' She seemed suddenly cheery and upbeat. 'Is this for a family? Are you looking for a dog for your children?'

'No, just for me, I guess. And I only wanted that dog.' There was nothing more to say, so I turned and left.

When I climbed back into the car, Buster didn't say anything. He dropped it into gear and drove me home, the voice of the talk radio host our only companion. Buster stopped at the curb in front of the house, but neither one of us got out.

'Thanks for coming today,' I said. 'I'm glad you made it.' I extended my hand, which he shook.

'That's what brothers do for each other,' he said.

'I didn't even ask what you're doing these days.'

He shrugged. 'A cell phone company. Sales. It pays the bills. Look, I know why you're asking about that —'

'No —'

'I plan on paying you back. All of it, all five thousand.'

'I don't care.'

'Abby?'

I paused. 'She cares about it. But she's also given up on you. She tells me she's written off that money, like it was a business expense.'

He started tapping his right hand against the rim of the steering wheel. 'The price of being related to me.'

'Something like that.'

'How about you? What are you doing with your time off? Writing a book? Who's it about this time? Melville? Moby Dick? Dicky Moe?'

'Hawthorne. His short fiction. You know, it sounded

like there was a woman with you when I talked to you on the phone the other day. Are you dating someone?'

'Why the sudden interest?'

'I just don't want us to be pissed at each other. I know the stuff with your dad is tough. For both of us maybe, but certainly for me. I still dream about him, about him coming into our room at night, drunk and angry. The way he'd come after us, swinging at us. I see his figure there in the dark. Sort of a hulking presence. I can't forget it.'

'We're not going to solve all this sitting here in the car.'

'Do you remember the same things?' I asked. 'At least tell me that.'

He didn't hesitate. 'No, Tom. I don't remember it that way at all. Sorry.'

'We used to huddle together in the dark,' I said. 'Hell, you used to try to protect me. You'd lay on top of me and keep me safe. Are you going to tell me you don't remember? You're really going to stick to that? Really?'

'I'm not sticking to anything,' he said. 'It's a fact.' He looked at the console clock. 'I have to get back home, okay?' I opened the door, and before I was out he added, 'But, Young Goodman Tom, if you do decide to change your life – really change your life – give me a call. You have my number.'

Chapter Four

In the weeks and months after Caitlin disappeared, rumors had started to spread. New Cambridge, Ohio, is a small college town of about fifty thousand people, mostly middle class, mostly quiet and pleasant. It was primarily populated by professors and their families and students who came and went based on the academic calendar. Bad things didn't happen in New Cambridge, at least not bad things that people knew or talked about.

But even if friends tried to insulate us from the gossip, we still heard what people said: Caitlin was pregnant, and we'd sent her away. Caitlin met a lover over the Internet and ran off with him. Caitlin fell victim to an online predator who'd kidnapped her. Or Caitlin simply ran away. Tired of the boring life in a small college town, she'd taken matters into her own hands and run off for greener pastures. California or New York. Seattle or Miami.

The police, of course, interviewed all of our friends and family, and they talked to a handful of my students and examined police records, but they found nothing. In those first days and weeks after Caitlin didn't come home from her walk, the police treated us with the due deference owed to the parents of a missing and possibly murdered child. They spoke to us in soothing tones, they offered us platitudinal encouragement – which actually felt wonderful to hear – and they answered our calls and questions promptly. But it didn't take long for cracks to appear.

It began with Buster and his indecent exposure rap. He lived an hour away in Columbus and wasn't in New Cambridge the day Caitlin disappeared – as far as we knew – but he couldn't provide a rock-solid alibi. He said he was at his house. An ex-girlfriend claimed to have spoken to him on his cell phone an hour before the disappearance, but she didn't know where he was while they talked. For a while, Buster became something of a suspect, even though the police refused to call him that to either Abby or me. He endured some heated questioning, and some not so subtle threats in the interview room. While he never requested a lawyer or offered anything close to a confession, and while no evidence linked him to the commission of a crime, word leaked to the newspaper that Caitlin's uncle – unnamed – was a *person of interest* in the case.

I never offered a particularly strong defense of my brother. Not to Abby and not to the police. I did tell them I didn't believe he would harm Caitlin. In fact, he was a surprisingly doting uncle to Caitlin, one who often sent birthday gifts and, on the rare occasions when he visited us, went out of his way to talk to Caitlin as though she were more adult than child.

'But that's just it, Tom,' Abby said to me on one of the days Buster was going a few rounds with the cops. 'He paid so much attention to Caitlin. Didn't it seem out of character to you?'

It did. It really did. And I allowed the suspicions of the police and Abby's doubts to become my own to such an extent that they never fully went away, even when the police finished with him and let him go. I still found myself returning to those questions again and again: Where was he that day? Why did he seem to care about Caitlin so much? Was his indecent exposure charge really just a drunken misunderstanding?

But if my doubts about Buster remained alive, even in the back of my mind, the police – absent any conclusive proof of his involvement – moved on to other things. They examined every scrap of mail, every phone call, every bill and financial statement we possessed, and none of it led anywhere – except for the computer we'd purchased for Caitlin, the one she used in her room. There were no unusual e-mails, no evidence that she made contact with a man who might have lured her away or taken her. But Caitlin had been searching the Web the day she disappeared, and in the hours before she walked out the door with Frosty, she'd visited Web sites for Seattle, horses, Amtrak, the U. S. presidency. I didn't see anything nefarious or unusual in this list. A curious child surfed the Internet, following her train of thought wherever it might go. I do the same thing every day.

But the police jumped on two items from the list – Seattle and Amtrak – and decided there was a decent chance that Caitlin had run away. They questioned us about it, placing special emphasis on whether or not there were difficulties in the home. They asked her friends, her teachers, our neighbors, and many of them said that, while they didn't believe anything was wrong, they did think Caitlin was something of a distant child, one who kept to herself, one who really didn't allow others to know what she was thinking. All true, and all things Abby and I had told the police from the very beginning. We didn't always know what Caitlin was thinking, but what parents of a twelve-year-old do?

From that point on, a slight rift grew between the police and us. They slowly drew down their resources – the SBI removed their consulting agent from the case, the New Cambridge PD cut back to one detective – and we sensed, both Abby and I, that the authorities were no longer taking us seriously, that we were being moved to the back burner as long as no new information came forward to propel the case along.

Did I really believe that Caitlin had run away? I like to tell myself I never did. But I have to admit there were nights – lying in bed, staring at the ceiling – when the results of those Internet searches cycled through my brain like trains themselves. And I had to ask myself, there in the dark: What was Caitlin really thinking or doing? Did anybody – even me – really know?

Chapter Five

The Fantasy Club was removed from all the respectable businesses, a small, sturdily built structure with a gravel parking lot and a blinking sign that promised adult entertainment – couples welcome.

The lot was almost empty when I parked, my tires crunching over the gravel and kicking up a puff of white dust. The lack of windows made the place look a little like a fortress, a distant entertainment outpost. When I walked in, my eyes struggled to adjust to the gloom; no one tended the door or asked me to pay a cover charge. The stage was empty, the music off. The lone bartender and his only customer stood watch over a newspaper and a TV playing a daytime talk show. The bartender managed to pry his eyes away from the paper.

'Help you?'

My head was still buzzing a little from the beer I'd drunk with Buster, so I ordered a club soda. The corner of the bartender's mouth curled a little.

'You want a lime with that? I'm all out of limes.'

'No lime.'

He sprayed the soda into a plastic cup and placed it on the bar. 'We're between shows,' he said, 'so I won't charge you for the drink.'

'That's fine.' I dug around in my pocket and found

a dollar bill, which I placed on the counter as a tip and a peace offering.

The bartender raised his eyebrows but didn't pick it up. 'Thanks,' he said.

I took a seat at the end of the bar. I drummed my fingers on the bar top and swallowed the club soda in less than a minute. I jabbed at the ice with my little red cocktail straw, tried to focus on the argument raging on the TV, then asked for a refill. The bartender provided it without looking up from his paper.

'Tonight we're having a lingerie show,' he said. 'You ought to stick around.'

'I have to face my wife at some point today.'

The bartender looked up and winked at me. 'Hell, bring her. Didn't you see the sign? Couples welcome.'

'You haven't met my wife.'

The bartender and his customer both laughed at my joke, and for a moment I entered their masculine circle.

'Can I ask you guys a question?' I asked.

Their laughter broke off. The sound of the TV filled the space, the tinny voice of an acne-faced kid who stood accused of fathering two children by two different high school girls. He was protesting to the host, his voice rising like a siren.

I reached into my wallet and brought out the picture of Caitlin I always carried with me. Her last school portrait, the one the police circulated to the media in the wake of her disappearance. I held it up in the space between me and the two men. I tried to make my voice casual.

'Have you ever seen this girl in here?' I asked.

The customer, an older man with a deeply lined, sagging

face, looked away, deferring responsibility for dealing with me to the bartender.

'You a cop?' he asked.

'No.'

'Private investigator?'

'I'm her father.'

A hint of sympathy flickered across the bartender's eyes. He leaned in a couple of inches and looked at the photo, his brow furrowing.

'Yeah, I've seen her,' he said. He flipped the newspaper closed and tapped his index finger against the front page. It was the *New Cambridge Herald*. 'Right here.' It wasn't above-the-fold news, but it had made the front near the bottom, tucked next to the weather forecast. A picture of Caitlin along with the story – the same photo I held in my hand. 'But I haven't seen her in here. We don't allow underage kids in. No, sir.'

'Did you really take a look at the picture?' I asked.

He sighed a little, then looked again. He studied the picture longer than before, even going so far as to tilt his head back and to the side to get a better angle.

'No,' he said. 'She's just a little girl. I've never seen her.'

'She'd be sixteen now.'

'Sixteen? How old is she in the picture?'

'Twelve.'

'Do you know how much a kid changes between twelve and sixteen?'

I put the photo back in my wallet.

'I wish I did,' I said. 'I really wish I did.'

Chapter Six

The woman with Liann looked young, college-age young, and she wore a T-shirt, short cutoff denim shorts, and flip-flops. She carried a blue and red gym bag, and when they came abreast of the bar, the bartender, the same one who'd served me, grunted.

'You're late, Tracy.'

'Did someone die and put you in charge, Pete?' she asked.

Liann looked as out of place in the Fantasy Club as I felt. She wore a no-nonsense brown business suit, and her brown hair was pulled back in a short ponytail. Liann was older than me – she was approaching fifty – but she maintained a rail-thin figure through a combination of jogging and biking. She looked strong and determined as she brought the young woman toward me, a motherly hand resting on the girl's arm. Her presence comforted me as it had ever since she'd shown up at our house the day after Caitlin disappeared.

I stood up as they approached my table – one in the corner and out of the way – and I shook the woman's hand as Liann introduced us.

Up close, in the glow from the stage lights and neon beer signs on the wall, I saw that while my initial assessment was correct – the girl named Tracy was only about twenty years old – the years didn't look like easy ones. Her hair looked thin and brittle from repeated bleachings, and lines were already forming at the corners of her mouth and eyes. She was thin but not in a healthy, youthful way. Instead she appeared tired and worn, like someone who didn't sleep or eat right.

I offered to get everyone a drink, but Liann shook her head. They both sat down.

'We should get started,' Liann said. 'Tracy has to work.'

I took my seat, my hands folded on the table.

'Okay, Tracy,' Liann said. 'Go ahead.'

'Wait a minute,' I said. 'How do you two know each other?'

Tracy looked down at the tabletop. Liann turned to me and said, 'We're short on time here, Tom.'

'I understand that,' I said. 'But I want to know where this information is coming from. Liann, you work with women and families who have been affected by violent crime. And you're a lawyer. I want to know which role you met Tracy in.'

'Tom, Tracy has had some issues —'

'I got busted, okay?' Tracy said, raising her head to look at me. 'I got busted for drugs, and Liann was my lawyer. She kept me out of jail.'

I nodded. 'Okay, I get it.'

'It's not really relevant,' Liann said. 'Tell him what you saw, Tracy.'

Tracy took her time getting started. She reached into the gym bag and brought out a pack of cigarettes – Marlboro Lights – and a lighter. Once the cigarette was burning, she let a stream of smoke go up toward the ceiling, then waved her hand around out of consideration for Liann

47

and me. The ceremony completed, Tracy fixed on me with a level gaze.

'I've seen you before,' she said. 'I used to dance at the Love Shack, and you would come in there showing that picture of your little girl around. You showed it to me one night.' She took another drag, exhaled. 'I have a little girl, too. She's almost five. Cassie. She stays with my aunt while I work, but I see her sometimes.'

She wanted a response, so I provided one. 'That must be tough,' I said.

Tracy nodded as though my words carried some eternal truth. 'It is. It sure as hell is.'

Most of the twenty-year-olds I interacted with at the university came from privileged backgrounds and were often more worldly and widely traveled than I was. Tracy didn't have that life. She didn't spend her winters in Vail or her summers in Cancún. More likely, she spent her whole life in the counties surrounding New Cambridge, and she'd carry the rough features and country accent common among locals with her the rest of her life, markers of who she was.

'What's your little girl like?' Tracy asked.

'Tracy —'

'I want to know, Liann, that's all. I'm curious.'

'It's okay,' I said to Liann. 'I don't mind.'

But then I felt stuck. Four years of interviews with cops and reporters, four years of encapsulating Caitlin for flyers and Web sites. I never felt able to adequately sum her up so someone who didn't know my daughter would recognize her. And I couldn't help but wonder: would the picture I created of the twelve-year-old who walked out the door that day bear any resemblance to the sixteen-year-old young woman I hoped she lived to become?

'She's smart,' I said. 'Really smart.'

'You're a professor at the college, right?'

'Yes.'

'Figures she'd be smart then.'

'She's kind of quiet, too. She kept to herself a lot.'

'Is she pretty?'

'Yes. She has blonde hair, very blonde. And her eyes were – are – blue. Bluer than yours even.'

Tracy smiled, and I couldn't help but think I was looking into the face of some older version of Caitlin, the one who never came home.

The bartender, Pete, came by carrying two cases of beer. His biceps pressed against his shirt like cannonballs.

'You're almost on shift, Tracy.'

'Fuck off, Pete.'

Pete sighed and kept walking.

Tracy waited until he was gone, then leaned in and stubbed out her cigarette.

'I saw your little girl once. At the Love Shack.'

Despite the club soda, my mouth felt dry. I didn't say anything; I didn't move, not wanting to create a vibration that might prevent her from telling me what I needed to know. Instead, I sat perfectly still while an icy sensation grew beneath my shirt collar and spread down my back. I waited.

Tracy dug into her pack and lit another cigarette.

'This was about six months ago, about six months after you came in there showing that picture around. Do you still have that picture with you?'

'Tracy, tell him the story, just like you told me,' Liann said.

Tracy glanced at Liann and nodded, looking a little like a chastened teenager. She flicked her ash onto the floor.

'It was a regular night, just any old night. I don't remember what day of the week it was. Probably not a weekend since we weren't that crowded. This guy came up to me and said he wanted to buy a lap dance. I told him, "Twenty dollars," and he said, "Sure," like it was no problem with the price. Some of them come in there and try to get the price down, or else they're real careful how they ask because they're hoping they're going to get something more than a lap dance. They say, "Twenty dollars to go back there with you," you know, because they're thinking if they don't specify we might go back there and do something besides the lap dance. Something extra.' She shook her head. 'They didn't let us do that at the Love Shack. No way.

'At the Love Shack they have little rooms off to the side, three of them. That's where we went for the lap dances. They weren't much bigger than closets really, but there were those vinyl bench seats built into the wall, and usually another chair just sitting there in the room. Sometimes we got guys who came in who were shy, and they'd sit in the chair for a while, waiting. We'd let them do that for a little bit, but not too long. If they didn't hurry up, they needed to go. There was money to be made.'

Tracy stared at the table and picked at a chip in the Formica. 'Anyway, I went behind the curtain and into room number three to wait for the guy. I got kind of a bad vibe from him, just the way he talked and handed over the money.'

'What kind of bad vibe?' I asked.

She looked away. 'I don't know. Some guys I can tell are just going to be relaxed and easygoing. Regular guys who are just doing this for fun.' She kind of smiled, as though thinking of a distant but pleasant memory. But the smile passed quickly, and she looked back at me. 'But there are other types. I know all about them. They have something else on their mind. Do you know what that is?'

She seemed to be waiting for an answer, so I provided one.

'Sex?' I asked.

She shook her head. 'I wish.' She shook her head again. 'No, these guys want to hurt somebody. Girls, mainly. They want to control a girl or clamp down on her. They want to use her for something, overpower them.'

'Did this man hurt you?' I asked.

'He came into room three,' she said, 'where I was waiting. He was older, in his fifties probably. His hair was kind of long and greasy, and it was going gray. He was ugly. His nose was wide and fat, his skin was kind of puffy. He looked right at me and came over to the bench, and I almost just gave him his money back right there and told him to forget it. We have bouncers and everything. They listen for trouble, and they're good, but being in the room with that guy made my skin crawl.' She shivered just thinking about it, and I assumed her feeling was a cousin to the icy sensation that still possessed my body. 'Then I saw the girl behind him.'

'Caitlin?' I asked.

She nodded.

Liann reached over and placed her hand on top of

mine. She didn't say anything, and while her touch felt warm, it brought no real comfort.

'I've danced for couples before,' Tracy said. 'Plenty of times. It wasn't that weird. But I'd never danced for a couple like that. At first I thought maybe they were father and daughter. Hell, maybe he was her grandfather. But then he reached out and took her hand and pulled her close, and I got it. I understood what was going on between them two. They were a couple.'

'Tom?' Liann asked. 'Are you okay? Are you going to be sick?'

I didn't know. I didn't answer. But I did feel like I was coming down with something. For a moment, I wasn't sure if I was going to keep everything down, if the beer and greasy food was going to come pouring back out of me in a hot, messy rush.

Liann was up and almost immediately came back with another cup of club soda. The sickness eased; my temperature regulated.

'Do you want to stop, Tom?' Liann asked. 'We can do this another day.'

I shook my head.

'I know it's hard to hear,' Tracy said, although she didn't sound all that sympathetic.

'Why didn't you tell this to the police back then?' I asked. 'Why are you telling us this now?'

Liann stepped in. 'Tracy didn't make the connection until she saw the stories and the picture in the paper this week, the stories about Caitlin's service. When she saw them, she called me. Like Tracy said, I've helped her out before when she's had a little trouble. And some other members of her family as well. It was no big deal, just kid stuff. She's over that now, though.' Liann reached out and placed that comforting, motherly hand on Tracy's arm again. 'She trusts me.'

'You remembered Caitlin all that time later?' I asked Tracy. 'You recognized her picture in the paper?'

'I'd seen you before,' she said. 'And then . . .' Her voice trailed off.

I looked from her to Liann, waiting for the rest. 'And?' I asked.

'Go on, Tracy,' Liann said. 'Tell him.'

I wanted to tell her to stop. I wanted to say, *No more*. It felt like the muscle fiber in my heart was rending, tearing apart.

But I couldn't stop listening.

'He went and sat down, the guy. And the girl —' She paused. 'Your daughter sat in the chair across from him. You know what a lap dance is, right?'

I'd been to enough bachelor parties to get the picture, and Liann nodded, too. 'They make us do it reverse cowgirl style,' Tracy said. 'They want us to face away from the guy, so only our butt touches his lap. And we're dressed, of course. That's the law. And with us facing away, I guess they figure it's less likely the guy's going to get all handsy or something. I don't know why they think that. If a guy's going to get handsy, he'll do it no matter what, right? But when this guy asked me to face him, I felt nervous. I mean, he was already creeping me out and everything, and then he brought the girl with him, your girl, and I just didn't feel right.' She sighed. 'But I didn't feel like I could say no to him. We're not supposed to say no unless we really feel like we're in danger, and I couldn't say I felt in danger. And I needed the money and the job. So I went along. And everything went fine. He didn't lay a hand on me.'

She paused and lit another cigarette.

'But?' I asked.

'He didn't even look at me,' Tracy said. She might have tried, but she couldn't hide the trace of disappointment in her voice. 'He looked right past me at the – your daughter. He kept his eyes locked on her the whole time I danced in his lap. She's younger than me, I guess.' Tracy shrugged. 'We only do it for one song. When the song ends, we get up. I turned around and saw the girl. She wore this blank look on her face, no emotion. Nothing. She looked kind of dead. But she was staring right at him. Her eyes were locked on his, like she was under hypnosis or something and couldn't move without him saying so. It gave me the creeps even more, even worse than if he'd hit her or something.'

Tracy paused, and fished yet another cigarette from her bag. 'I left the room first,' she said. 'I stepped outside the little closet, and I'm supposed to go right back to the dance floor, you know, and start working all over again. But I didn't. I stayed right outside the door. I didn't have a plan or anything. I just felt like doing it. I felt like I needed to be there for some reason. Maybe I was thinking of my own little girl. Cassie. Maybe I was thinking if she were ever in that situation I'd want somebody to try to do something for her.

'But the two of them didn't come out right away. I waited a minute, two minutes, and nothing. No sign of them. Like I said, I'd danced for couples before, and I know sometimes it gets them . . . excited, you know? Some couples get off on that kind of stuff. But they're not allowed to do anything about it, not on our property, you know? That would get us in trouble, and we're supposed to look out for that kind of thing. So I went back in to check.'

She stopped and looked at Liann. It seemed to be some kind of sore spot between them and Tracy was silently pleading her case one last time in the hope that Liann would let her off the hook.

Liann shook her head. 'We talked about this, Tracy,' she said. 'You have to tell the whole story. It's your story, and you have to own it.'

After a long pause, Tracy turned back to me. 'I'm sorry,' she said.

'It's okay,' I replied, even though I didn't believe it was okay. In truth, I wanted to run and hide.

'When I went back in, the girl was on the floor, on her knees, facing away from me . . .'

She didn't have to complete the picture. I got it. We all did. Even if it hadn't been Caitlin, if it had been somebody else's daughter, I'd want that man brought to justice. I'd want him castrated and tortured. No one's daughter should have to do that. No parent should have to hear about it. The fact that it might be my daughter, that I hoped it was my daughter, made it almost too much to bear.

'I guess they stopped when they heard me come into the room. Then they came out, and they were walking side by side. He kept his arm around her, like they were a couple, but when I looked close, I saw it was a real tight grip. His arm was around her waist, like he didn't want to let her go.'

'Or like he was afraid she would run,' Liann said.

'Yeah,' Tracy said. 'Like that. He held his head real close to hers, real close, like he was whispering something to her . . . or kissing her.'

I swallowed and waited for more.

'She was on my side, the girl. It was just lucky that way. I put my hand out, real slow and gentle, and I touched her arm. I didn't think he'd see me, but I wanted her to know I was there if she needed something or wanted to say something. The girl turned to me. She looked right at me. Her face still looked blank and all zombielike, but her eyes showed something else. Fear, I guess. Emotion. Like she wanted to say something to me. She really wanted to, I could tell. And the girl actually started to – she opened her mouth and looked right at me, and I thought she was going to ask me for help. And I would have done it, too, right there. I would have.'

'What did she say?' I asked, my voice getting louder.

'Nothing,' Tracy said. 'Right when her mouth opened, the guy saw me there, and he must have seen my hand on her arm, because he jerked her away, pulled her right back to him the way you pull a dog on a leash, you know? He didn't say anything to me. He didn't have to. He just stared at me as they walked away, his eyes telling me to stay back, to butt out, to mind my own business.' Tracy seemed to have forgotten her cigarette. Its ash was growing and tipping toward the floor. 'I wish I'd done something or said something. I think about it all the time.'

Her last words sounded scripted, almost insincere, but Liann reached over and gave Tracy's hand a squeeze.

'You're doing something now,' Liann said. 'This is how you can help that girl.'

Tracy looked at me. 'I saw that picture in the paper last night, and I called Liann right away.' She looked over at Liann and smiled. 'I do trust her. I got busted once —'

'That's not important, Tracy,' Liann said.

Tracy shrugged. 'Whatever, right? It all came together. I want to see this man stopped. I want to see him punished.'

Her voice took on an edge that wasn't there before, one that sounded personal. She stabbed the dying cigarette into the ashtray as if to punctuate her point. She looked away from me then, her hand near her mouth.

The crowd in the Fantasy Club picked up. Businessmen in ties sat at tables side by side with truckers and farm-workers. True democracy. There was a stirring behind the curtain on the stage, and somebody clapped. It looked like the show was about to begin.

'We need to tell the police,' I said.

Tracy's head whipped around toward me.

'No,' she said, the same edge in her voice. She turned to Liann. 'You said I didn't have to.'

Liann gave me a quick glance, letting me know I was crossing some boundary. She leaned in toward Tracy and adopted the motherly pose again, speaking to the young woman in a gentle, comforting tone of voice.

'You said you wanted to help,' Liann said to her. 'And this is the way to help. This is the way to make a differ-ence. The only way to find this guy is to call the police. I'll watch out for you and make sure they don't bullshit you.'

But Tracy shook her head. She pushed back from the table and grabbed her gym bag.

'You didn't say anything about the police, Liann. You

told me no cops. You know that's how it has to be. You know that. I trusted you.'

She stood up, a swirl of motion, and not even Liann calling her name slowed her down as she walked away. So I stood up and said her name, louder than I'd intended apparently. Tracy stopped and so did a lot of other people. They were all looking at me, their heads half cocked, their mouths partly open. Some of them smirked, and others nudged their friends as if to say, *Here's the show! Watch this guy get all crazy over a fucking stripper.*

'Tracy, wait. Wait!'

She stopped in her tracks, her back to me. She didn't turn around, didn't encourage me, but she appeared to be waiting. Listening.

My audience listened as well.

'This is my daughter,' I said. 'Like you said, you'd want someone to help your little girl if she needed it.'

Someone let out a long, sarcastic '*Awwww,*' and someone else shouted, 'Show us your tits!'

Tracy still didn't move.

'Please, Tracy. You're our only lead here.'

I couldn't see her face. I couldn't read what she was thinking or if my words were sinking in at all.

'I don't like the police,' she said, her voice small and childlike.

'Liann's right,' I said. 'They have to be involved. They can help us.'

Tracy didn't say anything else, but her head moved ever so slightly. A quick nod with her eyes squeezed shut. It looked like surrender.

'Thank you,' I said. 'Thank you.'

Chapter Seven

A dark sedan entered the parking lot of the Fantasy Club and came toward the building. It was Detective Ryan. Liann and I stood next to each other while he parked and exited the car. Ryan was taller than me and thick through the middle, with a bushy mustache that more than compensated for his thinning hair. His belt buckle always hung low, beneath his gut, and Ryan frequently used his large, powerful hands to hitch his pants higher. He had come to us the day Caitlin disappeared and he led the investigation the entire time. Early on, he was a comforting presence in our house, a distant but protective father with the power to restore order.

We shook hands as he stepped into the glow from the Fantasy Club's entrance lights. They were orange and yellow and cast Ryan in a surreal wash. I knew Ryan wouldn't like seeing Liann there. She asked questions and second-guessed the police in a way that must have made Ryan feel like he was getting nibbled to death by ducks. But I always appreciated Liann's efforts. I figured the more questions being asked, the more pressure being exerted, the greater the likelihood something good would result and Caitlin would be found. Ryan nodded at Liann, his lips pursed into a forced smile.

I gave Ryan a quick rundown of what had happened, with Liann filling in details when needed. He listened, not saying anything or commenting in any way. Ryan wore what I thought of as a cop mask. He kept his face impassive regardless of the circumstance and frequently began his sentences with the phrase 'I don't have a horse in this race ...' But I never failed to notice the way his eyes appraised me while I spoke, absorbing my every gesture or inflection and recording it somewhere.

When I'd told him all there was to know, he still didn't say anything, so I pushed.

'So what do you think?'

'I think I need to talk to this woman,' he said. 'If she seems credible, maybe we can get a sketch of this guy out to the media.'

At last, something. A step might be taken.

'She doesn't want to talk to you, Ryan,' Liann said.

Ryan looked a little startled, like he'd forgotten Liann was there.

'Oh?'

'She doesn't trust the police. She's been in some trouble, so getting you to talk to her is going to be a tough sell.'

'Nobody likes talking to the police, Liann. Tom, do you like talking to the police?' I could tell it was a rhetorical question, and Ryan didn't allow me to answer. 'But sometimes we just don't have a choice, do we?' he said.

'I really had to work on her just to get her to tell the story to Tom,' Liann said. 'I'd like to be there when you go inside to talk to her.'

Ryan shook his head. 'Negative.'

'I'm acting as her counsel,' Liann said. 'She has that right.'

Ryan made a snorting noise that might have been a

laugh. 'Liann, make up your mind. When you want to be a lawyer, you act like a lawyer and work cases. But when you want to be a victims' rights crusader, you put on that hat and ride herd over the police and the prosecutor's office and everybody else.' He raised his index finger in the air. 'You don't always play well with others, and you haven't stored up many favors with the police.' He dropped the finger. 'Besides, this girl doesn't need counsel. Not that I'm aware of anyway.'

'Let me go back,' I said.

'No.' Ryan's voice took on an edge. 'In fact, why don't the two of you clear on out? I'll call you when I know something.'

'Forget it,' I said. 'I'll wait here. I want to talk to you as soon as you come out.'

Ryan studied me again, then nodded. He took a step toward the door, but Liann stopped him.

'Look, Ryan,' she said. 'That's a scared girl in there. She's lived a tough life. So none of your storm trooper bullshit, okay? She's not a criminal; she's a witness. She has rights.'

'Are you saying criminals don't have rights?' the detective asked. Liann started to respond, but he held up his hand and cut her off. 'I know how to do my job, Liann. I know how to handle witnesses, and I know how to handle criminals. And I do know the difference between the two, even without you on my back. And I'll even go a step further – thank you for bringing her to our attention. I do appreciate it.'

Liann still looked like she wanted to say something, but she didn't. I didn't care about their back-and-forth, their little power plays and gamesmanship. I wanted to know something else, something most important to me.

'Ryan, wait,' I said. 'I forgot to ask her something, that woman in there – Tracy.' I searched for the right words. 'I wanted to know if she thought . . . did she think Caitlin was . . . I know she wasn't okay, of course, but . . . was she – is she okay?'

Ryan came over and placed his big hand on my shoulder. Beyond a handshake, I don't think he'd ever touched me before. I felt like a little boy being comforted, and it was reassuring.

'Wait here with Liann,' he said. He gave me a couple of good pats and started back toward the door. 'I'll talk to you when I come out.'

Chapter Eight

Liann refused to sit. As soon as Ryan went inside, she started to pace back and forth. It was like some portion of my nervous energy had been transferred to her.

'I know what he's doing in there,' she said. 'It's the way the police operate, especially male cops. He's in there trying to knock all the supports out from under her story. He's trying to get the whole thing to collapse. That's his goal, Tom – make no mistake about it. He doesn't want to believe her. He wants to doubt her.'

'I don't think so, Liann. This is it. This is real. Once he talks to her, he'll see it.'

She spun toward me and jabbed her finger toward the door of the Fantasy Club. 'The cops are the ones pushing the possibility that Caitlin ran away. You know that, don't you? It's shown up in the papers, right? "Police department sources say . . ." Maybe it's not Ryan himself. He may not think that. But cops like to push the runaway theory. It makes it easier on them. It gets them off the hook.' She slowed down and turned away. She seemed to be cooling off a little. 'It's what the police always do. They criminalize the victim. They blame her.'

'But could she have run away? What if what Tracy said in there . . . ?' I made a futile gesture behind me, toward the club. I couldn't say it, but Liann knew what I meant.

Caitlin, on her knees in front of that man ... Doesn't that mean she wanted to be there?

'No, Tom.' Liann came back over and sat next to me, her index finger raised like a stern schoolteacher's. 'You can never think that,' she said. 'That's the way the police think. You know your daughter. Do you think she ran away? Really?'

I shook my head. 'No.'

I wished I could get the image out of my head, the picture created by Tracy's words. But I did want to know *him*. I wanted to see the face of that man, the one who took Caitlin.

'You can't waver, Tom. I've been telling you that from day one. That's why you needed to hear that story in there. You can't forget what this is about.'

'Right,' I said. 'It's about finding Caitlin.'

Liann nodded, but not as vigorously as I would have expected. It seemed like she was holding something back, some other part of the answer that I hadn't provided. Before I could ask for clarification, my phone rang. I allowed myself to hope, for just a split second, that it was Ryan calling from inside the club, needing me to come in and participate, to hear some key piece of information he'd just uncovered. But the name on the caller ID screen made much more sense.

Abby.

I told Liann.

'Are you going to answer?'

'No.' I silenced the ringing. 'She's going to be mad.' I looked over at Liann. 'I skipped out on the service at the cemetery today. I went out for a drink with my brother.'

64

'Jesus, Tom.'

'It's worse. I didn't tell her. I just didn't show up.'

Liann shook her head. 'You have your work cut out for you. Of course, you have this news to tell her. You could call her back and let her know.'

'I'll tell her when we know more from Ryan,' I said. 'Besides, I'm not even sure how much Abby will care about this. She wants to turn the page. It might interrupt her mourning.'

Liann fiddled with the large bracelet on her left wrist. 'I'm not a big fan of Abby's decision to move on, either.'

'What do you mean?' I asked.

'I just think that closure isn't the best thing in a case like Caitlin's,' she said. 'You don't want anyone – not the police, not the community – to think you're ready to move on until you really are. And I don't think you're ready to move on, Tom.'

'I guess it was different for you. You knew Elizabeth was really gone.'

'We had a body,' she said. 'And a real funeral. Not a memorial or whatever you had today.' She raised her index finger to make the next point. 'And we had a conviction. Don't forget that. We got the guy.'

'Did that really help?' I asked.

Liann kept her finger in the air. 'It didn't hurt,' she said. 'It sure as hell didn't hurt.'

'What about your marriage?' I asked. 'I don't want to be a fucking cliché, you know? The parents of a missing child who can't keep their marriage alive. How did you two do it?'

She lowered her hand and shook her head. 'It's a long road, Tom,' she said. 'A long, long road.'

It took Ryan nearly an hour to come out. An hour, or what felt like twenty twangy thumping songs I didn't want to hear, and by the time Ryan reemerged I was cursing the first person who'd ever banged on a drum to create music. Liann and I stood up when we saw him.

Ryan's face was unreadable, obscure. 'Tom,' he said, and made a gesture indicating he wanted me to move a little way off and talk to him alone.

'It's okay,' I said. 'Liann can hear.'

He didn't look at Liann. 'I'd rather talk to you alone.'

'Liann is a friend,' I said. 'She knows all about Caitlin's case. She's been there from the beginning. I'd like her to hear. I'd like the extra set of ears.'

Ryan's expression didn't change, but his eyes shifted so that he considered me with a sideways glance.

'Okay,' he said. 'What do you want to know, Tom?'

'I want to know what you thought of her story. Do you think she saw Caitlin?'

'Well, I like to take a long view of these things,' he said. He stood with one hand in his pocket and the other rested on his belt. 'I'm skeptical of stories like these —'

'Here we go,' Liann said.

Ryan took a deep breath and went on, ignoring her.

'I'm skeptical of these stories that show up in the wake of an event like Caitlin's service today. This woman says she saw the story in the paper and remembered, but it's just as likely the story in the paper suggested something to her that wasn't already there. It happens all the time in these cases.'

'But she's not talking about what's in the paper,' I said. 'She's telling a different story, one that no one else has heard.'

Ryan nodded. 'I agree. She does tell an impressive story. It's well detailed, convincingly so.'

'You're saying it's just that, a story?' I asked.

'I'm saying consider the length of time that passed before she came forward. Six months.'

'She didn't know —'

Ryan raised his hand, cutting Liann off.

'Six months later. And consider her profession. A dancer in a club like this.' He turned to Liann. 'No doubt with a record?'

'Criminalization of the victim,' Liann said.

'She's not the victim,' Ryan said. 'She's a witness.'

'She's been a victim in the past,' Liann said.

'She has?' I asked.

'Most of these girls have been.'

'She's a witness now,' Ryan said, 'and who she is counts just as much as what she says.'

I waved my arms, cutting them off. 'So you're just going to do nothing?' I asked.

The door opened behind me, and we all turned. Two men in suits strolled out, and they turned and looked at us, almost coming to a stop. They didn't say anything, and when Ryan gave them the stare down, they moved on, chuckling to themselves over our little show.

When I spoke again, I tried to keep my voice under control. But I couldn't keep the desperation out of it. 'This is our only hope right now, Ryan. Shit, this is the only hope we've ever had.' I spoke through gritted teeth. 'You've got to do something, god-damn it! Ryan —' My voice almost broke. 'This is it, you know? This has to be it.'

'She's agreed to meet with a sketch artist from the Columbus PD,' he said. 'We'll set it up in the next day or two. We'll get the sketch out to the media.'

'Is that all you can do?' I asked.

'The sketch should get us a lot of attention,' Ryan said. 'We'll hear things, but not necessarily the right things. It's not a magic bullet. I don't want you to think it is.'

'You need to get behind the sketch, Ryan,' Liann said. 'You need to push it to the press like you believe in it. And no mention of Tracy's occupation or past criminal history. It's irrelevant.'

'Tom,' Ryan said, 'I don't want to downplay what happened here tonight. It's a good lead, maybe the best we've had. We should all be glad about that, and we'll work it as far as it will take us.' He took a deep breath. 'I'm sorry, but I've got another case we're wrapping up, so I have to get back, but if you or Abby' – he emphasized our names, excluding Liann – 'have any questions, please call. Anytime, just call.'

I fell back onto the bench, my weight carrying me down. I let my elbows rest on the tops of my knees and watched Ryan go around and open his car door. He stopped before he climbed in.

'I'm sorry I wasn't at the church today,' he said. 'I meant to be. I try my best to attend those events, but this other case . . .'

He didn't finish the thought. He started the engine, and the tires kicked up gravel while Liann and I watched him go.

Chapter Nine

A light burned in our living room when I came home, and at the end of our driveway sat two cars – Abby's and Pastor Chris's. He must have driven her home after the graveside service and the potluck, and he must have stayed to keep her company while waiting for me. A knot of jealousy twisted in my gut. Buster was right – there was little or nothing left between Abby and me. In fact, for the past six months, I'd been sleeping alone in the guest room. Our hand-holding at the church felt, just hours later, like a forced gesture, one given in to out of the emotion of the moment.

I entered the kitchen through the back door. The house was quiet, the kitchen clean. The red light on the coffee-maker glowed, and the rich aroma of freshly brewed coffee hung in the air. I remembered the evenings I came home from work when Caitlin was still a toddler. The excitement I felt at just coming through the door, being with my wife and child. The comfort of having such a secure and solid home and family. I thought it would never end.

'Abby?'

I moved down the hallway to the front of the house, past a wall of framed photos. Our wedding. Caitlin through the years, including the one I carried with me at all times, the one I'd shown Pete at the Fantasy Club. But I also saw the empty spaces where Abby had removed some photos of Caitlin – her kindergarten portrait, a photo of her as a newborn, a snapshot of her soccer team. Pieces of Caitlin disappeared before my eyes as I walked down the hall.

Abby sat on the end of the couch but didn't look up or meet my eye. Pastor Chris did. He sat legs crossed, a mug of coffee in his hand, and when he saw me he smiled, his face full of cheery judgment.

'Evening, Tom,' he said, as though he and I were old friends getting together to shoot the breeze on a fall evening.

'I need to talk to Abby,' I said.

'Of course,' he said.

'Alone.'

Abby kept her head down. She held balled-up tissues in her hand, and her cheeks looked blotchy and raw. I waited, my lips pressed tightly together.

Pastor Chris leaned in close to Abby and whispered something I couldn't hear, even in the small room. She nodded her head in response. The intimacy, the closeness of the gesture, carried out as it was right before my eyes made me mash my lips together even tighter.

Pastor Chris set down his mug, uncrossed his legs, and stood up. He placed his hand on Abby's shoulder.

'I'll see you tomorrow, Abby,' he said. He nodded at me. 'Tom.'

'You won't see me tomorrow,' I said.

Pastor Chris didn't blink or appear thrown off stride. He held his smile and considered me with the perpetual placidity of the truly certain.

'But our door is always open to you,' he said, and left

the house as though he didn't have a care in the world, leaving Abby and me alone.

'Abby?'

I settled into an overstuffed chair across from her.

'Abby, I have something to tell you. Something pretty amazing.'

'You humiliated me today, Tom.'

Her words hung between us, a thick cloud of recrimination. I knew the way Abby acted when she was angry or hurt. She was a lot like me in that regard. She seethed, quietly.

'I know, but —'

'Everybody wanted to know where you were, why you weren't there with us. What was I supposed to tell them?'

'Tell them you lied.'

'What?'

'All that bullshit at church, all the stuff about heaven. Pastor Chris saying I believed Caitlin was in heaven.'

'I don't have control over what Chris says.'

'Right.'

'I don't.'

'Okay,' I said. 'Okay.' I didn't want to fight; I wanted to tell Abby about Tracy, about my conversation with Ryan, about the sketch. I forced a calm into my voice that I didn't feel. 'I felt trapped there, Abby,' I said. 'It felt like I was watching a play, and I was in the play but I was also watching myself. And I felt no connection to any of it. It didn't seem like they were talking about me anymore, about my life, so I needed to leave. I should have told you. But I found something out. That's what I came home to tell you.'

'You left me standing alone at our daughter's grave.'

'It's not her grave. Don't say that. It's not her grave at all. That's what I'm telling you. Someone saw her. Someone I met today. They saw Caitlin. Alive. She's alive. The police came, Ryan came, and he took a statement, and they're going to do a sketch and everything, and it means she's alive.'

Abby looked at me for the first time. Really looked at me. The tip of her nose was red from where she'd rubbed it with the Kleenex. Something stirred inside me for this woman. Not as simple as pity, which I might feel for a stranger. It was something more complicated, something deeper. The thick roots of love and resentment tangled together and were almost impossible to unravel. I thought I was reaching her.

She swallowed and took a deep, phlegmy breath. She sounded mucus-choked from the tears and snot.

'I'm not sure I understand what you're saying.'

'Someone saw Caitlin,' I said, speaking slowly, enunciating clearly. 'A witness. She saw her.'

'Who saw her?'

'A dancer from a club in Russellville.'

She rolled her eyes. 'A stripper.'

'Abby, don't. Just listen.'

'You're back to that again . . .' Her voice trailed off, and full realization dawned. 'You were in a strip club during our daughter's funeral.'

'It wasn't a funeral.'

Abby stood up and started to walk away. 'I can't hear this. I can't do this again.'

'Wait, Abby. Wait.'

She was in the hallway, but she stopped, her back to me.

'Listen, will you? Just listen. This witness went to Liann. She knows Liann. It wasn't me, okay?'

She still didn't turn around, but she said, 'Liann knows her?'

'Yes.'

'How does Liann know her?' Abby asked.

'Can you at least look at me while I tell you this?' I asked. 'Please?'

She turned around, slowly, and when she faced me, she raised her eyebrows as if to say, *Hurry up, let's get on with this.*

'Do you want to sit down? It's not all pleasant —'

'Just tell me, Tom. How does Liann know her?'

'I guess this girl, the one who saw Caitlin, has been in some trouble before, and Liann helped her out.'

'Oh.'

'It's not really relevant, is it?'

'Okay,' Abby said. 'Just tell me what she saw. I can handle it.'

She showed no inclination to leave the hallway or return to her seat, so I plunged into the story. I didn't tell her everything, but I told her a lot. When I reached the part about the man and the lap dance, Abby's composure broke ever so slightly. She looked down at the floor, and the movement shook loose a strand of her hair. When she went to tuck it back behind her ear, her hand shook. I felt sick to my stomach just repeating it, so I left out the worst part . . .

Caitlin on her knees, in front of the man . . .

'You said this was about six months ago?'

'Yeah, about that long.'

Somewhere a clock ticked steadily, a monotonous back-and-forth sound.

'That's a long time, Tom,' she said.

'Not that long.'

'It is in this instance. The police told us —'

'The police? You're telling me about the police? Abby, they're not working on the case that hard anymore. They're on to other things.'

'The police have told us that we have a twenty-four- to forty-eight-hour window here. After that, leads grow cold. They dry up. People forget things, or else they fabricate memories . . .' Her voice sounded flat. She was repeating talking points.

'Yeah, I get it.'

'And this woman's a stripper. She's probably on drugs. Or drunk. Is that how she knows Liann? Is Liann her lawyer? I value Liann's advice about Caitlin's case, but if she's bringing this girl around with some crazy story —'

'Okay, okay, forget the witness. Forget what she said.' I moved forward and stood in front of Abby. I put my hand on her shoulder, rested it there gently, offering her support. She looked a little surprised but didn't pull away or brush me off. 'The point isn't the witness here, okay?' I said. 'What matters is that six months ago someone saw Caitlin. Our Caitlin. Alive. Not ten miles from here.'

I knew I'd reached her. When I'd said, 'Our Caitlin,' she took a little breath, a quick intake of air that told me those words still meant something to her.

'We thought she'd be far away . . . or we thought —'

'She'd be dead.'

'Yes. That. We thought that about our own daughter. Abby, we shouldn't have to think that about our daughter. We shouldn't. And now we don't. We have hope again, Abby. Real hope. For the first time in years . . .'

She looked at me, straight into my eyes, then down at my hand, where it still rested on her shoulder. She seemed to be considering me. Not the news or the witness, but me.

'But this is all dependent on this woman having really seen what she says she saw. She doesn't know Caitlin. She saw a picture of when Caitlin was twelve, but she'd be so much older.'

'But Ryan came. He talked to her. They're going to do a sketch and send it out.'

'Did he believe her?' she asked. 'Did he say this was solid?'

'You know how Ryan is. He's cautious. He has other cases he's working. He doesn't want to give us false hope.'

'Did he believe her?'

I hesitated. That told her all she wanted to know. She started to pull away, but I applied pressure on her shoulder, trying to keep her from backing up.

'Ryan wouldn't be having the sketch done if he didn't believe her,' I said.

'I thought you had such a low opinion of the police.'

'I know they haven't always told us the truth. They never once told us they thought she was dead, did they? But you know damn well they were thinking it. They just string us along, make vague promises and offer platitudes. "We're still working on things . . . We still have leads . . ." They don't care. Liann's right. They can't care as much as we do – that's just a fact of something like this. The cops go home to their own wives and kids, and the parents of the victim have to keep carrying the flag. That's why we have to keep her memory alive. That's why Liann is so important. She cares like we do. She understands. Her daughter was —'

I stopped myself.

Abby didn't say anything. Where just a few moments earlier it felt as though I had been making progress with her, slowly thawing the ice and reaching an essential part of Abby, just as quickly things turned back away. I was losing her again. I could sense a turn in the air as palpable as the arrival of a cold front.

'What?' I asked.

'We've never talked about it, Tom.'

'About what?' I waited. 'That she might be dead?'

Abby shook her head. 'That she did run away from us.'

'No, Abby. Never.'

She became more animated. 'She was so moody and withdrawn. I never knew what she was thinking or feeling. She could have lived a whole life we didn't know about. And those Internet searches. Seattle . . . the trains . . . She was taking the dog to the park. Maybe she met somebody there, somebody she was talking to. We wouldn't know.'

'What are you saying?'

'And now this story about the girl in the club. If it is Caitlin, if she was doing those things . . .' Abby's lip curled as she spoke. 'Maybe she wants to be gone and stay gone. Maybe . . . if she was right here, so close to us and . . .' She turned away, starting up the stairs to the bedrooms. 'I can't do this anymore. I can't.'

'What?'

She stopped near the top of the stairs and looked back. 'This has been difficult, Tom.'

'Of course. I know.'

'No, you don't. I'm not talking about Caitlin's disappearance.' She sat down on the top step. Her body weight seemed to go out of her. She almost collapsed. 'I'm not talking about that. I'm talking about how difficult it's been for me to watch you go through this over the last four years. Ryan's going to send out this sketch, and you come home all excited. Well, Ryan doesn't know what hope has done to this house. To this marriage. Does he?'

'Abby —'

'Every time a piece of news comes in about Caitlin. It could be just a scrap. A girl would get assaulted across town, and you'd want to know who did it. Or there'd be an abduction attempt an hour away, and you'd be on the phone to the police telling them to check it out. Ryan humors you, doesn't he? He always takes your calls, right?'

'He came out today as soon as he could.'

'I love and miss Caitlin as much as you —'

'No one said you didn't.'

'I know. And I do appreciate that.' She rubbed her palms together, as though scraping something off them. 'You asked me once why the church meant so much to me. You acted confounded by the fact that I wanted to go and spend my time there, as though just nurturing my faith wasn't reason enough. I know you think people who talk that way – who say things like "nurturing my faith" – are beneath you, but there's nothing I can do about that. Is there?'

I didn't respond.

'I went to the church because your unreasonable hope didn't leave room for anything else in our life together. I was squeezed out. And while you may not have questioned my love for Caitlin, you did question how invested I was in keeping her memory alive. You thought that if I didn't pore over every missing-persons case in the country, or if at some point I wanted to stop spending my weekends organizing search parties, that I just didn't care enough. That I was deluded or out of touch. But that's not the case. I just chose to go on. It's a little selfish, I admit, but I chose to go on with my life rather than to spend all my time as the poor, unfortunate woman who lost her daughter. And the church helps me do that.'

She paused. I still didn't say anything. But I noticed a different kind of look on her face, a newfound relief or ease. She was unburdening herself.

'I didn't want you to get rid of Frosty because he bothered me. I know you think that, but it's not the case. I wanted you to get rid of him for you. I thought maybe if you did it, you'd be able to move on. It was a last-ditch attempt, I guess. I thought it might have worked. The last few days seemed better, and this morning at the church —'

'What do you mean by "last-ditch"?'

She looked down at her hands. 'Chris and I have been talking. He's been counseling me. Ordinarily, he doesn't encourage people to divorce – Well, I guess if we had children to consider . . . But we think – *I* think – it would be for the best. It seems inevitable in a way. This happens to a lot of couples who lose a child.'

She looked up at me for a quick moment, her eyes full

of tears. Then she stood and walked into what used to be our bedroom.

'Hold on.' I scrambled along behind her. The evidence was all over the bedroom. Two suitcases open and full of clothes. The closet door thrown wide and nearly empty.

Abby stood in the middle of the room, chewing on a fingernail.

'You're really doing it?' I asked.

'One of us has to, Tom.'

I pointed behind me, toward the stairs and the lower level of the house. 'Is there something else going on here? Is this about . . . ?' I couldn't say his name. It tasted like ash in my mouth. 'Him?'

Abby looked at me, her eyes full of pity. 'Oh, Tom. If it were only that simple.'

'If you're fucking another man, it *is* simple. If you're not the person I thought you were, the person you claim to be —'

'Don't be crude,' she said. 'Chris is helping me. There might be a job at the church, something to get me started. They have a place I can stay, in their retreat housing. It's temporary, of course. I talked to someone at Fields, someone in the School of Ed. I think I'd like to go back to teaching. It wouldn't take me long to get recertified here. And there are jobs. Maybe working with children again, teaching them, would fulfill me in some way my life isn't fulfilling me right now. I wouldn't expect you to leave this house. You've always liked living here, and I know you think one of us should always be here in case Caitlin . . . if she ever came back.'

We were quiet then. I sat on the edge of the bed, letting my body weight sink into the mattress. Abby came over and bent down. She planted a kiss on the top of my head. I reached up and took her hand. We clasped tightly for a moment; then she slipped loose.

'I know you think this is my fault,' I said.

'It's no one's fault. Not really.'

'I don't mean us,' I said. 'I mean Caitlin. I know you think I let her get away with too much, that she shouldn't have been allowed to walk the dog in the park alone. She was too young, and Frosty . . . Frosty was too big . . .'

'That's all over, Tom.'

'I just wanted her to run toward life and not be afraid of it. You know, my family, growing up – it was awful, so smothering. It was like living without oxygen.'

'I know, Tom.'

But I wasn't sure she did. Abby's parents were frighteningly normal: upper middle class and traditional. A little repressed, a little concerned with appearances, but next to my family they looked like royalty. I don't know if Abby ever really understood what it was like to come from a family like mine, even though she often said she did.

'I didn't want her to be tied to us,' I said. 'Like we held her back.'

'It's late, Tom . . .'

'Do you remember what it was like when Caitlin was little?' I asked. 'Just the three of us in the house together. Watching TV or playing games. Hell, it didn't matter what we were doing.'

'It was good, Tom,' she said. 'Back then, it was good.'

'Back then,' I said, repeating her words, letting them

hang in the air between us. 'I tried to get Frosty back today. I went to the shelter and asked about him, but he was already gone.'

Abby raised her hand to her mouth. 'Oh,' she said. 'It happened that fast?'

I shook my head. 'Not that. Somebody adopted him. Some family, I guess. They wouldn't give me the name, even though I said I wanted to get him back.'

'He's probably okay then. Somebody wanted him.'

'He and I could have lived here together. He was good company.'

'It's going to take me a little while to get all my stuff out. There isn't much room over there at the church. It's like a dorm, I guess.'

'Hell, maybe I'll just go get another dog.'

Abby made a noise deep in her throat. No one else would have recognized it, but I knew. She started to cry. Her tears always began that way, and then she quickly began taking deep, sobbing breaths, so it sounded like she couldn't get enough air. Then I started crying, too, the tears stinging my cheeks and falling into my lap. I wiped my face with the back of my hand, first one side, then the other. 'One dog's pretty much the same as any other, right?'

Chapter Ten

Ryan showed up with a sketch the following week. Abby was slowly moving her things out of the house, one box at a time, so there was some disarray, which caused Ryan to raise an eyebrow. But he stepped around the mess without saying anything or making a comment. It was one of the few times he didn't wear a tie. He wore the collar of his white shirt open, revealing a strip of T-shirt and some straggly black chest hairs.

'You've got it?' I asked before he took a seat.

He nodded and lowered his body into the big chair in our living room.

I couldn't bring myself to sit. While Ryan sat calmly, patiently, almost Buddha-like in the chair, I paced back and forth among the boxes. It had taken him three days just to arrange a meeting with Tracy. First her phone was disconnected; then someone at her apartment told Ryan she was out of town. I called Liann and asked her – told her – she needed to find this girl and apply some pressure.

'We need her,' I'd said.

And that only earned me an extended lecture from Liann, one in which she explained to me how delicate it was to deal with women like Tracy, women who were living victimized lives. I wanted to be sympathetic, I did. But I wanted the god-damned sketch more. I didn't have anything else to think about. Finally, Liann met Tracy at the Fantasy Club and brought her to the police station.

And so Ryan sat in front of me, holding the Rosetta stone.

'Can I see it? Please?'

'Abby isn't home,' he said, more of a statement than a question.

'She's . . .' I pointed at the boxes. 'This has been . . .'

He nodded. He'd probably seen it a million times.

'Do you want me to call her?' I asked. 'Get her over here? I really don't want to wait. I want to see the sketch.'

'Tom, let's talk first.'

'Jesus,' I said. 'I don't need another lecture.'

'I don't lecture you.'

'Liann set me straight about this. Now you.'

Ryan raised a finger. 'Liann doesn't work for the police. She doesn't speak for me. I appreciate what she did, getting this girl to meet with the artist, but she doesn't speak for me. If I have something to say, it comes from me.'

Finally, I sat, hoping to speed things along.

'Okay, okay,' I said. 'Tell me.'

He cleared his throat. 'I was there the whole time she worked with the sketch artist, and then I spoke with the artist after she left. She gave the same story and approximate description she gave to me at the strip club, and apparently the same one she gave to you.'

'That's good, isn't it?'

Ryan's facial features grew pinched.

'It's not good?' I asked.

'I believe she saw the man she says she saw. Her description of him is quite detailed. It led to a very good sketch, as far as those things go. In fact, it's very possible she knows this man. Well.'

'Did you ask her about this? Did you ask his name?'

Ryan gave me a supercilious look, the kind I use on my students. It said, *Do you think I don't know how to do my job?*

'Okay, so you asked her, and she stuck to the original story. But I get the feeling you're hinting at something larger.'

He hesitated, then shook his head. He chased the thought away or held it back.

'I have some other concerns.' He reached into his interior jacket pocket and fumbled around. I thought he was going to bring out the sketch at last, but instead he pulled out a small pocket notebook, the kind he wrote in whenever he was conducting business. He reached into another pocket and brought out a pair of half-moon reading glasses and worked them into place on the tip of his nose. He leaned back in his chair and studied the notebook. 'This woman, Tracy Fairlawn, has been arrested twice for drug possession, once for prostitution, and has also been investigated by the child welfare department. These things call into question, to some extent, the reliability of whatever she says.'

'No, it doesn't. You said you believed her story —'

Ryan raised a finger of caution. 'I said I believe she knows this man.'

'But you can't throw her story out because of these arrests. That's —'

'Criminalization of the victim,' he said. 'I know. Liann's taught you well.' He flipped the notebook shut and put it away. He took off the glasses. 'I detected something both

84

times I spoke to Miss Fairlawn about this man. There was something underneath her words, an anger or sense of grievance lurking there, something I couldn't quite place my finger on, but it gives me reason to stop for a moment. Tom, I want to give you the choice about something. We can go ahead and distribute this sketch, or we can hold off a few days until we know more about where this information is coming from.'

'Let me just look at the thing.'

'I think if we run with it, we risk getting a lot of information that won't be helpful because we don't know if we're starting from a good place or not. We risk shooting our last good bullet here —'

'Can I see it?' I asked. 'Will you just hand it over so I can see it? I don't want to talk about it anymore. I want to see it.'

Reluctantly, he started digging into his jacket pocket. He brought out a white piece of paper, folded like a letter. He shifted his bulk, leaning forward, and the paper hovered in the air between us.

But I didn't make a quick grab for it. My hand moved slowly, as though weights were tied to it, and the farther I extended the more I felt it shake. Ryan didn't seem to notice. He held the paper in the air until I took it.

As I unfolded it, Ryan spoke. 'Take a long look. See if it jars your memory. Co-workers, service people. The guy who cuts the grass or cleans the floors at work.'

I unfolded the paper and took it in. It was a simple drawing, black on white. I saw the wide, fat nose Tracy had described. It filled the middle of the page and made the man depicted look brutish, almost simian. His brows were thick and dark, and the eyes beneath them looked small and narrow, as though the artist had depicted the man in midsquint. I scanned the other features quickly – the hard set of the jaw, the thin lips – and absorbed a sense of menace from the simple drawing.

'I don't think I know him,' I said.

'I would like Abby to take a look at it,' Ryan said.

I continued to stare at the drawing and tried to retrofit that face to all the images of the kidnapper that continually ran through my head. A car pulling up at the park, or a man talking to Caitlin, making a grab for her arm.

The man in the strip club, in the little booth with my daughter.

'Do you think it's him?' I asked.

'Like I was saying before . . . Tom?' He wanted me to lower the sketch, so I did. Slowly. 'We need to think carefully about what we do next,' he said. 'It's been a long time since Caitlin disappeared. The public has a short attention span. Over time, people understandably forget. They move on to other things, other news stories. Their memories get muddy.'

I held up the paper. 'I want to run it. I don't want to wait. I've been waiting four years, and this is the best lead we have. Run it.'

Ryan rubbed his hand over his cheek as though he were tired.

'It's my choice ultimately,' he said. 'If I don't think it's in the best interest of the case to run it, I won't.'

'How could this not be in the best interests of the case?' I asked.

'It is, of course,' he said. 'What I said the other night is true – this is the best lead we've had in four years. But I'm thinking of you and Abby as well as the case.'

'What about us?' I asked.

'How well do you know your daughter, Tom?'

And there it was, just as Liann had predicted. Just as I'd suspected all along. Ryan believed his own counternarrative of Caitlin's disappearance, and he intended to share it.

'I guess it's hard for me to answer that since I haven't seen her in four years.'

'Before that. Before she disappeared.'

'I knew her very well then.'

'Are you sure?'

'Yes. We were happy.'

Ryan raised his eyebrows. He glanced around the room at the boxes. 'Were you?'

'What are you saying, Ryan? I'm not following you.'

'We don't always know people the way we think we know them, do we? People change. Our lives change.'

'Therefore . . . ?'

'You believe this was your daughter who was seen in this club, right?'

'I do.'

He nodded. 'Did the behavior described match what you think you know of Caitlin?'

'She was twelve when she disappeared. Twelve. And that man' – I tapped the paper – '*this* man has her. He has her against her will. Which is it, Ryan? Either you believe Tracy's story and you think this is Caitlin, or you don't. And if you don't, why are we having this conversation?'

Ryan took a deep breath. 'Four years have passed, Tom.'

'I know that.'

87

'Leaving aside the very remote chance that this is going to lead to anything positive —'

'Ryan —'

'Now, hold on,' he said. 'Let's play a little of the believing game here. Say this sketch *does* lead to something good. Let's say this story is true and somehow, someway, we do find Caitlin and bring her home to you. Those four years, the time you lost with her – would you be prepared for what that would be like, Tom?'

'Will this be in the news tomorrow?' I asked, holding out the sketch.

'You didn't answer my question,' he said.

'Ryan, will this run tomorrow?'

He looked around at the boxes again. 'Tom, have you and Abby been seeking counseling of some kind? Help? It's none of my business, of course, but this sort of thing places an enormous strain on a marriage. And on an individual. If you wanted, I could refer you to some of the resources we have available through the department.'

'You offered me that four years ago,' I said. 'And every year since. And I appreciate it greatly, but I'm not interested.'

'We have a program – it's funded by the state – where volunteers, private citizens, meet with and assist families affected by tragedy. Did I mention this to you? It's relatively new, and it's called Volunteer Victim Services. These people are trained, of course, but some feel it's less pressurized than conventional therapy. It's not as structured and it's even more comforting in a way. Professionals sometimes get constricted by their roles.'

'Ryan —'

'You could certainly choose to seek help through more conventional channels,' he said. 'There are a number of good therapists and counselors in New Cambridge. Even at the university —'

'There's only one thing I want and need. And you know what it is.' I held the paper out in front of me. 'Will this be in the paper tomorrow?'

'It will,' he said. 'We'll go public with it tomorrow. I'll call you and let you know the details.'

Chapter Eleven

Something woke me that night, thumping. I fell asleep in the guest room earlier than usual, after flipping on the porch light and making sure the house key still remained in its hiding spot. After hearing Tracy's story and seeing the sketch, the ritual seemed more urgent, more essential.

But Abby's words had struck a nerve: *If Caitlin were living so close to us . . . ?* I knew what she meant, what completed the thought: *Why didn't she just come home?*

Abby was gone already, sleeping at the church. Whenever she came to the house to collect more belongings, we were cordially, distantly polite to each other, and I didn't allow the sight of her to make me think she might have reconsidered her decision to leave.

I came awake disoriented. I checked the clock on the bedside table: 10:01. Not that late. My heart rate was up, my shirt a little damp. I'd been dreaming. Not a coherent narrative, but a series of disjointed and haunting images, a parade of all my fears. *Caitlin calling my name in the park . . . The man from the sketch reaching for her, taking her away . . .*

I heard the thumping again.

I lowered my feet to the cold floor. My mind started to catch up, shaking off the dream images and focusing on the real. Someone was in the house. Downstairs.

Caitlin?

I jumped up, started out of the room. I made no effort

to soften my steps. Whoever – whatever – was downstairs would hear me coming and know I knew they were there. I didn't care. I bounded down the stairs, wearing only a T-shirt and boxer shorts. At the bottom I called out into the house:

'Caitlin? Is that you?'

Light came from both the kitchen and the living room. I turned left, toward the front of the house.

'Caitlin?'

I entered the room. Someone was sitting on the couch. She didn't look up when I came in, but kept her eyes fixed on the paper in her hand.

Abby.

Some of the boxes were moved. More were packed.

And she held the sketch.

She stared at it, oblivious to my appearance. I didn't speak, even though I wanted to ask why she was showing up so late. Did she want to scare the crap out of me? But I left her alone to absorb the face on the paper.

While I stood there and grew colder, Abby raised her free hand and slowly, almost gently traced the outline of the man's face. It looked like she was trying to get a reading from it, absorb some psychic emanations. Finally, she put the sketch facedown on the table and leaned back against the couch cushions.

'Is that him?' she asked.

'It might be.'

'Ryan called me on my cell phone. He told me about the sketch being released. He said he didn't know if we'd be talking.'

'He came by.'

'Did you tell him I'm moving out?'

I gestured toward the boxes. 'He's a detective. I think he figured it out on his own.' I entered the room and sat on the opposite end of the couch from her.

'I must have woken you up,' she said. 'You said Caitlin's name on the stairs. You used to do that all the time, back then. Do you remember?'

'I do.'

'I used to think I didn't care as much as you because I didn't dream about Caitlin or mutter her name in my sleep. I thought I should have been doing that too.'

'They're just dreams. They're not a measure of your love for her.'

'That's nice of you to say.' She smiled a little. 'You were right about something. I have . . . blamed you for Caitlin's disappearance at times. I guess it was just easier than blaming some stranger, some unknown entity. I'm working on these things with Chris. We're trying to move on from all the things in the past and trying to get to a more positive place. Emotionally.'

'How neat and tidy.'

'Ryan told me he has doubts about the sketch and about the witness. He said if it was up to him he wouldn't go forward with it. I told him to go ahead and do whatever you wanted to do. I think this is important for you, Tom. Important for your process of moving on. You need to know that everything that could be done has been done.'

'And you don't need that?'

'We're in different places in many ways,' she said. 'It's strange, though. When Ryan called and told me about the sketch, I wanted to see it. Right away I did. I told him I didn't care to, but I really did. That's why I'm here tonight. I told myself I was getting more stuff.'

'This late? It's after ten.'

'Yeah.' She laughed a little. 'I knew Ryan gave you a copy, and I wanted to see it. I wanted to see that face.'

'I understand.'

'You know what I was thinking about earlier today?' she asked. 'That trip we took to New England when Caitlin was little.'

'What about it?'

'What a great time we had. How beautiful the scenery was. How easy it was to just be together, the three of us. I remember how you wanted to baptize Caitlin in Walden Pond. She was just three, but you took her down to the edge of the pond and splashed water on her head like you were in a church.' She smiled a little. 'I thought you were crazy, of course. But I also thought it was endearing. I could tell how much you loved her. And how much you loved the idea of baptizing her in that pond.'

'As I recall, you liked the idea too. You took a picture of it.'

'That's right.' Her mood seemed to have shifted a little. Her voice sounded a little colder, a little more distant. 'I did like the idea back then. But now when I look back on it, I see the whole thing differently. I see a couple and the husband wants to baptize his daughter in a pond and the wife wants her baptized in a church.'

'She did get baptized in a church, because you wanted her to.'

Abby didn't respond. She leaned forward and picked up the sketch of the suspect. She handed it to me, practically stuffing it into my hands, crumpling it a little.

'But I don't want to see it anymore. Just keep it away from me if I'm around.'

I straightened the paper, smoothed out the crumples.

'I know you know some things, Tom. I could tell by the way Ryan talked to me on the phone that there were things he was keeping from me. I guess they're the details of what happened in that strip club, what that woman saw.' She swallowed. 'I don't want to know those things, Tom. Ever. Those are just things you're going to have to endure alone. I can't —'

'I get it,' I said. 'In fact, it's not really anything new, is it? Me enduring these things alone.'

She let out a long sigh. 'We know, Tom. You're the saddest.' She stood up. 'I was going to stay here tonight, but I think I'll just take some of these things back to the church.'

I stood up, too. 'Do you mind keeping it down while you do? I feel pretty tired.'

I went back up the stairs, sketch in hand, and didn't wait for her to reply.

Chapter Twelve

The morning walkers and joggers still crowded the park. People went past me in waves, excusing themselves, occasionally brushing against me, and I wondered what they thought of me, a slightly disheveled man wearing jeans and a button-down shirt among their shorts and athletic shoes. Still, I welcomed their company, the push and jostle of other human beings. Aloneness without being lonely.

I knew what lay on the far side of the park – the cemetery and Caitlin's 'grave'. My reaction to it in the wake of the ceremony and the eyewitness account from Tracy seemed similar to Abby's reaction to the sketch of the suspect. I wanted to see that grave again, if only to confirm its reality in my head. It was, for better or worse, a memorial to my daughter, a stony testament to the fact that she existed on this earth at one time.

I started to sweat under my shirt. I rolled up my sleeves to my elbows and kept walking. I thought about how we'd made it to that point, how Abby's involvement with the church had led to that headstone in the ground. Abby had begun attending church with Pastor Chris before Caitlin disappeared, but her attendance at that time was sporadic. Once a month, maybe. Sometimes twice. Eventually, Abby announced that she wanted Caitlin to be baptized there by Pastor Chris. Caitlin was eight years old then and refused, but I took Abby's side and told Caitlin she should do it. I chose not to attend the service, but Caitlin grudgingly agreed, scowling and dragging her feet the whole way. When they came home, I asked Caitlin how it had gone.

'Weird,' she said, crinkling her nose.

'I figured as much,' I said. 'Do you buy any of it?'

'Nope.'

We laughed together, more like conspiring siblings than parent and child. Abby left the room.

'You're both so . . . *hard*,' she'd said. 'I can't get near either one of you.'

Her involvement with the church had increased steadily after that – a mission she undertook alone – and when Caitlin disappeared, Pastor Chris and a gang of his helpers set up shop in our living room, praying, bringing food, answering the phone. They kept a constant vigil, and when the media and police left, the church people left too, but Abby went with them and so did what remained of our marriage.

At the far side of the park, near the cemetery, I slowed my pace. More trees lined the path there, providing shade. I looked behind me and saw no one, so I wasn't in any danger of getting run over or becoming the obstacle clogging the path. I knew Caitlin's marker – *cenotaph*, as Buster would say – lay just beyond the trees, and where the foliage was thin enough I made out the rows and rows of headstones.

What if Ryan was right?

They would release the sketch, and for a time things would happen. A flurry of attention, the discovery of possibilities.

But after that? If none of the leads panned out, and the sketch proved to be a dead end . . .

What would I do then?

I turned my gaze away from the cemetery, and that's when I saw the girl on the path ahead of me.

We locked eyes for a moment. She saw me. I knew she did. And as soon as she saw me, she bolted, moving from left to right and through the small stand of trees that separated the park from the cemetery. She was blonde and young and looked just like –

Caitlin!

I ran forward, my shoes slipping and sliding against the gravel track. I felt like a man running through deep water. I couldn't move fast enough. Then I reached the spot and looked through the trees. There was a small break, a worn little path leading from the park to the cemetery.

I followed, ducking my head beneath the low branches, and came out onto the green lawn of the cemetery. I looked around. Nothing but the flat earth and the headstones. No sign of the girl.

'Caitlin!'

I moved left, out toward the main road. My breath caught in my throat, the sweat thickening beneath my arms. I crossed the small, winding road that wrapped through the cemetery.

I called out again. 'Caitlin!'

No girl in sight, but in the distance a graveside service was in progress. Several heads turned toward me, considering me. I didn't have time to think about the figure I must have been cutting. I didn't call out again, but worked my way up through the cemetery, keeping close to the boundary it shared with the park. I looked to the left, into the trees, hoping for another glimpse of the girl or even just the sound of rustling branches and leaves.

But there was nothing. I went all the way up the boundary, all the way to the parking lot by the small limestone chapel, where the cemetery held services. The lot was full of cars, including a hearse and two gleaming black sedans, but no girl. No Caitlin. I stood there in the sun, my breath coming in short huffs. But there was no girl there, no sign of a girl at all.

Chapter Thirteen

I wandered back toward the house in something of a daze.

The girl – blonde, thin, fast – definitely looked like Caitlin, and I'd spotted her in the park where Caitlin had disappeared. She looked younger than Caitlin should have looked after four years away.

But then, if it was Caitlin, if that was my daughter, why did she run at the first sight of me? Why did she bolt when we locked eyes?

The sun was passing overhead, and the sweat under my shirt itched at my skin like millions of tiny bugs. I unbuttoned the shirt, my hands shaking and struggling, and pulled it off. I walked the rest of the way in my sticky wet T-shirt.

My phone rang. Liann. 'Tom, where are you?' she asked, without even a hello.

'I just saw Caitlin in the park,' I said, also not bothering with pleasantries.

'What?'

'I saw Caitlin. I mean, it might have been Caitlin. It was a young girl, and she looked like Caitlin, but when she saw me she ran off and I couldn't catch her.'

'We don't have time for this now, Tom. Listen. The police, Ryan – they're having a press conference right now. They're releasing the sketch.'

'Now?'

'Yes. Now. You need to get down there. They need a parent, a human face, to give the story more impact.'

'Why didn't he call me?' I looked down at my sweaty T-shirt, the dust on my shoes. No shower. I probably looked crazed. 'I don't think —'

'You need to go, Tom. I'm coming to your house now. I'll see you in three minutes.'

I managed to mostly button my shirt by the time I slipped into Liann's car, and I looked at myself in the mirror on the passenger side, smoothing my hair down with the aid of spit applied to my fingers. Liann was all business. She barely looked at me when I entered the vehicle, and drove across town like a New York cabbie. 'What am I supposed to do when I get there?' I asked.

'Just stand there, be a presence. Answer reporters' questions. They need to see the toll this is taking on you. You need sympathy.'

'Should I call Abby?'

Liann made a dismissive noise deep in her throat. 'You can do this alone. We don't need her.'

'I look like shit.'

She took her eyes off the road for a second, giving me a quick glance. 'Even better. You look more desperate.'

We entered the square and approached the station. My right hand clutched the door handle so hard my fingers hurt.

'How did you know about the press conference?' I asked.

'I know people in the department. I talk to people every day.'

'Why didn't Ryan call me about it?'

'I've seen the police do this before,' she said. 'If they think a parent is a loose cannon or too distraught.'

'He thinks that about me?'

'Please, Tom. Look at yourself.' Liann stopped the car behind a news van. I expected more. Liann undid the locks and made a shooing gesture toward me. 'Go on. Go. You're late.'

'Aren't you coming in?'

'You're better off without me. Go.'

'What about the girl I saw at the cemetery?'

'Our minds can play tricks on us, Tom. Now go.'

I stepped onto the sidewalk and into the sunlight. As soon as I shut the door, she drove off, leaving me alone.

The police spoke to the media in a small conference room near the back of the station that felt small and cheap. The out-of-date wood paneling needed to be replaced. The bookshelves they used as a backdrop were covered with dust. But it played well on TV. When they placed a police official – either in uniform or wearing a suit and tie – in front of that backdrop, addressing a bank of microphones, it brought instant credibility and authority. I'd stood there on more than one occasion when Caitlin had first disappeared. Abby and I were asked to step forward, blinking against the burning glow of the TV lights, and plead for Caitlin's return. I imagined we looked like any other victims of tragedy – stunned and weary and desperate enough to make the viewers at home say to themselves, *Thank God it's not me.*

I told the uniformed officer at the front desk who I was

and asked to be allowed back. For a moment, he hesitated, studying me in the way only cops can, as though I were giving off a scent he recognized, some combination of fear and desperation. He reached for his phone.

'I'm sorry I'm late,' I said. 'Detective Ryan told me the time, and I forgot. Ever since my daughter disappeared . . .'

I tried to look helpless. I wasn't above using my status as the parent of a missing child to get something if I needed it. This cop didn't seem particularly moved. He picked up his phone, dialed an extension, and then spoke in a voice so low I made out only a few words.

Press conference . . . father . . . back there . . .

He nodded and hung up.

'Someone's coming to take you back.'

'I know the way.'

He shook his head. 'Someone needs to take you.'

I drummed my fingers on his desktop. I looked around. There were hard plastic chairs and copies of *Reader's Digest* to distract people. An old man waited alone, head down. A TV was mounted on a bracket in the corner. It broadcast a game show.

'Can you get the news on there?' I asked. 'Are they showing the press conference?'

'Not live,' he said. 'Why don't you have a seat?'

'Can't I just go back? I know the way —'

'Sir, you have to wait.'

'Why aren't they showing it?'

But the cop ignored me. I looked back at the TV. The host of the show threw a bunch of money up in the air, and it fluttered to the ground while contestants grabbed handfuls. The phone on the cop's desk rang. He listened, then nodded, looking up at me.

'Okay,' he said into the phone and hung up.

'Was that about me?'

'Someone's coming to take you back now.'

'You said that already.'

'Sir . . .'

The heavy steel door to the side of the desk opened. A uniformed female officer held the door for me and jerked her head down the hallway, indicating I should step through.

'Thanks,' I said.

'They're wrapping up,' she said.

The door shut behind us as we walked down the hall. Fluorescents glowed overhead and watery blue paint covered the walls.

'Wrapping up? I missed it?'

'We can't go walking in right in the middle,' she said.

I knew the way and walked ahead of the cop. I turned right and then right again and saw the conference room door. A uniformed officer stood outside, a cell phone to his ear.

'I'll just slip in,' I said to no one in particular, but the cop with the phone held up his hand like he was directing traffic. I felt another hand on my arm.

'Just wait here,' the female officer said. To make sure I did, she kept her hand in place, and we stood there, waiting for what seemed like another eternity.

Finally the door of the conference room opened. A few people began filing out. I didn't recognize anyone, and I tried to look over their heads and into the room.

'Can you let go now?' I asked the cop, and she did.

Just a few more people came out, and they stepped aside as I entered the room. I saw Ryan, and he saw me. He looked surprised and – maybe – a little disappointed.

I expected more. A lot of cameras, a lot of people. But I saw only one film crew and a handful of people who looked like reporters.

Someone said my name.

'Mr Stuart? What did you think of the press conference today?'

I thought I recognized the woman. Did she work for the *Daily News*?

'I missed it,' I said. 'I didn't know —'

'Are you encouraged by this lead?'

'Of course.'

'How have you managed to keep your spirits up during this ordeal?'

A few more people gathered around. I hoped they were all reporters. I saw Ryan come closer, his big head and body standing out in the crowd. He looked nervous, concerned. I remembered what I looked like. Unshaven. Unshowered.

But the questions kept coming.

'How is your wife holding up?'

'She's fine.'

'Why didn't she come today?'

'She's . . . I don't know. I guess she's moved on.'

'Moved on? How so?'

'She doesn't really think Caitlin's coming home.'

A TV light came on, and, beneath it, a glowing red dot. They were filming. I started to sweat again. Ryan said something, but the light kept me from seeing him.

'Mr Stuart's had a long morning,' he said. 'And I need to brief him.'

'Do you think your daughter is still alive? Do you think you'll see her again?'

I couldn't see who'd asked the question. The room swirled a little bit.

'Yes, I do.'

Camera shutters clicked and whirred. A flash went off. No one said anything, no more questions, so I kept going.

'In fact, I have seen her. Just this morning, I saw her in the park.'

The cameras clicked more rapidly. There were more flashes.

I felt hotter, more nervous, my clothes too tight and constraining.

'You saw her?'

'Your daughter?'

'Really?'

I felt a hand on my arm, a strong grip. Ryan. He started to lead me away.

I wanted to explain.

'I saw her – I saw a girl – in the park by the cemetery. I don't really know if it was Caitlin —'

Ryan pulled me out of the room and down the hallway, leaving the reporters behind. He ushered me into another office, a small room with two empty desks and a filing cabinet.

'That was not a smart thing you just did back there,' he said.

'Why didn't you tell me this was happening?'

He sighed. 'Isn't it obvious?'

'No, it's not.'

'Look, Tom. This came together quickly. I had to get that sketch out to the newspapers. Isn't that what you wanted? And, yes, we do like to have the families at these things, but given the strain you've been under and the strain in your marriage, we – I – thought it might be best to talk about this on my own.'

'I can talk about my daughter if I want. I have the right.'

'You repeated a ghost story. Now anything good that would have come from the sketch could be overshadowed by what you said in there.' He turned toward the door and opened it. He stuck his head into the hallway and looked both ways. 'Get out of here. Go out to your car and get out of here. And don't talk to any reporters. I'll try to make this right.' He gave me the once-over. 'I think they'll believe you're under a great deal of stress and don't know what you're saying.' He remained in the door, holding it open for me.

But I wasn't ready to go.

'Ryan, can I ask you something?'

He didn't encourage me, but he didn't walk away either.

'What do you think I saw in the park today? What was that?'

'You saw what you wanted to see,' he said. 'Nothing more, nothing less. It's human nature to do that. This is a difficult time for you, Tom. Very difficult.'

'Is that it? It's just an illusion?'

'The feeling is real,' he said. 'The desire to see your daughter.'

I shook my head. 'But it's not enough, is it? The desire? The wish? For me, it's just not enough.'

Chapter Fourteen

My cell phone buzzed on the nightstand. I kept my eyes closed, ignoring it, but it seemed to buzz louder, shaking and jumping against the varnished wood like a beached fish. I reached out and answered it without looking at the caller ID screen.

'Yeah?'

'What the fuck is going on up there?'

'Buster?'

'Did you see this shit in the paper? Did you really say this stuff?'

I didn't immediately follow what he was saying. I tried, through the fog, to reconstruct the events of the previous day and evening. It came back in a rush – my morning at the park and my encounter with the reporters at the police station.

'It's in the paper down there?' I asked.

'Are you kidding? Missing child possibly seen in strip club, in the company of an adult male, and then the father of the missing child goes on some loony riff about seeing the girl in the park —'

'I know the story,' I said. Through the window I saw a flat, gray sky. The house felt cool, as though the weather was turning. 'I'm just glad it's getting coverage.'

'Don't worry. Everybody knows your story now.'

I pulled the blanket over my bare legs and leaned back

against the soft pillows, letting them support my head and shoulders.

'I'm surprised you called,' I said. 'I thought maybe I'd pissed you off.'

'You did,' he said. 'But I've been thinking about you and how tough this is on you.'

'Really?'

'Sure. I haven't appreciated the toll it must take on you. And I don't mean in the obvious ways. Hell, look at you. You lost your dad when you were little. And then you lose your only child. I guess I don't think of you losing your dad since my dad was always around, but you did. You lost your old man when you were really young. And now you've got this with Caitlin. It's tragic.'

'Thanks.'

'It looks like I was wrong anyway. Shit, this is the real deal, isn't it? Did you meet this witness?'

'I did.' I told him the story of meeting Tracy in the strip club. He listened, interjecting with occasional exclamations of amazement and surprise. Telling the story to someone who was so into it, who was eager to hear it and who had the appropriate responses, felt gratifying. I felt better just laying the facts out there. 'So that's where we stand,' I said when I was finished.

'I hope they catch this guy. Fucking dirtbag pervert. Look at his fucking face. Have you ever seen such a son of a bitch? I'd like two minutes in a room alone with him – wouldn't you? I'd rip his fucking guts out for doing that to such a beautiful little girl.'

I didn't feel anything quite like Buster's anger. Other parents whose children were victims of violent crimes spoke that way, and I always felt something must have been missing in me since I couldn't summon the same sense of rage.

When I didn't answer his rage with my own, Buster changed the subject. 'How's Abby taking all this?'

'Oh, well, she's the same, you know? She's still "moving on". She doesn't want to hear about any of this. In fact, she's moving out. She's leaving me.'

'Oh,' Buster said, his voice flat.

'You're not surprised?'

'Not really. I could tell she was looking to make a break for it. I saw it in her eyes.'

I sat up straighter in the bed. 'You did?'

'Sure. She looked like a caged animal. And she's probably doing the bouncy-bouncy with that pastor guy.'

'You think that?' The twist of jealousy that knotted in my gut surprised me.

'Who knows?' he said. He sounded less certain now. He cleared his throat. 'I'm just saying . . . You know, you said you two weren't exactly kicking it anymore, so why bother with her? You're better off without her at your side. You need to know you have people there you can count on.'

'Yeah.' I stared at our ceiling. A long, narrow crack ran through the plaster, bisecting the room; it needed to be painted. 'I was hoping maybe you could come up for a few days. You can crash here. I don't know what's going to happen next with this suspect. Like you said, it would be nice to have someone here, someone who's on my side.'

Buster was silent. I waited.

'Well, you know,' he said, 'I can't exactly just break away at a moment's notice. I'm working and everything.' He cleared his throat.

'Just a couple of days . . .'

'Why don't we wait and see how this plays out,' he said. 'If you get big news or a break in the case, let me know. I'll come up.' I heard someone talking in the background, a woman. Then the sound was muffled, like his hand was over the phone. I heard his voice but couldn't make out what he was saying. Then the sound cleared, and he was back on the line. 'Okay?'

'Are you dating someone?'

'Here and there,' he said, his voice low. 'So we'll keep in touch and see what happens. Right?'

'Yeah. Right. I guess I need to work on my book.'

'Right. Idle hands and all that. Did I ask you what it's about? Is it Melville?'

'Hawthorne. Remember?'

'Cool. *The Scarlet Letter*. Man, I hated that book.'

I heard the voice again in the background.

'Okay, okay,' he said. I couldn't tell if he was talking to me or someone else. 'Okay, Tom, I've got to run.'

'Okay,' I said, but he was already off the phone.

Chapter Fifteen

I went to my office in the English department – more out of obligation than anything else – but I couldn't concentrate on anything. When I sat down at my desk, it felt as though I were sitting behind an unrecognizable wooden block, a piece of furniture whose purpose I no longer remembered or understood. The whole room felt that way. It smelled funny – different – and the proportions and angles of the walls seemed off, as though it had been years and not weeks since I'd been there. I made a half-hearted attempt to sort through the mail. I placed it into two piles: things I knew I would throw away and things I would probably throw away.

I turned on my computer and listened to it whir and grind as it booted. Occasionally a group of students passed in the hallway, their voices sounding like the chirps and calls of exotic birds. It was a mistake to come, I decided. There was no work I could do.

I checked my e-mail. More than eighty messages waited, most of them departmental and university announcements. I scanned the subject lines: *Health Fair. Estate Planning. Sandy's Baby Shower. Spring Teaching Schedules.* I didn't bother to go through them. They'd still be there later, and if anyone needed anything important from me, they could call. I might not answer, but they could call.

I looked at my overcrowded bookshelves. At eye level

sat a pile of research materials for the Hawthorne book. I rolled my chair over and picked them up. The top page was dusty, so I wiped it off with the back of my hand. Then I flipped through. A couple of photocopied articles and some notes I'd made on a legal pad. I knew it was my handwriting, but the thoughts on the page didn't mean anything to me. I couldn't remember what I was trying to say. 'Wakefield', it read, and the word was underlined three times. 'Opacity.' It was underlined three times as well.

Someone knocked on the door, quick, tentative taps. I decided to just ignore it. But they knocked again, louder and more insistent.

'Shit,' I muttered.

I put the Hawthorne notes away and opened the door. 'Yes?'

'Mr Stuart?'

'Yes?'

Something about her face seemed vaguely familiar, and at first I assumed she was a student from a previous semester, one of the anonymous multitudes who flew under the radar in an American Lit survey, knocking out the requirement with the same joy and gusto usually reserved for doing laundry. But then I noticed the limpness of her hair, the tiredness of her eyes. It registered.

'Tracy,' I said. 'I'm sorry. Out of context, I —'

'You don't expect to see a girl like me here on campus.'

I stepped back. 'Come in. Sit down.' She looked uncertain. Her eyes roamed the room as though she were across a boundary and into another world. She settled into my extra chair, the one where students usually sat. I took my seat behind the desk. 'Are you a student here?'

Her laugh possessed a bitter edge. 'Yeah, I'd have to rob a bank and not just take off my clothes to pay for this. I didn't even finish high school.'

'Thank you for talking to the police and working with them on the sketch.'

She didn't respond. Her hand was raised to her head, and her index finger twirled a strand of brittle-looking hair. Her eyes were focused on the desktop.

'It's going to help a lot, I think. The sketch.' When she didn't answer again, I said, 'Is there a reason why you're here? Is something wrong?'

'I guess that's what I wanted to talk to you about, all that stuff in the papers and on TV about your daughter.'

'It's there because of you.'

'Yeah . . .' She stopped twirling her hair and looked at me. 'I'm sorry about that.'

'What are you sorry for?'

'You believe my story, don't you?' she asked.

'Is there a reason why I shouldn't?' I asked.

She shook her head slowly, and while she did I remembered Ryan's comments about Tracy. *Well detailed. Convincingly so.*

'I saw what I saw,' she said. 'I did.'

'Then there shouldn't be a problem.'

'Have you thought about what you'd do if she came back?' she asked.

'You mean Caitlin, right? Have I thought about her coming back home?' I asked. 'Of course. Many times.'

In great detail. Convincingly so. Caitlin running into my arms. Caitlin saying my name. Caitlin happy and smiling, a beautiful young woman ready to resume her life.

'I hope you get to see that come true,' she said.

She smiled a little, but it didn't possess much warmth.

'Is something wrong, Tracy? Is there something you need to tell me that you're having a hard time getting out?'

'You're a religious man, right?'

'No.'

'Oh.'

'Why would you ask me that?'

'I just thought since you saw that . . . vision in the park yesterday.'

I squirmed a little in my chair. 'I wouldn't call it a vision.'

'But you saw something. Something you believe in. Like me at the club.'

For the moment, I followed the train of her thought. We were alike, she and I. We were both witnesses to things central to Caitlin's case, and while others may have had their doubts, we were both certain. We believed ourselves and each other at the very least.

She started twirling her hair again. 'I haven't had an easy time of things, you know.'

'Since we met —'

'In life.'

She looked at me again, without smiling. Her eyes were hard, impermeable. Like colored glass.

'I'm sorry,' I said.

I didn't know where our conversation was going. I thought she was looking for reassurances from me, for an understanding that I felt happy about her coming forward and telling her story to the police. But something hovered beneath the surface of her words, something slippery and elusive I couldn't get a handle on.

'See, I want to help you,' she said. 'That's why I called Liann, even though I'd been in trouble before and I don't really like the police.'

'I understand.'

'I'd like to help you more.' She still twirled the hair. And with her other hand, she tapped a fingernail – the polish chipped and dark – against the armrest of the chair.

'Let me show you something.' She bent down out of my sight and rustled around in her bag. She popped back up holding a business card. She brushed a loose strand of hair out of her face, then passed the business card across the desk to me. 'Here. I brought this for you.'

I reached out. It was a business card for someone named Susan Goff of 'Volunteer Victim Services'. A local phone number was listed under her name.

I knew my face betrayed my skepticism. 'What is this?' I asked.

'She's a lady who helps people.'

'A therapist?'

'She's not a therapist,' Tracy said. 'I don't even know if she went to school.'

I tried to hand the card back. 'I'm not really interested in that.'

'I met her through a friend,' Tracy said. 'But she works with the cops too.'

The name sounded familiar to me. *Volunteer Victim Services*. Ryan had mentioned them to us more than once, but we never called or followed up. 'The police are already working on this,' I said.

'She's not a cop,' Tracy said. 'She's . . . just someone to

talk to, someone who's willing to support you no matter what. She's not working any angles.'

'Everybody has an angle, don't they?' I asked.

'Susan's nice. She's not a lawyer or anything like that. She understands people and things.' Tracy rolled her eyes a little. 'I mean, I know Liann's trying to help me and everything, but she's only willing to do so much, you know? She wants to help me, but she wants to help me on her terms. If I ask her for something, something outside her agenda, she shuts me down.'

'Have you been in therapy?' I asked.

'That's all bullshit,' she said. 'Therapists, social workers – you just tell them what they want to hear. They check off their little boxes on their little forms, and they pass you on to somebody else.' Tracy bent down again and brought out her cell phone. She studied the display and frowned. 'I have to go in a minute. But keep that card and use it if you want. Maybe you could talk to Susan. I've talked to her before, and she's really helpful, you know, with life and relationships and stuff. She listens to me. Really listens to me. You know what it's like when someone really listens to you?'

'I know what you mean,' I said.

'Susan's not a bullshitter. Not at all. She tells you the truth if you want to hear it. And if you don't have a minister or a shrink or anything, you need someone to talk to. Right?'

'I don't know . . .'

'Think about it. Okay? She just . . . she knows things. A lot of things. Sometimes I think she knows me better than I know myself. And she's comfortable talking about stuff that's tough to talk about.'

'Is this what you came to tell me?' I asked, holding the card in the air between us. 'Is this all?'

She squirmed a little in the chair, shifting her weight from one side to the other as though fighting off an unpleasant itch.

'Tracy? Is there something else?'

'Remember how I said I had a daughter?'

'Yes.'

Her voice was lower. 'You know how kids are expensive to raise.'

'I don't follow.'

She squirmed some more. Side to side, rocking like a metronome.

'Are you asking me for money?'

'You see . . .' She paused, let out a long breath. 'I've been thinking about what I saw that night. Thinking and thinking . . .'

'And?'

She slumped a little, her body going slack in the chair.

'Tracy?'

'I want to remember more,' she said. 'I want to help more.'

She stopped short. Somewhere outside, a lawn mower engine kicked to life, making a low rumble across the campus.

'What do you know?' I asked.

She didn't answer.

'If you think you can come in here and mess with me, toy with my emotions —'

She moved quickly and was up out of the chair, reaching for her bag and brushing her hair back out of her face. She didn't even look at me, but turned for the door.

'Tracy, wait.'

My hand went to my back pocket. I never carried much cash. I dug around and found forty-two dollars. I held it out to her.

She turned and looked at me, looked at my hand and the money, but didn't make a move to take it. I tossed it onto the desk.

'Take it,' I said. 'I don't care.'

She still didn't move. Her top teeth rested on her lower lip.

'Buy diapers or something. But if you know anything else . . .'

She took two steps forward and picked up the money. She looked at it for a moment, then folded the bills in half and slipped them into the front pocket of her shorts.

'That man is very bad,' she said.

'Do you know him from somewhere? Have you seen him before?'

She backed away, her eyes averted from mine.

I started around the desk. 'Tracy, if you know something and you don't tell —'

She held her hand up between us, telling me to stop. I did.

'Tell Liann,' I said.

'I told the truth already,' she said. 'I told my story.'

'Is there more?'

She nodded toward my desk. It took a moment for me to understand what she meant. Then I saw it – the card. *Volunteer Victim Services*.

'Think about calling Susan,' she said.

Then she slipped through the door and closed it behind her almost soundlessly.

Chapter Sixteen

Abby's car sat in the driveway. It was filled with more boxes, more clothes, the remains of what she needed from the house.

Three boxes sat on the kitchen table with clothes on hangers draped over them. The clothes were from the winter – heavy coats and sweaters. I stood beneath the overhead fluorescents, a light fixture we'd always planned to replace but never did. I ran my hand over the fabric of her sweaters. I brought the sleeve of one up to my nose and took a deep breath. I always used to enjoy Abby's scents – the fruity shampoos, the sweet soaps, even the smell of her sweat when she exercised or worked on something around the house. But this sweater smelled musty, the product of a closed closet.

'You're home.'

I dropped the sleeve. Abby stood in the doorway, holding a canvas bag full of clothes.

'I was in the office most of the day,' I said.

'Good.' Abby came farther into the room and put down the bag. 'This is the last of it,' she said. 'I'll take it out to the car.'

'Do you want me to help?'

She shook her head. 'No. It's my stuff. I'll take it.'

'You'll hurt yourself.'

'I've got it,' she said. 'It's not that heavy.'

She picked up one of the boxes and elbowed the screen door open, letting it slam behind her. I went out into the other room and sorted through the mail. Bills mostly. A newsmagazine. I leafed through it, scanning the headlines about war and political crises. While I did that, the back door opened and closed a couple more times. I finally gave up on the magazine and tossed it onto the coffee table. I went back to the kitchen and saw just the canvas bag remaining on the floor. I looked outside and saw Abby bent into the backseat of her car, the dome light a tiny white spot in the darkening evening. She and I hadn't even talked about the property, about the cars and the bank accounts and the credit cards we still owed money on. Friends of ours who had been down the same road spent weeks working out every detail.

But then another thought occurred to me: those people all had children. They *had* to plan and hash things out. Abby and I were breaking up like young marrieds, like a boyfriend and girlfriend who'd shacked up and then simply grew bored with each other.

She came back in and wiped her forehead with the back of her hand. 'I need some water,' she said.

'Did you read the news stories?' I asked. 'I'm just wondering.'

She took a deep breath. She stood at the sink, her back to me. 'I did. I saw all the news coverage. People would have told me about it anyway.'

'You don't believe any of it?'

She put down her glass but didn't turn around. 'Tom, I think you should see someone. A professional.'

'A shrink?'

'Yes.'

'Why?' I raised my hands in an exaggerated shrug.

She turned around. She folded her arms across her chest but didn't answer. In the harsh light from above she looked older but still beautiful, not all that different from when we first met.

I stepped closer. 'Is it because of what I said in the paper? About the girl in the cemetery?'

'That's part of it.'

'You're the one who has so much faith. Why don't you believe me?'

She shook her head. 'Because God doesn't work that way.'

'How do you know? Did Pastor Chris tell you?'

'When Caitlin disappeared, I said we should go to counseling. Remember that? Not marriage counseling but counseling to help us deal with the loss. Remember?'

She wanted an answer, so I gave her one. 'I remember.'

'And you said you didn't want to go, that you didn't need it because nothing was really lost.' She hunched her shoulders and rubbed her arms as though she were cold. 'I didn't argue about it. I didn't push you. I thought we needed it – we both needed it – but I also knew that death meant something different to you because of your dad. When my dad died, I was older. We were married already and had Caitlin. But I know your dad's death is a wound for you, and so when Caitlin disappeared . . . I know how much it meant to you to have your own child since you were your dad's only child. It's complicated with Buster. He's your half sibling. And I know there was guilt on your part. Guilt about letting her go out that day, about letting

121

her cross the street with Frosty and go to the park. And to the extent I contributed to that, I'm sorry. I really am.'

'Do you want to sit down?'

I reached for a chair and Abby did likewise, but then she stopped and held out her hands as though the thought of sitting down disgusted her.

'No, Tom. I can't.' She was still holding up her hands, and she was crying. She started with two deep sniffles; then her chin puckered. 'I can't.'

'Abby . . .' I didn't sit either. I reached out for her. I placed my hand on her arm. My own emotions – pity, love – crept up on me unexpectedly.

She lifted her free hand to her face and wiped at her tears.

'Come on,' I said. 'Sit.'

'No, no.' She pulled back. 'I can't. Just listen.'

She backed away from me and again swiped at her face with her hands. She took a deep, sniffling inhalation of air and seemed to regain a measure of her composure. I didn't sit or move. I waited. I knew she had more to say, more to direct at me.

'You disappeared on me, Tom.' She cleared her throat. 'You wanted children more than me, remember?' Her composure slipped again. 'And I'm so very glad we did it. Even now. Even after all of this. I think of our girl . . . that sweet, baby girl.'

'We tried to have another one,' I said. 'We could try again. I don't think it's too late.'

Abby shook her head and looked away. She seemed more distraught, more upset. 'No,' she said. 'I can't do that anymore.' She kept shaking her head.

'You mean the toll —'

'Tom, it worked.'

'What worked?'

'I did get pregnant again, after Caitlin was gone. When we were trying. I did get pregnant, but I had a miscarriage. I didn't tell you, and I'm sorry.'

For a moment, I couldn't speak. The room felt closer, more contained. I became aware that my mouth was hanging open. 'We had another baby?'

'A miscarriage,' Abby said.

'And you didn't tell me?' I still wasn't sure I understood.

'I was protecting you,' she said. 'In your state of mind, with Caitlin gone, I didn't think you could handle it.' She reached up, wiped at her nose.

'Why are you telling me now?'

'Because . . . because I don't want to walk away with you thinking I wasn't willing to do all I could for this marriage.'

'By lying to me?'

'I have to go, Tom. I really do.' She bent down and grabbed the canvas bag, and without stopping her motion or slowing down, she breezed across the room and to the back door. 'Think about what I said, Tom. About getting help. See a therapist. Or ask Ryan. He might know someone. You can work with someone about your family, about your stepfather, about the rejection you felt there. I think you need it.'

And then she was gone.

PART TWO

Chapter Seventeen

My father died when I was four. Pancreatic cancer. Most of my memories of him are in fragments – little, tattered pieces I carry around with me. They come back at odd moments. I remember the musky smell of his cologne and the rough way his stubbled face scraped against mine. Sometimes when I'm shaving my own face, I wonder how much he and I would have looked alike.

I remember that his hands were big, with thick fingers, and when he picked me up and held me under the armpits, his grip was so tight and strong it hurt a little. A good hurt that I didn't mind. And I remember his voice, loud and strong, and the way it almost seemed to ring when he called my name or my mother's name from across the house.

But the most coherent memory of him occurred on a spring day about a year before he died. It's the only sustained narrative memory of him I have.

My mother wasn't home. I can't say where she was or what she was doing, but she wasn't there, which meant my father was watching me. And I don't know if he knew he was sick yet or not. If he knew, he would have just found out. More likely, he hadn't been diagnosed yet, but the cancer was already there, growing inside him, extending its tendrils into his healthy cells and tissue, destroying his body from the inside out.

Our backyard sloped down to the houses behind us. Some kids a little older than me lived back there. Our mothers knew each other, and from time to time they'd let us all run around together under their watchful eyes. On this particular spring day I'm remembering, I was out with those other kids, a boy and girl named Amy and Kevin. The weather was newly warm, the trees and flowers were starting to bud and bloom, and the parents were probably glad to be able to let us all out of the house to burn off energy.

But at some point that day, the skies darkened.

Enormous clouds, thick and purple and looming, grew above us. The wind picked up, making branches and leaves fall to the ground around us. It buffeted our small bodies until we swayed and struggled to stay on our feet.

There's a gap in my memory. It's possible the parents of the other children called them in, or perhaps the other kids decided to run home in the face of the threatening storm. I just know that I ended up in our backyard alone as the storm continued to blow. And it seemed as though the entire world had been set in motion. The trees bucked and bent, the fence that bordered the yard shuddered, and everything that wasn't anchored down – every leaf, every scrap of paper, every grass clipping – took to the air and swirled around me until I felt as though I were standing in one of those Christmas snow globes, the kind that when shaken produce the kinetic spinning of a blizzard.

I turned toward the house, moving my little legs a half step at a time. The wind pushed against me, holding me upright as though I were being restrained by invisible wires. Something flew into my eye, a quick stabbing pain.

I pressed my hand against the eyelid and kept walking forward as best I could.

By the time I reached the side of our house and came around into the front yard, rain had started to fall. Thick, pelting drops splattered against my face and into my hair. My breath came in jerking huffs. My one open eye blurred and burned from the tears. And I finally reached a point, standing on the side of the house, where I decided I just couldn't go on anymore. I let the wind push me back, let my body go slack and loose, and I sat down in the grass, my hand still pressed against my eye. I remember thinking, very clearly, that I was going to die right there, that my life was going to end in the storm, in the side yard of our house.

I don't know how long I sat there. It couldn't have been very long, because I don't remember getting very wet. But at some point I looked up and there he was. My father, standing over me, his face creased with concern. I thought he was angry with me for being out in the rain, but he didn't say or do anything to indicate anger. Instead, he bent down and gathered me in his arms and squeezed me tight against his chest. I went limp in his grip and buried my head against the side of his neck. I breathed in his familiar scent, and in that moment I knew what it meant to be home. To be protected. To be safe. And long after my father died and this became the only solid memory of him I carried with me, I used this moment as a measuring stick, a guide to remind me of what a father was supposed to be.

Chapter Eighteen

The business card with Susan Goff's name sat on the kitchen table amid the crumbs and the morning paper. I had picked up the phone twice and put it down twice, changing my mind, before I finally placed the call.

I was alone in the house. Really alone. Abby had been gone three weeks. Whenever I called Ryan for updates, he offered nothing new and told me to be patient. Liann e-mailed me a few times, just checking in, as she put it, but the lack of developments didn't give us much to talk about. And my occasional trips to campus only reminded me of how little interest I had in writing a book about Nathaniel Hawthorne.

Susan Goff answered her phone with a bright, energetic voice that made it tough for me to estimate her age. She could have been in her twenties, or she could have been pushing sixty. But her enthusiastic greeting did have one effect – it disarmed me and made me more at ease than I'd expected to be.

'I was referred to you by a friend,' I said.

'Wonderful,' she said. 'What can I help you with?'

'I don't know. Do we set up an appointment or something?'

'Yes, of course. But just a casual chat. I hate the word "appointment". It sounds so businesslike. Don't you agree?'

'Yeah, I guess so. Okay. Well, just so you know, my name is Tom Stuart, and I'm calling because of my daughter.' I started to tell her the details of Caitlin's disappearance, thinking she would want to know them up front, but she gently interrupted me.

'Oh. Oh, yes. Oh, I know who you are. Yes, yes.'

'You've heard about it on the news.'

'Yes.' She paused. 'From the news. And Tracy told me she'd be giving you my card. This is so very sad. I'm so very sorry for this.'

'Thank you,' I said. 'It was Tracy who referred me to you.'

'And have you been seeing someone else? A professional therapist?'

'No, I haven't.'

'You need to know up front that I'm not a licensed therapist or a professional counselor. If you need that, I can't help you.' She laughed a little, a self-deprecating sound. 'I volunteer through the police department, but I don't work strictly for them. I'm not any kind of police officer, and I don't investigate crimes. In fact, I don't just work with the victims of crime. I might work with someone who has a loved one who has committed suicide. Or families that have lost someone in an accident. That sort of thing.' She made it sound as casual as helping someone choose wallpaper.

'So you're just a person who helps people?' I asked. 'Couldn't I just go out in the street and start talking to someone?'

'I've been trained,' she said. 'They don't just throw us out into the community and turn us loose on people in their most vulnerable moments. That wouldn't make much sense, would it?'

'Do you hold a license or degree in something?' I asked.

'Everyone in Volunteer Victim Services goes through an eight-week training session. At least once a year we go back for a continuing ed course, and we all have criminal background checks. Hell, once a month I pee in a cup so the state of Ohio knows I'm not doing any illicit drugs. It's all to give us a grounding in the basics of helping people in need.'

'And what do you do for them?' I asked. 'What can you . . . ?'

'What can I do for you?' she asked. 'I'm really just a support system, Mr Stuart. Someone to listen to your problems. You know, the police officers are so busy with other aspects of the cases they work on. The investigating, the testifying, the prosecuting. That's not what I do. Mostly I listen. I try not to judge or offer heavy opinions, but if you ask me for one, I'll share it. That's up to you. Does that sound like something you would be interested in?'

I didn't feel like I could say no, even if I wanted to. She was so *there*, so in the moment for me. She was so ready to help. And the fact that she wasn't a police officer or a minister or even a crusader on behalf of victims' rights made me feel better. She did seem like someone who wanted to help me.

'Okay,' I said. 'Yes. Do you want to make an appointment – a meeting time – for next week?'

'Let's get together tomorrow at four,' she said. 'Do you know the Courthouse Coffee Shop downtown?'

'I do.'

'Let's meet there,' she said. 'If you don't like me, at least the coffee will be good.'

A year or so after Caitlin had disappeared, around the time Abby would have been having her miscarriage, she and I discussed what to do with Caitlin's room. We had been keeping it just as it was the day Caitlin disappeared – the clothes in the closet, the personal items on the shelves. But Abby started to make a case for change. She went out of her way to tell me we wouldn't throw away anything, but she wanted to pack up some things and move them to the attic, and then paint the walls and rearrange the furniture.

'The room is an obstacle, Tom,' she said, no doubt using language she'd heard from Pastor Chris in one of his 'counseling' sessions. 'We can't move on with it there.'

I categorically told her no. I left no space for argument.

And the room stayed intact.

Just before I left the house to go to meet Susan Goff for the first time, I stopped by Caitlin's bedroom. I went in there several times a month. I liked to sit on the bed or run my hand over the desk and the bedclothes, picking up the stuffed animals and putting them back down exactly where Caitlin had left them. In the first hours after Caitlin's disappearance, I combed through the room, digging into the drawers, opening school notebooks, looking for anything that might give us a clue. Then the police took over that job, and they discovered the Seattle and Amtrak information that conjured the possibility of Caitlin being a runaway.

When I went in there before seeing Susan, something felt different. The space seemed foreign to me, almost forbidden, as though I were about to enter a room belonging to a stranger, one who wouldn't want me intruding upon her world.

And while I stood there, my mind ran through the *what-if*s: What if Abby and I had had another child; what if she'd carried that baby to full term? Would it have taken over this space? Would Caitlin's memory have been effaced from our lives?

I pushed open the door.

The blinds were closed and little light entered, giving the room a gray, wintery cast. It smelled musty, as I'd expected. I ran my hand across the top of the dresser to my left, acquiring a thick layer of dust on the tips of my fingers. The floor squeaked beneath me as I moved across the carpet. A cluster of young adult books sat on a shelf; a group of stuffed animals lay at the foot of the bed. On a small shelf above her desk, two trophies from the two years she'd played soccer through a local youth group. She didn't want to play and insisted, even in the car on the way to the first practice, that she wasn't going to do it or go along. But go along she did, and she ended up loving it, and even talked of playing in high school someday, all of which amounted to a rare display of interest on her part in a group activity.

The bed remained unmade. I went over and sat on it, felt the springs bounce beneath my weight, and remembered the nights when Caitlin was small and too scared to go to sleep alone. Either Abby or I would take turns coming in and lying next to her until she fell asleep – her soft, whistling breaths assuring us we could go – but we always made sure to leave the door cracked so she could see the faint light in the hallway.

I pushed myself off the bed and went to the closet. This time, before this door, I didn't hesitate. I pulled it open, then reached up and yanked the light cord. I took a step back. The closet was packed full. Her clothes were crowded together so tight they could barely move from side to side. I recognized and remembered certain things. A pink sweater we gave Caitlin one Christmas. A Fields University football jersey, girl sized and bearing double zeroes. At the far end of the closet, I came across Caitlin's winter coat, a puffy red parka. I touched it, squeezed the soft sleeves in my hand, and with a stabbing ache was taken back to a winter day six years earlier when Caitlin and I had built a snowman in our yard.

The pain I felt was literal and real. It went through my chest and into my back. I closed my eyes, clenched them shut, and heard Caitlin's laughter in the yard, a giggling trill. I felt the sting of the cold wind on my cheeks and the wet burning from the snow she'd dumped down the back of my shirt. For that moment, that one painful, glorious moment, she was there, Caitlin, and then just as quickly it passed. The pain eased; the memory receded. I opened my eyes and it was just me, a middle-aged guy standing in a closet, clutching a child's coat.

And the child was gone.

The thought popped into my head, just like the memory of playing in the snow. I never thought it so clearly and with such finality. *She's gone. Caitlin is gone.* And I knew, as time passed, the memories would fade, and the haunting, stabbing moments would come back to me with less frequency until, someday, they might be gone forever, and with them all tangible sense of my daughter.

I pulled the coat tight to me, pressed my face deep into its fabrics and folds. I inhaled. It smelled musty like the closet, but I didn't care. I breathed deeply again and again, letting the musty smell fill me.

I took the coat and placed it back on its hanger, then started working it back in among the other clothes on the rod. I stepped back, my hand on the closet door, when I saw the flash of red. I thought it was a hat or glove. The weather had been cold in the days leading up to Caitlin's disappearance, but on the day she disappeared, we'd experienced a brief late-winter warm-up, so Caitlin had left the house that day in a lighter jacket instead. I noticed that the red object looked fragile, almost papery, and parts of it fell to the ground.

I reached for it, and it crumpled more. It was a flower, a red carnation. It felt brittle in my hand, a handful of dust. A single stem, with no note or adornment. No ribbon or lace. I didn't know where it came from, except that Caitlin must have gotten it in the days before her disappearance. Where she'd come across that red carnation, I couldn't guess.

Chapter Nineteen

I saw them together in the parking lot. I'd gone to the grocery store looking for better food. My bachelor diet was making me feel sluggish and drained, a corpulent lump on the living room couch. I forced myself out into the world, out to where living people ate things that were green or yellow or red and not in a box or a can.

I was leaving the store when I saw Abby and Pastor Chris getting out of a car together. He waited for her, even went so far as to place his hand on the small of her back as she walked by. I stopped where I was and watched them. I held my plastic bag in one hand, the car keys in the other. It took them a moment to see me. They walked close together, leaning in toward each other as though sharing secrets.

Chris saw me first. Something crossed his face – momentary guilt? – but just as quickly his happy mask snapped into place. His smile grew wider than normal and he called out to me like we were old friends.

'Tom!'

His hands fell to his sides, stiff and straight as tent stakes.

I didn't say anything. I watched Abby. She looked away, first at the ground, then at the sky; then, when left with no choice, she looked at me.

'Hello, Tom,' she said.

'Hello.'

They stopped, and for a long moment the three of us stood there, Mexican standoff style, while shoppers pushed their carts past us and minivans full of kids and groceries navigated the lanes.

I tried to keep my voice level.

'You two look awfully domestic together, don't you?'

Chris kept smiling. 'Just buying groceries,' he said. 'We have a youth group meeting tonight at the —'

'Shut up.'

He blinked his eyes a few times, a hurt puppy.

'Come on, Chris,' Abby said.

'Yeah, go on,' I said. 'Go on with another man's wife. Isn't there a commandment about that? Or does your church not do the commandments anymore? Is that why people like it so much?'

'Now, Tom,' Chris said, bringing the smile back. 'I don't think there's any need to say these things to me.'

'Didn't I tell you to shut up?'

Abby took Chris's arm and pulled him toward the store.

'Go home, Tom,' she said. 'Think about what I said about getting help.'

I managed to switch my keys from my right hand to the left, leaving me free to reach into my pocket. I pulled out a plastic sandwich bag, the kind with a zipped top. It held the remains of the flower I'd found in Caitlin's closet.

'Do you know what this is, Abby?' She stopped and squinted at the bag, confused. 'I found this in Caitlin's closet. It was in her coat pocket.'

She shook her head but didn't say anything.

'It's not over, Abby. I know you want it to be over. I

know you want to move on. Apparently, you have moved on. But it's not time yet.'

Abby stared at me for a moment. I thought she was going to say something – anything – but she just turned and started for the store, leaving Chris behind her.

'She had a miscarriage,' I said to him. 'Our baby, about a year after Caitlin disappeared. And she didn't tell me.'

Chris pursed his lips. 'It was a difficult decision for Abby,' he said. 'I counseled her about it. We prayed about it. She decided it was the best thing to do, to keep it from you.'

'You knew?'

But he was already gone. Having given me a little wave good-bye, he hustled to catch up with Abby, leaving me standing alone in the middle of the parking lot.

Courthouse Coffee sat on the opposite side of the square from the police station and served a very different clientele. During the day lawyers and businesspeople stopped there for lattes and cappuccinos, and at night college students congregated there with their books and laptops. At least once a month, Courthouse Coffee hosted a poetry reading, and a rotation of local artists hung their work on the walls. Because I considered it a student hang-out, I didn't spend much time there, and my awkwardness at entering the coffee shop was exaggerated by the fact that I had no idea how to identify Susan Goff. I had hung up with her without asking how we'd know each other. But as soon as I walked in, I heard my name.

'Dr Stuart? Tom Stuart?'

I looked around. Most of the tables were occupied, but

only one was occupied by a woman who was halfway out of her chair, waving at me. She called my name again and continued to wave, and it felt as though everyone in the room had turned to look at me.

'Yes,' I said. 'That's me.'

I crossed to her table and took her in. She wore her gray hair short and a little mannish, and a pair of half-moon glasses sat perched on her nose. She took the glasses off when she stood to shake my hand, and I saw that she was wearing beige cotton pants, white sneakers, and a loose, baggy shirt. Her grip was firm, and her no-nonsense appearance seemed in opposition to the cheeriness of her voice.

'I recognize you from TV,' she said, loud enough for everyone to hear.

'Lucky me.'

'Do you want a coffee?' she asked. 'I love the coffee here.'

'I'm okay,' I said.

We sat on opposite sides of the small table. She maintained a wide yet sympathetic smile, and her gray eyes studied me as though I were the most fascinating person she'd ever met. I placed her age in the midfifties.

'Well,' she said. 'You're on quite a journey.'

'Like I said, Tracy Fairlawn sent me your way.'

'She's on quite a journey, too.'

'Have you been able to help her?' I asked.

'I listen to Tracy a lot,' Susan said. 'I think she needs that.'

'And you think that helps her?' I asked.

'Why don't I tell you a little more about what I do, and

then you'll understand where I'm coming from,' she said. 'Like I told you on the phone, I'm not a professional. I'm a volunteer. I'm not a therapist or a licensed counselor. About ten years back, the state realized there were people falling through the cracks. They may have suffered a personal tragedy of some kind, and they may have been reluctant to seek remedies through traditional mental health venues like a therapist or counselor. Volunteer Victim Services was created to fill that gap. It's just people like me helping people like you. The police or other social service agencies dispatch us if they think there's a need. We know how to spot larger troubles if they're there, and we know where to refer people whose problems go beyond the scope of what a volunteer can do. Believe me, we know our limits, and we're overseen by social workers who know them too. Otherwise, we're here to listen and help people cope with the transitions tragedy brings to their lives. Does that make sense to you?'

'How did you get involved with this?' I asked.

'My children are grown, and my husband and I split up about five years ago,' she said. 'I retired from the school system around the time of the divorce.'

'You were a teacher?' I asked.

'No, a secretary. Sorry, an administrative aide. I worked in the superintendent's office. When I retired and got divorced, I was looking for something to do, some way I could help people. I didn't want to just sit around living off my pension and gardening. It sounds really corny and noble, doesn't it?'

I had to laugh. 'It does. It really does.'

'Guilty as charged,' she said. 'Are you sure you don't want anything? I was just about to go up for a refill.'

'Okay. Coffee.'

While Susan went up to the counter, I studied the crowd. Normal people having a normal day. I recognized a former student who didn't look over at me, and a colleague from another department who waved and went back to his laptop. And there I was talking to a complete stranger about the most important thing in my life.

Susan returned and placed a mug before me. 'So,' she said, 'what's it been like since you were on TV?'

'Not what I was hoping for,' I said.

She didn't say anything. She just held that steady, considering gaze on me, the one that said she was ready to hear anything and everything I might have to say. Before I knew it, I was saying more.

'The sketch and the press conference led to a lot of crank calls and not very helpful information. People claiming to see Caitlin's ghost, or perverts saying they had Caitlin with them right there. I know it's not unusual for that to happen.'

'No, it's not,' Susan said. 'It makes people feel important, even the pranksters.'

'Has anyone in your family ever been the victim of a violent crime?' I asked.

'We've been lucky.' She sipped from her mug. 'We don't have to talk about your daughter,' she said. 'We can talk about other things. We can talk about your job, for example. I saw in the paper you teach at the university. What's that like?'

'Oh, God,' I said. 'No one wants to hear about that. I'm writing a book on Nathaniel Hawthorne. That should tell you all you need to know.'

'I love to read,' she said. 'I was a literature minor —'

'I don't want to waste your time,' I said. Despite Susan's openness, a discomfort gnawed at my insides, a raw rubbing I couldn't shake. Being there and talking felt unnatural to me. 'Maybe this isn't the best thing for me. It's unusual —' I stopped and turned away from Susan, letting my gaze wander out the window to the traffic circling the square. I felt muddled and unfocused. 'You're a complete stranger, and I'm somewhat of a private person.'

'I understand that this is difficult,' she said. 'We can talk about the weather if you'd like.'

'I don't know. It's just . . . this sketch, the drawing of this man. It's the best lead we've had, you know? But in some ways it's making things worse for me.'

'How?'

'I don't know.'

Susan Goff didn't say anything. She just sat there, coffee mug before her, waiting.

'I'm afraid,' I said finally.

'Of what?'

I paused. 'I'm afraid if I admit my doubts, they'll become reality.'

She kept her steady gaze on me. 'What are you afraid of?'

I didn't answer. I couldn't say it. I refused to say it.

'Are you afraid she's dead?' Susan asked.

'Jesus Christ. You can't just say that to somebody. You can't just be so cavalier about it.'

Susan straightened a little in her chair. 'You're right,' she said. 'I can't. I'm sorry.'

'Jesus.'

'Maybe I'm overstepping too soon.'

'Maybe.'

'But I was just trying to give voice to what you were already thinking.' She cleared her throat. 'You're here because you want to know something about yourself. You feel guilty. And you want to know if it makes you a bad father to allow yourself to think the worst. It's not an unusual response. I worked with a woman a few years back. Her sixteen-year-old son had been killed in a car accident. Sixteen. About a year after the accident she decided to give his clothes to Goodwill. She felt so guilty and like such a bad mother, she practically collapsed. She went to bed for a week. I had to go and talk to her in her bedroom. Do you see how this can affect people?'

'I guess you're right.' My voice sounded thin and distant even to my own ears.

'Why would you think she's dead?'

I felt small in the chair, like a child. 'It's been four years. With no real advances in the case. Even the recent events, this man —'

'This is the man from the strip club? The one in the sketch in the paper?'

'Yes.'

'The man who Tracy saw.'

'Has she talked to you about him?' I asked. 'Has she said anything about this man?'

She didn't answer.

'You can't say,' I said. 'Or you won't say. Which is it?'

'If one of your students came to you and asked about another student's grade, what would you say?'

'I get it,' I said.

'Let me ask you this – why would it be such a problem to admit that your daughter is in all likelihood dead?'

'I'm not supposed to. I have to believe she's not gone.'

'Why?'

'I'm her father.' It was the best and simplest answer I could summon.

'But you don't really seem to believe this. I can tell. You're full of doubt. And that's why you're here, right? That's why you're talking to a complete stranger after all this time, when I know you've had plenty of opportunities to talk to shrinks and social workers. You're here because you've been playing the big, strong man all this time, and now the doubts are starting to win. Right?'

'I thought you didn't offer opinions or judgment unless asked?'

'You seem like you can handle it,' she said. 'So, am I right?'

My throat felt constricted and phlegmy. 'When I look around, I see that everyone else is moving on, has moved on, and maybe I should do the same.'

'Maybe?'

'I *should* move on,' I said.

'But why? Why now? What's changed?'

I reached into my coat pocket and brought out a ziplock bag. I handed it across the table. Susan took it, examined it, and then looked at me.

'A wilted flower,' she said.

'Before I came over here today, I went into Caitlin's room. I do that from time to time.'

'Is it still her room?' Susan asked. 'Have you changed it?'

I shook my head. 'It's exactly the same.'

'Ah,' she said as though my answer meant something. But she didn't explain.

'She wore her coat to the park in the days before she disappeared. Then the day she disappeared she wore a different coat. I think the man who took her – the man in that drawing – gave her the flower. It was right before Valentine's Day.'

'Hmm.' Susan held the bag in her hands, turned it over, and looked at it from all sides. Her nails were short and unpainted. She seemed to be taking the flower very seriously. 'Maybe she picked it up off the ground. Or took it from the cemetery, off of a grave. Or a school friend gave it to her. There are other possibilities.'

'Why would she keep it in her coat if that was the case? It's like she was hiding it.'

Susan shrugged. 'I think you should share this with the police. It's over my head, to be honest. But if it's evidence, if it's important, they should see it.' She handed the bag back.

I took it and held it in my hand for a long moment. I couldn't imagine giving it away to the police. It was foolish, I knew, but it seemed like a strong link to Caitlin, and I couldn't just give it away.

'It's like an artifact, isn't it?' Susan asked.

'You read my mind.'

'I don't do that. But I will tell you that when my husband moved out of our house he left some of his things behind. Some old clothes, some books. I couldn't bring myself to get rid of them.'

'When did you finally do it?' I asked.

'Never,' she said. 'They're still right there and probably always will be. That's why I understand how that woman I mentioned felt about her son. And how you feel about this.'

'I don't know if that's encouraging or disturbing,' I said.

'Neither do I.'

I slipped the plastic bag into my coat pocket. 'Well, since we're telling each other all our dirty little secrets, I thought I could ask you one more thing.'

'Shoot.'

'You read the paper, right? And saw the story about the press conference where the police released the sketch? You know that I mentioned seeing something – someone – in the park where Caitlin disappeared.'

'The ghost,' she said, holding her hands up and making air quotes.

'What do you make of that?' I asked. 'Is it possible? Did I see something . . . ?'

'You saw something,' she said. 'I'm an open-minded person by nature. I tend to think it's possible there are things we just don't understand in this world. People and things we don't understand. Maybe you just saw what you wanted to see.' She paused and studied my face. 'We all have ghosts, Tom. We trail them along behind us like banners.'

'Or like weights,' I said.

'What are you going to do with your weight?' she asked.

I didn't know. I really didn't know.

But I didn't get up to leave. I stayed in my seat.

'The police . . .' I said.

'What about them?'

147

'The police think Tracy might know the man she saw in the strip club. And she came by my office at the university and hinted at the same thing.'

'I told you I shouldn't —'

'And then she asked me for money.'

She raised her eyebrows. 'Did you give it to her?'

'Am I being played here?' I asked. 'Is she up to something?'

'Tracy is not fully healed. You need to keep that in mind when you have dealings with her. If she asks you for money again, I suggest you don't give it to her. I've made that mistake with her before.'

'I guess it's hard to resist the urge to help,' I said. 'It's hard to forget she's somebody's daughter. Somebody somewhere.'

'We all are, aren't we? We all are.'

Chapter Twenty

The cell phone woke me the next morning. My eyes fixed not on the buzzing, vibrating phone, but on Caitlin's red coat, which I'd tossed across a chair the night before. The coat that had held that red flower.

I looked at the clock: 6:15. Early. It was still dark beyond the curtains. Predawn.

I didn't recognize the number on the caller ID. I thought about letting it go to voice mail, but I looked at the coat again. Something wasn't right. The phone shouldn't be ringing so early . . .

'Hello?'

'Tom? This is Detective Ryan.'

'What's wrong?' I asked.

'Tom, I need you to come down here right away.'

I kept my eyes fixed on the coat. I felt cold, the blood in my body icy.

'What is it? What happened?'

'We may have found Caitlin, and we need you to come down here and see this girl for yourself.'

I tried to work my mouth, but no sound came out. My jaw moved up and down like a broken hinge.

'Tom? Can you come down here, or should I send a car to get you?'

'You found her,' I said. 'And you need me to identify . . .'

I couldn't say it. I couldn't refer to my daughter as

simply a body, a pile of remains or dust scattered by the wind and wild animals.

'No,' Ryan said. 'She's alive. This girl is alive, and we need you to come down to the station right away. Now, can you drive yourself or do you need me to send that car?'

'Alive . . . Caitlin? Are you serious?'

'No joke, Tom. This girl is alive.'

I closed the phone and spoke at the same time.

'I'm on my way.'

My hands shook. I gripped the wheel tight to steady them, and the pressure I exerted made my knuckles ache. I thought they might crack open and bleed. My speed crept too high, so I over-compensated and drove so slow other drivers came within inches of my bumper. My heart thumped at twice its normal pace, and my extremities felt numb, as though they'd been severed from the rest of my body.

When I reached the station, I parked my car at a crazy angle and barely managed to shut the door before running inside.

She's here. She's here. This is it. She's here.

I was two steps inside when Ryan intercepted me.

'Where is she? Where?'

'Come with me.'

He clamped his big hand on my biceps and led me down a short hallway to the familiar conference room. He guided me inside. My eyes darted around the room. It was empty.

Ryan closed the door behind us.

'Where is she?' I asked. 'Are you bringing her in here?'

'Sit down.'

'I want to see her.'

'You will. But sit down first.'

'I don't want to sit down. I want to see my daughter.'

I started past him, my right arm brushing against his left. Ryan took hold of me again, but this time I shook loose and reached for the door. Ryan grabbed me from behind like a wrestler and pressed his mouth close to my ear. I felt his hot breath as he spoke.

'Not yet,' he said. 'You need to sit down.'

His voice was steady but laced with steel. His arms encircled me, dug into my rib cage. I couldn't get loose. He was too big, too strong. Surprisingly so. I struggled a little more, but we both knew it was futile.

'Are you going to sit?' he asked, his voice practically inside my head.

I nodded, went limp. 'Sure, sure.'

He didn't really let go, but with less force turned me away from the door and back toward the conference table.

'Sit here,' he said.

I sat, straightening the collar of my jacket, which had shoved up under my chin during our struggle.

'We need to talk about a few things before this goes any farther,' Ryan said.

'Is it her?' I asked. 'Is it really her?'

Ryan nodded. 'We think it is. Caitlin wrecked her bike when she was little, right? It left a pretty distinctive round scar.'

'Yes, of course. She got eight stitches.'

'This young woman allowed a female police officer to look at her knee. She rolled her pant leg up. The scar is there. We've gone ahead and fingerprinted her in order to make a comparison with the prints that were taken when she was little. That will take a few hours, but I don't have any doubt, looking at her and comparing her to the pictures of your child. This is your daughter. It's Caitlin.'

I felt the sharp pain in my chest, the same one I'd felt in Caitlin's closet. My heart swelled like a balloon, expanding until it reached my throat and choked off the passage of air. I put my head in my hands, closed my eyes. I squeezed them tight until I saw firework patterns on my eyelids, great starbursts of red and green. *Caitlin. Here.*

Alive.

Ryan's hand landed on my shoulder. I let go of everything – the runaway theories, the unreturned calls, the suspicions. I stood up and wrapped my arms around him.

'Thank you,' I said. 'Thank you.' I squeezed him tighter, a reversal of our little struggle from a few minutes earlier. He smelled like shaving cream, and I felt his own gentle but awkwardly delivered man-pats against my back.

'It's okay. We have some things to talk about, Tom. Just sit down. Go ahead there. It's okay.'

I ended up back in the chair, my vision blurred by tears. I wiped them away with the backs of my hands. Ryan handed me a box of tissues. I don't know where he found them, but I took one and continued wiping at my eyes.

'Do you want some water?' Ryan asked.

'No, I'm fine. What happened?' I asked. 'What the fuck happened?'

Before Ryan could tell me, someone knocked on the conference room door. I looked up.

'Is that her?' I asked.

Ryan went to the door, but it opened before he reached it. Abby stepped into the room, the whites of her eyes prominent, the corners of her mouth turned down. She took short, tentative steps across the carpet and didn't look up or make eye contact with anyone.

'Who invited *her*?'

Ryan's head turned toward me. 'I called her, Tom. She's Caitlin's mother.'

'She hasn't acted like it. A mother wouldn't give up on her child.' I stood up. 'You were wrong, Abby. You and Pastor Chris. She's alive. She's right here, alive, and you were dead fucking wrong about it.'

Ryan held his hand out toward me. 'Please, Tom. Not now.'

Abby didn't look toward me. She sat in a chair across the room. She dropped her hands into her lap and twisted them around and over the top of each other.

'Are you okay, Abby?' Ryan asked.

She finally spoke in a low church whisper. 'It took me a while to get here. I was so . . . surprised when you called.'

Ryan grabbed one of the rolling chairs and moved it out into the center of the room so he was between us. He sat down, feet splayed, his knees far apart.

'I'd like to tell both of you what's going on and how we got to this point,' he said.

'Yes, please. *I'd* like to know,' I said.

'Abby,' he said, 'do you want to hear this?'

For a moment, it looked like she wasn't listening. Then she nodded.

'This morning, at approximately three-thirty, officers on a routine patrol saw a young woman walking along the side of Williamstown Road, out near the mall. She looked too young to be out at that time of night, so the officers questioned her. She appeared to be in good health. A little dirty, but with no obvious signs of injury. She didn't appear to be drunk or under the influence of drugs. She didn't have any identification, and the officers on the scene were going to take her to juvenile detention for processing – that's routine when a kid turns up like that with no ID – when one of them, a female officer, thought she recognized the girl from somewhere. She remembered the coverage of Caitlin's burial and the sketch of the suspect. She asked the girl, pointedly, who she was.

'The girl got nervous and agitated. She told the officers, "I know you think I'm that Caitlin Stuart girl, but I'm not." That seemed to confirm things for the officers, so they brought her here for further inquiry, and they decided to call me.'

'Jesus,' I said. 'Was she brainwashed? What was wrong with her?'

Ryan held up his finger, indicating there was more to tell.

'When I arrived at the station, I questioned her about her identity and where she lived. She wouldn't tell me anything else except to repeat that line. "I know you think I'm that Caitlin Stuart girl." When I asked her why she was out walking so late at night, who her parents were, where she went to school, she just stared at me like she was deaf or didn't understand English. I offered her something to eat, and she asked for a cup of coffee.'

'Caitlin doesn't drink coffee,' Abby said, her voice just above a whisper.

'Did she ask about us?' I asked.

154

Ryan shook his head. 'She kept asking us to let her go.'

'Are you sure it's her?' Abby asked. 'It might not be her.'

Ryan nodded. 'It's her. She looks smaller and younger perhaps than the average sixteen-year-old. Maybe she hasn't been eating as well. I don't know. But that means she looks more like the pictures taken before Caitlin disappeared than we would have suspected. Then I told her we were going to fingerprint her, which she went along with. It's going to take a few hours to find out if they match, but – I told Tom already – this girl has the same scar on her leg from a bike accident.'

'She was eight,' Abby said. 'She needed stitches.' Abby finally looked up and faced Ryan. 'But that's not proof. Lots of people have scars. Until you have DNA or the fingerprints or an X-ray . . .'

'Jesus, Abby,' I said. 'You really don't want her back, do you?'

She looked at me. 'I don't want to get crushed,' she said. 'I don't want that for either of us.'

'I understand that. I do, Abby,' Ryan said. 'And, ordinarily, I would try to wait for something more conclusive. I don't want to wind you both up for nothing. But in a town this size, people are going to know that girl's here, and before things get too far away from us, I want you to be able to see her. I wouldn't have brought you both here if I weren't certain. My gut tells me this is it.'

'Let's go see her then,' I said.

Ryan held up his finger again. 'We have some things to take care of once you've seen her. We have to get her to the hospital to be examined by a doctor. You won't get a lot of time, and the time you spend with her here, today, might be the last quiet moments you have for a while. This is going to be a hell of an adjustment for you two, and since we don't know where she's been or who she was with, we all need to be prepared for anything.'

'We know who she was with,' I said. 'That man in the sketch. Did you ask her about him?'

Ryan shook his head. 'It's best in a case like this not to press too hard at the outset. Not to ask too many questions too soon, even if we want to.'

'A case like this?' Abby asked. 'Are there other cases like this?'

'I just mean when a child has been kidnapped or run away.'

'No, no, no, no. Not a runaway,' I said. 'That man, the sketch – that proves it. She didn't run away. Someone took her – they took her from us.'

Ryan nodded along, placating me. But then he said, 'I know this has been a long road for the two of you, but I can promise you what we already know and see is just the tip of the iceberg. There's much more to the story here, and we're going to have to get to it.'

'What are they going to do at the hospital?' Abby asked.

I knew. *I knew I knew I knew.* I didn't want to hear it, but I knew.

Ryan confirmed it.

'They'll do a complete exam. Gynecological included. They'll be looking for evidence of sexual assault and pregnancy.'

Abby made a small noise in the back of her throat.

'Someone who needs to be checked for those things didn't run away,' I said.

Ryan stood up. 'Wait here, and I'll go see if things are ready. I thought I'd give the two of you a moment together before we bring you back. I think maybe you have some things to get straight before you see Caitlin.'

'Ryan?' I asked. 'Is this going to be all right?'

He offered me a small smile. 'Your daughter's back. Doesn't that mean this is a good day?'

When he was gone, I turned to Abby.

She didn't look at me.

'Abby?'

She remained rigid as a block of wood.

'Abby? Are you okay?'

'I was at the church, working, and then Ryan called me.' She was looking at the floor. 'I knew something bad was happening, something about Caitlin. I wasn't expecting this today, Tom. This just comes out of nowhere.'

'It's not a bad thing, Abby.'

'Why did you say such awful things about me?' she asked, raising her head.

'Are you looking for an apology? Because I'm not offering one.'

'Do you really think I don't deserve to be here?'

'It's not about you, Abby. Your feelings have nothing to do with this day.' I stood up. 'But I can tolerate the idea of you being along for this. I'm willing to put up with that . . . for Caitlin. But I'm also not going to wait for you. They should be ready for us now, so get up and let's go.'

Her upper body tilted forward, then back, and she slowly rose to her feet. She stood there for a second, looking like an unsteady drunk, one who didn't trust that the world wasn't about to tip over and throw her to the floor.

'Tom?'

'What?'

'I can't do it.'

'You can't —?'

'I can't do it. I can't go see her.'

'Oh, Abby. Come on.'

'Don't push me, Tom.' She held her hand out. 'Don't give me some guilt trip about how I'm some kind of bad mother because I don't want to . . . *can't* . . . go see Caitlin right now.'

I looked to the door, my anxiety rising. *She was here. Caitlin.*

'Why don't you want to go back there? Tell me.'

'I'm scared, Tom. Okay? I'm scared.'

'Of what?'

'Of what I might see. Of what Caitlin is going to be like now. Of what she's been through. We've talked about a lot of things since she's been gone. Is she still alive? Who took her? We never talked about what we'd do, what it would be like, if she did come back. I never really thought about it. Not in detail. And now . . .'

I went to her and crouched down, so we were at eye level.

'Abby, this is what we wanted. This is what we've been waiting for. You should go back there.'

She didn't move.

'Abby?'

'I just need more time.' She looked away. 'Give me more time.'

Ryan stuck his head in the door, looking like a giant turtle emerging from its shell.

'We're ready,' Ryan said.

I straightened back up.

'Abby's going to take another minute while I go back.'

Ryan's eyes shifted from me to her and back to me again. He looked uncertain, but went ahead.

'Whatever works,' he said, holding the door open for me. 'Let's do this, Tom.'

I took one last look back at Abby, expecting her to change her mind. But her head was down, and she didn't look at me.

Chapter Twenty-one

Even though I'd spent a lot of time in the police station, it still felt like an incomprehensible maze of hallways. We passed small rooms with closed doors, the brass finish on their knobs rubbed off to reveal the darker metal underneath. Two uniformed cops sat in a small office, one that overflowed with paper. They laughed as we approached and then, seeing us, lowered their voices. They continued laughing after we'd passed. Ryan didn't speak. He walked in front of me, his head bobbing with his movements, his broad shoulders and thick middle nearly filling the entire hallway.

Something like adrenaline burned through me. Every pore and hair follicle in my body tingled with anticipation. I tried to swallow, but my mouth was dry. And I resisted the urge to reach out, shove Ryan to the side, and charge ahead to the room where they were keeping Caitlin.

Finally, Ryan stopped in front of a metal door.

'Okay,' he said. 'Take your time. But remember, she does have to go to the hospital at some point.'

I nodded.

'Did you work things out with Abby?' he asked.

'Don't worry. I'll cover for her.'

Ryan opened the door and made a gesture into the room. I couldn't see who was in there, even as I stood on my toes and craned my neck to see around Ryan's big body. A female police officer came out. She nodded at me as she passed, and Ryan pushed the door open wider.

He turned to me. It was time.

'You can close the door behind you for privacy,' he said.

How many times does a life turn in a moment? For me, twice in four years. Once when Caitlin disappeared, and then again, right there, when she came back.

I moved through the doorway. It was a small, cramped room, a kind of lounge or break area for the employees of the station. A round table with four chairs sat on the left, the morning's newspaper scattered across it. Along the back wall, there was a percolating coffeemaker and a refrigerator covered with handwritten notes and newspaper articles. And then on the right, a long, low couch, where a teenage girl sat holding a mug of coffee.

I pushed the door shut behind me.

I'd imagined this moment many times, but I could never allow my brain to work through the scenario completely. I could picture a young girl, that twelve-year-old who'd vanished while walking Frosty, squealing and jumping into my arms. As time passed, I couldn't update it, couldn't conceive of what she might look or act like. So I left it blank. But now, here I was, being considered by the cautious eyes of a teenage girl who was supposed to be my daughter.

Was she? Really?

Ryan's words and observations had promised it. But a lot of people bore scars. The fingerprint evidence wasn't back yet . . .

'Caitlin? Honey?'

Her eyes looked large, as always – just like Abby's – but

this was accentuated by how thin she was. She looked sickly, like someone recently recovered from a long illness. Her skin was pale, her cheeks almost without color. Caitlin always wore her hair long, but this girl's hair was cut short, almost chopped, as though someone who wasn't a professional had used a pair of household scissors to whack it off. She wore a loose, baggy NCPD sweatshirt with the sleeves pushed up, and her shoes were scuffed and dirty.

She didn't say anything. She watched me with those big eyes, white and blue orbs that tracked me from across the room.

I watched her, too. Studied her. The facial features, the shape of her nose, the set of her jaw. I saw Abby in that face, as always. My mother, too. And, yes, a touch of me somewhere.

It was her.

It was Caitlin.

'Caitlin?'

She didn't answer.

'Do you remember me?'

'Of course I remember you.'

Her voice was flat, emotionless, as though I were a passing acquaintance. And the voice was huskier, more raw. Not the voice of a little girl but that of a postpubescent young woman.

I approached the couch and sat down next to her. She eyed me a little suspiciously, but didn't pull away or get up.

I couldn't hold back.

I wrapped my arms around her, pulling her close to me, crushing her against my body. I kissed her head, her cheeks.

'Oh, Caitlin, my Caitlin, my sweet baby girl. I missed you. I missed you so much. My baby . . .'

She let me hold her and hug her, but she didn't return the gesture. She remained stiff under my touch, and I only let go when my fingers and hands began to ache.

I leaned back, taking in a full view of Caitlin's face. The changes only accentuated her resemblance to Abby, and, in fact, the Caitlin who sat before me looked remarkably like the high school photos of Abby – slender, big eyed, not entirely confident under the gaze of the camera.

'Are you okay?' I asked.

'I'm fine.'

'Really? Fine? Are you sure, honey? They're going to take you to the doctor in a minute.'

'Why?'

'To check you over, to make sure you're not hurt.'

She squirmed a little, looking uncomfortable. 'They won't find anything. I'm not hurt.'

I brought my hand up to her cheek, then cupped her chin like when she was a baby. There were some blemishes, teenage acne. I soaked her in until my vision blurred and grew watery.

Caitlin either didn't notice or chose not to comment.

'You were gone for so long. We thought you . . . I started to think . . .'

I noticed how greasy her hair looked, a few days unwashed. Caitlin was a neat child, almost fastidious, yet she smelled a little, the rough scent of an unwashed body and stale cigarettes. I remembered the admonition to not ask questions, not to press, but my mind spun like a wheel.

'Who did this to you?' I asked. 'Where were you?'

She looked away. 'It's over, I guess.'

'What's over? No —' I said. 'Where were you? Who took you?'

'Where's my mom? Is she here?'

'She's here.' I hesitated. Was Caitlin trying to change the subject? 'She's in the other room.'

'I'd like to see her. Can I see her, please?'

'Of course, honey. Of course.' I held her hand. 'She's upset by all of this, your mom. It's hard on her. It's been hard on both of us. I know it's been harder on you – don't get me wrong – but we've been so worried.'

'Did you get divorced or some shit like that?'

Shit?

'No. Why would you ask me that?'

She stared straight ahead and spoke in a monotone, almost programmed voice, like she was repeating something she'd heard somewhere.

'I just know that relationships can be strained, they can be put under a lot of pressure when things change. Sometimes relationships don't survive the changes. That's part of life.'

She nodded when she finished speaking, a kind of exclamation mark to the statement. For the first time, I saw real emotion in her eyes. She looked upset, as though she didn't really believe or understand what was just said. I wondered where those words had come from, if she'd been coached to say them.

'Who told you that, Caitlin? Where did you hear all that?'

'I'd like to see Mom now, I guess.'

I didn't want to leave her, even for a minute, but her

164

little speech unnerved me in a way I couldn't explain. I stood up and looked out the door to where the female officer waited. I told her Caitlin wanted to see her mother.

'Tell my wife, Abby, I think she needs to come back here, please.'

When I went back in, Caitlin stared at me.

'What is it?' I asked.

'I need to ask you to do something, something pretty important.'

I went across and resumed my place on the couch. I started to reach for her hand but saw she was keeping them both in her lap, intertwined with each other. I settled for resting my hand on her shoulder.

'Of course. What do you need?'

'I need a favor from you, a big one.'

Her voice took on a slight tremor. It picked up a hint of the emotion I saw – and which still remained – in her eyes.

'After four years, I owe you a few favors, I guess.'

She looked down at her hands, bit her bottom lip. 'I don't want you to ever again ask me where I was or what happened while I was gone. Please.'

I let my hand slide off her back. 'We don't have to talk about it today. I shouldn't have asked.'

She shook her head. 'Not just today. I don't ever want you to ask me about it. Ever. You have to promise me that. Please.'

'But, honey, they . . . People are going to want to know. They have to know. If a child disappears for four years, they have to know —'

'I'm not a fucking child.'

I leaned back. 'Who taught you to talk that way?'

165

'Come on. Promise.'

'If something happened to you, something that embarrassed you or made you feel ashamed, it might be better to talk about it.'

'I'm not ashamed.'

Now she looked up, locked her eyes onto mine. If I'd been offered this deal the day before – have your daughter back, but you can't ask her where she's been – I'd have taken it faster than the speed of light.

'Okay, I promise,' I said. 'No more questions.'

She nodded and looked at her hands again, her face displaying no real sense of satisfaction or relief.

The door clicked open, and Abby entered. She held her head up and displayed a genuine smile. Her eyes were full of tears.

'Oh,' she said, her hand to her chest. 'Oh. Oh.'

She didn't come across the room toward us. She stood by the closed door, staring at us, her hand still to her chest, like a patron struck speechless by a beautiful work of art.

Then Abby dropped her purse and rushed across the room. She fell onto the couch next to Caitlin, wrapping her in her arms. I looked away but heard the sound of Abby crying and sniffling.

Caitlin stood up suddenly. Without warning, she left the couch, slipping out of Abby's grip and taking a few steps toward the center of the room. I thought Abby might have overwhelmed her, piled too much affection and attention onto her too quickly, but Caitlin didn't look bothered or distressed. She still wore the same preternaturally calm expression on her face, her features as smooth and undisturbed as the unbroken surface of a quiet lake. She didn't say anything. She simply moved away, the coffee mug still in her hand, and stood there in silence, her gestures suggesting she was tired of hugging her long-lost parents and now she wanted to be left alone.

Abby and I looked at each other, as puzzled as we were when a newborn Caitlin cried and cried for hours for no apparent reason. But we could always guess then. Colic. Gas. Hunger. Fear. My mind scrambled, and I concluded it was all too much, too soon. I needed to remember not to push too hard.

I tried to think of something to say, but we were saved by another knock on the door. Abby and I said, 'Come in,' at the same time, and Ryan appeared.

'I'm sorry to interrupt,' he said, 'but we really need to get Caitlin to the hospital to get checked over.'

'Sure,' I said.

'Did you hear that, honey?' Abby asked. 'They need you to go to the hospital for some tests.'

Caitlin didn't look at us. I wasn't sure she'd heard, but then she said, 'What if I don't want to go?'

'They just want to make sure you're not hurt,' I said.

'Do I look hurt?'

'Well . . .' I could tell Abby was scrambling. She looked at Ryan. 'Maybe she doesn't have to go right now.'

Ryan shook his head. 'She has to go,' he said. 'It's standard procedure in these cases. It won't take long.'

I looked at Caitlin, met her eye. 'They might find evidence.'

'Evidence?' she asked. Her voice didn't rise. She sounded truly puzzled. 'Evidence? What evidence?' She turned and looked at all three of us. 'I don't understand what you all are talking about.'

Ryan stepped forward. 'Like your dad said, we need to make sure you're not hurt.'

'And then I can leave?'

I heard it. *Leave*. Not go home. *Leave*.

'One step at a time,' Ryan said, and placed his hand on Caitlin's arm.

She looked down at it as though it were a giant fly. But she didn't resist. Abby stood up and took the coffee mug from her, and the four of us left for the hospital.

Chapter Twenty-two

Abby and I waited together in a small family area while they took Caitlin back for a series of tests. Ryan paused and told us what the tests would entail: a general physical and psychological exam, routine blood work, and, of course, tests for rape, pregnancy, the DNA of the perpetrator, as well as STDs.

After ten minutes of Abby and me not speaking to each other, and right when I was considering picking up a magazine to distract myself, Abby spoke.

'We should be back there with her,' she said. 'She's never even been to the gynecologist before. One of us should be back there.'

'You didn't want to go back with her before, at the police station.'

'Don't be bitter, Tom. This is hard for both of us.'

'Besides, we don't know if she's never been to a gyne-cologist, do we? We don't know what she's been doing.'

'I doubt she's been to the gynecologist.' Abby shud-dered a little. 'What did she tell you before I got back there, Tom? What did she say?'

'She didn't say anything really.' I looked around at the sterile walls, the cold tile. 'She did ask for you.'

'She did? What did you tell her?'

'Don't worry,' I said. 'I covered for you. I told her you were with the police.'

'Did you tell her anything else about us? Our situation?'

I shook my head. 'She cursed like a truck driver, though.'

'She did?'

'And she wouldn't call me Dad.'

After a long pause, Abby said, 'Tom? What are we going to tell Caitlin about us? They're probably going to let us take her home today. My room at the church is small, but Chris wouldn't mind if she stayed there with me.'

'No,' I said. 'No and no.' I made a quick, cutting gesture with my right hand. 'You left. I stayed in our home. That's Caitlin's home, too. That's where her room is. She's not going to live with Pastor Chris and his traveling sideshow.'

'What are we going to do then, Tom? Pretend?'

'You can tell her you left,' I said. 'That's fair. Hell, Abby, you didn't even believe she was still alive. You let her go. You gave up. Why don't you tell her that while you're at it?'

For a long while, we were quiet. I heard voices in the hallway, the rumbling of something on wheels.

'If you want me to tell her the truth, I will.' Her voice was calm, almost detached. 'I can accept responsibility for this.'

'Why didn't you want to go back and see her earlier? Ryan practically held me back. He grabbed me and put me in a chair. That's our daughter, and she came back to us after four years. Why wouldn't you want to see her?'

'Why are you so focused on me and my reactions?'

'Because I'm trying to understand you. I've been trying to understand you for a few years now. The religion. The lack of hope for Caitlin's return. Moving out. Now I want to understand this, but I'm not sure I can. I'm not sure you could say anything that would make sense.'

Abby brought her hands up to her face and covered her mouth with them. She looked like she was cold, like she needed to blow on her hands for warmth, but I knew she was thinking and choosing her words carefully. She lowered her hands and spoke. 'I was afraid, Tom. I was afraid to see Caitlin. Right before you went back there, it went through my mind that she's been gone for four years. She's changed. And who knows what has happened to her. And I got scared just thinking of that.' She reached up and moved her hair out of her face. 'I probably felt guilty, too, for thinking she wouldn't come back. But the longer I sat out there, thinking about Caitlin being just a few rooms away, the harder it was for me not to go back there. I needed to see her. I guess it had been a long time since I really felt like a mother, and that instinct finally kicked back in for me.'

'Then you should go with that feeling,' I said. 'It's a good one.'

'She seems so cold, so cut off from us.'

'You should come home with us, Abby. The three of us, back in our house. The way it's meant to be.'

Abby started shaking her head before I even finished the sentence. 'Oh, Tom . . .' She kept shaking her head. 'She doesn't need two unhappy parents.'

When Ryan returned two hours later, Abby and I both asked how she was doing before he could even sit down.

'They're finishing up. She's getting dressed,' Ryan said. He settled into a chair. 'The physical exam shows no real problems. She has a bruise on her abdomen that could have come from a fist, but it's not a serious injury. She wouldn't say what caused it. No broken bones or evidence of past broken bones. Her teeth are in good shape, although it doesn't look like she's been to a dentist in a while. She's a little on the thin side for a girl her age and height. But her vital signs are normal. The lab will process the blood work over the next few days. It's possible she's anemic, but other than that, I don't think they'll find anything. Bottom line – wherever she's been and whatever she's been doing, she's been pretty well taken care of.'

'That's a relief,' I said.

'What about . . . the other things you tested for?' Abby asked.

'The doctor did a rape kit to check for any evidence that might be left behind after a sexual assault. We won't know those test results right away, but based on the exam, she doesn't think it will reveal anything. There's no obvious evidence of sexual assault. No vaginal bruising or bleeding. No defensive wounds on her hands, no scrapes or scratches. Just the one bruise I mentioned. And the pregnancy test was negative.'

'Thank God,' I said.

'That doesn't mean there wasn't a sexual assault at some time in the past. It just means that there hasn't been a recent one. Now, the exam did reveal something that I feel I must share with you. It could be difficult to hear, especially considering all you've already been through.' He paused. 'The examination revealed that Caitlin's hymen is no longer intact. That would most likely indicate some type of sexual activity. Again, we can't say if it was consensual or not, but it's a fact we're all going to have to deal with.'

I started to feel sick. The room, which to that point seemed perfectly comfortable, started to feel hot and close. My clothes clung to my body as though they were shrinking.

'What did she say about it?' Abby asked.

'Nothing,' Ryan said. 'The doctor didn't press, considering the situation. In fact, Caitlin didn't respond to any of their questions about her health. She acted like she couldn't hear them. She's been like that ever since we brought her in. She's barely spoken. I was wondering if she said anything to either of you when you were with her?'

Abby shook her head. 'Nothing of substance. Right, Tom?'

I felt sweat beading on my upper lip. 'Nothing.'

'Are you okay, Tom?' Ryan asked.

'I'm fine. Just a little overwhelmed.'

I leaned back in my chair and closed my eyes, trying for just a moment to escape. But I heard another voice speaking to Ryan, and when I opened my eyes again a man was standing there. He wore a polo shirt, khaki pants, and loafers, and looked like he was on his way to a golf game. His thinning hair was cut close to his head and his face was round and his cheeks smooth and rosy, giving him the appearance of an oversized baby. He must have been in his thirties, but he could have passed for much younger.

'Tom, Abby, this is Dr Rosenbaum,' Ryan said. 'He works with the police department as a psychiatrist, and he specializes in adolescent cases like Caitlin's. He's going to help you with the transition as you take Caitlin home.'

Dr Rosenbaum took a seat next to Ryan and offered us a small smile intended to convey both sympathy and support. It looked forced, and it didn't make me feel any better.

'Mr and Mrs Stuart,' Rosenbaum said, 'today is really just the beginning of a long journey to reacclimate your daughter to a normal life. I know that seeing her again is cause for celebration and high emotion – as it should be – but the real work begins now, both for you and for the police. I'm here to assist you with the work that transition entails.'

'How long will she be in the hospital?' Abby asked.

Rosenbaum looked at Ryan, and Ryan nodded.

'We're going to release Caitlin to you today,' Ryan said. 'We see no reason to have her stay here overnight or for any further observation. Medically, she's cleared and okay. We've asked her the questions we wanted to ask her. We'll do more soon, though – don't worry. Our investigation will continue.'

Rosenbaum cleared his throat. 'I know you're going to have questions about even the most basic things in Caitlin's life. Does she go back to school at some point? Does she resume the life of a typical teenager?'

'Exactly,' Abby said. 'I was wondering about school. Has she even been in school? What has she been doing?'

Rosenbaum offered the same forced smile. 'We don't have to tackle them all today. Like I said, this is a long road.'

'The press has no doubt gotten wind of this story,' Ryan said, 'so we have to go put that fire out. I guess you can expect them to be knocking on your door soon enough. We'll put out a statement asking for privacy. It will help some.'

'What are we supposed to do with her?' Abby asked. 'I mean . . . what do we do?'

Rosenbaum nodded. 'You have to understand something about taking Caitlin back to your home. It's not going to feel like her home to her, at least not right away. Wherever she's been or whoever she's been with . . . *that* was home to her. Even if she was sleeping on the streets. She may not feel immediately safe in her old environment, the way we would expect her to be.'

'But it is her home,' Abby said. 'It's the only house she's known. Her room is just the way it was when she disappeared.'

'The best thing you can do is make her feel safe,' Rosenbaum said. 'That's the biggest concern for victims of crimes like this. Keep her safe and secure. Expect some nightmares. But follow her lead and don't rush her. You're still parents, even after all this time. Trust yourselves. And she's still your daughter. But she's not going to be the same kid who walked out that door four years ago.'

'What do you mean?' I asked.

'Four years have passed,' he said. 'And who knows what trauma. The passage of time and events have shaped her just like they have shaped you. She's not going to be the same person.'

Ryan cleared his throat. He had something to say.

'I wanted to check in with the two of you concerning your marriage. I'm merely trying to think of the best situation for Caitlin to come home to.'

'She'll come home with both of us,' Abby said.

Ryan cocked his head, a little confused. 'How's that?'

'We'll all go home together,' she said. 'As a family.' I didn't speak up, but Abby looked at me and spoke in my direction. 'Caitlin needs me. She needs both of us. I don't

175

want her to think that her disappearance brought down her parents' marriage.'

'It's okay to tell the child whatever —'

She cut Ryan off. 'No. We're going home together. All of us.'

Ryan nodded. 'Fair enough. Well' – he pushed himself to his feet – 'I still have a lot of work to wrap up.'

'Doctor?' I said. 'When we were at the police station, Caitlin said she wanted to leave. She didn't act like she wanted to go home with us.'

'I explained the situation to her,' Ryan said, fielding the question. 'She knows she's leaving with you.'

'How did she respond to that?' I asked. I wasn't sure I wanted to know, and I almost couldn't look him in the eye while I waited for the answer.

'Caitlin has a lot of things to get used to,' Rosenbaum said. 'And being home with you is one of them. If you'd like, I can come to your house with you now, when you take Caitlin home. I could just observe her there and answer any questions you might have. I've done it before in similar situations.'

Abby turned to me. 'What do you think, Tom? It sounds like a good idea.'

I considered it, but more than anything else, I wanted Caitlin home. With us, in our house. No strangers. No impediments or barriers between my daughter and me. 'No, thanks,' I said. 'I think we should just be there for Caitlin ourselves.'

Rosenbaum looked a little disappointed, but he stood up. He reached into his pocket and brought out a business card. 'Do call me if you need anything tonight,' he said.

'My cell number is on there. Otherwise, we'd like you to come to my office in the morning, and we can start working through the things we need to get through.'

'I've already been talking to someone,' I said.

'You've what?' Abby asked.

I looked around. Rosenbaum and Ryan were both studying me, waiting for an answer.

'I took your advice, Ryan,' I said. 'I called one of those people from Volunteer Victim Services. We met once and talked about Caitlin and the case.'

'Who did you talk to?' Ryan asked.

'Susan Goff.'

Rosenbaum spoke up. 'I think it's best if we talk to Caitlin in a formalized, professional setting. My experience tells me that's most effective.' He still held the business card in the air between us. 'Is that okay with you?'

I took the card and handed it over to Abby.

'Ryan,' I said, 'you referred to her as a victim of a crime. Does that mean everyone's certain she didn't run away?'

'It's obvious a crime was committed somewhere along the line. Now it's up to me to find out what it was.' Ryan jiggled the loose change in his pockets. 'And for what it's worth, I know Susan Goff. She does excellent work for us through Volunteer Victim Services. They're good people.'

'But still,' Rosenbaum said. 'I'd like to see Caitlin.'

'Of course, of course,' Ryan said. 'See Dr Rosenbaum first thing tomorrow.'

Ryan turned to go, and Rosenbaum followed him, leaving Abby and me to sit there and wait for Caitlin to be released to us.

Chapter Twenty-three

We drove home in awkward silence. Caitlin rode in the back, just like in her childhood, except now she stared out the window, her face blank and indifferent. She didn't ask questions or comment on the passing scenery. She didn't try to convince us to change the radio or CD to something she liked, so I asked her if she wanted to listen to something.

'I'm fine,' she said.

I didn't know what else to say, and apparently neither did Abby.

Caitlin broke the silence for us.

'Where are you going to drop me off?' she asked.

'Drop you off?'

'You can do that anywhere,' she said.

I tried to talk to her with one eye on the road and one eye on her profile in the rearview mirror.

'We talked about this at the hospital, remember?'

She ignored me.

'We're going home,' I said. 'To the house you used to live in.'

Nothing.

'Your room is just the way you left it,' Abby said.

But that was it. Caitlin didn't speak again the rest of the way home, not even when we turned down our street and saw the news van from the local TV station parked at the end of our driveway. A police department spokesperson had met with us at the hospital, and we gave our approval to a fairly standard statement, one that said we were happy to be home, thankful to have our daughter back, and eager for privacy. When I hit the turn signal and angled toward our driveway, the cameraman moved out of our way but kept his lens trained on the car. I took a quick look at Caitlin in the rearview. She seemed not to notice.

The reporter and cameraman didn't follow us farther onto the property, so we were able to pull to the end of the driveway and the back of the house.

Abby and I climbed out, but Caitlin stayed in the car. Abby shrugged and pulled open Caitlin's door.

'Are you ready to go in?' Abby asked. 'Do you need a minute?'

Caitlin looked up, her lips slightly puckered. 'This is where you're taking me?'

'This is home,' Abby said. 'Remember it? Here's the yard and the back door. We left the front porch light on every night since you were gone. Every night. And the key was right there so you could come in if you wanted.'

'Really?' Caitlin said.

'Really,' Abby said. 'We were waiting for you.'

Caitlin nodded a little, then stepped out of the car. I hustled with the keys and undid the back lock, opening the door ahead of them and stepping aside.

'It's all pretty much the same as when you were last here,' I said.

Inside, Abby and I followed behind Caitlin as she went from room to room on the first floor, looking around and taking in the sights with the passivity of an unmotivated home buyer. She took a quick glance out the front window where the news van was still parked. The cameraman appeared to be putting his gear away, and the reporter, a young blonde woman who I recognized from the news but whose name I couldn't remember, was talking on a cell phone as she smoked a cigarette.

'Where's Frosty?' Caitlin asked.

'Oh,' Abby said. 'Oh, honey . . .'

'Is he dead?' Caitlin asked.

'Honey, when you . . . went away, we thought . . . We put him to sleep. He was old . . .'

'He'd only be nine,' Caitlin said.

'He wasn't put to sleep,' I said.

They both turned to look at me.

'I took him to the pound, and someone else adopted him.' I looked at Abby. 'I checked. In fact, if you want, I can try to find out who adopted him and we can try to get him back. Under the circumstances, I would think —'

Caitlin turned away, but I went on.

'We know you loved Frosty. And he was crazy about you. When you left, he used to sit by the door and cry. Didn't he, Abby?'

'He did,' she said. 'He was so sad not to see you.'

'You didn't like Frosty, did you?' Caitlin asked. She turned and directed the question at Abby.

'I liked him,' Abby said.

'You didn't like me to walk him. You thought I was getting away from you.'

'No, honey. I worried about you, of course. That's what moms do.'

'We can get another dog,' I said. 'Or we can try to get Frosty back.'

Caitlin turned away and shrugged a little. 'Whatever,' she said. 'Just don't say everything's the same, because it isn't. That's bullshit.'

Abby jumped a little but kept her cool.

'Your room is the same,' Abby said, staying on message. 'Maybe we need to update it a little. And clothes. The clothes you have here wouldn't fit anymore, I guess. Do you have any clothes from ... where you were staying?'

'No. Nothing.'

'Whenever you're ready, we can go out and buy some things,' Abby said.

When Caitlin remained silent, Abby looked at me, helpless.

'Would you like to go up to your room? Maybe you'd like to take a nap?'

It took a long time, but finally Caitlin nodded.

We trudged upstairs, the three of us. Caitlin went and sat on her bed, while I remembered standing in that closet and feeling the piercing pain of her loss go through me like a lance.

'I bet the sheets aren't clean,' Abby said.

'I got used to dirty sheets,' Caitlin said.

Abby sat next to Caitlin and leaned in close.

'Where was that, honey? Where were you sleeping without clean sheets?'

Caitlin didn't answer. She stared at me.

Abby pressed on.

'If you tell us, the police can help find the man responsible. It was a man, right? An older man who did this to you?'

Caitlin's eyes widened, expressing an urgency to me, so I spoke up.

'Why don't we let the kid sleep, okay, Abby?'

Abby looked a little wounded, a little betrayed by my comment. But it was just a flash.

'Honey,' she said, 'I know this is tough, but you can talk to your dad or me about whatever you want, whenever you want. You know that, don't you?'

'Who's been sleeping in the guest room?' Caitlin asked.

'Why do you ask that?' Abby asked.

'I saw the door open when we came up here, and the sheets were messed up. Did you have company?'

'Buster was here visiting,' I said.

'Really?' Caitlin perked up a little.

'Have you seen your uncle Buster?' Abby asked. 'You know, since you've been gone.'

'Why would you want to know that?' Caitlin asked.

'Don't worry about it,' I said. 'It's nothing.'

'We do have to be honest with you about something,' Abby said. 'Dad and I . . . we've been having some tough times in our marriage. It happens when people have been married for a long time. We're trying to sort it out.'

'You mean with counseling or something?' Caitlin said.

'Yes,' Abby said. 'Some of that. But we're both here for you now. We're both going to be in the house with you and helping you any way we can. Together. Right, Tom?'

'That's right.'

'You're taking me to a shrink tomorrow, aren't you?' Caitlin said.

'The police think it would be best,' Abby said. 'They have things they want to talk to you about.'

Caitlin looked at me when she next spoke, her eyes locked on mine, a reminder of the promise I'd made to her at the police station. 'I don't want to go somewhere and answer a bunch of fucking questions. I'm not interested.'

'Caitlin . . .' Abby looked shocked, even hurt. 'When the police ask you to do something, you have to do it. And I think it will be good for you. Don't you, Tom?'

Caitlin held her gaze on mine, waiting for my help. But I'd promised only that I wouldn't ask, not that I wouldn't let a professional do it. 'Right,' I said. 'You should go tomorrow.'

'And I don't think you should talk to us that way,' Abby said. 'I know it's been a long time . . .' She stood up, gathered her composure. 'Do you need something to sleep in? Clean clothes or anything?'

'This is fine,' Caitlin said. She kicked her shoes off, revealing gray, dirty socks, and flipped back the covers on her bed.

'Just call us if you need anything,' Abby said on her way out.

I lingered in the doorway, watching my daughter settle into bed.

'It must be weird being back,' I said.

She didn't respond. She turned over on her side, showing me her back, and as far as I knew, closed her eyes and went to sleep.

An hour later, I slipped upstairs, moving carefully, stealthily, trying not to make any noise that might wake Caitlin.

The door to her room was still cracked. I slipped up to the door and pressed my ear close, listening. It took me a minute to separate the sound of Caitlin's breathing from the fuzzy background noise of our house. The hum of the refrigerator, the soft whoosh of the heat, the traffic noise outside, the wind. But I managed to hone in on Caitlin's breath, and each exhalation and inhalation brought me a greater sense of ease. She was here. She was really here. She lived, she existed under our roof again.

Before I turned away, I heard a new sound, one that broke through the rhythmic breathing. At first, I thought she might be coughing, but as I listened, the sound crystallized and became recognizable as human speech. Caitlin's voice, murmuring.

I leaned closer, bent down so my ear was level with the doorknob. She was saying the same thing over and over, almost like a chant or a mantra, but I couldn't make it out. She stopped and, again, I thought of backing off, but then the words resumed, a little louder this time, a little clearer. I understood.

'Don't send me away,' she said. 'Don't send me away.'

I reached out and peeled the door open a little. A narrow band of light leaked into Caitlin's room from the hallway, crawling across the floor and stopping just short of her bed. She lay in the same position I left her in – facing the wall, back to the door. She was asleep. Dreaming. But her voice kept repeating the words in the dark.

'Don't send me away. Don't send me away. Don't send me away.'

Chapter Twenty-four

Abby dug through the refrigerator. One of the neighbors had brought us a dish of lasagna, and the oven ticked as it preheated.

'You don't have any vegetables in here,' she said.

'I guess not.'

'Were you just upstairs?' she asked, closing the refrigerator door. 'Is she okay?'

'Still sleeping.'

'Should we wake her to eat something?'

Don't send me away . . .

'No,' I said, still distracted by the words she'd spoken in her sleep. 'Let's just let her be.'

Abby frowned. 'If you're sure . . .'

I went over to the lasagna pan and lifted the foil. Lots of cheese, just the way I liked it. I actually felt hungry for a change.

'Tom? Where do you think she was?'

I let the foil drop. 'She was with that man.'

'You think I pushed her too hard upstairs.'

The oven beeped, indicating it had reached the right temperature. I opened the door and slid in the heavy pan of food. 'I guess we can eat in thirty minutes or so,' I said.

Abby wore a distant look, her eyes fixed on a point somewhere near the ceiling.

'What is it?' I asked.

'Do you ever think you don't want to know what happened to her?' she asked. 'What if it's too awful to hear? Those things they told us at the hospital, about the sex . . . What if she's been raped or abused? The way she's been acting . . . it's like she's been through something awful, something that stunned her. I would have been happy to have that psychiatrist come home with us.'

'We're fine without that,' I said. Caitlin's whispered sleep talk cycled through my brain, like a taunt. *Don't send me away. Don't send me away.* 'The police are going to push her to tell. If there's an arrest, she'll have to talk about it.'

The back doorbell rang.

'Who is that?' Abby asked. 'Could it be Ryan?'

I pressed my face against the glass.

'It's Buster.'

'Oh.'

'Could he have heard?' I asked.

I opened the door, and he answered the question for me.

'What the fuck is going on up here?' His voice was loud, almost crazed. 'What the fuck? Are you fucking kidding me? I mean, Jesus Christ. Are you kidding me?'

His voice rose and squealed with excitement, like a pre-pubescent boy.

'Yes, it's amazing,' I said.

'Why didn't you call me? Why didn't you call?'

I led him into the other room, away from Abby, who didn't even look up or greet him. 'It's been kind of crazy here, you know? It's been a long day.'

'I wanted to come visit. I want to see the girl. Shit.'

He was almost hysterical. Bizarrely so.

'We're trying to get our bearings.'

'Oh,' he said. 'I see. You need some family time and all that, try to put the pieces back together again.' He stood in the middle of the living room, rubbing his hands together and nodding. 'I guess that makes sense. I'm family, too. I thought I could help.'

'You can. In a couple of days. In fact, I mentioned you to Caitlin, and her eyes lit up.'

'Really?'

'Really. She'll want to see you.' I looked up at the ceiling, listening. Wondering. 'But she's asleep now. Really zonked out. It's been a hell of a day.'

'Goddamn.' Buster looked up at the ceiling too, his face curious. Then he cleared his throat. 'I love that kid,' he said.

'Yeah ... Abby asked Caitlin about something, just before.'

'Did she ask about that guy? Did they arrest him?'

'No, there's been no arrest.'

'I want to tell you, Tom, I want to go out and find this guy.' His voice sounded heavy, heated. He leaned in close to me with a caninelike ferocity. 'I want to get in my car and go looking for him. What are the fucking cops doing? Sitting on their asses?'

'I don't know. They're taking it slow.'

'Fuck them.'

'Look, like I started to tell you ... Abby asked Caitlin something upstairs, something about you.'

'She did?'

'Yeah.' I moved slow. Cautious. 'She asked Caitlin if she saw you during the four years she was gone.'

He fell quiet. I hesitated, wondering if I'd pushed too hard.

'I don't understand what you're asking me . . .'

I kept my voice even lower. 'It's just that Caitlin didn't answer the question exactly. She didn't say no, so I wanted to ask you.'

'You're asking me if I saw Caitlin during the last four years, right? Right? Is that what you're saying, just so we're clear on this?'

'Buster, just answer the question.'

'You're a real motherfucker, Tom — you know that? You're as bad as the fucking cops. Worse. I'm your brother. To ask me a question like that . . .'

'Did you see her, Buster?' My voice rose. 'Do you know what happened? Answer me.'

'Why don't you ask Caitlin again? Oh, wait.' He thumped his hand against his forehead, an exaggerated gesture. 'She probably can't stand to talk to her fucked-up and crazy parents, can she?'

'Buster —'

He stormed to the front door and tugged against the lock until it came open.

'Go to hell, Tom. Go straight to hell.'

Abby was waiting for me in the kitchen, her hands knitted together. 'What were you two arguing about?' she asked.

'We weren't arguing.' I distracted myself by picking at the salad she was making.

'I heard you raise your voice.'

'I asked him if he saw Caitlin during the last four years.'

'And?'

'What do you expect? He got pissed off and yelled at me. He acted like it hurt him.'

'What was his answer?'

'He didn't really give me one.'

'Don't you see?' She pointed at me. 'That's how Caitlin acted. I know he's your stepbrother, but —'

'Half brother.'

'I think we need to talk to the police about all of this, don't you?'

'It's not that simple, Abby. He *is* my brother. We grew up together. He was always there for me when we were kids. No matter how bad our home life got, Buster was with me. He stood by me.'

I opened the oven door and looked in. The cheese on the lasagna was bubbling.

'This food is ready,' I said. 'Have you heard anything from upstairs?'

'She was pretty sound asleep when I was up there, but I thought I just heard some footsteps.'

I closed the oven door, then looked up. 'Probably going to the bathroom.'

'Tom, I need to know you're taking this seriously. I've always been nervous about Buster, with the way he seemed so . . . fascinated by Caitlin, you know? Like they were two kids with crushes on each other instead of uncle and niece.'

'Abby . . .'

'You've seen it, too. You've commented on it. Don't make this all about me, Tom. You can't.'

She was right. I'd noticed Buster's interest in Caitlin. I'd always managed to chalk up the closeness between them to the fact that she was his only niece, so he showered her with attention whenever he was around. But still . . . an older man, a younger girl. Buster's checkered past. His absences from our lives over the past four years.

Abby jerked up her head.

'Did you hear that?'

'What?'

'She's moving around up there again.'

'Okay, I'll go tell her we're ready to eat.'

When I reached the bottom of the stairs, Abby said my name. I stopped.

'This isn't going to go away,' she said. 'This Buster stuff.'

I nodded. I knew it wasn't.

At the top of the stairs, I could see the bathroom light under the closed door. Caitlin's bedroom door stood open. I didn't want to stand around, hovering outside the bathroom door while she was inside, so I stuck my head in the bedroom. The covers were thrown back, the lights off. A thick, musty odor hung in the small space. I remembered Caitlin's greasy hair at the police station, her dirty clothes. I listened for but didn't hear water running in the bathroom. She needed to shower. She needed new things to wear. I looked at the floor. It was empty. No discarded clothes, no shoes or socks.

I went back to the bathroom door. I rapped lightly with my knuckles.

'Caitlin? Honey?'

Nothing. My heart started to thump. I knocked again, using more force.

I raised my hand to try the knob, but didn't. I couldn't

just barge in on her, in whatever delicate state she might be in.

'Caitlin? If you don't say anything, I'm going to open the door and check on you.'

Still nothing.

I tried the knob, expecting it to be locked, but it gave right away. I pushed in. The lights were on, gleaming off the polished surface of the vanity and mirror. The window was open too, wide open, the curtains swelling in the cold breeze. Caitlin wasn't there. She was gone, out the window and into the night.

Abby stood at the bottom of the stairs.

'Tom?'

'Call the police. She went out the window.' I didn't break stride. I went out the back door and into the yard, calling her name. 'Caitlin! Caitlin!'

Nothing. No sign of her. The car still sat at the end of the driveway. I looked in the windows, cupping my hands against the glass. Empty. An unbidden thought popped into my head – I didn't know if Caitlin knew how to drive.

I turned away from the car. 'Caitlin!'

I looked back at the house. She'd gone out the window and onto the porch overhang. From there, it was about a ten-foot drop to the ground. Hardly a challenge for someone young and in any kind of decent shape.

Abby came to the back door. 'Tom? The police are coming.'

'We should call Ryan.'

'They said they'd tell him.'

'I'm going to take the car and look,' I said, already

moving. 'She can't have gone far. Jesus Christ, Abby. I should have seen this coming. The way she acted in the car . . .'

'I think you should stay.'

'I'm going,' I said. 'Around the neighborhood.'

'Tom, I want you to stay. Please. I don't want to be here alone.'

I held my keys in my hand and moved toward the car. I looked back at Abby under the glow of the back porch light. Her face was full of pleading and fear.

Last time, I sat in the house, waiting. A fool. Not again, I thought. Not again. I couldn't let Caitlin disappear this time without doing something. Immediately.

'I have the cell,' I said. 'Call me if anything changes.'

'Tom.'

I didn't look back. I got into the car and sped off.

Chapter Twenty-five

He took her.

As I made my way through the streets around our house, up one and down the other, peering into front yards and up driveways, trying my best to see through the darkness, one thought circled through my brain: *He took her. Buster took her.*

Televisions glowed blue behind drawn curtains, and regular people washed dishes or put out trash cans. They lived their lives, ignorant of and unaffected by my drama.

I didn't see Caitlin anywhere.

The cell phone buzzed in my pocket. Abby. I answered. 'Tom, the police are here.'

My heart raced even more. 'Did they find her?'

'No. They want to talk to you.'

'Tell them I'm looking.'

'They don't want you to look,' Abby said. 'They want you back here.'

'*You* want me back there,' I said. 'The cops don't care.'

'Tom —'

'Tell them to call Buster.'

'Do you really think —?'

'Tell them.'

Once I drove through our neighborhood, I headed toward campus and looked along the streets there. Students filled the sidewalks, shuffling to evening classes.

I quickly felt like a man adrift, without hope. Engaging in a fool's errand. Even in a town this size, what were the odds of finding one person, especially one person who apparently didn't want to be found?

The phone buzzed again.

'Shit.' I checked the display, expecting to see Abby's name. I was relieved to see it was Ryan. 'Hello? Did you find her?'

'Tom, you should come back here. We have men looking.'

'Where? I'm over by campus, and I don't see them.'

'Your wife needs you at home. If Caitlin comes back, you need to be here.'

'If, if, if, Ryan. I'm not going to be passive this time,' I said. 'I should have seen this. I should have stopped it. I'm not going to sit at home while my daughter is lost, God knows where.'

'Listen to me, Tom —'

I hung up. I decided to head out toward the mall, to Williamstown Road, where they'd found Caitlin walking just that morning. It seemed like the next logical step. I backtracked through our neighborhood to get to Williamstown Road, but I avoided our street, figuring that if there was news, someone would call. And if there wasn't, I didn't want to get sidetracked. I took a longer way around and ended up abreast of the cemetery. I hit the turn signal and pulled in through the gate, heading toward the back to Caitlin's headstone. I wasn't supposed to be there. It closed at dark, but they didn't always shut the entry gates. This was one such night.

The road through the cemetery was narrow and closely

lined by trees. My headlights illuminated the gnarled trunks and bounced off the headstones, showing the names and dates in brief flashes. I took a fork in the road, one that bent to the left, and I knew I was getting close to the headstone.

Then I saw the girl.

First she was a white blur in the headlights, held in relief against the darkness. I hit a bump in the road, and the headlights jostled up and down. I lost sight of her for a moment, then picked her up again. She stood in front of Caitlin's headstone, her hands resting on the top, as though she needed it for support. It was the same girl from the park that day, the one who ran off into the trees when I approached her.

Caitlin?

I hit the brakes, skidding to a stop. I pushed open the door.

'Hey!'

The girl turned and ran off, dashing into the darkness like a frightened animal. I went after her, dodging around the tombstones. But there was next to no light. As I ran, I saw the girl ahead of me, her light clothes showing up in the darkness, but in a short while she faded from my view, swallowed up by the night.

'Hey!'

I stopped running, my breath coming in short, huffing bursts. She was gone. I listened but didn't hear the sound of twigs snapping or grass being trampled. If she was still out there, she was being stealthy and quiet, moving in the night like a guerrilla.

Beyond the edge of the cemetery were tracts of new

and fairly expensive subdivisions. She could easily be from one of those homes, I reasoned, a kid who wandered out of her yard to play.

But what did she want from me? What did she have to do with Caitlin?

When my wind came back, I turned for the car. The headlights were angled toward Caitlin's headstone and held it in a cone of light that carved through the darkness.

A fresh bouquet lay at the base of the stone, below Caitlin's name and dates. It looked like the kind from the grocery store, fresh-cut flowers wrapped in cheap and crinkly cellophane.

I hadn't been back to the cemetery since the first day I saw the girl, a few weeks earlier. I didn't know if Abby was visiting the plot. I imagined she would – Abby on her knees at the headstone, her hand reaching out to brush away a stray leaf or spiderweb, then bowing her head in prayer or reflection. She might even bring Pastor Chris with her, a spiritual companion to share her journey of grief. I shook my head, allowed myself a little moment of I-told-you-so triumph. I'd been right. Caitlin was still alive. She'd come back. No need to turn the page or move on.

There was a piece of scrap paper affixed to the cellophane with a paper clip, a note written in pen, a scrawled, scratchy handwriting. Not a child's writing, and not a woman's either. I could read the note without bending over.

Good-bye, it said. *Don't come back.*

My knees felt jittery, like they were full of sand.

I grabbed the bouquet and brought it with me to the car.

I returned home just before nine o'clock. Ryan and Abby were in the kitchen. They sat at the table, sipping coffee. I carried the bouquet.

'I found these,' I said. 'At the cemetery.'

They didn't say anything, but I could tell they didn't get it.

'At Caitlin's headstone,' I said. 'There's a note. Somebody left a note for her.'

Ryan came out of his chair.

'Put it down,' he said. 'Put it down.'

I laid it on the counter.

'Did you touch the note?' he asked.

'No. It's still there.'

He put his glasses on and read the note. 'Do you know the handwriting?' he asked.

'No.'

'Abby,' Ryan said, 'will you get me a ziplock bag, one of the large ones for the freezer?'

Ryan carefully picked the note up by its corners, his fat, sausagey fingers looking almost delicate, and dropped it into the bag Abby was holding open. He sealed it with a quick motion of his thumb. 'It's unlikely there will be any prints, but we can try.'

'Who is that note for?' Abby asked. 'Is it for her? Or us?'

'It might be a joke,' Ryan said. 'Some sort of hoax.'

'I don't think so,' I said. 'Earlier, when Caitlin was asleep, I looked in on her. She was saying something in her sleep. She said, "Don't send me back. Don't send me back." At first I thought she was talking about us, that she thought we were going to send her back to wherever she came from. But the way she said it . . . I don't know.'

'Let's not jump to any conclusions,' Ryan said. 'I'm going to take this with me. And I'll call as soon as I hear anything. Just hang in there.'

'I guess we know all about that,' Abby said.

'Ryan,' I said. 'My brother, Buster.'

'Abby mentioned —'

'He was here, right before. I think . . .'

I didn't know what I thought. Not really.

'We're looking into everything,' he said. 'But no promises, no guarantees.'

And that's the way he left us, waiting for our daughter again.

Chapter Twenty-six

I fell asleep in a living room chair. Someone knocked on the front door and it took a moment for the cobwebs to clear, for the events of the day to reappear in my mind. Caitlin at the police station, the hospital, back home. Then Caitlin out the window, into the night, the cemetery, the note . . .

They knocked again.

'Tom?'

Abby's voice reached me from upstairs.

'Tom, it's the police. I'm getting dressed.'

I went to the door and opened it. Ryan stood there in the porch light. He looked haggard, unshaven. I feared the worst. They found her, but she was dead, and Ryan was here to bring me the bad news.

'Is she . . . ?'

'She's in the car,' he said. 'We got her.'

Abby appeared beside me, and then we both moved out of the way, letting Ryan in. I gestured toward a chair, but he shook his head.

'I have to get home,' he said. 'This won't take long.'

'Is she in trouble?' Abby asked. 'Did she do something?'

'No, we found her north of downtown, not far from the police station actually. She was walking, but we're not sure where. There isn't much out there really.'

'Thank you for bringing her back,' Abby said.

'Is there something we need to sign?' I asked. 'A report or something?'

Ryan shook his head. 'No need.' He didn't make a move to leave or sit down. 'I know how difficult this is, and that the two of you have been kind of thrown into the deep end here,' he finally said. 'This is a huge adjustment for both of you. I'll help in any way I can, but . . .'

'What are you saying?' Abby asked.

'It can start to get dicey when manpower is being diverted in this way. If the media finds out, it becomes a spectacle. And you and Caitlin don't need that right now. Let's just utilize the resources we have at our disposal. We're in a critical stage with Caitlin, and we all have to be on alert. Especially the two of you. You're on the front line here.'

'Of course,' Abby said.

'Who was she with?' I asked.

'No one,' Ryan said. 'She was alone.' He looked me in the eye. 'We never got ahold of your brother.'

Someone knocked lightly on the screen door, so we turned. In the faint porch light, Caitlin looked calm, unaffected. Two uniformed cops walked behind her, but they didn't appear to be forcing her to move along or into the house. She came in on her own, as though it were perfectly natural to be brought to our door by the police at sunrise.

I took a quick look up and down the street. The neighbors had received quite a show. News vans and cops and now this.

Neither one of us touched Caitlin when she came in. She stopped in the living room and stood with her hands jammed into the pockets of her hooded sweatshirt. She looked like any slightly grubby teenager waiting for a bus.

Ryan nodded at us. 'I'd like to see you keep that appointment in the morning,' he said.

Rosenbaum. I understood what he was saying.

'We'll be there,' I said.

'You could even call him now,' Ryan said. 'He might have some ideas —'

'We're okay,' I said. 'We've got it.'

When Ryan was gone, Abby broke the silence.

'Do you want something to eat, honey?'

Before Caitlin could form a response, I cut her off.

'No,' I said. 'She needs to sit down. We have some things to talk about.'

'Tom —'

'Sit down,' I said. 'All of us.'

Caitlin didn't move. She stayed rooted in place, her eyes a little vacant, her mouth a narrow line.

'Caitlin?' I said.

'I don't want to sit,' she said.

My voice rose and I pointed at a chair. 'I'm telling you to.'

'I want to go to bed.'

'And run off again?' I said.

She didn't say anything else. She stared past me toward a point somewhere in the air.

'Where were you going tonight?' I asked.

When she didn't move or respond or even change the expression on her face, I felt anger welling up within me. I wanted to reach out and take her by the shoulders and shake.

'Tom, why don't we just get her something to eat?' Abby said.

I stormed off toward the kitchen. I wasn't going to eat. I took a piece of paper from the counter and returned to the living room. Caitlin and Abby started to follow me, but when they saw me coming back, they stopped in the dining room. My dirty dish was still there, the tomato sauce hardening like dried blood.

I held up the sketch.

'Who is this man?' I asked Caitlin. 'Is this the man you were going to see tonight? Is it?'

She blinked a few times and leaned closer. She studied the sketch like it was a rare bird that fascinated her.

'Is this the man who took you?' I asked.

'Tom.'

I moved the paper closer. 'Is this the man who took you to strip clubs and made you watch him?'

She blinked again, surprise showing on her face.

'Did he give you flowers in the park? For Valentine's Day? What's his name, Caitlin?' I asked.

Her chin puckered. 'You . . . said . . . you weren't going to ask me those things.'

And then she crumpled. She fell into Abby's arms, sobbing, her face pressed against Abby's neck, her body shuddering so much that Abby had to hold her up. Abby rubbed her back and held her tight and looked over Caitlin's shoulder at me, her face sending me a clear message.

I hope you're happy now. I hope you got what you wanted.

Chapter Twenty-seven

Abby woke me by knocking lightly, then coming in the guest room before I could say anything. Light spilled in from the hall.

'Where is she?' I asked.

'She's in the shower. She needed to take one.'

I sat up quickly. 'You left her —'

'It's fine. The door's open, and the water's running. I helped her get undressed. She doesn't have anything else to wear.'

'Where did she sleep?'

'In the bed. She slept a couple of hours at least.'

'Did she say anything?' I asked.

'She apologized for leaving and for scaring us.'

'Did she say where she went?'

'I didn't ask.'

'Did she say anything in her sleep?'

'I want to tell you something else. Something important.'

I was more insistent. 'So she didn't?'

'I was asleep, too, Tom.' Abby looked behind her, checking on the bathroom. When she turned back around, I took note of the fact that she looked calmer, more relaxed than the day before. Even with a lack of sleep, she looked refreshed. 'I want to tell you that I feel good about the way things are going.'

'You do? Our daughter goes out the window, and you feel good?'

'I had a dream last night, while I was sleeping next to Caitlin. In my dream, there was this woman, and she came to our door here, the front door of this house. She was maybe twenty-five years old, and she was pregnant. She didn't look like Caitlin, not at all. She didn't even resemble her. But when I opened the door and saw her, I knew it was Caitlin. She was coming here to tell us she was pregnant. You see?'

'I'm not sure I do.'

'It means she's going to be okay,' Abby said. 'She has a future, one that's going to turn out fine. We just have to accept that this is the path we've been set on, and know that eventually we'll get to the place we want to be. Like Dr Rosenbaum said yesterday, this is a long road.'

Abby smiled down at me, with a forced smile I recognized. As Abby became increasingly involved with the church, I saw that smile more and more. The church believed in the power of positive thinking, and its members were encouraged to present a happy face to the world. I wasn't sure if Pastor Chris actually taught his followers that they could change the world through smiling, but I wouldn't have doubted it.

'And this dream made you feel better?' I asked.

'The dream and the way things worked out last night. Caitlin came back.'

'You know they told us the pregnancy test was negative? I don't think I want a grandchild out of this deal.'

Abby's façade melted. 'Why would you say a thing like that, Tom?'

'I'm helping you interpret your dream.'

'Why do you always have to see the negative side of things?' She looked behind her again. 'I was thinking of it metaphorically, that it was saying Caitlin could be happy again.'

'It just seems silly to place that much stock in a dream, doesn't it?' I settled back against the pillows. 'It's wish fulfillment. Did you used to have dreams about Caitlin coming back?'

'Sometimes.'

'I did, too. And in those dreams, she would come home and she'd be happy to see us and we'd be happy to see her. And when she came in the door, we'd know where she'd been and how she'd been taken, and it always, always made sense, just like your dream made sense to you.'

Abby looked at the floor. I could tell she wasn't showered yet, and I was reminded of the first nights we'd spent together, the mornings when Abby wouldn't believe me that I thought she looked beautiful even then, just after waking up.

'We almost had another baby together,' I said.

'Oh, Tom.'

'Where was I when it happened? How did you hide it from me?'

She shook her head. 'Tom . . .'

'I want to know. I have a right to know.'

'You were at school. It was early in the day. The cramps were terrible, then bleeding. I knew what was happening.' She looked up. 'I almost called you. I did.'

'But?'

'I couldn't do it. I couldn't tell you.'

The water shut off in the bathroom. Abby turned away and said, 'Are you okay, honey? I'm right here.'

Caitlin said something I couldn't make out. Abby started to leave, but I said her name, stopping her.

'You called Pastor Chris, right?' I said. 'He took you to the doctor.'

Abby nodded slowly. 'When you came home that day, I was in bed. I said I had a stomach thing. You slept in here so you wouldn't catch it.'

Before Abby could go again, I spoke up. 'I just wanted to ask you one other thing, about this dream of yours. Something about it doesn't make sense.'

'What, Tom?'

'Why – if Caitlin is coming to this house in the dream and in the future – why are you the one who's here and opening the door for her? I thought you wanted to go.'

'It's a dream, Tom . . .'

'So it doesn't mean anything? Or does it?'

Abby turned away.

'I'm going to help her get ready,' she said.

We went to a bland brick and glass office building downtown where Dr Rosenbaum kept an office for his private practice. He met us in the reception area, and I expected him to have something to say about the night before and Caitlin's attempted escape. But he didn't. Maybe it was because she was there, or maybe he was simply in a hurry, but he told us he wanted to talk to Caitlin alone first. We let him lead her behind a closed door into his office, while we sat in uncomfortable chairs filling out the insurance forms the receptionist gave us.

No other patients came or went. There was no TV, no piped-in Muzak, and few magazines. I wished I'd brought a book, anything to distract me. Abby picked up a women's magazine, something with the promise of diet tips plastered across the front, and started paging through. She turned the pages quickly, snapping them from the right to the left. Things hung in the air between us, heavy as lead. Her dream. The miscarriage. Pastor Chris.

We didn't talk about them.

My phone rang. Liann.

I took the call out in the hallway.

'I was going to call you last night, as soon as I heard the news,' Liann said. 'I wanted to scream when I saw it and come right over. But I figured you were occupied. How does it feel? How is she? Tell me.'

'We're at the shrink's office right now.'

'What's wrong? You sound awful.'

I told her about the night before, about Caitlin coming home and almost immediately running away again.

'Now don't even worry about that. That's just a bump in the road. And there are going to be bumps along the way, I promise. That girl's been through a lot. She's confused. Very confused. You just have to hang in there.'

'Right.'

'I just wish . . .'

'What?' I waited for an important insight.

'Shit. I wish we could have followed her,' Liann said. 'She would have led us right back to that snake who took her. It would have been so easy, like a trail of bread crumbs. The cops are so dumb. They just want to run right out and grab her and bring her back. They don't even want to stop and think.'

My face flushed a little. 'I think they were concerned with her safety and getting her home again.'

'Did she say anything about the guy? Has she offered anything?'

'Pretty much the silent treatment,' I said. 'She made me promise not to ask her any questions about where she'd been.'

'You didn't agree to that, did you?'

'Of course I did.'

'Oh, Tom. You can't make deals with her. She's a child, and she has to tell us things.'

Us?

'Who's the therapist you're seeing?' Liann asked.

'Rosenbaum.'

Liann made a little humming noise.

'What?' The hallway was empty, and my voice echoed.

'He's okay. He's fine, really. He works with the police a lot. He's very experienced.'

'Isn't that good?'

'Can I come over and see her later?'

Before I could answer, Abby opened the office door and made an impatient, hurry-the-hell-up gesture at me. I held up my index finger, and she pulled her head back inside.

'I have to go, Liann. Look, I'll call you. Things with Abby . . . and Caitlin – it's weird.'

'Of course, of course. Just call me tonight. We have a lot to talk about now.'

'Okay. I will.'

'Tom, this is a major break. We'll find this guy. This is good.'

'And Caitlin —'

But she was already off the phone.

Rosenbaum came out with Caitlin. He asked us to come into his office and directed Caitlin to a waiting room chair. I hesitated.

'Caitlin will be fine right here. Won't she?' Rosenbaum said. Caitlin sat down in the chair without looking up at us. 'Mary?' He nodded at his receptionist, who nodded back, as though she understood the drill without anything being said. 'Shall we?' Rosenbaum said to us.

Abby took a hesitant step forward but kept her eyes on Caitlin.

I felt torn.

I didn't want to let her out of my sight, fearing a repeat of the night before.

But something else entered my mind, a sudden, darting thought I hadn't anticipated:

Might it be better if we let her go?

Would everyone be happier if Caitlin wasn't here?

I chased the thought away, pushed it down below the surface of my mind. I pointed to the door Rosenbaum had emerged from. 'It's okay,' I said to Abby. 'They'll keep an eye on her.'

We settled into chairs in Rosenbaum's inner office. It held a small, uncluttered desk, several comfortable chairs, and even a chaise longue a patient could recline on. A pitcher of water and several glasses sat on a side table, and next to every chair – except the one Rosenbaum landed in – was a box of Kleenex.

'I received a call from Detective Ryan this morning, and he told me about your adventurous night last night. Remember, you could have called me if you needed to.'

'It was late,' I said. 'Very late.'

'You'd be amazed at how many late-night calls I get,' he said. 'Keep it in mind for the future. But I guess she did settle down and sleep a little?'

'She did,' Abby said.

'Good,' he said. 'Her attempt to run away isn't completely surprising. Although going out a second-floor window is pretty bold. That's a first for me. Like I said, home is the unfamiliar environment right now.'

'What about —?' I pointed toward the waiting room.

'I don't really think Caitlin's going anywhere right now.'

'How can you be sure?' Abby asked.

'I can't be,' he said, offering that same kind of forced smile. 'But I think I am. Right now, none of us can really know anything for certain.' He crossed his legs, ankle on knee, and looked at us, his face pleasant. 'I just wanted to touch base with you both about Caitlin and share my initial impressions of our first session.'

'What did she tell you?' I asked.

'Nothing. She didn't open her mouth. That's not unusual for someone who's been through what she's been through.'

'What has she been through?' I asked. 'We really don't know.'

'If I can be candid with you, the medical and police reports already tell some of the story. Based on that and other cases like this one, I suspect she has been the victim of some sort of sexual assault, most likely at the hands of whoever took her out of that park that day. And most likely this assault was repeated over the last four years.'

The same piercing pain hit me, but this time it came on like someone punctured my lungs, letting the air evacuate from my body. I looked at the floor while my mind raced, trying to find a glimmer of hope.

'So you don't think she ran away?' I asked.

'She doesn't fit the profile of a runaway. And whether she ran away originally or not, if a twelve-year-old girl has sexual relations with an adult man, it's sexual assault.'

Abby remained silent, so I looked over at her. She looked dreamy, distant. While I stared she spoke up.

'Why did she leave again? You said she didn't feel safe at home.'

'We don't really know where she was going, but it's possible she was trying to get back to whomever she was with. As for why she would go back, that too is fairly common in these cases. Quite a lot has been written about this phenomenon. A lot of case studies and research. You see, the victim identifies with the attacker as a defense mechanism. She becomes more attached to him than anything else. After four years, those attachments to this man run deep, much deeper than what she now feels for either of you.' Rosenbaum's voice was calm, almost soothing, and somehow that made the impact of his words even more terrible. 'I won't kid you – this is a long, uphill climb here. Some of these victims never testify against the people who've harmed them. They never see it as a crime.'

'Jesus,' I said. I still didn't feel like I could get enough air.

Rosenbaum's eyes wandered over both of us. There was more to say, and it looked like he was gauging whether or not we could handle it.

'Caitlin may think of this man as her husband. She may have been told this for the last four years. Adolescence is a profoundly important time in someone's development. To have such trauma intrude upon that time can have catastrophic psychological consequences. I remember a case in Columbus during my residency. The young woman corresponded with the man who took her for many, many years, even while he was in prison.'

'Oh, God,' Abby said.

'We're talking years of therapy here, not days or months. And we may never know exactly what happened while she was gone.'

He paused, but neither one of us said anything.

'It's not just trauma for her, you know,' he said. 'It's trauma for you. How are the two of you handling the adjustment so far?'

'It's only one day,' I said, grasping to put a positive spin on things.

'And an eventful one at that,' he said.

He smiled again. It seemed less forced and more natural. But I sensed his question for us was probing at something.

'I think —' Abby said, then hesitated before she began again. 'I think Tom has some unrealistic expectations for Caitlin.'

'Oh?' Rosenbaum said.

'He wants to push, and like you said, it's going to take time. A lot of time.'

'Tom?' Rosenbaum said.

'I came down hard on her last night.'

'This is before she ran away?' Rosenbaum asked.

'No, after.' I told him about it: grabbing the sketch and sticking it in Caitlin's face, bringing her to tears. 'Aren't fathers supposed to ask those questions?'

'Yesterday, at the police station, Caitlin told Tom not to ever ask her any questions about where she'd been or what she'd been doing while she was gone,' Abby said.

'Very interesting,' Rosenbaum said. 'And you said you'd honor that wish?'

'I did. At the time. Yes.' I tried to sound reasonable, to get them both to understand where I was coming from with the promise. 'I was so thrilled to have her back, I would have said anything.'

Rosenbaum nodded, the wise sage. 'I think it's best if you honor that promise for now. If you make promises and don't keep them, you'll only widen the gap between the two of you.'

'But you're going to get her to talk, right?' I asked.

'I'm going to try,' he said. 'But she's a teenager now, one with a lot of trust issues. At some point, I can't force another person to say or do things they don't want to say or do. Building trust with her will be a big key for both of you right now. It's the best way to start to work against the events of the last four years. It's like you're starting from scratch in a way.'

'Don't you think we should try to focus on the positive aspects of Caitlin being at home?' Abby asked. 'We should welcome her and support her.'

'What do you think of that, Tom?'

I looked at Abby. 'Abby and I are separated. Abby left me and moved out of our house. It's tough for us to be supportive and put up a united front if I don't know whether we're united or not.'

Abby glared at me. 'I've moved home for Caitlin's sake,' she said. She turned back to Rosenbaum. 'And we've already told Caitlin about our separation. She understands about our rough times, but we're trying.'

'You know,' Rosenbaum said, 'this process of recovery will be twice as difficult if there are unresolved issues between the two of you. We're here for Caitlin, remember?'

'Okay,' I said. 'I guess none of the other stuff is as important.'

'Abby?' Rosenbaum said.

'It's not going to be a problem with me,' she said. 'I'm focusing on the positive.'

Rosenbaum didn't look entirely convinced, but he kept his concerns to himself. 'Then I think we should go with that,' he said. 'In the meantime . . .' He leaned over to his desk and picked up a prescription pad and pen. 'I'd like to put Caitlin on an anti-anxiety drug, something to help her feel less defensive and more at ease in your home. It might even help her sleep.' He scribbled, then extended the paper toward us. Abby took it and put it in her purse. 'And remember,' he said, 'I'm also here to help the two of you. If either of you find yourselves struggling with this adjust-ment, you can give me a call. Or I can recommend someone.'

'Doctor?' I said. 'One more thing. When Caitlin came home last night, she fell asleep in her old room. I heard her talking in her sleep. She said, "Don't send me back." She said it over and over. What do you think of that?'

'You mean do I know who she was talking to?'

I nodded.

'I'm sorry, but experience tells me she probably wasn't talking to you.' He asked if there was anything else. I couldn't imagine there could be, so I let him walk us to the door.

Chapter Twenty-eight

We stopped at a department store on the way home to buy Caitlin clothes. Abby led the way. She took Caitlin into the young women's section and picked out several pairs of jeans, shirts, and sweatshirts, as well as underwear, bras, and socks. They disappeared into a dressing room while I sat outside, watching older women with oversized purses hanging from their arms poke around on the sale racks.

How had this become my life?

How really, truly far gone was my daughter?

They came out with a stack of clothes, and Abby paid for them all with a credit card. I didn't pay attention to the price. We then stopped in the shoe section, and we bought two pairs for Caitlin. I watched my daughter, hoping to see some glimpse of the child I once knew. A sign of joy or contentment, even vulnerability. It wasn't there. At least not to my eyes. I remembered taking her to buy her first pair of soccer cleats. I remembered her excitement over getting a Happy Meal at McDonald's. I remembered her squeals and her energy. None of that was there. No life, no happiness.

In the car, on the way home, Abby tried to converse. 'We have plenty of food at home,' she said. 'The neighbors have been bringing it by.'

A long pause. Abby started to turn around, but Caitlin's voice stopped her.

'Like someone died,' she said.

Her voice sounded distant and small from the backseat. I looked in the rearview mirror, but she was still staring out the window. Abby turned back toward her.

'People bring food at happy times, too,' she said. 'Like when a baby is born.'

I watched in the rearview mirror when I could. Caitlin didn't move her head or make any effort to look at Abby.

'You know,' Abby said, 'this is kind of like you were born again, though. Isn't it?'

'Kind of like the Prodigal Son, right?' Caitlin said. 'You used to tell me about that.'

'Right,' Abby said, brightening. 'You remember that story from when you were little, don't you?'

Caitlin didn't answer. Abby didn't get discouraged.

'Honey?' she asked. 'Have you been going to school? Or church?'

I alternated my eyes from the road to the rearview mirror and back again.

'No,' Caitlin said. 'And I didn't miss it either.'

'Well,' Abby said, trying to remain cheerful and not succeeding very well. 'We can certainly take care of that one of these days.' She turned back around, and I kept my eyes on the road as well.

When we reached the house, I asked Abby to give me a moment alone in the car with Caitlin.

'Sure,' Abby said, but she didn't leave right away. She moved her eyes between the two of us, considering us. Then she went to the trunk, gathered the bags, and headed inside, leaving me alone with Caitlin.

'Caitlin?' I said. She didn't move. 'I know you can hear

me, right?' Nothing. 'Okay. I'll assume you can.' I took a breath. 'I'm sorry if I upset you last night when I showed you that sketch and asked you those questions. I just want to make sure you're okay, and if someone hurt you or did something to you, I want to know – *I want you to know* – that, whoever he is, that person is going to be punished and held accountable. We taught you that when you were little, and it hasn't changed. People are accountable for what they do, and they suffer the consequences for their actions.' My awkward position brought a crick to my neck. 'Are you hearing me? Do you understand what I'm saying?' My voice started to rise, but I brought it under control. 'Well?'

'You're not going to ask me anymore?' she said, her voice low and steady. 'Those bullshit questions?'

I took a deep breath.

'I won't,' I said. 'I promise.'

She pushed open the car door and stepped out, slamming it shut behind her.

Chapter Twenty-nine

As I came through the back door, I heard Abby gasp. I rushed in and found Abby and Caitlin standing at the entrance to the dining room – and Buster sitting at the head of the table, a mug of coffee steaming in front of him.

'How did you get in?' I asked.

'You need to find a new place for the Hide-A-Key,' he said. 'I would think a family that – you know – you might be more careful. Besides,' he said, standing up, 'I wanted to come by when she's awake. Right?'

Caitlin stood close to Abby, uncertain. Abby rested her arm on Caitlin's shoulder, a protective gesture. But Buster didn't relent. He opened his arms wide.

'You remember me, don't you?' he said.

And Caitlin nodded, almost spasmodically. 'Buster!' She went to him quickly, allowing herself to be folded up in his arms. He squeezed her tight. I watched them, saw the real emotion on Buster's face as he held on to my daughter. He eased his grip and held her back at arm's length, looking her over.

'Goddamn,' he said. 'Look at you. You're all grown up.'

Abby cringed at his language, but Buster didn't notice.

'I never thought I'd see you again, girl. I really didn't. This is like some sort of dream come true. You're back from the dead.'

A blush rose on Caitlin's cheeks, but she didn't say anything.

'You're going to have to tell me all about it,' he said. 'Where you were, what you were doing. All about your adventures.'

'Maybe Caitlin needs to come upstairs and change her clothes,' Abby said. 'We got her a bunch of new clothes just now.'

'Yeah?' Buster looked Caitlin over again. 'You're right. It looks like you're wearing your mom's clothes. No sixteen-year-old should have to do that.' He let her go. 'Okay, but we'll talk after that.'

Before Abby and Caitlin left the room to go upstairs, Abby looked back at me. 'Maybe you can fill William in on all that's been happening,' she said.

When they were gone, Buster sipped his coffee.

'What is your deal?' I asked.

'What do you mean?'

'You were talking to her like she'd been on a cruise or something. After you came by last night, she ran off. Or did you know that already?'

'What are you talking about?' he asked. 'What happened?'

'Do you know?'

'Jesus, Tom.' He shook his head. 'Can you for once – for five fucking minutes – just forget about your own bullshit? And Abby's? Will you?'

'What are you doing here?' I remained standing, watching him.

'I came to see my niece. I'm family, too. Remember?

I know sometimes you want to act like we're not, but we are, even if you want to deny it.'

My hand was on his shoulder. I hadn't realized I'd reached out to hold him, but my grip was tight. I let go.

'No more interrogating, okay?'

'Okay. Jesus.' He stared into his mug. 'She looks different.'

'She's older.'

'She's skinny. Worn. Like she's been through it. And she has that awful, dykey haircut. What are the cops saying?'

I went over to the table and sat at the opposite end from him. 'I don't know. All we do is hurry up and wait.'

'We'll never know what happened to her,' he said. 'The cops, they're never going to get anywhere.'

'Why do you say that?' I asked, studying his face.

'Do they think she ran away?'

'Maybe.'

'Or they think I did it, right? They're chasing their tails.'

'She's back,' I said. 'That's what's important.'

But the words felt put on, like I was speaking lines from a script.

I heard Caitlin and Abby on the stairs, then in the kitchen. Before they entered the dining room, Buster said, 'You keep telling yourself that, Tom. Just go ahead and keep telling yourself that.'

I knew it would bother Abby, so I asked Buster to stay and eat with us. The four of us sat down at the table together, facing a meal of ham, scalloped potatoes, and green beans left by someone from Abby's church. Between the church and some neighbors, we had enough food to last for weeks. We were all ready to eat, even Caitlin, but Abby bowed her head and closed her eyes. She reached out for Caitlin's hand, and I was happy to see that Caitlin made no effort to return the gesture. Instead, she grabbed her fork and started eating while Abby murmured a prayer, her eyes shut so tight it looked like it hurt. When Abby opened her eyes again and saw Caitlin eating already, she pursed her lips a little but didn't say anything.

Caitlin's eating made me cringe, but for a different reason. She ate quickly, shoveling the food from the plate to her mouth with the rapidity of an automated machine. She didn't pause long enough to take a breath or use a napkin to wipe her face. And when she chewed, she kept her mouth open wide, the food on display for all to see, her teeth and lips making smacking sounds that would have put Frosty to shame. Abby and I had ridden Caitlin hard when she was little, making sure she knew good table manners, but it was all out the window now. She conducted herself like she'd been living in a zoo for four years. Abby and I didn't even bother to look at each other during the meal. We each knew what the other was thinking.

All that effort wasted . . .

But Buster spoke up.

'Settle down there, girl. You're eating like the Iraqis are coming up I-75.'

Caitlin ignored him and kept going.

She did look better in her new clothes – a long-sleeved T-shirt, jeans, and new sneakers. She didn't say anything, didn't acknowledge any of the mindless conversation the three of us made, and when her plate was clean, she laid her fork aside and belched. She began fidgeting with a necklace. It was a simple gold chain with a small amber stone. Topaz maybe? She took the stone between her thumb and forefinger and pulled it back and forth on the chain.

'That's pretty,' Abby said, her teeth gritted just a little.

Caitlin just nodded.

I watched Caitlin swing it back and forth, a nervous tic. I wanted to know what made her touch it that way and who she thought of when she held it.

'That's your birthstone,' Abby said. She kept eating, but the skin around her mouth drew tight. She looked like she was chewing broken glass. 'Very pretty, very pretty.'

Detective Ryan called as we were finishing our meal. He said he was on his way over to talk to us, the sooner the better. I shared this with everyone when I hung up the phone. Buster poured himself another cup of coffee, but he squirmed in his seat and checked the clock on his cell phone repeatedly. Finally, he stood up and said he was leaving.

'Really?' I asked. 'Don't you want to stay and find out what's going on?'

'I don't want to stay and get hassled by the cops. Besides, I have the drive back . . .'

'Makes sense,' Abby said.

Buster bent down and gave Caitlin a hug.

'We'll talk soon,' he said.

She nodded, almost smiling.

'I'm glad you're back.'

I walked with him to the front door. 'We took her to a psychiatrist today, and she didn't say a word.'

'A shrink? Really? Jesus, Tom. That's worse than that fruity pastor at Abby's church. What's he going to do for you?'

'He can tell us what's wrong, or get her to tell us what happened.'

'You need a shrink for that?'

The doorbell rang.

'Shit,' Buster said. 'I should slip out the back.'

'Yeah, that would look good.'

I opened the door for Ryan. Momentary surprise passed across his face; then he held out his hand to Buster and they shook. Buster's posture stiffened. He pulled back his shoulders and lifted his chin.

'Are you living here, William?' Ryan asked. 'In New Cambridge?'

'Over in Columbus.'

'Nice,' Ryan said. 'Actually, it's a good thing you're here. I need to talk to Tom and Abby, and if you don't mind . . .'

Buster nodded. 'Sure. I'll sit with Caitlin and watch TV or something while the grown-ups talk.'

'Don't you have to go?' I asked, trying to move things along.

'It's fine. I'll make sure I only speak to her in declarative sentences.'

'I'll get Abby,' I said. 'The three of us can talk on the porch.'

The late afternoon was warm, unseasonably so, and a light breeze rustled through the trees. It felt good on the porch, like we were doing something normal.

'Is she doing better?' he asked.

'We bought her some new clothes today,' Abby said. 'We're adjusting.'

'What did you think of Dr Rosenbaum?'

'It was fine —'

'What are you here for?' I asked. 'Did you make an arrest?'

'No, we didn't. Can you tell me how things went with Rosenbaum?'

'We learned that our daughter doesn't like to talk to shrinks,' I said. 'And we learned that she doesn't like being with us as much as she liked being gone.'

'Tom . . .' Abby said.

'Okay, he told us a lot of things, things a parent wouldn't really want to hear.' I kept my eyes on Ryan. 'What did you learn today? There must be something.'

He reached into his inside jacket pocket and brought out a small spiral notebook. He wet his index finger and started flipping through the pages while he talked. 'One of the benefits of Caitlin's recovery is that it puts her story back in the public eye in a big way, even more than the composite sketch of the suspect.' He licked his finger again, turned a few more pages, and stopped. 'In the last twenty-four hours, we've been getting a lot of calls about Caitlin's case, and we've only just begun to wade through them. But a picture has started to emerge.'

'A picture of what?' Abby asked.

'A number of people have called and told us that they saw Caitlin during the four years she was missing.'

'You mean people who thought they saw Caitlin and were mistaken?' I asked.

Ryan shook his head. 'No, they saw her. Not all of them, of course. Some of them are crackpots, but there's a consistency to the sightings that makes us believe them.' Ryan looked down at his notes again, and I sensed a reluctance on his part, a hesitation about what he was about to tell us. 'People saw Caitlin out in public in the company of the man from the sketch. The stories are similar to the one you heard from the young woman at the Fantasy Club. Caitlin and this man were seen in out-of-the-way places. Strip clubs or diners. Always in rural or isolated areas. Never here in New Cambridge. Never in town or near the campus.'

I felt a sickness churning in my lower gut, a slow roiling, as though I might at any moment have to run to the bathroom to relieve it.

'I don't understand,' Abby said. 'What does it mean that Caitlin was out with this man? She must have tried to get away or asked for help.'

'No, she didn't. At least not that any of our witnesses saw.'

I leaned forward in my chair, hoping to ease the pain in my gut. I didn't think I could say anything.

'How can that be?' Abby asked. 'Some strange man takes her, and she doesn't run away. He must have held a gun to her or something, right? Tom? What are you doing, Tom? Are you okay? Are you hearing this?'

'We don't know if there was a weapon involved or not,' Ryan said. 'We're looking into that. But in cases like this, it's not unusual to hear that the victim was intimidated into not running away.'

'She has that bruise,' Abby said.

'We don't know what that's from,' Ryan said, 'but it

wouldn't be out of the realm of possibility that she was physically assaulted by whoever took her.'

'Why are you telling us all of this?' I asked. I shifted my position on the chair.

'I'm really just trying to keep you informed. This is going to somewhat change our approach to this investigation,' Ryan said. 'Caitlin was a child when she disappeared. She's still a child in the eyes of the law. We need to remember that. But this information could suggest a different and potentially more complicated relationship with whoever took her.'

'Let's not use the word "relationship",' Abby said.

'I'm sorry,' Ryan said. 'That was a poor choice of words. But Caitlin may very well be seeing it as a relationship.'

'Who is this guy, Ryan?' I asked. 'If he showed up in public places, he must have left a trail. Credit card statements, signatures. He must have talked to people, given someone his name or something.'

'We're going to do everything we can,' Ryan said.

His words were just nonsense syllables, though, meaningless mutterings that made no impact on me. I felt myself tuning out, fading away from a conversation that should have held so much importance for me. When Abby spoke again, her voice came to me from a great distance, as though she were speaking through a long tube.

'Are you going to ask Caitlin about this?' she asked.

Ryan nodded. 'That's the other reason I'm here. I have to see if she'll talk to me. We gave her a break yesterday, but the sooner we can get some answers out of her, the better for the investigation. I was hoping . . .' Ryan hesitated. 'I was hoping you wouldn't mind if I was a little more aggressive with my questions. I'm going to press her a little bit now just to see if anything shakes loose. We'll know pretty quickly if she's going to respond to my approach.'

Abby looked over at me, her face uncertain. I got the feeling she wanted me to object or tell Ryan he couldn't talk to Caitlin, that it was too soon, give us time. But I didn't. The pain in my gut was starting up again, and I liked the idea of someone trying to provide me with answers.

'Go ahead,' I said. 'I'll tell her.'

Chapter Thirty

Buster and Caitlin sat on the couch in the living room, the
TV tuned to some kind of talk show. The volume blared,
and Buster was leaning over to Caitlin, saying something
into her ear. He straightened up when I entered the room.

'What's all this?' I asked.

'Nothing. Just hanging out and doing a little uncle and
niece bonding.'

'What are you saying to her?' I asked.

'I'm telling her a stupid joke, Tom. Easy.'

'Caitlin, Detective Ryan needs to ask you a few
questions.'

I felt Ryan behind me, his bulk looming there like an
eclipsing planetary body.

Caitlin kept her eyes on the television.

'Maybe now isn't the best time there, Sipowicz,' Buster
said. 'Maybe another couple of days to settle in.'

The left corner of Ryan's mouth went up in a half
smile, but there was no humor in it. 'Maybe you could give
us some privacy, William,' Ryan said. 'But don't leave. I'd
like to ask you some questions as well.'

Buster smirked. He leaned over to Caitlin and gave
her arm a squeeze. 'I'll be out there if you need me,'
he said, loud enough for all of us to hear. 'And don't take
any shit.'

Ryan walked across the room and took a seat on the

opposite end of the couch from Caitlin. He reached out, picked up the remote, and clicked off the TV.

Abby slipped in the front door as Buster went out to the porch. She closed the storm door, blocking out the sounds of the outside world. 'Is it okay if we're here with her?' she asked. 'I'd like to be here.'

'Sure,' Ryan said. 'We're just going to have a friendly chat.' Ryan adjusted his bulk on the couch, settling into the cushions a little like a bear choosing a spot to hibernate. It took long seconds, and when things were just right, he let out a long sigh. 'Okay, Caitlin, do you want to tell me anything? Do you feel like talking about where you've been?'

Caitlin stiffened visibly and gave Ryan a quick glance out of the corner of her eye, but she didn't respond.

'I know this might be difficult, but we've got to get to the bottom of some things here, and the sooner we do that, the better. A crime's been committed, and it's my job to figure out who did what. Can you help me with that?'

Ryan reached into his inside coat pocket again. He brought out a piece of white paper, folded into thirds. He unfolded it and held it in front of Caitlin.

'Do you know this man? Do you know who he is?'

Nothing.

'You know his name, don't you? He took you when you were little.'

'Maybe —' Abby began to say.

Ryan held up his hand without turning around, cutting Abby off.

'Caitlin, did this man hurt you in any way? Do you know the kind of ways I might mean?'

Abby gasped, but Caitlin turned and faced Ryan for the first time. She spoke to him through gritted teeth. 'You think you know so much, but you don't. You don't know anything.'

'I want you to tell me those things, Caitlin,' Ryan said, his voice softer. 'I want you to tell me what I need to know to find this man and convict him.'

Caitlin's eyes darted back and forth ever so slightly, and she used her tongue to moisten her lips.

'Did this man threaten you? Did he say he'd hurt you if you talked to the police? Did he threaten your family? Your parents? You don't have to worry about all of that. You're safe here. Your parents are safe. We can protect you and your family.'

'Yes, Caitlin,' I said. 'Listen to him.'

Ryan paused, letting his words sink in. I'm sure he was hoping the fatherly, protective approach might break Caitlin down, but when it didn't, he pressed ahead.

'You know, people saw you out with this man,' Ryan said. 'They saw you in public places, acting as though you were a couple. Let's see, you were at the Fantasy Club with him, Pat's Diner over in Leesburg, the Country Inn and Buffet in Russellville. You weren't in handcuffs when these people saw you. You weren't tied up or shackled or anything like that. In fact, some people saw you go off and use the restroom, which means you could have run away if you wanted to. Why didn't you, Caitlin? Were you scared? Did he say he would hurt you if you ran?'

The sick feeling in my gut, the one that had started on the porch, came back even stronger. I bent down into a squatting position, resting my back against the wall. Abby

231

was looking away, off toward the blank TV screen. Her right hand was raised to her chest and clutched a handful of fabric from her shirt.

Ryan sat back a little. He refolded the paper with the sketch on it and placed it back in his pocket. 'I think I know what's going on here,' he said. 'I think you were trying to go back to this man last night. That's why you went out the window and ran away. Do you love him, Caitlin? Is that what you think? Do you think you love him?'

'I do love him,' she said. 'And he loves me. He does. Still. He loves me.'

I stood up, my mouth dry. I felt on the edge of panic. 'Who does, Caitlin?' I asked. 'Who is this man who's been telling you these things?'

Ryan held up his silencing finger again, and when he did, Caitlin turned away from him and folded her arms across her chest. She looked younger than her years, like a small child throwing a tantrum, and to complete the effect some tears ran down her cheeks. It wasn't full-fledged sobbing like the night before, but it was enough to signal the end of the conversation.

Ryan pushed himself up from the couch, the springs groaning with relief.

'Okay, Caitlin,' he said. 'I'll leave off there. But I do hope we'll talk about this again. And I'll be sure to tell Dr Rosenbaum about our conversation. Maybe you'd rather talk to him about it at some point. Would you prefer that? Would you prefer to talk to Dr Rosenbaum?'

Caitlin didn't answer.

'Okay,' he said. 'That's fine. Well, I'm glad you're home with your parents and getting settled in.'

Ryan left the room, and as he passed, he placed his hand on my arm and nodded, indicating he wanted us to follow him. We did, but before we left the living room, I looked back at Caitlin. She still sat on the couch in the same position – arms folded, jaw set. She looked stubborn and determined. Not only did I wonder about the secrets she held inside her, but also about the nature of the effort it would take to pry them loose. Before I left the room, Caitlin reached up and took hold of the topaz necklace. She rubbed the stone between her thumb and forefinger as if it were some kind of charm.

The three of us gathered in the kitchen, presumably out of Caitlin's earshot, although a part of me suspected Ryan wanted her to hear our conversation.

'Continue to keep a close eye on her tonight,' Ryan said. 'She may bolt again.'

'Oh, God,' Abby said. 'Those things you said to her . . . Why . . . ?'

'I'm sorry if it seemed too harsh. She has a strong wall up, and she's strong willed. I had to try to get through it. The sooner we answer these questions, the sooner we can catch the person who did this to Caitlin. This guy's out there, and I think he's close.'

'Close?' Abby asked.

'In town. Or at least he was. Where did your brother go?'

'The porch, I guess,' I said.

'I'll catch him on my way out.'

'Why do you want to talk to him?' Abby asked. 'Frankly, given some of his past behavior, I thought maybe you should . . . examine him more closely.'

'This is just routine,' Ryan said. 'Really, keep a close eye on her tonight. She's still attached to this guy.' He gave Abby a gentle pat on the shoulder. 'Stay strong. We're getting there.'

Abby and I walked with Ryan to the front of the house, back to the room where Caitlin was sitting. She'd turned the TV back on. Through the large picture window, I saw Buster sitting on the porch, smoking a cigarette. I thought he'd quit, but there he was, the long tendrils of smoke leaving his mouth and nostrils and being carried away on the wind.

'I'll just have a word with William and be on my way.'

'Tom?'

I followed Abby's gaze. She stared out the window to the porch, where Ryan stood over Buster. Ryan's face displayed the same unfriendly grin, and Buster was shaking his head back and forth, back and forth.

She said my name again.

'Tom?'

I looked over at her. She jerked her head toward the kitchen, so I followed her back there. She leaned against the one counter and I leaned against the other, facing her.

'It's true, isn't it? All that stuff Ryan was saying to her? It's true. She lived with some man, and she . . . lived with him or whatever.'

'She was taken.'

'Are you sure? What if she ran away? What if she wanted to be away from us? Someone else seemed more appealing. Better.'

'Stop it.'

'It's possible, Tom. Admit it's possible. Don't all kids wish they could be away from their parents? Maybe Caitlin . . .'

I went back to the living room and looked out the window. Buster wore a large smirk, and for a moment, he looked as childish and pouty as Caitlin under the heat of Ryan's questions. He flicked his cigarette butt out into our yard and kept smirking.

Chapter Thirty-one

I turned back to Caitlin. It was getting late in the afternoon, and the light was going. I sat in a chair across from her and didn't bother to see if she would move her eyes from the TV screen to me. I knew she wouldn't.

'I know Detective Ryan was kind of hard on you,' I said. 'He's just doing his job, trying to find out what's going on.'

Silence.

'He left you a note.'

'Fuck him.'

'I don't mean Detective Ryan.'

She cut her eyes toward me. I waited while the realization showed on her face.

'He left it in the cemetery, with a bouquet of flowers. Ryan took it, but I'm sure he'll show it to you at some point. I think they're looking for fingerprints.' I paused, letting that hang in the air a moment. 'The note said not to come back. It told you to go away and not come back.'

'Why would anyone leave a note in the cemetery?' she asked.

'Maybe because that's where he took you.'

She started to turn back to the TV, but stopped. She looked at me again, still processing. 'Was my name on it? The note. Was my name on it?'

'No.' I didn't know where she was going with this.

'Then how do you know it was for me?'

'He left it someplace special,' I said. 'Someplace just for you.'

She had never been a stupid kid. She was always two steps ahead of Abby and me, even when she was little.

'What could be just for me in a cemetery?'

I didn't say anything, but Caitlin stared, her eyes a little wider.

'No,' she said. 'You fuckers.'

I was trapped. 'You were gone a long time, Caitlin. We wanted to celebrate your life somehow.'

She started shaking her head.

'You buried me,' she said.

'No.'

Her mouth hung open, her face disbelieving.

'He was right,' she said.

'Who?' I asked. But I knew. *The man.*

'He said you'd forget about me. You'd move on.'

'He lied to you, Caitlin. We *never* forgot.'

'It's bullshit.'

'It's a headstone, Caitlin. It's just a memorial, a tribute.'

She turned back to the TV, her jaw set like granite.

'I'll show you the note when I can. He's done with you. Stop protecting him.'

'You'll never know what happened,' she said. 'Never.'

'I will.' I raised my hand, index finger extended. 'I promise.'

She shook her head, speaking one word.

'Never,' she said. 'Never.'

*

I looked outside, where Buster paced back and forth on the porch, a new cigarette burning in his mouth. It looked like Ryan was gone, so I went outside.

'What was that all about?' I asked.

'Breaking my balls, I guess.'

He kept pacing.

'What did he ask you?'

He stopped pacing and came up to me. The cigarette smoke curled up into his face, and he squinted.

'He showed me that sketch and asked if I knew who the guy was. Then he asked if any of my associates might know the guy. *Associates*. Can you believe he used that word? Associates.'

'What did you say?'

He took the cigarette out of his mouth, still squinting. 'What do you think I said? I told him I didn't know the guy. I told him the same stuff today I told him four years ago. Did you put him up to this?'

'I need to know.'

He broke off eye contact with me and walked away, turning his back. I was surprised to see his hair was thinning at the crown of his head, allowing pale skin to show through. He was younger than me, so much younger than me, I always thought. He took a last drag on his cigarette and dropped it on the porch, grinding it beneath his shoe.

'Your brother?' he said. 'You'd really question your brother?'

'I don't know . . .' I paced a little, back and forth on the porch.

'You've got all this anger, Tom. All this anger toward

me. Toward the family. We were close as kids. We looked out for each other. I looked out for you. Always.'

'I know,' I said. 'But you should have heard the things Ryan was saying back there . . .'

'What kinds of things?'

I sat down, taking the same seat I was in when we talked to Ryan. Buster sat down, too, using Ryan's chair. He waited for me to talk, leaning forward expectantly. I wasn't sure where to start.

'Ryan came by today to tell us that people saw Caitlin out in public with this guy.'

'You're kidding,' he said.

I shook my head. 'Restaurants, strip clubs. Hell, maybe they went to church together for all I know. She was with this guy, in public, and she could've gotten away from him – several times – and she didn't. She stayed with him. I don't know what I'm supposed to think of that.'

Buster leaned back in his chair and folded his hands. He looked like a wise sage, absorbing my story. But I noticed that his fingers were intertwined and squeezed so his knuckles turned white. 'I'm sorry,' he said. 'That's fucked-up.'

'At the hospital,' I said, 'they did a bunch of tests. They wanted to make sure Caitlin was in good shape and everything.'

'Sure.'

'They did a gynecological exam.' I felt deflated. 'She's not a virgin anymore.'

Buster lowered his hands and gripped the armrests of his chair. He looked like he'd been slapped. 'He raped her,' he said, his voice low and hoarse. 'It figures, the fucking pig.'

I made a helpless, hopeless gesture with my hands, somewhere between a shrug and a surrender.

'What are we going to do?' Buster asked.

'I need to get back inside.'

'You didn't answer my question. What are we going to do?'

I couldn't look at him. 'I need time to think about all of this.'

'Sure.' Buster stood up. 'The thoughtful, scholarly man. Consider all the angles. Mull it over. We've got time, right?'

'You want to go beat the guy up? Find him and kill him?'

'It's a start.'

He didn't sound like he was kidding.

'I thought you didn't know who he was,' I said.

'That's just it, professor. You find out. You've got the sketch. You've got two good legs. Can you do any worse than the cops?'

'Did Caitlin tell you anything when you were alone with her?' I asked, jerking my thumb toward the house. 'Did she talk to you?'

'Not really. We talked about TV. She said she's watched the last few seasons of *American Idol*. It's her favorite show.'

'So she could watch TV, wherever she was.'

'I guess so.' He seemed to be thinking about something. 'Hey?' he said.

'What?'

'Is she . . . ? I mean – did they do a pregnancy test at the hospital?'

'They did. At the time, I thought it was ridiculous.'

He nodded. 'So then, it was cool, right? I mean, there's nothing else to know about that, is there?'

'That's one thing off my list.'

I stood up. Buster reached for the door and pulled it open.

'If you don't mind,' I said, 'I think we need to be alone now. Abby's upset . . . and Caitlin . . .'

Buster gave me the same smirk I saw him give Ryan.

'I was just getting the door for you, chief. I thought you could use a hand.'

He held it open while I went in, then let it slam shut behind me.

Chapter Thirty-two

I wasn't sure what brought me awake.

It was a few days after Ryan's visit. Abby and Caitlin were sleeping in the master bedroom, and I was deep asleep in the guest room when something woke me up.

I wondered if Caitlin was stirring, trying to get out. I had suggested to Abby that we call a locksmith, that we have the windows and doors secured better than they were. Abby vetoed that idea. She said we had to resume normal life as much as possible, that we couldn't all live like prisoners in our own home.

Did something make a noise?

Rain?

I swung my feet to the floor, listening.

The house was quiet, deathly so. The evening was clear, the stars bright.

I'd imagined it. Maybe it was a dream, the subconscious emergence of some unremarkable phantom.

I needed to roll back under the covers and close my eyes, but a part of me couldn't let go. I wanted to – needed to? – look outside, into the yard and the street.

I stood up in my drawstring pants and T-shirt. I parted the curtains.

The streetlights glowed. The shadows beneath the trees were thick and black. Nothing moved. No cars.

Then I saw the girl.

She stepped into the bright circle created by the street-light, looking like a stage actor. She stopped there, seemingly without destination or intent. She looked the same as in the cemetery, like Caitlin.

I pressed my hands against the glass, almost shouted.

She looked up and darted out of the light.

I ran.

I hit the stairs going full speed, trusting to the fates that I wouldn't fall and break my neck. I knew I'd wake Abby and Caitlin, but I didn't care.

She looked so much like Caitlin.

I scrambled to open the door.

She's gone. Too late – she's long gone.

I got the door open and ran in the direction I'd seen the girl go.

I was still barefoot. I slipped on the dewy grass, almost went down. Then I ran into the street, the small bits of dirt and road grime pricking my soles.

Except for where the streetlights glowed, everything was inky black. I ran down the center of the street, heading toward the park. My neighbors' houses were dark, the world closed up and in bed.

Why was the girl out there?

I finally stopped halfway up the street. She was gone. Disappeared.

And I was out of breath and feeling foolish.

But she'd been at the house. She'd wanted something from us.

From me? From Caitlin?

243

Huffing and puffing, I turned and went home.

Lights were on upstairs and downstairs. Abby and Caitlin were awake.

I limped up the front steps, my feet aching and bruised, and was greeted by Abby, who held the door open for me.

'What the hell's going on?' she asked.

I came in and sat down in the living room. I was sweating. My T-shirt clung to my body. I wiped my forehead with the back of my hand.

'The girl,' I said.

'Caitlin?'

I shook my head. 'The girl I saw in the cemetery. She was outside tonight, in the street. She was looking at our house.'

Abby didn't say anything. She just stared.

I knew what she was thinking:

Poor man. Poor, poor man, driven crazy by stress.

I looked past Abby. Caitlin stood at the top of the stairs. She wore the Fields University nightgown Abby had bought her, and she looked down at us, her feet on different steps like she'd been frozen in midstride.

'You know that girl, don't you?' I asked.

'Tom —'

'You know who she is and what she wants.'

Caitlin turned to go, back up the stairs and to the bedroom.

'That girl knows that man, doesn't she?' I asked. 'She looks just like you, Caitlin, like when you were a little girl. I'm going to get ahold of her.'

She was gone. Abby placed her hand on my shoulder.

'Easy, Tom. Take it easy.'

244

I didn't realize I'd been shouting. I tried to calm down, but it took a long time for me to catch my breath.

We returned to Dr Rosenbaum's office a few days later. He asked to see Abby and me first, leaving Caitlin again under the watchful eye of Mary the receptionist. Rosenbaum sat without notes or pen, just the coffee mug in his right hand and the same casually expectant look on his face.

'Anything different at home?' Rosenbaum asked.

Abby and I looked at each other. Before she could say anything about my adventure from a few nights earlier, I said, 'Nothing unusual.'

'Things are better then?' he asked.

'I wouldn't say better,' Abby said. 'Do you think it's a good idea for Detective Ryan to press Caitlin about what happened already?'

'How do you mean?'

'He came over the other day, and he really pushed her hard about what happened to her. He was almost aggressive. I didn't think it was best for her to hear that already.'

Rosenbaum pursed his lips. He set the coffee mug down. 'Right. Detective Ryan mentioned to me that he had talked to Caitlin at your house. Sometimes the police press like that because they think the case is time sensitive. Say, for instance, the man who did this is thinking of leaving the area, or even committing another, similar crime. Detective Ryan would like to get to him before that happens.'

'So you think it's okay for her to hear these things so soon?' Abby asked.

'I didn't say that,' Rosenbaum said. 'I've worked with the police a lot, and we don't always agree on how to approach these things. We have different priorities sometimes. But Detective Ryan is a good man. Give him a chance.'

Abby didn't seem placated. Neither was I, but we didn't say anything.

Rosenbaum apparently decided to move forward. 'I wanted to try to get a picture of what your home was like before Caitlin disappeared,' he said. 'Just some background information for me.'

'I guess we were normal,' Abby said.

'Whatever that means,' I said.

Rosenbaum smiled a little. 'But you two are separated now, so something must have been going on.'

'I think those issues arose in the wake of Caitlin's disappearance,' I said. 'I don't think either one of us dealt with it all that well.'

'Abby?' Rosenbaum said.

'I guess I feel as though the problems were beginning back then,' she said. 'I felt that over the years Tom and I grew apart. Our lives were kind of going in different directions. It's not that we didn't love each other. It's just that we were becoming different people. He was pursuing his academic life and work, and I was developing in other ways. I wanted to work on my spiritual life. Caitlin may have been aware of all that. She was a smart kid.'

'Is,' I said. 'She *is* a smart kid.'

'Tom, do you share Abby's assessment that problems might have been brewing that far back?'

'Abby would know about her unhappiness better than I would. Maybe there were issues brewing back then that came to the forefront when Caitlin disappeared. Sometimes it did feel like we were traveling on parallel tracks.'

'What about Caitlin at that time?' he asked. 'Had she shown an interest in boys yet?'

'Not really,' Abby said. 'I'm sure she liked some boys at school. Some names came up from time to time.'

'She didn't have a large number of friends,' I said. 'She's kind of a loner. It's no surprise really that she's being so tight-lipped now. She could be like that sometimes.'

'But she had friends,' Abby said. 'She was a well-liked girl.'

'Had she reached puberty yet?'

Abby nodded. 'About six months before,' she said.

Abby had taken Caitlin out to dinner about a year and a half before she disappeared, just the two of them. Abby explained the changes that were going to be coming over her body and the ways women coped with them.

'Were there emotional changes associated with puberty?' he asked. 'Mood swings? Anger?'

'She was turning into a teenager,' Abby said. 'There was more eye rolling, more snippy answers. Caitlin always played things close to the vest.'

'Did it bother you that she played things "close to the vest"?'

'It's just the way she was.' I caught myself. 'Is.'

'Did it force you to be more strict with her?'

'Not at all,' I said. 'We didn't have a lot of rules.'

'Who was the disciplinarian?'

'Abby probably was more than me.'

'Were you around a lot, Tom?'

'I worked.' I looked down and picked a piece of lint off my pants. 'But my job at the university allowed for a flexible schedule. I was home more than a lot of dads.'

'Were you a factor in Caitlin's life?'

'A factor?' I asked. 'I'm her dad.'

'He was very involved with her life those first twelve years,' Abby said.

'Why do you ask that?' I said.

'Sometimes young women who are in restrictive homes or who aren't getting significant attention from their male parent seek that attention through other avenues. They engage in reckless drinking or sexual behavior. Drugs even. Or they seek that attention they think they're being deprived of in other people. Substitute male authority figures.'

'What are you saying?' I asked.

'I'm speaking in generalities, of course,' Rosenbaum said. 'Caitlin hasn't offered us much, so I'm working through some possibilities that might explain what happened.'

'I don't think she ran away, if that's what you're saying,' I said.

'I'm not suggesting that,' Rosenbaum said. 'In fact, I'm glad to hear your certainty about the issue. Abby, do you share that certainty?'

'No, she didn't run away,' Abby said. 'I know my daughter. She wouldn't have done that.'

'Do you still know her?' Rosenbaum asked.

Abby tapped her chest three times. 'In here, I do. In here, always.'

I admired her in that moment, her certainty, her bedrock belief that things made sense. I didn't have it, and I wasn't sure Rosenbaum did either.

'Fair enough,' he said. 'If you'll step outside now, I'm going to chat with Caitlin.'

Chapter Thirty-three

Sunday morning, a few days later, and Abby came into my bedroom. I didn't hear her knock. She was just there, wearing her robe, her hair still disheveled and her eyes puffy from sleep.

She sat down on the side of the bed.

'Is something happening?' I asked.

'*Shh*. It's fine.'

'What?'

'Caitlin's fine.'

I sat up, rubbed my eyes. The clock read 8:45, later than I would have thought.

Abby looked distracted. I couldn't read her mood.

'It's weird, sleeping in the same room with her,' she said. 'It makes me think of when she was little and she'd crawl into bed with us. Or if she was sick and she'd come to our room and watch TV. It's hard to believe sometimes . . .'

'What?'

'She's the same girl. She's so different in so many ways.'

'I understand. I think about the fingerprints and the scar on her knee. Those seem to ground me a little, remind me it's really her.'

And deep down, I knew. She possessed the same qualities. The stubbornness. The willfulness. The obstinacy that could burn like hate.

The secrecy.

'Will we get her back, Tom? All the way?'

It hurt for me to say it, but I began to formulate an answer to that question. 'She'll never be the same as if she'd spent those four years here. With us.'

Abby nodded. 'We won't be the same either, will we? I think about everything that might have been different. If I'd continued to work. If you'd worked less. If we'd had another baby . . .'

I reached out, placed my hand on her upper arm. I felt her beneath the fluffy robe, our first real contact since the hand-holding in church. 'We still could,' I said.

'Tom . . .'

I applied some gentle pressure, drawing her toward me. She gave in, leaned her head down close to mine. I brushed my lips against her cheek, then moved to her mouth.

She pulled back. 'No, Tom,' she said, her voice gentle but firm.

'Why?'

She stood up and pulled her robe tighter around her. 'We can't.'

'We're married,' I said. 'We're here. Our child is here.'

'Our energy needs to be on helping her,' she said. She fussed with her hair. 'That's why I came in here. I want to go to church today. It's been a while.'

'So go then,' I said, leaning back.

'I want Caitlin to go with me.'

'No.'

She ran her tongue over her teeth. 'I could take her with me. It would be good for her to get out of here, to see some other people again.'

'No.' I shook my head. 'Not there.'

'You can say no to this now, as I figured you would. But at some point, she has to leave the house. She's going to have to go to school and have friends and have a life. We can't keep her here at home forever.'

'We should start small and get her to speak again.'

'She speaks to me.'

'About what?'

'Little things, Tom. Little things. Is the bed comfortable, or do her clothes fit? It's a start.'

Abby left the room on that note, so I got out of bed and looked in on Caitlin. The blinds were drawn, making the room gloomy, so it took me a moment to see that Caitlin's eyes were open. She was lying on her back, the covers pulled up to her chin. She was looking at me but not saying anything. 'Mom's going to church,' I said. 'Looks like it's just you and me, kiddo.'

She rolled over, turning her back to me.

Once Abby was gone, I made toast and coffee in the kitchen, then ate a bowl of cereal. I went outside and brought in the Sunday paper and found a story on Caitlin's return in the local news section. The reporter had called for a week straight, and we'd stuck to the script of no comments and making requests for privacy, but someone with the police must have spilled the beans, because the story mentioned all the sightings of Caitlin with the man in the sketch. Ryan was quoted – at the end of the article – and simply said the investigation was continuing and that they still considered it a case of abduction and kidnapping.

I heard stirrings upstairs. Footsteps in the hall, the

toilet flushing. Caitlin didn't seem eager to shower on a regular basis. Most parents of teenagers saw their water bills shoot up. Abby reminded Caitlin to shower every few days. But I heard the water running upstairs, which I took as a good sign.

I resisted the urge to go check. I poured another cup of coffee and started the crossword puzzle, listening with one ear for the water to stop. I waited as long as I could and was about to throw my pencil down and check when it did stop. I breathed a sigh of relief. I heard more footsteps above me and managed to drink my coffee in a little bit of peace. That lasted a few minutes, until the cup was empty; then I couldn't wait and decided to go upstairs and check in on her.

She wasn't in the bathroom – the door was wide open, the mirror still steamed over from her shower. And then, with some alarm, I saw she wasn't in the master bedroom. The windows were all still closed.

'Caitlin?' Calling out for someone who wasn't speaking to me anymore seemed odd, but at least she'd know I was looking. I checked Caitlin's bedroom. Nothing. 'Caitlin?' I stuck my head in the guest room door. She was there, sitting on the bed. At first, I didn't know what she was doing. Then I saw the phone – my cell phone – in her hand. She was entering a number. 'What are you doing?' I asked.

She slammed it shut and tossed it onto the bed.

'Who are you calling?'

I grabbed the phone and opened it, but whatever number she'd been entering was gone. I checked the called numbers. The last one was a call I'd made, so she hadn't actually placed it, meaning there was no record of the number.

If only I'd waited . . .

'Were you calling that man?' I asked.

She started to stand up. I held my hand out, a silent request that she stay seated and listen to me. She didn't like it. She stared at me through slitted eyes.

'You don't get to make calls or do anything else until you talk to us. And I mean for real. Not just bullshit.' I jabbed at the air with my index finger, but my hand shook. 'Who was it?'

Her glare slowly turned into a smile. A smirk, really. I saw some of Buster in her. It made me even angrier.

'Stop it,' I said.

'Someday I hope you do find out where I was and everything that happened to me,' she said. Her voice sounded deeper, huskier. She sounded more like a woman, more like Abby. 'I can tell the truth will hurt you more than not knowing.'

I slapped her across the cheek.

She looked shocked more than hurt. She raised her hand to her cheek, her mouth wide open.

'Fuck you, asshole.'

She was up and past me, storming out of the room. I thought about reaching out for her again, or following her, but I couldn't find the will to do it. I let her go.

Caitlin closed herself in the master bedroom. I didn't bother knocking on the door or apologizing. I went back downstairs but didn't eat or drink. I tried to look at the paper, but my eyes couldn't focus. No way I could do the crossword puzzle. Rather than helping my daughter, I'd failed her once again. I didn't seem able to understand what she needed from me as a father.

I replayed the scene with Caitlin. I wished I couldn't remember it. I wished it were gone. Erased. But it played in my head on a loop. Every word. Every gesture.

The slap.

About the tenth time through, something stuck out. A phrase. It caught in my brain like a fishhook. Something Caitlin had said:

Everything that happened to me, she'd said.

Not *everything I did* or *everything we did*.

Everything that happened to me.

Abby's car turned into the driveway.

Then I heard two voices coming in the door. Abby's and a man's.

Pastor Chris.

He was there, the smile plastered across his face. He held out his hand. 'Tom, I haven't seen you since Caitlin's return to us.' *Us?* 'I want you to know I'm here in a strictly pastoral capacity,' he said. 'I want to help Caitlin.'

'How is she?' Abby asked.

'She took a shower. I took that to be a good sign.'

Abby smiled. She looked pretty.

I tilted my head toward the dining room. 'Can I . . . ?'

She hesitated and looked at Chris, then back at me. 'I think if you have something to say, you can say it in front of Chris.'

I hesitated. 'I don't think that would be a good idea.'

'Is this something about Caitlin? You said she was okay.'

'I can go —' Chris said.

Abby cut him off. 'No. Tom? Is it Caitlin?'

'She's fine,' I said.

'Then what is it?'

254

I shook my head. 'She said . . . she tried to talk to me . . .'

Abby came closer. 'That's good, Tom. It's good she tried to talk to you. What did she say?'

The doorbell rang.

I looked at both of them. 'You didn't invite more church freaks, did you?'

'Tom . . .'

'I'll see who it is,' Chris said.

'Tell them to go to hell,' I said.

Abby stayed close, still watching me. 'What did she say, Tom? Is it important?'

I shook my head. 'She said . . . something happened to her . . . while she was gone . . .'

'What? What happened to her?'

'We didn't get that far. I . . . we didn't . . .'

Chris came back, a tentative smile on his face.

'Someone's at the door for you, Tom.'

'Who?' I asked.

'It's a woman,' he said. 'She says she's a friend of yours, and she knows something about Caitlin. Her name is Suzanne or Susan.'

I found Susan on the porch, where she stood smoking a cigarette. She wore the same kind of clothes as the first time we'd met, except her sneakers had been replaced by muddy hiking boots. When I came outside, she turned to face me.

'Ah, Tom.'

'I didn't know you made house calls.'

'We go wherever we're needed.' She pointed to the two

empty porch chairs, so we sat. 'I apologize for the intrusion on your family life, but I've been thinking about you.'

'You were?'

'I saw your good news in the newspapers,' she said. 'Your daughter is back. You must be a happy man.'

'It's a complicated adjustment in a lot of ways.'

'Right.' She dropped the cigarette on the porch and ground it under her boot. 'I'm sorry about this. It's a bad habit I picked up in college and then returned to a few years ago. I do it when I'm anxious.'

'What are you anxious about today?' I asked.

She rubbed her hands together as though keeping them warm. It was a cool day, and I wished I'd worn a jacket.

'What has your daughter said about where she was?'

'Nothing.' I looked down. 'She won't talk about it. She told us not to ask her about it. Why do you want to know?'

'And so you haven't asked her?'

'The therapist told us not to.'

'It's best to follow the lead of the experts in these cases,' she said. 'At least that's been my experience. They know what's best.'

'I take it you didn't just come to talk to me about the merits of therapy,' I said.

'Like I said, I've been thinking about you. This story. It's been in the papers, so it's been in my mind. Do you still have that flower, or did you give it to the police?'

'I still have it. I should have given it to the police —'

'You probably should —'

'You know, I'm sort of in the middle of a larger crisis here. I appreciated talking to you the other day, but I don't think I have time for whatever you're thinking about. Just get to the point or go.'

'You're right. Of course.' She dug into the pocket of her shirt and brought out a pack of cigarettes. Her fingers shook as she dug one out and struck the lighter. 'Sorry,' she said, blowing the smoke plume in the opposite direction of where I sat. Around us, normal life went on. A few doors up, our neighbors raked their leaves onto a large blue tarp. A child laughed somewhere, a bright, distant trilling. 'This man,' she finally said, 'the man from the sketch, you believe he's the one who took your daughter from you?'

'Yes, I do.'

'I think you're right, Tom. I think he did.'

'What are you saying? Because of the flower? What?'

She shook her head. 'Not because of the flower.'

'Then what?'

'Tracy,' she said. 'Tracy Fairlawn.'

'What about her? Did you talk to her?'

'Not for a while,' she said. 'But I've spent a lot of time talking with her in the past. She's a very troubled young woman. When you and I met the other day, I was trying to protect her, to value her privacy, the confidentiality of the things she has told me over the last year.'

'Drugs?'

'Among other things.'

'Are you saying she's not reliable? Or believable?'

'I think she's believable, Tom. Especially about this matter.' She looked down at the burning tip of the cigarette as though she didn't know how it had ended up in her hand. 'Tracy knows this man, the one she saw in the club. She knows who he is.'

I held tight to the armrests of the chair. My neighbor dragged his tarp full of leaves out to the curb.

'What's his name?' I asked.

'I don't know.'

'Tell me.'

'I don't know it,' she said, her voice acquiring an edge. 'I don't.'

'Tracy sent me to you.' My words came out sharp, ringing through the afternoon air. A picture formed. 'You two are doing this together, aren't you? She sends me to you, and you lead me around by my nose —'

'I can only guess at Tracy's motives, but the thought crossed my mind that she wanted me to communicate something to you on this account. She was right. I knew about this when you came to see me the other day. Then I saw the news in the paper. I couldn't keep it to myself. I looked your address up in the phone book and came over here.'

'You're quite a saint,' I said.

'I thought long and hard about whether I should get involved farther,' she said. 'About whether I should tell you. But if I had to guess, I think Tracy wanted me to tell you about this. I think that's why she gave you my card and name. She has a difficult time talking about this issue, and she probably wanted to use me as a kind of proxy. I have incomplete information as it is, and it feels like – it *is* – a violation of the trust Tracy and I built.'

'Don't make yourself out to be more important than you are,' I said. 'You're not a priest or a therapist. Now where is Tracy?'

'I told you – I haven't been able to get ahold of her.'

'I'm calling the police.' I started to stand. 'They'll find her. They'll come down on you, too.'

'That's not the solution, Tom. And neither is this anger.'

I was still on the edge of my seat. 'What else do you know? There's much more to this story, and you know it. Spill it.'

She didn't say anything.

'Goddamn it, spill it!'

'Have you seen that ghost girl lately, Tom?'

'Don't change the subject.'

'Have you?'

I paused. 'Yes, she was outside our house one night.'

'Did she say anything?'

I slid back in the chair. 'I went after her, but she ran away.'

'Remember what I told you about that?'

'That sometimes we see what we want to see. That it's a form of wish fulfillment to see that girl.'

'Right.' She dropped the cigarette and ground it out. 'And it's the same for Tracy.'

'Why would Tracy *want* to see what she saw in that strip club?' I asked.

'Not why she would want to see that man, but why would she want to tell her story. To you. Why would she care about that man being captured or revealed?'

'Because it's the right thing to do.'

'You've met Tracy. Do you think that's a primary motivation for her?'

I stood up. I fumbled in my pocket for my phone. 'Get out of here,' I said to her. 'If you're not here to help – if you're just here to talk in riddles – then get lost. I'm calling the police.'

'Tom?' she said.

'Fuck off.'

She reached out and put her hand on the phone. 'Tom? Are you sure you want to know what Tracy knows?' She nodded her head toward the house. 'Your daughter is home. She's alive. When we talked, you were worried about her being dead. That was your fear. Well, you have your answer.'

'I'm calling,' I said.

She kept her hand on mine. I waited.

'Put the phone away,' she said.

I held on to the phone, but I sat down.

'Tracy Fairlawn,' Susan said. 'She was taken.'

'What do you mean?'

'Tracy told me about this as I got to know her. It took a long time for her to confide in me, which is why I struggled with telling you this.'

'Go ahead,' I said. 'I'm listening.'

'About six years ago, when she was fourteen. She was walking home one night, alone, and a man stopped and offered her a ride. She took it. The man took Tracy to his house. She doesn't know where he lived. He drove around a lot, in the dark, and she didn't know the streets very well because she wasn't driving yet. When she got to the man's house, he fed her and gave her something to drink. They talked and listened to music, and when Tracy wanted to leave the house and go home, he wouldn't let her. He held her there against her will, in his basement. He locked her in. He raped her repeatedly.'

For a long moment, I couldn't say anything. I felt cold again, even though the wind was calm and the trees still.

'How did she get out?' I asked finally.

'He let her out,' Susan said. 'After about six months – six months of rape and terror in a locked basement room – he put her in his car again, blindfolded, and drove her around and around. Eventually he let her out on a country road in Simms County, twenty miles away from here. She made it to a gas station and called her mother.'

'What did the police do?' I asked, fearing I already knew the answer.

'What do you think they did?' she asked.

'A girl was kidnapped and raped.'

Susan shrugged. 'A girl with a drug problem, a girl already in trouble with the police. A girl who couldn't say where this man was who'd held her. She couldn't identify the house, the car, even the neighborhood. All she did was tell this wild story of being taken against her will and held in a basement, and then miraculously being let go.' She shrugged again. 'They didn't pay much attention to her. I only got involved through my volunteer work.'

'The police sent her to you?' I asked.

'Not directly. The police didn't see her as the victim of anything. But we had a mutual friend, a woman who taught at Tracy's high school. This teacher knew about my work for the police, so she put us in touch. I just tried to be a sounding board, a sympathetic ear. Tracy needs much more help than I can provide, but it was a start.'

'Do you know Liann Stipes?' I asked.

'That's Tracy's lawyer, right? The woman whose daughter was murdered? Tracy mentioned her. Complained about her really. I get the feeling I was a better listener than Liann or anyone else in Tracy's life.'

'And that man . . . ?'

'She says it's the same man, the one she saw in the club with your daughter.'

'How did she see him in that club and still dance for him? Why didn't she run or call the police right then and there?'

'She was terrorized, Tom. Terrorized. She thought that he came back there to taunt her, to intimidate her. It was like he wanted to remind her he still held some power over her. Which he did. Why didn't she say or do anything? It's a miracle she's ever said or done anything. She feels as though saying anything is taking her life in her hands. She went to Liann because she couldn't stand to not do anything about it.'

'And now Tracy's gone.' I brought my hand to my face and chewed on some loose skin around my thumbnail. 'This man released her over five years ago, about a year before Caitlin disappeared. And now that Caitlin is back, Tracy is gone again. You think . . . ?'

'Frightening, isn't it?'

I thought back to the first time I'd met Tracy, our conversation in the strip club. I calculated. 'Tracy told me her daughter is almost five,' I said.

Susan nodded. 'She has a constant reminder of what this man did to her.'

I curled my hands into fists, and when I did, they shook. 'He let Tracy go because she was pregnant,' I said.

'Who knows? I wouldn't assign humanitarian motives to him.'

'What should I do now?' I asked.

'I'm not sure, Tom,' she said. 'But I wanted you to know

everything you needed to know. The police, they might have their own agenda. There are things they don't want to tell a crime victim. Or they want to tell them on their own schedule and terms.'

'And Liann? Why didn't she tell me?'

'I don't know Liann,' Susan said. 'I can't speak for her. But you've been chasing ghosts. Maybe this will make things more concrete.'

'And what happens if I catch up to the ghosts?' I asked.

'You'd be lucky to put them to rest.'

Chapter Thirty-four

Ryan didn't answer. I tried two times after Susan left, leaving two messages. Before I could call a third time, Abby came out onto the porch, letting the screen door slam closed behind her.

'Who was that, Tom?'

I shut the phone. 'She's helping me.' I pointed to the house. 'Did you leave Caitlin in there alone?'

'Chris is talking to her.'

'Lovely.'

'Is that woman a therapist of some kind?' Abby tried to stop me from going inside. 'Tom, I think you do need help. Real help.'

I went past her and up the stairs. At the half-open door of the master bedroom, I heard Pastor Chris's cheery voice chirping inside. I pushed in. They were sitting on the floor.

'Tom,' Chris said. 'I was just counseling Caitlin here —'

'Do you know someone named Tracy Fairlawn? She's a stripper at those clubs you used to go to with the man in the sketch. Did you talk to her?'

'If I say I don't know,' Caitlin replied, 'will you slap me again?' She scooted closer to Pastor Chris.

'Tom, if you'd like to join our conversation, it might —'

I turned and left the room, letting him talk to my back.

*

When Liann came home from church, her family in tow, she found me waiting on her front porch. She told the family to go on, and when they were inside, she still didn't say anything.

So I spoke.

'Why didn't you tell me?' I asked.

Her shoulders sagged a little. She knew what I meant.

The phone rang in my pocket. I ignored it. 'You knew this about Tracy all along,' I said. 'The man, the baby . . . you kept it all from me. You told me you were her lawyer for a drug case. You didn't mention she'd been the victim of a violent crime.'

'Tom, she did come to me needing legal help. That's where my contact with her started. And in the process of helping her with the drug case, I found out that she had been taken and assaulted. The police turned their backs on her, Tom. They just turned their backs on her. Someone had to help that girl. She trusted me, and I couldn't —'

'No. I don't want to hear any bullshit.'

The phone rang again, so I checked it. Abby. I silenced it.

'So you decided not to tell me everything you knew about Tracy?' I asked. 'Answer the question.'

'I didn't think it was relevant.'

'Not relevant?'

'What mattered was catching the guy,' she said. 'Tracy was skittish. She was scared of the police. But she did see Caitlin in that club, and it was easier for her to talk about that than about what he did to her. That's why I brought Tracy to you with her story. I helped you.'

'I trusted you,' I said. 'You came to us when Caitlin disappeared. You cut through the bullshit and helped us.

I thought you were on our side. But you kept this information from us. From me.'

'What do you want me to do, Tom?' she asked.

'All those things that happened to Tracy. The kidnapping, being held hostage. The rape. That's what happened to Caitlin, isn't it?'

'What matters now is that we find that man —'

I was up and past her. 'Call me if your agenda changes, Liann.'

Chapter Thirty-five

I sat in my car in front of Liann's house. I wasn't ready to drive off. I didn't know where to go or who to turn to.

I looked down at the phone. Two more calls from Abby. Three messages.

The slap. My confrontation with Caitlin.

There was music to face on all sides. And what did they say about home – when you go there, they have to take you in . . . ?

So I drove home.

I stepped inside the back door. 'Abby?' She didn't answer my call, but I found her in the living room, sitting on the end of our couch, her elbow on the armrest and her chin cupped in her hand. It looked precarious, as though her head could slip loose at any moment. 'Abby?'

She still didn't look up, but I could tell something more was wrong, something besides the fight and the slap. The room felt devoid of air, like someone had died.

'What's the matter, Abby?'

She jumped a little. She looked over, moving her head slowly, as though turning took a great deal of effort. 'Oh, Tom. It's you.' She held the phone next to her on the couch.

'What gives?' I asked. 'Why did you call me so many times?'

'Ryan called,' she said. 'They found that guy, the one from the drawing. They made an arrest.'

Abby told me the little she knew. Ryan had called shortly after I'd left the house and told Abby they had someone in custody, someone who matched the description given by Tracy. Someone they believed to be the man Caitlin was seen around town with. Abby didn't know how or where they'd found him or what tipped the police off, but Ryan was going to come by the house at any minute to fill us in. And talk to Caitlin.

I couldn't stop thinking about the morning.

If the man was in custody, where was Tracy? She hadn't been seen in weeks.

'Caitlin told me about the fight this morning,' Abby said. 'Actually, she told Chris about it.'

The fight and the slap seemed so distant somehow, something that had happened in another life.

'I lost my cool. And I'm sorry for it. She must have gotten a thrill out of being able to tell Chris about it and make me look like the bad guy.'

'It's not like that, Tom.'

'I know. In a strange sort of way, I'm glad he got her to talk to him. About anything. I thought slapping her was going to wake her up.'

Abby didn't respond. She still wore the slightly stunned, slightly spacey look she had been wearing when I'd first come into the room.

'Abby? Does Caitlin know about this?'

She shook her head. 'I'm scared, Tom.'

'Of the man?'

'I thought we'd turned the page,' she said. 'I was ready

to just go on. When she talked to Chris today, I thought things might really be moving ahead.'

'I'm going to go tell her,' I said.

'I couldn't do it, Tom. I thought telling her would make it more real. I called you. I was glad when you didn't answer.' She knotted her hands together, a lump of flesh and fingers. 'Chris left, so I was alone.'

I heard something and turned my head. I held a silencing finger up to Abby. A rustling at the top of the stairs. Faint. I listened and heard nothing more.

'I'm going to go tell her,' I said. 'She has to be ready to face Ryan.'

'I didn't like the way he talked to her last time,' she said. 'It was too harsh.'

'I know,' I said. 'But he was trying to push her a little.'

'It sounded like he was blaming her,' she said. 'Do you think they'll let Chris be there or talk to her? She opened up to him.'

'She wasn't opening up to Chris,' I said. 'She was getting back at me.'

Halfway up the stairs, I stopped. They were holding the man, physically. He was in custody. He could answer for — explain even — everything. For ripping the fabric of our lives to pieces. For Caitlin. For Tracy. For God knew how many others.

My grip tightened on the banister. Something clouded my vision. Red and white splotches. My heart thumped. When the splotches disappeared, I found myself pulling against the banister, trying to rip it out of the wall. It didn't give and my grip slipped. I fell back against the opposite wall of the staircase, making a loud thump. It hurt my

269

back, and I welcomed the pain. It brought me back to reality. My home. My daughter.

The man in the sketch.

I took several deep, gasping breaths. Abby appeared at the bottom of the stairs.

'Tom?'

'It's okay,' I said. 'I fell.'

She took a step up. 'You look sick, Tom.'

'I'm fine.' I held my hand out. 'I'm going to talk to Caitlin.'

She was in the master bedroom, the door closed. I knocked, and when I didn't get any response, I knocked again. 'It's your dad,' I said, trying the knob and feeling it give. Not *Dad. Your dad.* A more distant and formal designation, as though I were talking about two strangers.

Caitlin was lying back on the bed, reading a book. I couldn't make out the title, but it looked like the kind of thing she used to read before she left, something aimed at preteen girls. She didn't look over at me when I came in but kept her eyes on the pages of the book. Her brow was furrowed and her lips moved as she scanned the words. She looked like a certain kind of kid who passed through my classrooms, the ones who came from areas with poor public schools and adults who never attended college.

'I need to tell you something, Caitlin.'

She didn't look up from the book.

'Did you hear what we were talking about downstairs? Were you at the top of the stairs?'

'I heard some,' she said. 'You were talking about the

police. And Pastor Chris. Then I heard you try to rip the banister out of the wall.'

'Detective Ryan's coming over again.'

She stiffened a little. 'Why? To ask me more sex questions?'

'They found him, Caitlin. They arrested him.'

She considered this for a long moment without looking at me. 'You're a fucking liar,' she finally said. 'You'd lie to me about anything.'

'No.' I kept my voice firm. 'He's in jail, right now. Detective Ryan is coming over to talk to you, and this time there's no point in keeping everything a secret. They have him, so we're going to find out what it's all about. He's hurt other people, Caitlin. Other girls like you. He's not going to be able to do that to anyone else.'

'He wouldn't hurt someone.'

'He did.' I took a step forward into the room. 'Remember, just this morning, you said that he did things *to you*. He hurt you.'

She sat up on the bed, letting the book fall to the floor. Her face showed real animation. 'Are they bringing him here?' she asked.

'No, they're not bringing him here. He's in jail. Didn't you hear me?'

She looked at the floor, her chin quivering. She took hold of the necklace and rubbed the stone.

'What's the matter with you?' I asked. I stopped myself, gathered my thoughts. 'Caitlin, I know this is confusing for you. I know that after what's happened, you might be confused about your feelings, especially your feelings for

271

this man. It's part of what you've been through, but you need to start getting through that. This man . . . he needs to go to jail.'

'They're not going to hurt him, are they? Tell me you won't let them hurt him.'

She turned away and flopped back onto the bed, burying her face in the covers so I couldn't see her. It sounded like she was crying.

Chapter Thirty-six

Ryan looked more tired than usual when he showed up at our door. He wore a polo shirt, tan pants, and no jacket despite the cool temperature. He didn't come inside, but instead motioned the two of us out onto the porch.

When we were all seated, Ryan started talking.

'I imagine you want to be brought up to speed as soon as possible.' He flipped open the small notebook. 'Yesterday, just before five a.m., the fire department responded to a call for a house fire out on Smith Springs Road. When they arrived, they found the house engulfed and beyond saving. A neighbor had seen the flames and called it in, but no one was certain if anyone was home at the time. It's still too hot to do a thorough search of the house, but the preliminary investigation hasn't revealed any evidence of human remains yet. Records indicate that the house belongs to a John Colter. Does that name mean anything to either of you?'

'Is that the man?' I asked. 'Is that his name?'

'Does the name mean anything to either of you?' Ryan asked.

Abby shook her head. 'I don't think so.'

'Tom?'

I scanned through every student name I could remember, every coworker, every maintenance person who ever passed through school or our home. 'I don't think I know him.'

Ryan went on as though I hadn't spoken. 'The preliminary investigation shows that the cause of the fire was arson. A pretty amateur job. Whoever set the fire didn't make much of an attempt to cover their tracks. They simply poured gasoline over everything, and investigators even found the melted plastic gas cans in the debris. Initially, we thought it looked like insurance fraud of some kind.'

'Jesus,' I said.

'They also found something else in the basement of the home.'

'Do we want to know?' Abby asked, more to herself than to us.

'They found a room. At first, it looked to be a bedroom, something created after the home was built. It didn't appear to be part of the original structure. The door to this room was heavily fortified. Several different locks as well as some sort of reinforced steel sheeting.'

I stared at the sky. It was perfectly blue like a robin's egg. I was numb.

'It looked like it was meant to keep someone locked up.'

'You think . . .' Abby left her thought unfinished.

'Like I said, it's going to take some time before they can complete a more thorough examination of the house, especially the basement. Given the nature of the fire damage, it seems unlikely we'll be able to find any definitive proof that any individual, Caitlin or otherwise, was ever in that basement room. It seems possible the fire was set for that very reason. To obscure evidence.'

'Maybe he didn't want the police to know he held Tracy Fairlawn there as well,' I said.

'Excuse me?' Ryan said.

'Tracy.' I looked at Abby. 'You know, the girl from the strip club?'

'Why are you bringing her up?' Abby asked.

'Maybe Detective Ryan should tell us,' I said.

'I don't think this is relevant, Tom,' he said.

I turned back to Abby. 'Tracy was held captive by a man for six months about five years ago. He took her off the street and brought her to a house. She didn't know where. He held her there. He raped her repeatedly. She managed to get away, and then she had a baby.'

Abby looked stricken. 'Are you going to tell me there's a connection?'

'We don't know —' Ryan said.

'She says it's the same man.' I kept my eyes on Abby, boring in. 'The man she saw in the strip club with Caitlin was the man who took her and held her and raped her. The same man. Detective Ryan here just declined to share that information with us.'

Ryan stiffened. 'Where are you hearing these things, Tom?'

'I have my sources, too.'

'Well, I came here because I'd like to talk to Caitlin,' Ryan said. 'And I'd like to be able to talk to her alone.'

'Shouldn't we be there?' Abby asked. 'Someone to look out for her.'

'Our attorney?' I said.

'Why would she need an attorney?' Abby asked.

'Caitlin isn't guaranteed access to a lawyer during questioning,' Ryan said. 'We may allow her to have one present, as a courtesy. Some kind of advocate. I can decide on that —'

'She has fewer rights than this guy in the jail?' I asked.

'Hold it, Tom.' Abby held her hands out for silence. 'Hold it.'

'Abby, he doesn't care about Caitlin . . .'

She kept the hand up in the air between us, and I stopped talking. Abby looked calm and determined, so I yielded. 'Who is this man?' she asked Ryan. 'And are the things Tom is saying true? Did he hold Tracy there?'

Ryan shifted his eyes between the both of us. 'Late last night, police in Union County pulled Mr Colter over for speeding. Do you know where Union County is?'

Abby nodded. 'About seventy miles away.'

'When they ran him through the system, the warrant for the arson came up, so they took him in and called us. We collected him in the morning and brought him back here to have a little talk about the house fire. Let's just say we caught a lucky break. Caitlin's story has been in the news, so our officers have seen that composite sketch on an almost daily basis. One of our officers raised the question, and we put it together with the house with the room in the basement.'

He held his hands out. *There you go.*

After four years, a speeding ticket wrapped it up.

'What did he say?' Abby asked.

'Nothing yet. When we brought up Caitlin's name, he said he'd read about her in the paper. But that's it.'

'And witnesses?' Abby asked. 'The girl from the club? Tracy? Is it true he took her too?'

'She's gone,' I said.

Abby whipped her head toward me.

'She's disappeared,' I said. And my voice was quieter, distant even to my own ears. 'No one can find her. Not her mother, not Liann. Two weeks and no sign of her.'

'She'll turn up,' Ryan said. 'They usually do. Like I told you, that girl has problems, drug problems. She's not reliable.'

'Who is this guy?' I asked. 'What does he do?'

'He's on disability. Some kind of knee injury. He used to work at the Hearn plant, but it's been about ten years since he did that. He hasn't been in much trouble with us. One assault arrest about fifteen years ago. Otherwise, nothing.'

'How old is he?' I asked.

'Fifty-three.'

The number stabbed me like a knife. Fifty-three. Older than me.

Ryan leaned back and worked his hand into his pants pocket. He brought out a Polaroid photo. 'I'd like you to look at this and tell me if you know this man.'

He held it out in the air between us, but neither Abby nor I made a grab for it. Finally, she moved and took it. The corners of her mouth turned down with revulsion.

'I don't know him,' she said.

She passed the photo to me. My hands shook as I took it.

I looked down at a stunned face, one that didn't appear prepared to have its picture taken. His surprisingly blue eyes were open wide, his lips slightly parted. He bore a strong resemblance to Tracy's description and the sketch the police had created. There was the same long, greasy hair, the wide nose. His skin was ruddy and pocked, like twenty miles of bad road, as my stepfather used to say. I didn't recognize the man from anywhere in my life, but I continued to stare, searching for something. A mark of

277

evil, a sign of malicious intent. But I couldn't find the marker that would tip me off, the thing that told the world this man aimed to destroy lives. It was an ugly face, not an evil one.

'Do you recognize him?' Ryan asked.

'No,' I said.

'You're sure?'

'I'm sure.'

I held on to the picture, and Ryan reached out and took it back. He didn't put it in his pocket, but held it in his hand. He tapped it against his thigh a few times. 'I need to talk to your girl,' he said.

'You said you don't need our permission,' I said. 'Are you just going to drag her out of here while we watch?'

'I don't need your permission, but I'd like it.' He continued to tap the photo against his leg. 'I'd also like to talk to her away from here. Since it didn't go so well the last time, I thought we might try it at the station. She might take it more seriously.'

'Will she have to see him?' Abby asked.

Him. We all knew who she meant. *The man.* John Colter.

Ryan shook his head. 'No way,' he said.

'But she would have to see him at a trial?' I asked.

'That's why we'd like her to talk now. Maybe this guy agrees to plead to something and save us all a lot of trouble. If we can get to the bottom of this sooner, it might save Caitlin some grief.'

Abby looked at me. 'Tom?'

I recognized my cue. 'Ryan, I – we – were a little concerned about the way you spoke to Caitlin the last time. It

278

seems as though you were treating her like she had done something wrong. She's the victim here, remember?'

'Of course, Tom.' Ryan shrugged, and the gesture seemed too large, overexaggerated. 'We all have the same goals here, to understand what happened and to get Caitlin the help she needs.'

'She's only sixteen now,' Abby said. 'Sixteen is so young . . .'

Her voice trailed off, fading like the wind through the trees.

Ryan stood up. He slipped the photo back into his pocket. 'We're still tying some things up from the morning,' he said. 'But if you could bring her to the station in an hour or so, that would be great.'

'Are you going to get this guy, Ryan?' I asked.

'That's the plan.'

'And will we know what was said, what she tells you?'

Ryan nodded. 'I will keep you in the loop.'

'Tom?' Abby asked. 'Are you sure you want her to do this alone? I'm really not. Caitlin is so fragile right now. She's been so hurt by this.'

What happened to me.

'That's exactly why she needs to do this,' I said. 'Don't you think?'

Abby didn't respond, so I pressed on.

'Because she's been hurt, she needs to tell the story,' I said. I felt the need to convince her. 'This man has hurt other girls. He needs to be put away. Caitlin can do that.'

'You just want to hand her over to be questioned?' Abby asked.

'A crime's been committed, Abby,' Ryan said. 'I have to

find the answers, and Caitlin has them. I'm not trying to harm her, but we need her to try to help us as much as she can. Even if it's just a little.'

'There are a lot of people involved in this, Abby,' I said. 'Not just us.'

'Is that who you're thinking of, Tom? All the other people?'

'It's necessary, Abby,' I said.

'Right.' She stood up and folded her arms across her chest. 'I guess I better be the one to go tell her she's being handed over to you *men*.' She nearly spat the last word at us, like it was a stone she'd found in a loaf of bread. 'You two have such a good rapport with her these days.'

She whisked away, leaving the two of us on the porch. We didn't have anything else to say to each other, so Ryan turned and went, reminding me as he left that we should bring Caitlin to the station in an hour.

Chapter Thirty-seven

Abby stared out the cloudy front window of the police station at the traffic passing on the street. She didn't appear focused or fixed on anything. I sat down beside her, and she pretended not to notice me. I waited a few moments, not sure if I should even bother to say anything. Finally, I decided to try. 'I'm not trying to hurt Caitlin,' I said. 'Or you.'

She didn't say anything, but I saw a muscle in her jaw twitch.

'I think this is our last, best chance, letting her talk to Ryan today.'

Abby turned to me. 'You talk about last chances, Tom. Caitlin is the one who matters. Our focus needs to be on her. She's what matters – to both of us.'

I stared at the floor. Then my phone rang. I stood up and took the call.

'Hey,' a voice said through the line. It sounded flat, almost unrecognizable.

'Buster?'

'Where are you?' he asked.

'What's wrong?' I said.

'Where are you? I came by the house.'

'We're at the police station,' I said. 'They made an arrest.'

'Look,' he said. 'I'm sorry.'

'For what?'

'For everything you've been through. You and Caitlin.'

There was something about his tone, something off.

'Where are you?' I asked. 'What are you doing?'

'We'll talk soon, I think. Okay?'

'Buster . . .'

But he was gone. I called right back, but it went to voice mail immediately. Three times in a row.

Ryan appeared again and summoned the two of us with a quick wave of his hand. He led us to the conference room. No Caitlin.

'Where is she?' I asked.

Ryan pointed to the chairs. 'She's fine, Tom. I wanted to talk to you alone.'

'Did she have to see him?'

'No,' Ryan said. 'Please. Just sit. You can take Caitlin home in a minute.'

Abby nodded at me. *It's okay.* So we sat.

'We really didn't make much progress today,' he said. 'At least not with Caitlin.'

'Talking to her alone didn't help?' Abby asked.

'She told us a few things,' he said.

I scooted to the edge of my seat. 'Like what?'

'She didn't so much say anything,' Ryan said. 'But she did ask something. Over and over again. She asked to be allowed to see John Colter. She asked to see him multiple times. Repeatedly and passionately. Finally, I told her to stop asking because it wasn't going to happen.' He sighed, shifted his weight a little. 'And then Caitlin said that she'd tell me whatever I wanted to know if I would just let her

282

see Colter again and spend a few minutes with him. I told her that we couldn't allow that to happen, that the victim of a crime couldn't speak to the alleged perpetrator.'

'How did she respond?' Abby asked.

'Like a pouty teenager.' Ryan rubbed his hand across his chin. 'You asked me to let you know everything that was said in there. If you still want to know all of that, I can share some more details.'

'Yes,' I said.

Abby moved in her seat, but she didn't say anything. She didn't object.

'Caitlin told me that she's in love with John Colter. She said he didn't do anything wrong, that no one did anything wrong, and she wants the police and the two of you to drop all of this and let her life go back to the way it was before.'

'Meaning . . .'

'Meaning she wants to go back to her life with him, not with you.'

He let that settle over the table, a deadweight dropped into our lives.

'We're going to hold Colter on the suspicion of arson charge. We're still talking to witnesses and waiting for the arson investigator's report.'

'So he'll stay behind bars,' Abby said.

'We need Caitlin's story,' he said. 'She's the only lead-pipe witness we have. Without that, and without the evidence that went up in the fire . . . Have the two of you thought any more about that picture I showed you of John Colter?' He dug in his pocket and brought the photo out. 'Why don't you look at it again?' He slid it across to us. I didn't look.

'Do you know something else?' I asked.

'Do you?' he asked. 'Are you absolutely certain you've never seen that man?'

Abby picked the photo up and looked it over. 'How can I answer that?' she asked. 'Maybe I passed him in the grocery store. Maybe he came and fixed our plumbing. How can I remember every face I've ever seen? But, no, I don't *know* him, if that's what you're asking. I don't. Do you, Tom?' She held the picture out to me, but I didn't take it.

'Is there something you're not telling us?' I asked.

Ryan held my gaze, unblinking. I didn't look away either. He was digging for something, pushing. I couldn't imagine what it was. He took the photo back.

'Nothing,' he said. 'But we need to be sure.'

'Nothing?' I said.

He stood up, hitched his pants. 'I'll have Caitlin brought right out to you,' he said.

Chapter Thirty-eight

I really didn't feel like dragging ourselves back to Rosenbaum. But we all climbed into the car, our jackets zipped against the cooling fall weather, and backed out of the driveway.

Then Abby surprised me. She turned to me while I was still backing out and said, her voice casual and effortless, 'How would you feel if I went to the church today?'

'Now?'

'I just . . .'

She didn't finish her thought. But I understood. 'You want to talk to Chris. I mean, Pastor Chris.'

'It's not that simple.'

I didn't drive away. The car sat in the middle of our street, idling. No traffic came either way, and Caitlin sat in the back quietly. 'What is it then?' I asked.

She looked back at Caitlin, then shrugged, as if to say, *Who cares if she hears?* 'It's been a difficult time, and I get something out of being at the church,' she said. 'It's not just Chris.'

'Not just.'

'Let's just go to Rosenbaum's,' she said. 'I should be there.'

When I came to the turn that would take us to Rosenbaum's, I went right instead of left. We didn't say anything else about it, but I headed for the church. We passed a

couple of strip malls and a long, low building that manu-
factured machine parts. Then I turned into the church lot.

'Head toward the back,' Abby said. The complex of
buildings went on and on, like a small corporation. 'Stop
by this door,' Abby said. I did. It was a nondescript side
entrance flanked by some evergreen shrubs. Ten cars were
scattered through the lot, most of them later models.
Abby sat with her hand on the door release. 'Are you sure
you don't want me to go?' she asked.

'It's fine.'

'We could take her in there,' she said, nodding toward
the door. 'She could talk to Chris again. The last time . . .
Do you really think she talked to Chris just to get back
at you?'

I turned and looked into the backseat. Caitlin stared at
me. 'Yes, I think so,' I said. 'Isn't that right, Caitlin? You
talked to Chris just because you were mad at me? Because
I slapped you, right?'

'You have it all figured out, don't you?' Caitlin said.

Abby turned around now, too, letting her hand slip off
the door. 'Did that man at the jail hit you?' she asked. 'Did
he hurt you? What about that bruise on your stomach?
I've never asked, but I worry that he abused you.'

'You don't know,' Caitlin said.

'What? What don't I know?' Abby asked.

'Anything,' Caitlin said. 'You just don't know anything.
Either one of you. You're both a couple of fucking
idiots.'

Abby let her eyes linger on Caitlin a moment longer;
then she turned back. 'I guess I don't know anything, do
I? I want to. Very much, Caitlin. But I'm trying to remind

286

myself that there are things in this life I just won't know or understand. And I guess I'm okay with that. I've tried to accept it.' She turned a little, back toward Caitlin. 'But the less you talk to us, the more you have to talk to the police. And you know how that's been going. So really it is your choice. I hope you understand that.'

With that, Abby climbed out of the car. We sat and watched while she disappeared into the building. When she was gone, I dropped the car into gear and headed out of the lot.

'How do you feel about skipping out on the shrink today?' I asked. 'Seriously. Do you want to go somewhere else?'

'Where?'

I was out in traffic now, heading back toward town. 'To see a friend of mine,' I said, trying to sound normal, almost cheery.

'You have a friend?'

'It's either the friend or the shrink,' I said, an edge creeping into my voice. 'You pick.'

'I pick neither.'

'Then it's Rosenbaum.' I paused. 'But she'll be disappointed. She wants to meet you.'

'Your friend's a woman? Is she your girlfriend?'

'I thought you weren't interested.'

She clammed up and sat back against the seat. I kept driving, leaving her to her own devices. After a few minutes, she spoke up. 'I did talk to him because I was pissed at you,' she said. 'You're right.'

I didn't say anything.

'Is it weird for Mom to have a boyfriend?' she asked.

'You think he's her boyfriend?'

'He is. She told me.' She waited a beat. 'She said she loves him.'

'Bullshit.'

'She does. I can tell she loves him.'

'You mean the way you love John Colter?' I asked.

She looked out the window. 'It's not like that at all,' she said, almost dreamy. 'You've never been away from someone you love.'

'Yes, I have.'

'Who?'

'You.'

I waited for a response and again looked for one in the mirror. This time, I thought – hoped – I saw something there, some registering of emotion. A slight swallow, a blinking of her eyes, a flush to her cheeks.

But she said nothing. She stared out the window, silent.

I called Susan from the car and explained what I wanted to do and who was with me. We agreed it wouldn't be a good idea to meet in public again, so she gave me directions to her house. Susan lived in a small bungalow not far from campus in a neighborhood dominated by run-down student rentals. Her house was the nicest and best kept on the street.

When I parked in front of the house and turned the engine off, I said to Caitlin, 'We're here.'

'Who is this?' she asked. 'Someone you work with?'

'No.'

'Is she a shrink? I'm tired of that.'

'She tries to help people figure stuff out.'

'Sounds like a shrink,' she said. 'Have you figured any-thing out?'

'I'm not sure yet. I'm sort of in the middle of things.' I looked back at her. 'Do you want to go in and talk to her?'

Susan must have seen the car pull up. She came out onto the broad front porch that stretched the length of the house. She wore the same plain pants she always wore and an oversized flannel shirt with the sleeves rolled up to her elbows. She held up her hand and gave us a tentative wave.

'She kind of looks like a man,' Caitlin said.

'She's not,' I said. 'In fact, I thought you might like to talk to a woman for a change. I know these things can be difficult to talk about, especially with men. Maybe a female perspective would help.'

Caitlin seemed to be considering this. She nodded. 'Okay. I'll hear what she has to say. Anything's better than that idiot shrink.' She reached for her door handle.

'Hold on,' I said.

She let out a long, exasperated sigh. 'I'm not running off. Don't worry.'

'It's not that,' I said. 'I want to tell you something.'

She settled back against the seat, her eyes cautious.

'I know I shouldn't have hit you the other day,' I said. I chose my words carefully. 'But I was angry. You know, as a parent, I feel responsible for everything that happens to you. I feel like there must be something I could have done differently, and if so, we would have gone down a different path. You might have gone down a different path.'

'What's wrong with the path I went down?' she asked.

'You were gone for four years. We missed you. We lost you.'

'You mean you didn't choose it for me.'

'Nobody chose it,' I said. 'I know that.'

She turned away, her gaze drifting out the window to the small trees, their leaves turning orange and dropping to the ground. She didn't answer. I backed off, changed gears.

'I've been thinking a lot about when you were little. I remember the time – you were just six years old, I guess – and you crossed the street when you weren't supposed to. Do you remember that? You thought I couldn't see you, that I didn't know what you were doing, but I did. I came out to call you home, and instead I saw you cross the street and a car almost hit you. You ran right in front of it, and they slammed on their brakes so they didn't run you over. Do you remember that?'

She was still looking out the window, but she spoke. 'I remember. I can still see the grille and the headlights right in front of me. I think they honked their horn at me. I remember it that way.'

'I didn't know what I was supposed to do,' I said. 'Was I supposed to stop those people and yell at them? Was I supposed to drag the guy out of the car and beat him up?'

'It was my fault,' she said. 'I ran out there without looking.'

'Were you scared?'

She nodded. 'At first. When it first happened I was. But I also felt like it couldn't touch me, like it wasn't meant to run me over. I guess I felt protected in some way.'

'Protected by what? God?'

She shook her head immediately. 'Not God.' She kept shaking her head. 'Not God.'

'What then?'

'I don't know.'

'I didn't yell at you or hit you when you crossed the street because I didn't think it was necessary. Kids do things like that. They test their boundaries. They make mistakes. It bothered me, of course. It scared me. But I never told your mom about it. She wouldn't have been able to handle it. She never would have let you leave the house again.'

'She likes to overreact. I guess you both do.'

'You know, I look back at that, and I really wonder about the way you just stood there and looked me right in the eye, probably the same way you looked at the grille of that car, and you lied to me like it was nothing. Why did you think you could do that? Where did you learn to lie like that?'

'I guess I didn't think it was any of your business,' she said.

'But you were a child,' I said. 'Everything you did was my business.'

'That's what parents think,' she said.

'This is a second chance, Caitlin, for all of us. And I'm not going to let it slip past me. I'm not.'

'Are you going to hit me again? Would that make you feel better? Some men like to do that.'

'Did that man hit you?' I asked. 'Did he hurt you? You said things happened to you. What happened to you, Caitlin? Tell me.'

She shivered, her shoulders rising, her body quaking. But she didn't yield. 'It's cold,' she said. 'I either want to go in or go home.'

'Were you kept in the basement? In that room?'

She didn't look at me. She scrambled for the door handle and tugged against it. She pressed against the door with her shoulder, but it didn't give. The child safety locks were on. She couldn't get out. 'Locks,' she said. 'You all use locks.'

'I'm protecting you, Caitlin. There's a difference.'

She kept her eyes straight ahead. 'If you want to go in, let's go in,' she said. 'I already told you I'm cold.'

Chapter Thirty-nine

Susan greeted us on the porch. 'Well, I think I know who this is,' she said, stepping aside and sweeping her arms out, directing us through the front door and into a wide, cluttered living room. The house smelled of something like fried onions, and a national news program played over the radio.

Caitlin looked uncertain. I nodded at her, letting her know it was okay to go in. Susan pointed to an overstuffed chair, and after a brief hesitation, Caitlin sat down.

'Would you like some tea, Caitlin? I have some tea in the kitchen,' Susan said.

'No.'

'Would you like anything?' Susan asked. 'Water? A Coke?'

Caitlin's eyes wandered around the room before settling on me. 'My dad wants me to talk to you,' she said. 'Instead of the shrink.'

'Very good,' Susan said. 'What do you think of that?'

Caitlin kept her eyes on me when she spoke. 'It's fine, I guess,' she said. 'But if he wants me to talk to you, he has to leave.'

'No,' I said. 'That's not the deal.'

'What deal?' Caitlin asked.

'Tom.' Susan's voice cut through the room. 'Tom, listen. I've talked to girls like Caitlin before, and sometimes they want to have their privacy. At least initially, while they're getting to know me a little better.'

'Can we talk?' I said to Susan.

We moved off toward the doorway to the spotless kitchen. We stopped there so I could talk to Susan in a low voice but still keep my eye on Caitlin.

'I don't like this,' I said. 'I brought her here to learn something. For *me* to learn something.'

'I'm a stranger to her, Tom. She has to learn to trust me too.'

'All the more reason for me to stay.'

Susan looked behind her, then turned back to me. 'Tom, you and I have trust issues to work through, don't we? You're feeling angry because I wasn't up-front with you the first time we met, and I understand that. Maybe if I can talk to Caitlin alone, we can make up for that.'

She fixed me again with her wide-open eyes, and they worked on me. Despite what I considered her betrayal over Tracy, I believed this woman when she said she wanted to try to help. And beyond that, even if I didn't completely believe her, I didn't have anyone else to turn to.

'What am I supposed to do?' I asked.

'You can wait on the porch. It's a nice day.'

I looked at Caitlin, who was pretending to ignore us. 'She likes to run,' I said.

'I've been there before, Tom,' Susan said. 'I'll keep a close eye on her.'

I broke away from Susan and stopped by Caitlin's chair. 'Is this what you want?' I asked. 'Me outside and you in here?'

She nodded.

'Okay,' I said. 'I'll be outside if you need me.' Susan walked with me to the door, and I whispered to her, 'There's more to this story, you know.'

'There usually is,' she said.

'And you'll find it out?' I asked.

She placed her hand on my chest, gently but insistently, and moved me back. 'I'm going to do whatever I can, Tom.'

It took fifteen minutes for Rosenbaum's office to call my cell phone. When I answered on the porch, it was the man himself speaking, not his secretary.

'Tom, we were just wondering where Caitlin is. She's missing her appointment with me.'

'I don't think we're going to make it in today. To be honest, I've decided to take her to someone else, another professional, someone who I thought might have a better rapport with her.'

'You can't do that,' he said, his voice rising. 'It is not advisable to take a patient from one specialist to another. Who did you bring her to? Does your wife know about this? I know we haven't made much progress yet, but a case like this can take a long time to work through.'

'I have to go.'

'Who have you taken her to? What's the doctor's name?'

'It's not a doctor.'

'Not a doctor? Tom, I'm going to have to tell Detective Ryan. This case is at a critical juncture. If she's not getting consistent care —'

I hung up.

*

I paced on the porch after I hung up with Rosenbaum, listening to the birds and watching the comings and goings of the students in the neighborhood. Soon enough, Abby called, and I knew I needed to reassure her.

'It's okay, Abby. She's with me.'

She sighed on her end of the line. 'Did you really take her to another doctor?'

'No, not that.'

'Who then?' A pause. 'Oh, Tom.' She didn't sound angry. Instead, her voice dripped with judgment and concern. 'That woman from the porch?'

'She works with the police department. She's a counselor – a support system – for victims of crime.'

'Is she a doctor?'

'No, she's not, but she's trying to help,' I said. 'She listens. She's trained to work with people who are having crises. She doesn't have an agenda. She just listens and works with me.'

'Caitlin's my daughter, too. You need to tell me what you're doing with her, especially now.'

'I didn't plan this. I just did it.'

Someone spoke to Abby in the background. She muffled the phone with her hand and said something that sounded like, 'It's okay, it's okay.' Then she came back on the line. 'I feel bad that you think this woman was the only person you could turn to in a crisis. You're so alone, Tom. I worry about you.'

'I have to go, Abby. Caitlin's going to be ready soon.'

'Will you talk to me about this later? I don't think this should be the end of our conversation.'

'I have to go, Abby. Good-bye.'

Chapter Forty

It took another thirty minutes for Susan to come out onto the porch. Her face impassive, she made a beckoning gesture toward me, summoning me back inside. I followed.

Caitlin sat in the same seat, but she clutched a ragged ball of Kleenex. She'd been crying, but when we made eye contact, she looked away, apparently ashamed.

'What is it?' I asked.

'Sit down, Tom.' Susan pointed at an empty chair.

So I sat. My hands were clenched in my lap. I didn't know what to do with them. I reached out to Caitlin, but she pulled back. Her rebuke felt physical, like a sting. When Susan was settled, I said, 'Well?'

Susan rested her hands on the tops of her knees. 'Caitlin has been through a profound experience, one beyond her very young years.'

'I can imagine.' Then I shook my head. 'I can only imagine.'

'I'm not sure you can. I'm not sure any of us can, Tom.'

'Okay, you're right. I can't. I'm starting to understand that.'

Susan looked at Caitlin. I wasn't certain, but it seemed as though Caitlin made an almost imperceptible gesture, a quick, tiny nod of her head. Susan nodded back, confirming something. 'Tom, Caitlin doesn't want you to ask her any more questions about this subject. She has shared some things with me, and she told me it's okay if I share them with you.'

'She told you,' I said, looking over at Caitlin again. 'But she didn't tell me. Why won't you tell me?'

I became aware of a wheedling, pleading tone in my voice, so I stopped.

'She fears your reaction. Like this. She fears you will think too much like a parent and not really hear what she is saying.'

'Okay. I'll listen. I'll listen to you, or I'll listen to her. I'll listen to whatever is sent my way.'

Susan looked at Caitlin. 'Honey, are you sure you want me to be the one to tell him these things?'

Caitlin nodded, still clutching the Kleenex.

'Okay.' She turned back to me. 'Tom, Caitlin has fallen in love with this man, the man at the police station. She wants you to know this so that you will understand why she tried to leave that night and why she doesn't want to cooperate with the police. She doesn't want this man to go to jail.'

A pause, and I realized Susan wanted a response from me. The room felt smaller, closer and more cramped. It seemed as though I were heading down a blind alley, so I tried to turn around. 'What exactly is your interest in all of this?' I asked. 'I thought you wanted to help me.'

She didn't ruffle or back down. 'I am.'

I turned to Caitlin. 'What do you want then?' I asked. 'You just don't want me to ask questions? You want the police to stop with the questions? Is that all you want?'

Again the look passed between the two of them, and this time Caitlin spoke, although she didn't look at me. 'I want to see him,' she said.

'No,' I said. Then I said it again. 'No.' My voice was flat, but firm. It lacked emotion this time, at least to my own ears.

Caitlin still didn't look at me. 'I won't tell the police anything. They won't have a case.'

'They have other witnesses. People who saw the two of you out together. In strip clubs and God only knows where else. They're going to nail him to the wall, with or without you. And I'll be thrilled to watch it happen.' I stood up. 'Come on. We're going home.'

'Tom —'

'Enough,' I said. 'You've done enough. Come on, Caitlin.'

Again Caitlin looked to Susan, and again Susan nodded, but this time she nodded in my direction, telling Caitlin she needed to go with me.

But Caitlin still didn't move. She held the Kleenex, but her eyes were dry. And I feared I was about to truly see the limit of my own power. What would I do with her if she didn't want to move, if she wanted to curl up in the chair, an inert mass of teenage resistance? How would I move her or reach her?

But she wasn't ready to make her last stand yet.

She stood up, her shoulders hunched, her posture folded in on itself. When we reached the door, I placed my hand on her, my fingers encircling her bony arm, feeling its scrawniness through her sweatshirt. She looked up at me, then down at the place where my hand made contact with her body. She gave a little tug back, so I tightened my grip, adding not so subtle pressure. I didn't care if she bruised.

Before we went out the door, Susan said my name. 'Tom? I'm happy to see Caitlin again. Or you. Together or alone. But some of this is beyond my expertise. She should – you all should – be dealing with the professionals as well.'

I guided Caitlin out to the car. It felt like we were an odd pair of conjoined twins.

When we were in, and the child safety locks were activated, Caitlin spoke up. 'Okay,' she said. 'I'll tell you what you want to know.'

'Everything?'

She nodded. 'One condition, though.'

'What's that?'

'When it's done, when I've told you all that bullshit, you let me go. Back to John. Back to the life I want to have. Let me go, and I'll tell you everything.'

'He's going to jail for the rest of his life.'

'Then you don't want the deal.'

I shook my head. I put the car into gear and drove us home.

Chapter Forty-one

I was outside collecting the paper on Wednesday morning. The weather had swung back to warm again, and the trees and their dying leaves were putting on a red, orange, and gold show that was enough to lift my spirits in that quiet moment on the lawn. My neighbors had begun to embrace the spirit of the season by putting out pumpkins and corn sheaves and fake spiderwebs. A couple even placed fake tombstones in their yards, RIP scrawled across their front in dripping spray paint.

I took a deep breath.

Once, the Halloween after Caitlin had disappeared, a group of children came to our door. One of them was a teenage boy who almost looked too old to be trick-or-treating. He wore a floppy blonde wig and a girl's dress. He must not have known who I was or whose house he was at, because when I asked him who he was supposed to be, he replied casually, 'Caitlin Stuart, that girl who disappeared.'

I shut the door then and turned out the lights inside the house, leaving our bowl of candy on the porch for the kids to pick through if they wanted.

It wasn't possible to have a normal life. Not then, and it wasn't possible even with Caitlin back. But in the yard that morning, just for a moment, I felt like a guy collecting his paper while his family slept inside. If I unrolled the paper and saw a news story about Caitlin or the arrest of John Colter, the spell would break.

I didn't go inside right away.

I sat on the porch, barefoot and wearing my robe, the rolled-up paper in my hand, and just watched the morning unfold for a few quiet minutes. It was all waiting for me: Abby and Caitlin, John Colter, Ryan and the police. A light breeze blew and I took a deep breath, taking in the clean morning air, the sweet scent of decaying leaves.

I must have lost myself to the reverie for a few moments, because I didn't notice Liann's car pull up in front of the house. It swept dead leaves in its wake; then she stepped out, her sunglasses pushed onto the top of her head. She smiled at me, some strain on her face, and I saw she carried a briefcase in her left hand.

Something was happening.

'Good morning, Tom.'

'Is it still?'

She sat down next to me on the steps. 'Have you talked to Ryan today?' she asked.

'No. What is it?'

'I was down at the courthouse this morning. I know a lot of people there. They still talk to me. Anyway, I found out there's a bail hearing for John Colter,' she said. 'Ten a.m. I think you should be there. You and Abby, if you can both stand it. I'm sure Ryan will be calling you about it. Colter's lawyer has been pushing for it, and if it goes before a judge —'

'They're not —'

'I can't locate Tracy. And while there are witnesses to say they saw John Colter with Caitlin, that in and of itself

302

doesn't prove he's guilty of anything beyond being a slimeball.'

'Statutory rape?'

'According to who? Is Caitlin ready to go down there and testify against him? All they have is the fire,' Liann said. 'It's a crime, and when the investigation is complete, they'll prosecute . . .'

'Insurance fraud.'

'He hasn't filed a claim, and I doubt he will. His lawyer's pushing for bail. It will be high, but he'll get it.'

'Can Colter afford that? He's on disability.'

'His mother's putting up her house, some other assets.' She frowned. 'He's going to be out, Tom.'

I dropped the paper, put my head in my hands. My guts twisted and turned like my midsection was full of snakes. 'Why should we go then?'

'It can't hurt. It might pressure the judge, even just a little. I'm going to be there, too. We have to try, Tom.'

I looked up again. The same quiet street, the same falling leaves. Nothing would ever be the same. Truly. 'I'm tired of trying, Liann. You can carry the flag for me.'

PART THREE

Chapter Forty-two

My stepfather, Paul, died when I was in graduate school. When I told Abby – Buster was the one who'd called and given me the news, his voice hoarse and halting – I added that I wasn't traveling home for the funeral.

But Abby told me I had to go, that not only did my mother and my family really need my support, but I also needed to face and ultimately close the door on the things I carried with me from the past.

'That's why I don't want to go,' I said. 'I've already closed the door.'

Abby shook her head. 'No, you haven't.'

When I saw my stepfather in his casket, his face painted and sunken, a Bible tucked between the fingers of his gnarled and wrinkly hands, I felt nothing. It wasn't him. At least, it wasn't the version of him I once knew. My mom had told me during a couple of our infrequent phone conversations that he was changed, a different and better man. No more drinking. Better, steadier employment.

I didn't care or believe it.

And if I'd hoped to feel some kind of glee standing over his coffin, that didn't come either. He was just a dead body, an empty sack of flesh.

Later, after the service and the burial, the muttered 'Amens' and the repetitious words of the minister, we all went back to my mother's house, the house I'd grown up in with my stepfather, Paul, and Buster. I told myself and anyone who wanted to listen that I couldn't stay long, that I needed to get back to school as soon as possible. In my mind, I planned to stay for just an hour. No more, no less.

But as the reception went on, as more and more relatives and friends came by and offered their condolences to me, condolences that I accepted even though I didn't feel I had lost anything, my eyes were continually drawn to one particular feature of the house – the staircase leading up to our old bedroom, where my stepfather used to terrorize us in his drunken rages. I hadn't been up there for many years – not since I'd left home to go away to college – but in the wake of Paul's death, I felt a curiosity about the space that figured so prominently in my nightmares.

At an opportune moment, I wandered over to the foot of the stairs.

The same drab brown carpet covered the stairs, worn at the edges and apparently not vacuumed recently. My heart thumped a strange, accelerated rhythm as I stood there, and the palms of my hands felt greasy and slick, as though a thin sheen of oil coated them. I almost turned and walked away, back through the party and out the front door to my car, back to the life I'd made for myself away from that place. But Abby's influence must have worked on me. She'd pushed me to go that far. I decided to go all the way and I took slow, measured steps up the staircase.

The boards creaked as always. The staircase felt narrower, more constricting than in my childhood. I was bigger, of course, and their world was shrinking. But where my hand made contact with the banister, I still felt that greasy slickness, a film my body seemed to be secreting as a defense against the past.

At the top of the stairs, I paused.

It still smelled the same. Faintly musty, a space in need of a good airing out.

To the right was the bathroom, a cramped little space with flaking wallpaper and rust-stained fixtures. And to the left, the familiar room I'd shared with Buster. I went to the doorway, my legs feeling stiff and awkward. I didn't enter right away. I stood at the door, my hand resting against the jamb. It didn't look the same. A queen stood in the place of our two twin beds, and the American flag wallpaper was gone in favor of white paint. But without a doubt I recognized the curvature of the ceiling, the shape of the window, the familiar view of the very top of the neighbors' red brick house.

And it wasn't lost on me that, when I stood in the doorway, I was standing in the exact same space and nearly the exact same manner as Paul on those nights when he came up to the room. I felt cold, a deep chill the likes of which comes only on the worst of winter days. It was spring and pleasant outside, but being in that room frosted me and almost made my body quake with a shiver. I was about to turn and go when —

'You look like you miss this place.'

I spun at the sound of the voice, almost falling down. I came face-to-face with my mother, who'd somehow managed – squeaky stairs and all – to sneak up behind me.

She looked strangely pleased to see me standing in that doorway, as though I were any child reminiscing about the joys and happiness of the past. 'I guess we all miss our childhoods, don't we?' she said.

I shook my head. 'Not me.'

'Oh, Tom.' She reached out for my arm. My posture remained rigid. 'You should come back more. You should have come back more when Paul was alive.'

'Why would I do that?'

'Because we're your family,' she said. 'Don't you have any happy memories of being here?'

'I have to get back, Mom. There's school and everything . . .'

She didn't let go of me. 'Really, Tom. I know it was tough when your dad died and I got remarried. But we did okay by you, didn't we? Didn't Paul?'

I took a step back and studied her face to make sure she wasn't joking. But there was no smile there, no laughter in her eyes. Just a sadness I'd noticed ever since I was a child, its starkness emphasized by the age that was increasingly making its mark upon her – the graying hair, the deep lines around her mouth and eyes, the spots on the backs of her hands. 'Paul beat us, Mom. He beat me. He terrorized all of us, including you.'

For a moment, she looked confused, as though I were speaking of events from a long-ago time she knew nothing about.

She started shaking her head back and forth, slowly, the puzzled look on her face not fading but instead only deepening. 'Tom, Paul never beat you. He never laid a hand on any of my children.'

'You're crazy, Mom. You knew about it.'

'You say these things to me. I just can't understand why

you children hate me so much. Was I such an awful mother that you have to make these things up just to hurt me?'

'No one's making anything up, Mom.' I pulled loose from her grip, my anger swelling unreasonably. 'No one's making this up. Just admit what you know to be true.'

Her eyes filled with tears. She brought her hand up to her mouth. She looked like she wanted to keep the sobs from escaping from her throat. It worked, because none came. But she did manage to speak. 'Not today, Tom. Please, not on a day like this.'

'Why won't you say what I want to hear you say?'

Buster appeared on the stairs.

He reached the top, apparently having heard at least some of our conversation. The raised voices. My mother's pleas. He looked angry, but rather than taking my side – which I'd thought he would've agreed with – he took Mom's side against me.

'Tom,' he said, 'this isn't all about you and your hurt feelings. We're all hurting here today. We don't need you making this stuff up about Dad again.'

'I'm not making anything up. I just want her to admit it.'

Buster gritted his teeth. 'Tom, you asshole.'

Mom looked at the floor, wiping at her tears.

I stared, waiting. The two of them formed a Maginot Line of denial. I couldn't squeeze through. There wasn't a place for me there. There never was. Never once were they on my side. Not against Paul, not against anything.

I brushed past them and left the house.

And I never saw my mother alive again.

Chapter Forty-three

I wasn't sleeping. I knew that.

In the days since Liann's visit, my nights were spent staring at the ceiling of the guest room, the noise of an occasional passing car my only company. Caitlin was in our house, and John Colter was in someone's house too. Free on bail. Charged with arson, second degree, just as Liann had predicted.

Something tapped against my window.

I sat up quickly.

John Colter? Could he be there, trying to get into our house?

I crossed the room to the window and looked down. My palms were flat against the glass, feeling the cold from the outside.

Nothing.

The street, the yard were empty.

My imagination, nothing more.

But I couldn't go back to sleep.

Instead, I went downstairs and made a circuit of the house, checking every door, every window, making sure they were locked and secure. They were. The heat was down for the night, and my feet were cold against the kitchen tiles. I looked in the refrigerator. Finding nothing much, I picked up an apple but didn't bite into it. I thought about the girl from the cemetery and the noise against the window upstairs.

Was she out there again?

It didn't take me long to go back upstairs and dress. I paused on the landing and stuck my ear against the door to Abby and Caitlin's room. I heard faint, steady breathing. They were still there, as safe as they could be, so I slipped out of the house like a burglar.

The streets were quiet and empty. It was nearly one-thirty, and when I reached the main road a few cars passed. But even out there it was quiet. The streetlight flashed yellow, and in its strange glow, I scanned the sidewalk in both directions. I didn't see anybody, and certainly no sign of the girl. My hands were stuffed into the pockets of my jacket, but I still felt a chill that made me hunch my shoulders.

Even in the dark, the headstones were visible. Faint, stony outlines, solid and eternal. I crossed the main road, jogging slightly, cutting at an angle across the front of the park and toward the driveway that wound through the middle of the cemetery. A sign said the cemetery closed at dark, and on rare occasions a security car made a sweep through as the daylight faded. But mostly the security was lax.

Trees lined both sides of the main cemetery drive. The trunks and branches were thick and gnarled, and in many cases grew close to the graves and knocked long-planted headstones out of kilter, tilting them to the side like falling towers.

I slowed my pace the farther I moved away from the

street. I felt a little exposed. If the girl was in the cemetery, she could be anywhere, hiding behind any of the monuments or mausoleums, watching me.

And if she didn't come alone . . .

Even late in the season, with cool weather settling in, crickets still chirped in the grass. Above, through the breaks in the trees, the sky was clear, the stars bright. It was beautiful and peaceful. A wonderful place to spend eternity, if indeed we were granted an eternity to spend.

I reached the back where Caitlin's headstone – *cenotaph* – stood. I looked around, still not seeing or hearing anything.

But then something rustled to my left.

It was a quick sound, a crunching of fallen leaves. It could have been a branch falling or the skittering of a raccoon. But as I stood there, listening and looking for more, the sense grew within me that I wasn't alone, that more than just the legions of the sleeping dead were there in the night.

I waited, and the sound came again. It continued longer, a shuffling like footsteps through the carpet of leaves. And then I saw the girl.

She emerged from between two headstones, very close to Caitlin's monument. My heart jumped when I saw the girl. I took a step toward her. She backed up a half step, as though she wanted to run.

'No,' I said. I held my hand out in what I hoped was a calming gesture. 'Don't go.'

In the darkness, she looked as vague as the shadows between the headstones. I saw her blonde hair, and the loose, baggy Windbreaker she wore hung to her knees. Her big eyes glistened like pools of water in the darkness. She raised a finger to her mouth and chewed on the nail.

'Who are you?' I asked.

She kept chewing.

'What do you want from me? Do you know me?'

She studied me.

'He sent me,' she said.

'Who?'

She didn't answer, but the realization dawned.

'John Colter sent you?'

She nodded, the finger still in her mouth. 'He wants to see her,' she said. 'He wants to see the girl in your house.'

'He's going to jail.'

'No,' she said. 'He says he wants to see her.'

'Is he here? Is he in the cemetery?'

The girl craned her neck around, looking behind her.

'Who's back there?' I asked.

I stepped forward, squinting past the girl, but saw nothing. After a long moment, I heard the sound of footsteps, heavier this time and again stirring up the leaves.

I waited, and a figure resolved out of the darkness.

I expected to see that face from the sketch, the one from the photo Ryan had placed in front of me. That hulking, ugly, scarred face.

So it took me a moment to process the more familiar face I saw before me. The one that looked so much like my stepfather, Paul.

I must have blinked my eyes a few times until he said my name.

'Tom, take it easy.'

It was Buster.

Chapter Forty-four

He moved slowly toward me, his eyes wide, his lips slightly parted.

I felt the earth turning, the sky moving above me, the stars streaking through the night like fireballs. Everything welled within me, a burning taste at the back of my throat. Anger, frustration, confusion. My hands went out and took Buster by the lapels of his jacket. I gathered fistfuls of the material until I felt my fingernails bend back with the pressure.

'What are you doing here? What the fuck are you doing to me?'

'Calm down, Tom. Calm down —'

He grimaced as I shook him, his lips peeling back in a crazed-looking grin. But it was fear. He saw something in me. My own lack of control. My rage. I shook until he managed to get his own hands up. He gripped my biceps, slowing me down.

'Tom. Stop. It's me. It's Buster.'

'Paul —'

'It's Buster.'

'You took Caitlin. You took her —'

'No, no. Listen. Listen to me.'

I don't think I would have stopped, except the girl, the child who'd appeared outside my window, came up and grabbed ahold of me. She tugged on my belt loop and strained to be heard above our grunts and scuffling.

'Stop it!' she said. 'Stop doing that to him. Stop it! Stop it!'

Her voice reached me through the fog of my anger. I turned to look down at her, and when I did, I loosened my grip on Buster.

She was about twelve. This close, I finally saw her features. The greasy hair, the pale, almost translucent skin. Her clothes hung loose on her body, like she possessed next to no body fat. There were dark circles around her eyes. Malnutrition. The child hadn't been eating enough.

'Who are you?' I asked.

She looked scared of me, but held her ground. 'He wants her back,' she said again. 'The girl. *Your* girl.'

'John Colter sent you?'

She didn't answer.

'Tell me!' I shouted.

My voice echoed through the night. The girl swallowed, her throat bobbing. But still she didn't answer.

'Tom?'

I spun around. Buster stood about ten feet away, his right hand rubbing his throat.

'He did send her,' Buster said. 'Colter.'

'And you? What are you . . . ?'

He held his hands out again, asking for calm and patience. 'Let me explain, Tom. Just listen.'

I stayed rooted in place. My brain spun as fast as the planet.

Buster went on. 'I found the girl, Tom. This girl. She

317

was outside your house tonight. You mentioned her in the papers that time, so when I saw her there, standing underneath your window, I knew who it was.'

'What were *you* doing outside the house in the middle of the night?' I asked Buster. 'Were you there to take Caitlin?'

'No, Tom. I came here to see you. To help you. I saw in the paper that Colter was being let out, that they were only going to charge him with arson or some bullshit like that.' He brought his hands together and rubbed them against each other, steadily increasing the pressure. 'I tell you, Tom, I was angry when I saw that. I can't imagine how you felt. But I wanted to do something. I needed to do something about it.'

'What were you going to do?'

'I don't know.' He punched one fist into the palm of his other hand. 'I found something. I looked in the phone book. Do you know Colter's number was in there the whole time? All this time he held Caitlin, his phone number was right there in the book. There he was, getting calls from telemarketers, people asking him to give money to charity, to switch his long-distance service, and he was keeping Caitlin locked away in some room in the basement.' He dug into his pants pocket and brought out a small, wrinkled piece of paper. 'His mom bailed him out of jail, you know? She put up her house. Did you see that?'

'Yes.'

'Her number's in the book, too.' He waved the paper in the air. 'I called it. The old bitch answered, and I asked for John. She said, "Why can't you reporters leave him alone? He doesn't know nothing about that girl." I told the old bitch to fuck off. But you know what? That means we know where he's staying. He's staying there, at this address.' He waved the paper again.

'What are you suggesting?'

He shrugged. *What do you think?*

I pointed at the girl. 'What were you going to do with her?'

'I saw her outside the house when I came up,' Buster said. 'So I tried to grab her, to find out what she wanted. For you. But she ran this way, so I went after her. I caught up with her over here and asked her what she was doing outside my brother's house. I probably scared the hell out of her. I didn't mean to. But she told me something, Tom. Something really fucking freaky.'

'What?'

Buster looked at the girl. 'Tell him.'

'I already did,' she said.

'Tell him everything you told me.'

'Tell me what?' I asked.

The girl's eyes ticked between the two of us.

'Tell him,' Buster said again.

The girl nodded. 'Okay,' she said. 'Okay.' She started to bite her nail again but stopped. She curled her hand into a fist and let it fall to her side. 'He sent me to your house to get the girl back. He wanted me to tell her that he shouldn't have let her go. He thinks it was a mistake. He didn't mean it.'

'Let her go?' I said.

The girl nodded. 'He said he got scared, so he let her go. The story was in the paper, that drawing. He let her go during the night.' She crinkled her nose. 'She was too old, he said. And he had me . . .'

Buster made a disgusted gasping sound.

319

'Where are your parents?' I asked.

'He loves her. He says he misses her and he wants her back. He sent me to your house to get her back, but I didn't know what to do. I stood in the yard and tried to figure out which room was hers. I couldn't see. And then you ran after me that one night. And *he* ran after me tonight.' She pointed at Buster.

'Did he leave a note here telling her to stay away?'

The girl shrugged. 'He changed his mind, I guess.'

I took a step forward and bent down, trying to get closer to the girl's eye level. Buster came up beside me. 'Who are you, honey?' I asked. 'Who are your parents?'

'I go back to them sometimes. They don't care.' She ran the back of her hand across her nostrils. 'He said he doesn't need me anymore when he gets your girl back.'

'It's not right for you to stay with him like that,' I said.

'We should call the cops —' Buster cut in.

'No,' she said and took two big steps back. Her voice was full of fear, like a child waking from a nightmare. 'No. You can't call the police.'

'We have to,' Buster said.

'He'll run away,' she said. 'He wants to run away. He doesn't want to stay here. The police will take him. They'll lock him up.'

'That's what should happen,' Buster said. He reached in his jacket pocket and brought out a cell phone.

'No,' she said again.

'Hold it,' I said to both of them. 'Just hold it.'

Buster held the phone in his hand, but stopped. He didn't flip it open or dial. The girl stood still, staring at me, her eyes still wide.

'What does he want?' I asked. 'Colter. What does he want from Caitlin?'

'Tom —'

'Quiet. Listen.'

Again her eyes moved between the two of us. She looked like she could run at any moment. She finally settled her gaze on me. 'He just wants to see her again,' she said.

'You said he's leaving.'

She nodded. 'He wants to. He wants to go away.'

'So he wants to take Caitlin with him?' I asked.

She shrugged. 'I don't know.'

Buster's hand landed on my arm. 'Tom, you need to stop this.'

I shook free. 'Does he want to take her?'

The girl fixed her eyes on Buster. I looked. He held his phone and used his thumb to dial a number. 'I'm calling the cops,' he said. 'This is bullshit.'

'Goddamn it!'

I swung and knocked the phone out of his hand. Then I heard the scurrying.

I looked back. The girl was gone. She ran off into the darkness. I watched her disappear into the night, a faint blur moving jackrabbit quick. I took three steps in the same direction, then stopped. She was gone. Long gone.

When I came back, Buster was picking up his phone.

'Don't,' I said.

'It's dead. I never got through.'

'Good.'

'Good? That little girl is under the control of that creep. She must be the same age as Caitlin —'

'I get it.'

'Then what do you want?'

'I don't know.' I paced back and forth in the dark, moving between the headstones, my shoes kicking the leaves around. I started to sweat, and when the wind picked up and cooled the sweat, a chill came over me. 'He's going to get away with this, Buster. All of it.'

'You've got this girl right here. He took her.'

'She's gone. We'll never see her again. You scared her off.'

'They've got the other witnesses. They can put it all together.'

'And prove what exactly? That my daughter likes to date older men?'

'Don't joke about this, Tom. Don't fucking joke around. This is serious. This is your daughter you're talking about here.'

'Is she?' I asked.

'What are you saying?'

'Is she my daughter after four years?'

'Yes. Some animal came along and took your daughter, and he did do those awful things to her. Unspeakable things. But you can't just let that go. You've got to fight for this. You're in a fight, Tom.'

'Unspeakable things?'

'Yes.'

'That's the key right there, isn't it? Caitlin refuses to speak of them. Not to me or Abby or the police. But we all know what we mean when we say unspeakable. Right? Just because it's unspeakable doesn't mean I haven't thought about it. It doesn't mean I don't visualize it. Every night I see it.' My words came in a rush, so I paused to collect myself. 'I see them in a bed. Or on the floor. I see that pig grunting and breathing over her. Mounting her. Kissing her. Everything. And worst of all, she's doing it back and enjoying it.'

I couldn't look at him. My rear molars ground against each other.

'Do you think the truth is going to be worse than what you've imagined?' he asked.

'It can't be.'

He put the phone away and crossed his arms. He looked like he understood.

He reached into his pants pocket again and brought out the slip of paper. 'My car's over by your house,' he said. 'We can leave right now.'

I started to leave, then noticed Buster wasn't by my side. I looked back into the darkness and saw his shape leaning over Caitlin's headstone. He started grunting and huffing. I went back.

'Help me,' he said. 'I'm tired of this fucking abortion standing here.'

He started pushing against the stone again, trying with all his might to tip it over. I moved in beside him. It was tough, resistant, but after a few minutes it rocked loose and fell into the soft grass with a heavy thud.

Buster straightened, wiped his hands on his pant legs.

'Now I'm ready to go,' he said.

Chapter Forty-five

Colter's mother lived on the north side of town. I drove by the neighborhood on my way to the interstate, and from the highway I remembered seeing a few factories, some strip malls, and lots and lots of trailers and small homes, the kinds with debris scattered in their yards and blank-eyed occupants sitting on the stoops smoking and drinking soft drinks from plastic bottles.

'Looks like this is a pretty shitty neighborhood,' Buster said.

'That's fitting.'

'I guess not too many professors live on this side of town.'

'I wouldn't think so.'

Buster drummed his fingers against the steering wheel. 'You know, you called me Paul back there in the cemetery.'

'No, I didn't.'

'You did. You looked me right in the eye back there, when you were holding me by the collar, and you called me Paul. Clear as day.'

We took an exit ramp and came to a stoplight. I opened the glove compartment and took out a map. While we sat at the light, I located the correct street among the red and blue lines and told Buster which way to go. He made the first couple of turns, then started talking again.

'You've led a pretty good life,' he said.

'Yeah?'

'Yeah.'

I pointed to the windshield. 'I'm driving in the middle of the night to confront the man who kidnapped and raped my daughter. I'm a lucky man.'

'Your life has turned out better than a lot of people's. You've got a good job, some money. Okay, your personal life is in the dumper now. Your marriage is on the rocks.'

'My daughter . . .'

'Your daughter's back,' he said. 'Don't forget that.'

He made the last turn. We were in a subdivision called Skyline Acres. Every street was named after a heavenly body – Venus, Saturn, Aurora. Colter's mother lived on Neptune Way. I watched the house numbers and pointed. 'There it is. Stop here.'

Buster braked, and we stopped three doors down from the Colter residence.

'Well?' he said.

'You're telling me to appreciate all I have?' I asked.

'I guess so.'

'Tell me, did you feel like you belonged in our family? Did you believe there was a place for you?'

'I never thought about it,' he said.

'That's right. You didn't have to. There were the three of you, and then there was me. But that changed. That changed when Caitlin was born. I had someone like that. For me. I had a family. It was an even greater bond than anything I'd ever felt with Abby.' I fumbled around until I found the door lock.

'What are you doing?' Buster asked.

'I'm going to go look. Wait here.' I worked the door

open. My shoes against the sidewalk sounded ridiculously loud in the quiet night. I'd taken two steps when I heard Buster's door open behind me. I waved him back, but he kept coming. 'Wait in the car,' I said.

He shook his head and kept coming. When he came abreast of me, I put my hand on his arm.

'Why won't you wait?' I asked.

'I can't let you go alone,' he said. 'You don't know what to do in a situation like this.'

'And you do?'

'More than you.'

We stood at the edge of the glow of a streetlight. Our heads were in the shadows.

'Back there at the cemetery, with the girl, were you telling me the truth?' I asked. 'Did you just find her by chance?'

'What else could it have been?'

'Fuck if I know. I just don't know.'

We moved on. It felt good to have him by my side. He was right. I'd never been in a fight. Never confronted a criminal. The whole endeavor felt crazy, so much so that my hands shook and my knees felt loose and jangly with every step I took.

When we reached the driveway, Buster pointed, so I followed him. Light spilled out the side of the house, casting a large rectangle on the cracked and crumbling blacktop. Buster moved alongside the lighted window. He held his hand out to stop me.

The window sat at eye level, so it didn't take much effort for him to look in. He craned his neck and turned from side to side, scanning the room.

'What gives?' I asked.

'Nothing. It's a dump. Just a TV and a bed.' He pulled his head back. 'Shit.'

'What?'

'Some guy came in.'

'Did he see you?'

Buster shook his head. I grabbed his arm. Tight.

'Was it him?'

'I don't know. I got out of the way.'

'Let me.'

I stepped past him and eased next to the window. I risked a look.

The overhead light was on, a bright wash over the entire room. The walls were painted a pale green. A small TV, a thirteen-inch black-and-white that looked to be about thirty years old, broadcast a fuzzy picture despite its rabbit ears. Crumpled clothes covered the floor, and the closet door was open, allowing more clothes to spill out.

Then I saw the man sitting in a sagging chair. He stared at the TV, his head drooping.

I studied his face in profile. The prominent nose, the pock-marked cheeks. The stringy hair was cut but still streaked with gray. He wore a dirty gray sweatshirt and sweatpants. His feet were in house slippers.

It was him. Colter.

He didn't know he was being watched. His elbows rested on the arms of the beat-up chair, and his hands joined together before his chest, holding a steaming mug. While I watched, he lifted the mug to his face and blew gently on the hot liquid, then took a tentative sip and pursed his lips. I watched, waiting, but that was all he did.

Buster moved in next to me. He nodded toward the window, his face asking the question: *Is that the guy?*

I nodded, and while my head moved, something welled up within me. Colter looked pathetic, utterly defenseless and harmless, and it still didn't stop the rage bubbling within me.

Without thinking, I raised my fist and pounded it against the window.

'Colter! Hey, Colter!'

Buster made a grab for my arm, but it was too late.

Colter jumped when I hit the window, spilling the contents of the mug down the front of his shirt. I jerked free of Buster and hit the window again and again. The pane rattled in the frame, and for a moment my fist moved independently of my mind. I kept hitting the glass, wishing I could break it and smash through and grab the man who had taken my daughter.

Finally, Buster grabbed me from behind and stopped me.

'Easy,' he said. 'Easy. You'll cut your hand off.'

'I don't care.'

'Look, look —'

Colter was on his feet, peering at the window. Because of the interior light, he couldn't get a good look at the two of us, and from where he stood, we must have been indistinct ghostly shapes. Two pale, oval forms hovering in the night. He reached and flipped the light off, leaving only the glow of the television. He moved closer, his ugly face uncertain.

I expected him to reach for the phone. Or a weapon. Instead, he took two quick steps across the room and slid the window up.

'What is this?' he asked.

He didn't sound angry or agitated, just weary and defensive, like a man growing tired of answering questions.

I didn't answer. I was face-to-face with the man. I grabbed for his neck, but he was too quick. He ducked back out of the way with the skill of a boxer. I stumbled forward and caught myself against the window ledge.

Colter's eyes were alert now, like a threatened animal. He stared back and spoke in a low voice.

'Get out of here, you assholes. I thought you were reporters . . .'

His voice trailed off. He kept his eyes locked on me. Studying me. Examining me.

'Oh,' he said. 'I get it.'

'What do you get, shitwipe?' Buster asked.

Colter looked toward him and squinted before turning back to me. He raised his finger in the air as though just remembering something.

'What's your name?' he asked me.

'You think you know him?' Buster asked. 'You know his daughter, don't you? This is Tom Stuart. *Stuart*. Caitlin's father. The father of the little girl you snatched. My niece.'

Colter didn't look surprised. He didn't blink or nod, but I saw the recognition on his face.

'Why aren't you saying anything?' I asked.

'Please. My mother is asleep.'

'Fuck her. I ought to —'

'Be quiet,' Colter said. 'Jesus.' He held out his hands. They were surprisingly small, the fingers long and thin. 'The cops said they'd be keeping an eye on me, but I haven't seen a single car since they let me out. For all I know, some nutjob will want to come around and take a shot at me. All those lies in the papers.'

'Boo-hoo for you,' Buster said.

'Come around to the back,' Colter said. 'Quietly.'

I started to move, then noticed Buster wasn't coming with me. I waved at him.

He shook his head. 'I think you should go alone.'

'What? You brought me here.'

'I know,' he said. 'You have to do this alone. I'll be right here if you need me.'

I took a step back. 'What if he has a gun or something?'

Buster shook his head. 'You heard that stuff at the cemetery. You have something he wants. So go.'

I went toward the back of the house, leaving Buster behind.

When I reached the back of the house, no one was there. The wooden door, its paint cracked and blistering, stood closed, the single bulb above it dark. The door led into the kitchen, but the lights were off inside.

A light came on above the stove, and I saw Colter's bulky form moving toward the door. The light above the door came on as well, and a few late-season moths and gnats appeared instantly, drawn to the light and warmth. I heard locks untumbling, then a chain, and with some effort he yanked the door open.

His body filled the doorway, lit by the faint light behind. He didn't come out, but stood there on the step, his arms at his side.

'Does she ask about me?' he asked.

I still felt shaky. Something hot roiled in my chest. 'You're a pig,' I said.

He took two steps down so that we were on the same level. He was shorter than me, stockier, with a wrestler's body gone to middle-aged fat. 'What are you here for?' he asked. 'Are you here to shoot me or beat me? Do you want to kill me?'

I moved forward. My mouth was dry, but I worked my tongue around. When I thought I was close enough to him, I spit. It wasn't an impressive job, but some of it hit him in the face, making his head jerk back.

He kept his eyes on me while he brought his arm up and wiped his face.

'Okay,' he said. 'Is that out of the way?'

My heart pumped like an overworked engine, but I also felt foolish, my anger abating. A grown man spitting on another grown man.

He went on. 'Because I don't think that's what you really came here for, is it?'

'You called me back here.'

'And you showed up at my window. With reinforcements. So . . .' He spread his arms wide. 'How's she doing?'

'No, no. You don't get to talk about her. You don't get to know anything about her.'

'I know one thing about her. She won't testify against me.'

'Give it time.'

He shook his head. 'I love her. And more importantly, she loves me. That's why she'll never testify. Ever.'

'Is that what Tracy Fairlawn thought about you?'

He made a quiet snorting noise, a form of a laugh.

'I see she's been running her mouth. She never did understand the value of keeping quiet.'

'Where is she?'

'I don't know. Probably run off. Partying somewhere.'

'If you love my daughter so much, why did you make her leave?'

He hesitated a moment, looking at the ground. Light from the bulb above the door spilled over his feet. He still wore the slippers. 'I see you met little Jasmine. I guess that's how you all ended up out here tonight.'

'Why did you send Caitlin away?'

'And what do I get out of talking to you?' he asked. 'Are you going to forgive me? Grant me a pardon?'

'You . . . owe me.'

'What?'

'You heard me,' I said. 'I . . . gave her to you. I let her walk the dog in the park. I let her out of my sight for too long. Let me guess – you went up to her in the park. You'd seen her walking there. And you went up to her and you asked her something about the fucking dog, right? Something inane and stupid. Maybe something that made her laugh or giggle . . . and you had her. You had what you wanted. And I didn't.'

I stopped. My hands shook and were cold, so I rubbed them together.

'I really shouldn't be talking to you,' he said. 'For all I know, this could all be a setup. You could be wearing a wire.'

'I'm not,' I said. 'I don't care about any of that. I really don't. I want to know why she came back to us. Why?'

He considered me. I thought I saw real concern, real

pity in his eyes. He shrugged. 'I don't really care if you are wearing a wire, I guess. It wouldn't stand up in court, and I don't really plan on sticking around to see the judge.' He kicked at a pebble on the ground. 'At the time, I thought Caitlin needed to go. That stuff showed up in the paper, that stuff Tracy was saying. The sketch of me. I thought about just hightailing it out of here, packing the car and starting over somewhere else. But I didn't want to be on the run all the time. People wouldn't understand the two of us. We could pass ourselves off as father and daughter for a while. Caitlin was getting older, too. I thought maybe she needed a better life than the one I could give her. It was just me and her. I couldn't teach her about being a woman. Not everything anyway. I could always start over with a new girl, a younger one. Jasmine maybe.'

'Did Caitlin want to come back home?' Just asking the question made me feel weak, like I was a beggar. But I couldn't not ask. I needed to know.

'No, she didn't.'

Don't send me away. Don't send me away.

'How did you get her to go?'

'I told her I'd turn myself in. I'd call the police if she didn't leave. I forced her hand. I remember that night . . .' He paused again and stared past me, off into the darkness. 'You know what it's like to have a parting of the ways with someone you love. There were tears. It almost broke my heart – it really did. Before she left, she swore to me she'd never tell what we did together. I guess she hasn't, or you wouldn't be here.'

'What happened between you?'

'Now that's private, isn't it?'

333

One corner of his mouth ticked up, and one eyebrow as well. It set me in motion. I charged forward, trying to bury my shoulder in his midsection and knock him to the ground. But he handled me expertly. I was quickly spun to the ground, his thick forearm locked around my neck. He didn't apply full pressure to my throat. I could still breathe. But he applied enough to let me know he could do more if he wanted.

Buster came to the edge of the house and stopped. I heard his shoes against the driveway, but he remained in the dark.

'Easy now,' Colter said. I didn't know if he'd meant it for me or Buster. He said it again. 'Easy now, fella.' Colter was still on one knee. I saw Buster's shape out of the corner of my eye. 'Just stay there,' Colter said to Buster. 'We're calming down now, real easy like.'

'Let him go,' Buster said.

I tried to talk, but I couldn't. I hoped Buster would stay back. I hoped he could see Colter held control of my airway. Apparently he did. He moved back a little, giving Colter some space. 'You just go right on back where you were,' Colter said. 'We have a few more things to talk about here.' He eased the pressure on my neck so I could speak.

'Go,' I said. 'It's fine.' My throat was raw, like I'd swallowed thumbtacks.

'You don't look fine,' Buster said. 'You look like you're fucked-up.'

'Back off,' I said.

He did. He took slow steps backward until his form cleared the side of the building again. When he was gone, Colter released the pressure even more.

'Are you going to act right?' he asked.

I nodded like a fool.

He let go all the way and stood up. I fell to the ground, my face almost hitting the pavement. I reached for my throat and gulped air. It took a couple of minutes for me to feel right and push myself up. When I did, the night tilted a little like I might pass out. But I didn't. My legs came back to me, and I cleared my throat, making sure I could speak.

'You okay?' he asked.

'Fuck you.'

'I showed you mercy,' he said. 'I could have crushed your throat.'

'You'd never see Caitlin again.'

'I can see her anytime I want. I can snap my fingers and she'd be here.' To emphasize his point, he snapped his fingers in the air. 'You can't even deny it. I'm showing you mercy. I'll let you say good-bye to her, before she comes with me.'

'I'll call the police. I'll tell them what you said. You confessed.'

'Hearsay.' He laughed a little. 'But I guess I did make a little mistake with Caitlin. She isn't like the girls I typically date. Look at you – she comes from a good family. Good parents. You care. There are a lot of girls in the world without that. When they go away, no one notices. When they come back and go to the police, they get ignored. Still, this is all dependent on whether Caitlin wants to rat me out or not.'

He was right. There was little I could do unless Caitlin testified. 'Why show me mercy then? Why do anything for me?'

Colter looked me up and down. 'Because she'd want me to. She loves you, so I'll do this favor.'

'Did she talk about me? Did she remember me —?'

A sound from the house cut my words off. The back door was pulled inward again, and the light revealed an older woman, close to seventy, wearing a kerchief on her head and a housecoat. Her face was long and thin, unlike her son's, and the skin around her jawline hung loose.

'What's going on out here, Johnny? Who is this man?'

'He's a friend, Mom.'

'Is he a cop?'

'No.'

'I'm not a friend,' I said. 'I'm Caitlin Stuart's father.'

The woman raised her hand to her chest and gathered the loose folds of the housecoat tighter against her body. She looked stricken, almost ill. She'd put her house up to secure his bond, and if he left town before a trial . . .

'What are you doing at our house?' she asked, but she didn't wait for an answer. 'Johnny isn't . . . He just can't be seeing people, any people, right now.'

'Did you know about this, Mrs Colter? Did you know about Caitlin?'

She moved back into the shadow of the doorframe. 'Johnny, you come inside now. It's late.'

Colter walked toward the house like an obedient child. Before he went inside, he looked back. 'Remember what I offered, Mr Stuart. A chance to say good-bye this time.'

Chapter Forty-six

Buster didn't say anything until we were in the car and pulling away from the curb. 'What was that about? Colter said he offered something?' He kept his eyes on me and the car weaved across the road. That scared me even though it was late and there were no other cars out.

'Watch it.'

'What were you two talking about?'

I watched out the window at the passing houses. They looked dumpy and run-down, but I envied the residents their certainty, their comfort. They were likely sleeping the quiet sleep of the just.

'Tom? Tell me.'

I didn't turn to face him. 'He wants to see Caitlin again.'

'I bet.' He laughed.

'He says he loves her, and he made a mistake when he let her go.'

'Bullshit. Is he crazy? Is the guy fucking crazy?'

I kept my eyes straight ahead, but the side of my face burned. His eyes were on me.

'No, no, no,' he said. 'No.'

As we reached the base of the on-ramp to the interstate, Buster jerked the wheel to the right, forcing the car to the side of the road. He hit the brakes hard, skidding a little. My body jerked forward, and I used my hand to brace myself against the dashboard.

'You're going to do it? You're going to take your daughter to that man?'

'I don't know what I'm going to do,' I said.

'You don't know? That's not an answer.' He raised his finger in the air. 'There's only one answer, and the answer is no. That's it. End of story.'

'Just take me home.'

'She's your little girl.'

'She's not so little, is she?' I said. 'She's able to say she loves that guy. She's capable of feeling that, of thinking that. I know what the shrink says. I know about Stockholm syndrome. But, Jesus, what can I do with all of this? They were fucking, Buster.'

'He fucked her, not the other way around.'

I rested my hands in my lap. I turned them over and over, knotting the fingers together and twisting them until the knuckles hurt. 'Did you see him?' I asked. 'Did you see his fucking face? He's a fucking pig. And a loser. Living with his mom. She was with him for four years. We lost four years. That kills me.'

'He took her, Tom. Do you understand that? He took her. He's a criminal.'

What happened to me. The words cycled through my head, but I could no longer apply those words simply to Caitlin. They applied to me as well.

What happened to me.

I rubbed my eyes. 'I want to go home. It's late, Buster.'

'Not until you drop this,' he said. He turned to face me in the small car. The glow from the display panel lighted his face, turning it a pale and alien green. I could feel his breath. 'Tell me right now you won't do it.'

338

I watched occasional cars passing on the highway, their headlights creating bright white cones in the darkness. 'It's not your decision, Buster. She's not your kid.'

'She is my kid. We came out here in the night. We came together, side by side. As brothers. That means she's my kid. She doesn't just belong to you.'

'You don't have kids. You don't know.'

'Oh, fuck that, Tom. You know, I'm tired of your sad-sack routine. The "Nobody loved me" bullshit. I stood by you throughout our childhood. I was there for you. And now you throw it back at me and treat me this way. Fuck you, Tom.'

I took a short, futile swing at his face in the dark. I meant to hit him hard, to drive him back and hurt him. But he ducked away.

He reached back and pushed his door open. He didn't say anything. He came around the front of the car, his body passing through the headlights, and then he stopped at my door, pulling it open.

I didn't have time to react or think. He opened the door and reached in, taking me by the front of my shirt.

'What the fuck?' I said.

He kept pulling, the fabric of my shirt digging into the back of my neck, until I stopped resisting and allowed myself to be brought out into the night air. I tried to knock his grip free, but couldn't. He held on; then something jolted the side of my face. It took a second for me to realize I'd been hit, that Buster had punched me in the left jaw. I fell back against the car, but he pulled me forward and hit me again, stunning me. My knee joints loosened and I started to crumple. As I went to the ground, he swung a last time, catching me in the back of the head and knocking me flat to the ground beside the car. The ground was cold. Dirt and gravel pressed against my face. I didn't try to push myself up.

Buster's shoes came into my line of sight. He was wearing work boots for some reason. I knew what might come next, and it did. He drew one of the boots back and kicked forward. I managed to curl up a little, and the boot struck me just below the rib cage on my left side.

'You're lucky I don't kill you,' he said.

The pain seared through me, radiating out like an electric charge, into my back and down my left leg. I couldn't talk.

'I'm through with you,' he said, the words falling upon me like spittle.

I thought he'd kick again, but he didn't. He shoved my door closed; then the boots disappeared around the front of the car. I managed to roll away, putting a few feet between the car and me. He dropped it into gear and hit the gas hard, sending a spray of gravel into my face and over my body. And when he was gone, I just lay there on the side of the road, curled up in the dark like a broken and terrified child.

Chapter Forty-seven

I lay on the side of the road for a long while, staring at the stars, waiting for the pain in my side to go away. The stars and winking satellites offered no comfort or conclusions, nothing I could orient myself by or make sense of.

When the pain eased, I pushed myself up. The landscape whirled and tilted before me, the lights on the nearby highway blurring together and swimming. I thought for a moment I was seriously hurt, concussed or wounded in such a way I'd need to call for help. But after a couple of minutes on my feet, as I gathered my senses and balance, the world steadied. My equilibrium returned, and only the pain in my side remained.

I didn't have anyone to call. To wake up Abby would invite questions and examinations about how and why I'd ended up in that neighborhood in the middle of the night. To call *anyone* would invite such questions. And the only other person I could call had just left me here on the side of the road.

The walking did me good. Five miles to home, moving at a snail's pace. I worked the painful muscles loose, the ones that were clenched and stretched while not just one but two different men assaulted me. I tried to understand how I'd come to be in the place I was. The wheel of fortune had spun, and the arrow had landed on me: I'd been the guy whose daughter was taken. And then the wheel spun again, an even more unusual and perhaps crueler fate: I'd also been the guy to get his daughter back. Was it a mark of my confusion that I still couldn't decide which was the worse fate to suffer?

By the time I reached the house, the sky was turning gray with first light. My feet hurt, and all I wanted to do was fall asleep in my own bed. But the wheel of fortune would turn one more time.

I saw Ryan's car out front. It was just six-thirty, way too early for him to be there unless something was going on.

I thought I knew. Buster. He'd called them and told all. The girl in the cemetery, the trip to Colter's, my interest in dealing with the man who'd taken my daughter.

Having nowhere else to go and no energy with which to do it, I went up the steps to face the music.

Ryan and Abby were in the living room. Abby was dressed, but I could tell by her hair that she wasn't showered. When I entered the room, their heads turned in unison, as though they were part of a well-rehearsed stage act.

'Where have you been, Tom?' Abby asked.

'I was out taking a walk.'

'You've been gone for hours.'

'I couldn't sleep.'

'Are you hurt, Tom?' Ryan asked, sizing me up.

'I fell.'

Abby looked away, fixing her eyes on the coffee mug she lifted to her mouth and sipped from.

'Did you land on somebody's fist?' Ryan asked.

I stood near the door, let my weight rest against its frame. I ignored him.

'I'm here about your brother,' Ryan said.

'Okay.'

Abby put the mug down and started to cry. Her eyes were full of tears, and she brought both her hands up to wipe them away.

'Did something happen to him?' I asked.

'Oh, Tom,' Abby said. 'If only it were that easy.'

'Why don't you sit down, Tom.'

I did, gingerly lowering myself onto the opposite end of the couch from Abby. She looked over at me and shook her head, disbelieving and angry.

'Have you heard from your brother lately?' Ryan asked.

'Will someone just tell me what's going on?' I asked. I shifted so my side didn't hurt. 'It's been a long night.'

Ryan took a long moment, still studying my face. Then he relented. 'We've been continuing our investigation of John Colter and his relationship to Caitlin. We've been examining every angle, trying to understand how he ended up with your daughter. Work relationships, church relationships . . . these are the things we examine in a case like this —'

'I don't understand where you're going with this. And what does it have to do with my brother?'

'We've identified some points of commonality between your family and associates of John Colter. There's a connection there, a link.'

'Our family knew John Colter?' I asked.

'It was Buster, Tom,' Abby said. 'Buster. All along. It was Buster who gave Caitlin over to this beast.'

I still didn't move. While Abby wept, I stayed rooted in my seat, staring at Ryan.

Not Buster. No way.

Finally, Ryan jerked his head a little toward Abby. His motion broke the spell.

I slid down the couch and placed my hand on Abby's back. She jerked away.

'Don't touch me.' She looked up, her face tear streaked, her eyes on fire. 'Did you know about this? All along, did you suspect this and keep it from me?'

'I don't even know about it now.'

'Your brother gave our little girl away,' she said. 'He's a druggie and a failure, and he brought his own mess down on our lives.'

I looked to Ryan.

'Our investigation has revealed that John Colter was friends with a man named Loren Brooks. Do you know him?'

I shook my head. 'No, I don't.'

'Are you sure you don't know him, Tom?' Abby asked.

'I don't know the name. Should I?'

Ryan continued. 'Loren Brooks was a small-time drug dealer around here. Cocaine and marijuana mostly. Also some petty crimes. Burglaries, car thefts. He was an all-around malcontent and noncontributing member of our society.'

'Did you arrest him?'

'Many times, but not for anything relating to this case. He died two years ago. Drug overdose. I can't say the world is worse off without him. We did manage to locate his former girlfriend, a woman who'd lived with Brooks for several years. We asked her what she knew about John Colter. She told us that everybody knew one thing about John Colter.'

'What's that?'

'That he liked little girls. And, sometimes, he liked to keep them in his basement.'

I felt the air go out of me, like I'd been hit between the shoulder blades.

Abby spoke up. 'You can arrest him now. Rearrest him. You have a witness.'

'Buster . . .' I said.

I couldn't bring myself to say it all.

How does Buster fit into all this? What did Buster do?

'Your brother owed Loren Brooks money, the result of some drug transaction about five years back. This girlfriend of Brooks, she believes that your brother offered Caitlin to Brooks as some form of payment for the debt he owed.'

'But Buster never *had* Caitlin,' Abby said. 'She was never his to give. She was never with him.'

'But he knew where she lived,' Ryan said. 'He knew her routines. She trusted him and would have followed him if he asked her to. Right?'

The money Buster had borrowed from me . . . his phone call and apology . . . his appearance at the cemetery . . .

'Are you saying Buster led Caitlin to Colter and this other guy? That he tricked her into going and sold her to them like . . .' The only word that came to my mind sounded ridiculous, but I said it anyway. 'Like a concubine.'

'This girlfriend of Brooks picked Caitlin's photo out of a group of photos. She says she'll testify that she saw Caitlin in Colter's house. She's actually the kind of witness we've been waiting for. She's going to help the case a great deal.'

'Is she reliable?' Abby asked.

'More reliable than the men she'll be testifying against, despite whatever problems she's had,' Ryan said. He turned his attention to me. 'Tom,' he said, 'I need to ask you something very important. Do you know where your brother is?'

'Did you check his house?' I asked.

Ryan nodded. 'Of course. I need you to tell me other places we might find him.'

'I don't know —'

'And I need to know if you've heard from him lately. Anything at all.'

Ryan held his gaze on mine, his eyes boring into me like an X-ray.

'Buster is . . .' My voice trailed off. I tried again. 'Look . . .' I replayed the scene in the car early that morning. His words. He'd been right, I had to admit. He had always stood by me when we were children, and I couldn't underestimate that. Even if he had been involved – which I doubted, I really doubted – I wanted to find that out for myself. I couldn't bear the thought of handing him over to the police, to strangers. I drew the line there. 'I don't know where he is. We had a falling out. We often have them. I haven't spoken to him in a few weeks. In fact, the last time I saw him was right here at this house. And you were here, too. Listen, Ryan, are you really telling me Buster was directly involved? Just because this woman said something about him?'

'Like I said, we're moving forward on the case with the goal of placing Colter in custody again,' Ryan said. 'We need to talk to William as well. If he comes in voluntarily, it can be easier on him. If not . . .'

'Tom?' Abby asked. 'Where is he?'

'I don't know. I said I haven't seen him.'

Ryan let out a little sigh. He placed his hands on his knees and pushed himself up out of the chair. He straightened his jacket by tugging on the lapels.

'You'll let us know if anything else happens,' Abby said.

'I will.' Ryan pointed at my face. 'And if I were you, I'd put some ice on that eye. Whoever you fell on was probably trying to hurt you.'

Chapter Forty-eight

Abby and I remained on opposite ends of the couch, not saying anything to each other. Not moving. I shifted a little, adjusting my position, trying to get comfortable.

'Aren't you going to say anything, Tom?'

'What's there to say?' I looked to the hallway, to the space where Caitlin's pictures had been removed.

'I should have known it was him,' she said. 'I should have known it would be someone in the family, someone close to us. It always is. Statistically, you know, it's always a family member involved. And considering Buster's past, his record. And you defended him. You said he wouldn't hurt Caitlin.'

'Where is she?'

'Upstairs. Asleep. At least she was when Ryan called.'

I brought my hand up and touched my cheek. It felt tender and a little puffy. Ryan was right. It needed ice.

'Where were you?' she asked. 'Really. Where were you?'

'I thought I heard someone trying to get into the house. I came downstairs and looked. I couldn't go back to sleep, so I took a walk.'

'Someone tried to get into the house and you left us?'

'I *thought* someone tried to get into the house.'

'Did you really fall?'

I looked toward the stairs. 'It was wet. The dew. I was

wearing these shoes.' I pointed at my feet distractedly. 'I'm going to talk to her.'

'About what?'

'I'm going to ask her about Buster.'

'Good. Bring her down here.'

'No. I think it would be better if I went alone. She'll listen to me.'

Abby made a bitter, dismissive noise. It sounded like *Hut*. 'She hasn't listened to you for four years, Tom. She never listened to you. You were more like friends. That's why she liked you. She didn't have to hear or obey anything you said.'

I stood up. Slowly, gingerly, taking one step at a time, I went up the stairs.

I knocked on the door of the master bedroom and didn't wait for a response before I pushed the door open. Caitlin was sitting on the floor, her back against the bed frame, the bulk of a sleeping bag spread underneath her. She was wearing long underwear – tops and bottoms – and she looked wide awake, her eyes alert.

I moved over to the bed and eased myself down. A stitch of pain poked me in the side, and I winced. Caitlin showed no concern.

I pointed to my puffy cheek. 'Do you know who did this to me? Buster. Your Uncle Buster. We haven't fought like that since we were kids. It used to be more even then. But last night, he kicked my ass.'

Her eyes widened.

'Was he there, Caitlin? With Colter? Was Buster ever there?'

She looked down at her hands and started picking at the cuticles. Her nails were short, the skin around them red and scabbed, as though she'd picked them over more than once.

'Caitlin? I'm not going to tell Mom.'

I was ready to let it go when she spoke up.

'I thought I heard his voice once,' she said. She continued to stare at her hands. 'I thought maybe I imagined it. At first . . .' She paused a long time. 'I used to hear a lot of voices. I used to think a lot of people were there, looking for me.' She hesitated. 'I even used to think I heard you and Mom.'

'No, no,' I said.

'I couldn't tell if it was imagined or real,' she said. 'It seemed very real. It sounded just like both of you. I knew your voices. I could recognize them.'

'We were never there. If we were there, we wouldn't have left without you.'

Caitlin seemed to consider this for a moment, then went on. 'Once I heard someone talking and laughing, and it sounded just like Uncle Buster. I almost called his name, but I didn't.'

'Did you see him?'

She shook her head.

'Caitlin, this is important. Did you ever see Uncle Buster in Colter's house?'

'I didn't,' she said. 'Never.'

I put my hand on her shoulder, felt the textured fabric of the long johns. 'Were you in the basement?' I asked. 'Is that why you didn't see him?'

She shook her head again, more forcefully.

'You can tell me, you know? If you want to tell me something and not have Mom know, I can do that. It's okay.'

'I already told you what I want.'

I let my hand go limp and slip off her shoulder. 'Really, Caitlin? Still?'

She picked at her fingers and didn't pay attention. I touched her again.

'Come on, Caitlin. You can't still want that. Not that. It's okay to let that go.'

She spun out of my grip and crab-walked away from me.

'You don't know,' she said. 'Don't say that.'

'Caitlin —'

'No. I already told you.'

I went to the closed door, opened it, and looked into the hallway. No sign of Abby. I closed the door. Caitlin looked surprised when I came back into the room and took my spot on the bed again. 'You know how I said I was fighting with your uncle Buster? Do you know what we were fighting about?'

'I don't care.'

'We were fighting about you. And I'd think you would care, because I was on your side.' I could tell she didn't follow. 'We went to see your friend last night. Mr Colter.'

'You're lying.'

'We went to his house. Actually, we went to his mother's house, since that's where he's living these days. Do you know her? Did you know he burned his own house down? The one you lived in with him? He completely torched it.'

'He did?'

'He did. Why?'

'He said he would do that. I didn't believe him.'

'He's a man of his word, isn't he? He destroyed any trace of you, any evidence that you were ever there. He covered his tracks. Except he couldn't destroy that room in the basement, the one you must have lived in. The one you heard Buster's voice from, right? Remnants of it survived the fire, enough so the police could see what it was for.'

The sun came through the window, creating a rectangle of light that covered half of Caitlin's body.

'Why are you telling me all of this?' she asked.

'Because I talked to Mr Colter. About you.'

'What did he say?'

I took my time now. I leaned back a little and folded my arms across my chest.

'What did he say?' she asked again.

'You want to see him again, right?'

She stomped her foot against the floor. 'Goddamn it! What did he say?'

'We're going to make a deal,' I said, leaning forward again. 'Are you interested in that? If you want to know what he said, you have to agree to the terms of the deal.'

'How can I agree to this if I don't know what you're offering?'

It wasn't easy, but I pushed myself off the mattress, acting as though I intended to walk out of the room.

'Okay,' she said. 'Okay, I agree. Jesus. Just tell me what's going on.'

I backtracked and sat down on the mattress again. Caitlin

watched me eagerly, expectantly. I almost couldn't bring myself to say it. I almost walked away for real. But I couldn't. I needed to finish.

'He wants to see you again,' I said.

It took me a moment to read and understand her reaction. She blinked her eyes a few times, and at first it looked to me like she was crying. Then the corners of her mouth turned up, the emotion spreading across her face – and no doubt through her body.

Joy.

Joy at the prospect of reuniting with the man she claimed to love. It was the most emotion, the most happiness she'd displayed since her return.

Caitlin raised her hand to her chest and fingered the topaz necklace just below her throat. She looked like Abby – her narrow hand, her long fingers, the way only her left cheek dimpled as her smile grew. 'Will you take me there, Dad?' she asked.

Dad.

I didn't know when she'd last called me that.

'I might take you there,' I said.

'Okay,' she said, her voice just above a whisper.

'One condition,' I said. 'First you have to tell me everything that happened during those four years you were gone. You have to tell me how he took you and where you went. You have to tell me what he did to you there. And you have to tell me why you stayed and why you want to go back so much. If you tell me all of that, I'll think about taking you there.'

'Think about?'

'Think about,' I said.

'Does Mom agree with this?' she asked.

'No way. And if you tell her or mention it to her, the whole deal's off. Not only will the deal be off, but you'll be locked up like this place is Alcatraz.'

She thought this over for a long moment. 'But if I tell her what you're offering, she'll be mad at you, right? I mean, she'll throw you out.'

'Certainly. And then you'll never get to see your boyfriend.'

'When do we go?' Caitlin asked.

'As soon as you spill it.'

She shook her head. 'I don't trust you. I know you don't want me to be with him. If I tell you, you'll never take me there.'

'You don't have a choice. Give it up.' When she didn't say anything, I opted for putting more heat on her. 'The longer we wait, the less chance you'll see him. You heard what Detective Ryan said, didn't you?'

'Some.'

'They found a witness, some mouth-breather from a trailer park who says she saw you in Colter's house. Did you ever make the acquaintance of some guy named Loren Brooks? You know him?'

She nodded. 'He came by sometimes.'

'Did he hurt you?'

'What is that bitch in the trailer saying about me?' Her face was blank, but her voice sounded capable of cutting glass.

'Enough to put Colter back in jail. They're drawing up the papers today. He's going back to jail – and soon. And given your reaction to this news, I suspect they have enough to keep him there.'

'Then what does it matter?' she asked. 'There's no deal you can make. They're going to take him away.'

With great effort, I choked out the last words I needed to say. 'He's leaving town. And he wants you to go with him.'

Chapter Forty-nine

Caitlin continued to stare at me, her lips parted. The room, the house was silent. Outside a diesel engine rumbled. A school bus moved up the street, stopping and starting, collecting neighborhood kids for school. The simple routines of everyday life. Caitlin would have been driving herself to school that year. We would have bought her a cheap car, added her to the insurance.

Instead . . .

'Are you saying . . . ?'

'You want to go with him, right?' I asked.

She nodded slowly. She brought her hands together again and started picking at them.

'Are you sure?' I asked.

'Yes. I didn't think you'd let me go.'

'You want to go. And a father is supposed to make his daughter happy, right?'

She kept picking at her fingers.

I started to get up, but Caitlin spoke.

'Parents aren't supposed to let their children go, are they?' she asked. 'Not ever?'

I settled back down on the mattress. She wasn't looking at me but continued to study her hands. Still, I could tell she was listening. 'I've known since the day you were born I'd have to let you go someday. You were going to grow up and have a life. Get married maybe. Move away. Any parent who isn't aware of that is setting themselves up for emotional hardship.'

I waited. Finally she said, 'But it happens too soon sometimes, right?'

'It does. Like me and you. Are you reconsidering?'

'No.' She looked up. 'Not at all.' She shrugged. 'What about Mom?'

'She's a big girl.'

'Will the two of you stay married?'

'No. But we aren't going to stay married whether you're here or not.' I felt relieved having said it out loud. 'Does that bother you?'

She shook her head hard, almost too hard. She looked like she wanted to make sure I knew how little it bothered her. Abby knocked lightly on the bedroom door. Caitlin and I both jumped a little. I wondered how long she'd been out there and what she'd heard, but when I opened the door for her, she didn't look angry.

'What are you two talking about?' she asked.

I looked back at Caitlin. 'I was just telling Caitlin what Detective Ryan said.'

'Oh.'

'She heard most of it from up here,' I said. 'And as for the rest . . . I guess she didn't have much of a response to it.'

Abby looked like she wanted to say something to Caitlin, but she didn't. She turned to me and said, 'Liann's here. She said she wants to talk to you.'

I was halfway through the door when Caitlin's voice stopped me.

'Thanks, Dad,' she said.

I looked back. 'For what?'

'For telling me what you told me.'

'No problem,' I said and headed downstairs to see Liann.

Abby followed me to the stairs. Halfway down, she placed her hand on my arm. 'Did you hear that back there, Tom? She called you Dad. That's something, isn't it?'

I nodded. 'Yes, it is.'

'Did you ask her about Buster?'

'I did.' I paused. Something caught in my throat. My eyes burned. 'She thought she heard him one day. His voice.' I felt the tears coming. I choked back on them, held them in. 'She said she used to think she heard our voices.'

Abby reached out to me. 'It's okay, Tom.'

'I used to imagine her screaming. Calling my name in the park. I should have been there. I should have stopped it.'

'It's not your fault, Tom.'

I pinched the bridge of my nose between my thumb and index finger. 'I thought you thought it was.'

'It's not anybody's fault.' She took my hand and squeezed it in hers. 'She's home, Tom. She's here. And they know who did this, and they're going to arrest him. We can move on. What matters is where we are now.'

'Yeah, I guess so.' My hand slipped out of hers. 'I'm going to see what Liann wants.'

'And we need to get her back into normal life soon. School, church, friends. It's time.'

'Once Colter's taken care of,' I said and continued on down the steps.

*

Liann sat at the dining room table, a cell phone to her ear. When I came in the room, she folded the phone shut and slid it into her purse.

'You look like shit,' she said.

'Thanks.'

I wanted coffee, so I went to the kitchen and poured a cup. When I sat down, Liann cleared her throat.

'The atmosphere seems a little charged in this household.'

'You haven't heard?'

She shook her head. 'I've been distracted by other things.'

I told her about Buster and his connection to Colter. Liann listened, her face cool and dispassionate. When I was finished, I asked her what she thought of it all.

'I was going to ask you the same thing,' she said.

'He's my brother . . .' I didn't know what else to say.

'They've been looking at him hard from the very beginning,' she said. 'I can assure you of that. They always look hard at the family. And as you and I both know . . .'

'Family members are likely to be involved.'

'Amen,' she said. 'It's the gospel truth ninety-eight per-cent of the time.'

'But this time? Buster? He loves Caitlin. He's crazy about her. Always has been. I've had my doubts about it, their closeness. But I think he just loves her.'

'Love's got nothing to do with it. If he's mixed up with the wrong crowd, it's his butt that's on the line. If he tells the wrong guy the wrong thing.'

The coffee tasted burnt and bitter. It needed cream and sugar. I almost pushed the mug away.

'Have you talked to him?' Liann asked.

I looked toward the stairs. No sign nor sound of Abby. 'You're my lawyer, right?' I asked.

'Sure.'

I spoke in a low voice. 'I saw him last night. In the cemetery across the street.'

Liann's body stiffened. Her shoulders went up, then settled back down. 'What was he doing there?'

'He was coming to talk to me, I guess. At the house. It was the middle of the night . . .' I couldn't tell her about the girl, Jasmine. Not yet.

'And you're not telling the police about this?'

I shook my head. 'I can't turn him in.'

'After what he did?'

'Allegedly. You always say not to trust the police. And you don't understand, Liann – my relationship with him is complicated. This goes all the way back to our childhoods.'

'They could nail you for obstruction,' she said. 'You know something, and you're not sharing it with the police.'

'It's my fault. He wanted to borrow money from us. I didn't give him the full amount, so he owed these guys something. This could have been stopped . . .'

She leaned in close to me and placed her hand on top of my forearm. 'What are you planning on doing, Tom? What's going on?'

I worked my arm loose and choked down more coffee. 'Nothing. I just want to see the guilty party behind bars.'

She placed her hand on my arm again, forcefully enough that the coffee mug shook and liquid sloshed over onto the table.

'Hey.'

'I can't protect you from everything, Tom,' she said, her teeth gritted. 'I know what your motivations are.'

'You do?'

'You want to know what happened out there, during those four years she was gone. You're less concerned with justice.'

'I'm not as noble as you, I guess.'

'You think you want to know these things. But do you? Really? Do you want to stick your nose in all that darkness? Will it make you feel better to know that whatever you imagined isn't as bad as what really happened? Because I don't think you can – even on your worst day – imagine what really went on in that house.'

I didn't look at her. I traced my finger through the spilled coffee, smearing it around on the tabletop. She stood up.

'Are you even going to ask me why I came here today?' she asked.

Once we'd started talking, I'd forgotten. 'Why are you here?' I asked.

'They found a body floating in a pond over in Mayfair County. No ID on it yet, but they think it might be Tracy Fairlawn.'

She didn't say anything else. She let the news sink in. I felt sick. Hollowed out. A bitter taste filled my mouth, but not from the coffee.

'What do you think?' I asked.

'I don't need to wait for the official ID. I know it's her. Girls like her often end up floating in ponds like that. Or hidden in the woods. Or thrown in a ditch. It's the lucky few who don't.'

Like Caitlin, she meant. *The lucky one.*

'I'm going to go sit with her mother,' she said. 'Call me if anything else changes. Like your mind.'

She left me there, still smearing the coffee around like a troubled, distracted child.

Chapter Fifty

I was still at the table when Abby came down. I refilled my mug, stared at the dark liquid, and thought of Tracy's body facedown in the cold water of some country pond.

'What did Liann want?' Abby asked.

As I told her, Abby slid into a chair, her body seeming to lose weight and almost crumple. She raised her hand to her chest, her eyes unfocused.

'He killed her,' she said. 'They'll arrest him for that, too.'

'Maybe. How do we know they can prove it? A girl like Tracy, someone with those kinds of problems.'

I could hear Liann's voice in my head: *Criminalization of the victim.* I used to judge and blame parents with wild, uncontrollable children. Now I lived with a child I couldn't control. Who was to blame?

Colter.

'I was going to go to church,' she said. 'Maybe I shouldn't . . .'

'You can go. I'm fine.'

'You're not fine.' She waited for more of a response. I didn't offer one. Our marital standoffs could be like this. Abby probing, pushing; me resisting. Caitlin came by it honestly, the ability to wall out even those who could most do well by her. 'Tom, I'm scared. He's out there. He's free. And he killed another girl. What are we doing here?'

'Waiting, I guess.'

'What if he wants to hurt Caitlin? What if he comes here . . . ?'

I shook my head. 'He won't hurt her,' I said.

'How do you know that?'

'He thinks he loves her. And she thinks she loves him.'

I felt her gaze. She studied me. 'How do you know that, Tom? Do you know something I don't know?'

I waited. I shook my head again. 'I think you should go to church today, if you want. I'll stay here with her.'

'I can take her with me —'

'No. I want Caitlin to stay here. With me.'

She studied me more; then she nodded. 'Okay. If you change your mind, let me know. I can come right home.' She squeezed my hand when she stood up.

When she'd said her good-byes and left the house, I went to the foot of the stairs and called Caitlin.

We sat across from each other at the dining room table. My chest felt buoyant, like the ballast tank on a submarine.

Caitlin didn't look at me. She held her right hand near her mouth, her teeth working on a piece of loose skin around her thumb. I didn't bother to tell her to stop. She'd never stop the chewing, the cursing, the poor hygiene habits. All the things we could have helped, the disciplinary battles we could have fought, were lost. What was left?

'What do you want to know?' Caitlin asked. A large glass of water sat in front of her, and she took a drink.

'I want to know what happened in the park that day. I want to know how he got you to go with him.'

Her brow wrinkled as though she were thinking hard.

Four years. I'd assumed the facts would be right at her command.

'I was walking Frosty,' she said. 'He wasn't very good on a leash, you know. He used to tug and strain and make that weird hacking noise because the collar choked him. You know what I'm talking about?'

I did.

'Really, I was too small to be walking him. He wasn't trained well enough. So he was pulling me along and pulling me along, and I was holding on as best I could, but the leash started digging into my hands, deep into my hands. My fingers were all smashed together, the knuckles rubbed against one another. It hurt, really hurt. I tried to shift the leash from one hand to the other so it wouldn't hurt so much, but when I tried, Frosty took off. He just bolted through the park, toward the cemetery. He was gone, just gone.' She gave a pained, almost wistful smile at the memory. 'Anyway,' she said, 'I freaked out. I was scared. If something happened to him, I knew I'd be in trouble, and I knew you'd never let me walk him in the park again.'

'That would have been your mom's reaction,' I said.

'Whatever. I ran after him as fast as I could, but by the time I got to the cemetery, he was gone. I couldn't see him anywhere. I looked around. I called his name. Nothing. He was gone. I started to cry. I didn't like to cry – I thought I was too old for that, but I couldn't help it. I felt the tears burning my eyes, and I knew I was losing it.'

She stopped. I wished I could get a tape recorder, something to preserve her voice.

'I guess I was about to run home, to run back to you and Mom and tell you what happened, when a van pulled up beside me. A white van. The man rolled down his window and asked me what was wrong. I told him. He said if I wanted to hop in he'd drive me around a little and help me look for Frosty.' She took a drink of water, her throat bobbing as she swallowed. 'I knew I wasn't supposed to get in a car with someone I didn't know. I knew all that. You and Mom taught me all of that.'

She didn't go on, so I filled the gap. 'Why did you get in with him?'

'I didn't.'

'Then how . . . ?'

'I walked away. I turned around and started back for the house. And the guy in the van called after me – he kept saying he would help me. So I started to walk faster, and that's when John came up beside me. He was walking his own dog, and he'd heard what the guy in the van said to me. He came up beside me and told me I should just ignore that guy, and if I wanted help finding my dog, he'd walk around with me, with his dog on the leash, and he said he bet we'd find him. "He couldn't have gone far," he said. "Not with that leash around his neck." He seemed nice and safe, at least compared to the other guy. He seemed like a nerd, really.' She smiled. 'So we started walking around the park with his dog, looking for Frosty. I don't know what happened to the guy in the van. He drove off, I guess. Who knows what he wanted. I guess we'll never find out. The world's probably full of guys like that.'

She took another drink of water.

'So how did you end up going off with him?' I asked.

'We looked and looked for Frosty. We went around the

walking track in the park and up and down the rows in the cemetery. I was still crying a little, and John tried to talk to me and make me feel better.'

John. She called him John.

'I started to realize it was getting late, that you and Mom were going to worry about me if I didn't come home. I knew I'd have to go back and probably get in trouble over Frosty being gone. I told John I needed to go back to my parents. He offered me a ride in his car. He said he could drive me, and while we drove back we could look for Frosty some more. He said maybe Frosty just turned and headed for home, that dogs do that sometimes. They just follow their instincts.' She paused. 'I didn't know what to do. I was upset and scared, and John really did seem nice. He did.'

'We wouldn't have been mad at you.'

'Mom would have. And you would have too. You always act like you don't get angry about those things, but you do. Maybe you don't even know you do it, but you get this look on your face. This disapproval. It's there. I know it.' She looked at me, waiting for me to defend myself, I suppose. When I didn't, she went on. 'So I walked with him back to his car and got in. The car wasn't anything special, just an old Toyota. And it didn't feel that strange getting in and driving off.' She paused and held up her index finger. 'Wait. It did feel strange. It felt different, I guess, and that's really why I wanted to do it.'

'Different how?'

'Different like I wasn't supposed to do it, but it still felt safe doing it. I felt a little excited, even though I was scared and worried about Frosty. It just seemed like the most unexpected thing I could do – get in a car with a strange man, even though he was just promising to help me look for my dog and take me home to my parents.'

'But you didn't come home.'

'No.'

'Where did you go?' I asked.

'We went to his house.'

'How did that happen?'

'We looked for Frosty and drove back this way. We drove right past the house in fact.'

If only I'd been outside. If only I'd been watching for her.

If only.

'After we'd driven around looking for a while, he said I should go back to his house with him and clean my face off. He told me I didn't want to see my parents that way, that if I cleaned up and looked grown up, it wouldn't seem as bad as I thought it would be. I really think if I asked him, he would have just pulled into the driveway here and dropped me off. I don't think he was intending to force me to do anything I didn't want to do. I was in control of which way things went, and I liked that feeling. So I said to myself, "What the hell. Let's see what else happens." And I told him I'd go back to his house with him.'

'You know you weren't in control, right? You never were.'

But she had stopped. There was a finality to the way she broke off. She stood up and went to the sink for more water. She drank it down, then refilled and drank some more. She kept her back to me, acting as though I weren't in the room.

'But you had seen him before? Colter? Right?'

She turned around. 'Why do you say that?'

'In your coat, the coat you wore the day before you disappeared, there was a flower in the pocket. A red flower. It was right before Valentine's Day, and you kept that flower in your pocket like someone gave it to you.'

She swallowed but didn't answer.

'You know, it's not going to matter now,' I said. 'It's not going to change anything. I just want to know – did he give you the flower?'

'Yeah, he did.' She drank from the glass. I didn't say anything because I could tell there was more to say. 'I saw him at the park. I talked to him a few times.'

'How many times?'

'I don't know.'

'How many?' I said, tapping the table with my index finger.

She gave an exaggerated, exasperated shrug. 'Five or six?'

'A strange man, a grown man, spoke to you in the park five or six times and you didn't tell us?'

'Why should I have?'

'Because we are your parents. We are supposed to protect you from those things.'

'Well, you didn't, did you? You didn't.'

'Did he give you that necklace then? Before he took you?'

'No,' she said. She fingered the necklace. 'He gave this to me one year later. It's a token of what we mean to each other. As long as I wear it —'

'No, no,' I said. 'If you'd told us when you saw him in

the park —' I stopped. My anger and my voice rose. *If, if, if . . .* If I'd seen them drive by the house. If I hadn't let her walk the dog. If I hadn't allowed us to live with such an undisciplined pet. *If, if, if . . .* 'What made you stay?' I asked. 'Why, after all that, did you stay? People saw you with him in public places. You could have screamed and cried. You could have run away. Why did you stay with him? Why did you do that . . . ?' I resisted for a long moment. I tried to swallow it back, but finally I couldn't hold it in. 'Why did you do that to me, Caitlin? Why?'

She shook her head. 'To you?'

'Yes. Why?'

She looked at the glass and set it aside. 'No,' she said.

'No? What do you mean?'

'No, I'm not telling you anything else until you take me to see John.' She pursed her lips and set her jaw. 'I just gave you a down payment. I gave you something.'

'You just started. That's only the beginning.'

'What else do you want to know?' she asked. 'Do you want to know everything? Every detail?'

'Tell me that he made you stay,' I said.

'Take me to him. Or just stand aside and I'll go there myself.'

'But he did make you stay, right?' I asked. 'He held you there. He forced you.'

'I can't tell you something that isn't true.'

I pounded my fist against the table, rattling my mug.

'He made you stay. I know it. You wouldn't have imagined our voices if you didn't want to leave. Right, Caitlin? You wouldn't have imagined you heard us, would you?'

'What makes you think I imagined them?'

'Because I didn't know where you were. None of us did.'

'I don't know that. I don't.'

I stood up, almost knocking the chair over. I shoved it out of the way and moved toward her. 'No, honey, that would never happen. Never, ever. Never.'

She cringed. Her body locked when I approached, and she took two steps back. She held her hands out in front of me as though she wanted to shove me away. 'Just take me to him,' she said. 'We made a deal. Take me to John if you want to know anything else from me.'

She left the room before I could say anything.

Chapter Fifty-one

I pulled the phone book out and looked up the number. It took two tries for me to find the right one. An older woman answered, and I asked for John. A long pause followed, a staticky stretch of dead air. 'Why can't you all leave him alone?' his mother asked.

'I'm not a reporter,' I said. Another long pause. 'I'm the man who was at your house last night talking to John.'

'Oh, I see.' She sniffed. 'Are you really that girl's father?'

'I am.'

'Well ... Johnny ... he's always loved children. I mean ... he wouldn't really hurt anybody. He wouldn't. Not intentionally. Now did you ever think these girls — they ask for it, don't they? They wear certain clothes. Even the young ones ...'

'Just put him on.'

She breathed a deep sigh into the phone, then the receiver clunked against either the counter or the floor. 'Johnny?'

Someone picked up the phone; then I heard voices arguing. I couldn't make it all out, but Colter's mother said, 'I can't have you in trouble again. My house, Johnny.'

'Get out of here,' he said. He must have waited while she left the room, because it took a few more moments for him to come on the line and speak to me. 'Mr Stuart?'

His voice caused a shiver of revulsion to pass through my body.

'It's me,' I said.

'I'm glad you called. I knew you would, though.'

The phone felt warm against my ear. 'You're awfully confident.'

'Don't we both have things the other wants? Don't we have a . . . what you might call a symbiotic relationship?'

'Symbiotic?'

'It means that we mutually benefit.'

'I know what it means.'

'Hell, we're practically family. So what's your answer?'

'I spoke to Caitlin today.' I swallowed hard. 'She's game, and I am too. So . . .'

'You're agreeing to bring her to me?'

I hesitated. I wanted to know. I simply wanted to know. 'Yes,' I said.

'Okay,' he said. 'Okay.' What he meant was: *Now we're in business.* I heard a door close on his end of the line, and he must have moved into another room or outside the house for privacy's sake. When the movement stopped, he said, 'Okay, how are we going to do this?'

'Start talking.'

'I got a call from my lawyer this morning. Apparently, they have a new witness and new information about the case. He told me to expect an arrest and a new indictment any day now. For all I know, they'll be showing up today to put me in chains. What I'm saying is, if we're going to do this, we don't have much time to make it happen.'

'Maybe I should just let it all go then. You can go on to jail, and Caitlin would never have to face you in court.'

'I told you – I'm leaving no matter what. And if you don't ante up, you'll never know what you want to know.'

'I know some things. Caitlin told me a few of them just today. Hell, maybe I know enough already.'

I walked through the house to the living room and stopped, staring out at the front yard. The trees were almost bare, the leaves carpeting the ground or else piled at the curb by my industrious neighbors. The clouds hung low, seemingly just above the treetops. They were as gray as cold ashes.

Colter hesitated. 'What could she have told you?' he asked.

'She told me plenty. How you got her in the car, looking for the dog. She told me how you got her back to the house. Your dumpy little house.' As I talked and looked into the yard, I pictured that day. The car circling the park, then leaving with Caitlin inside. I pictured it driving right past our house, Caitlin in the front seat perhaps, staring out the window as she went by here for the last time. 'I can go to the police with that, tell them what Caitlin told me. I can add to what they already have.'

'Hearsay.'

'How did you get her to stay in your house?' I asked. 'How did you keep her there?'

He ignored my questions. 'No one will believe you. After you told the cops about seeing ghosts and all that bullshit, you have no credibility.'

'The parent of a crime victim always has credibility. Now tell me – how did you keep her there in your house?'

'I want to see her before I tell you anything. That was the deal I offered.'

I turned away from the window. 'If you want to see her, you have to give me something. You have to tell me some facts.'

'Why should I deal with you?' He lowered his voice, added a hint of menace to it. 'You want this more than I do. You're obsessed with knowing. I can hear it. You know, Caitlin told me some things about you. She told me about your stepdaddy. How he didn't love you. How he used to come in your room and scare you, like you were a little baby.'

'Caitlin didn't know that.'

'Somebody told her about it. Somebody in your family.'

'Do you know my brother?' I asked. 'You saw him at your house. Do you know him?'

'That's the angle the cops are working, right? That your brother put me onto Caitlin's trail?'

'Do you know him?'

'Let's just say I've crossed paths with a lot of people in my time. It's possible your brother was one of them.'

'Caitlin says she heard his voice there, in your house.'

'He might have been there. Like I said, I can't keep track of everything that happened in four years. And someone in Caitlin's situation – living in a strange house, away from everything that used to be familiar – she might imagine some things. It might even be that a guy like me might help her along in that direction.'

'What do you mean?'

'Did she say she thought she heard your voice?' he said, his voice almost jovial.

'She did.'

'It's not hard to convince a confused kid that certain things might be true. Like her parents don't want her back. That they came to the house and said it was okay if she stayed with me. Forever.'

375

My throat burned. 'No. No, you didn't.'

'How are we going to make this trade?'

'Is that how you kept her there? You filled her head with lies? Tell me if you want to see her. Did you lock her up? Did you force her?'

He let out a low chuckle. 'You wish I did lock her up, don't you? That's what you want me to say, isn't it?'

'I want you to tell me what happened. What really happened.'

'And then?'

'And then we'll make the switch.'

I heard his breathing through the line. My heart rate slowed. I sat on the couch, letting myself sink deep into the cushions.

'I didn't really have to lock her up,' he said. 'Not really.'

'What does that mean?'

'She stayed at first because . . . I don't know . . . I think she thought it was a game. Something different. Something new. Do you remember what it was like to be a kid? Everybody telling you what to do. Your life is never your own. You're always under somebody's thumb. Hell, I'm living with my mom now. It doesn't change.'

'You said, "Not really." You didn't really have to lock her up. But that implies you did something to keep her there. What was it?'

'Okay, okay. I guess she . . . got nervous . . . at the end of the first day, and she started asking if she could go back. Back to your house. Look, I knew at that point I was in trouble, you know? A guy like me can't just keep a twelve-year-old girl at his house all day and not expect repercussions. I knew the cops would be coming down on

376

me. I know how trouble falls in these situations, and who it falls on. And the cops never understand a deal like this. They don't see that two people like me and Caitlin can have something special. They want to call it a crime, make an issue out of it. It's not really that complicated when you get right down to it. It's love.'

'What did you do?'

'What could I do?' He sounded truly perplexed. 'I tried to talk to her, you know, reason with her. She seemed like a smart kid. I just asked her to stay. I told her that she could go home whenever she wanted the next day, but at that moment she needed to stay at my house. I even offered to help her look for the dog again in the morning before I took her back home. She didn't say anything for a long time. She looked blank. You know, she does that sometimes, just gives that blank look so that you're not even certain if she's heard you or not. Do you know what I'm talking about?'

I reluctantly agreed. 'I'm familiar with the look.'

'So she did that, just that blank look for a long time – minutes. I swear she could totally wear me down just by doing that. But eventually she said, "I prefer not to." It was so long, I didn't know what she was saying no to. Was she saying she preferred to stay with me, or was she saying she preferred to go home? So I asked her, and she said she preferred not to stay with me, that she preferred to go home. What am I supposed to do then, right? Like I said, I'm in too deep as it is. So I did the only thing I could do.'

My throat felt raw, scratchy. 'What was that?'

'I locked her in my basement. I took her by the arm – not too rough, because she really didn't resist or fight against me – but I took her by the arm and I led her to the basement door. I got her down the stairs. I put her in the room, and I told her there was no way out and no way anyone could hear her if she yelled and screamed.'

'And you knew that because you'd done it before?'

'There were other relationships, yes.'

'Tracy Fairlawn? You know what happened to her, right?'

'My lawyer may have mentioned something about that, but she was a girl with a lot of problems.'

'Like the child she leaves behind. Your child.'

He laughed again, a low huffing sound. 'You know, it seemed like – To be perfectly honest, it seemed like running into Caitlin in the park that day, with her dog lost and me right there, it seemed like destiny of some kind. Like we were meant to meet on that day and end up together.' Colter laughed some more. 'Hell, for all I know, you're taping this conversation, hoping to use it against me sometime. Is that what you're doing? Taping this? Look, you can't put a label on destiny. You can't explain it all away or call it names. However it happened, even if there was a little resistance at first, it was meant to be. It's that simple, isn't it? And if you just let me see her again, let me see the girl, you can know it all. For real. And she can be happy again. Let me guess what's going on over there – she's barely speaking to you. She's moping around, doing that stone-faced routine. I knew she'd be doing that. It's classic Caitlin behavior.'

'Don't. Don't act like you know her better than me.'

'I do. I've spent the last four years with her. Where can we meet?' he asked. 'We can all have what we want. Where can we meet?'

'Why did you let her go?' I asked. 'If you were so happy,

why did you make her leave? And why did you burn your house down after she was gone? What were you hiding?'

'You can't come here because of my mother. And who knows, the cops may be watching me. But I can get out for a little while. Later in the day. Where can I meet you both? You and Caitlin?'

I felt like he'd tied me to a leash and was walking me around the block. He was right. I wanted to know too much. And I needed to dial back, to pull away. I felt like a man tottering on a ledge. I could only windmill my arms for so long before I fell.

'Can I come to your house?' he asked.

'No. My wife . . .' I hesitated again. 'I think it would be best if we just —'

'Where then?' Colter asked, pushing.

I held the phone tight, felt the pressure in my knuckles. *You just want to know*, I told myself. *You just want to know. You don't have to give her away, but you do have to find out.*

The meeting spot was so obvious, I shouldn't have even needed to say it out loud.

'Why don't we go back to the beginning,' I said. 'I'll meet you in the park, on the cemetery side.'

'When?'

'How soon can you be there?' I asked.

He paused, no doubt calculating in his head.

'An hour after sunset,' he said. 'I have things to get together, and the park will be quiet and empty by then.'

'An hour after sunset.'

'And you'll have Caitlin with you?'

'It doesn't look like I have much choice, does it?'

Chapter Fifty-two

I went up the stairs. Caitlin had left the bedroom door open. She was sitting on the floor again, staring into space.

'Let me ask you something,' I said from the doorway.

'What?'

'Did you really believe your mom and I wouldn't look for you or want you back?'

She nodded, but her face was lacking some of its defiance, its certainty.

I pushed. 'Really?'

'Yes.'

'And how long —?'

I stopped myself. I'd wanted to ask her: *How long would it be before that feeling of rejection and abandonment went away?* But I already knew the answer: *Never.* It simply never would. We all would be living with it forever. And I was willing to accept that burden, to share it with my daughter, if only I knew what had really happened.

'You might want to pack a small bag,' I said. 'We're going to meet John Colter tonight. And we need to leave before your mom gets home.'

Caitlin didn't move. Her eyes were narrowed, her face suspicious.

'Well?' I asked. 'I thought this was what you wanted.'

My words released her from whatever spell she'd been

under. She jumped to her feet, and I left the room, leaving her to her packing.

My phone rang while I was waiting for Caitlin. It was Abby. I let it go to voice mail.

'Caitlin, hurry up!'

In a few minutes, Caitlin came down the stairs carrying a plastic grocery bag full of clothes. She wore the same jeans and sweatshirt combination she'd been wearing since she'd arrived, but something was different about her face. She was wearing makeup – presumably some of Abby's – and her hair appeared to have been brushed and styled, despite its short length.

'We've got to go,' I said. The phone rang again as we went out to the car.

'I wish there was time to take a shower,' she said. 'Is there?'

'No. I don't want to stay here any longer.'

We got into the car and Caitlin threw her bag of clothes onto the floor. I backed down the driveway. Quickly – too quickly. The car veered off into the grass. I stopped, pulled forward and corrected, then backed out again. We made it into the street, and as I swung the wheel around to go forward, another car approached.

'It's your mom.'

'So?'

'She knows something, that something's going on.'

Abby pulled alongside. She waved her arms back and forth, almost frantic.

I inched forward.

Abby threw open her door and stepped out into the street. 'Tom! Stop!'

I rolled down the window a little. 'We're just going out. It's okay.'

'Buster called,' she said. 'He told me what you're doing.' She reached for my door handle and started tugging. 'He acts more concerned for your daughter than you do.'

'Let go, Abby. Let go.'

She banged on the window twice, then reached for the rear door. I didn't give her a chance to get to it. I hit the gas and pulled away. I looked back only once. She stood in the middle of our street, her hands raised to her head. I looked over at Caitlin, whose eyes were straight ahead, looking toward what was to come.

There were a few hours to pass before the sun went down. We drove around aimlessly for a while, crisscrossing town, passing through the campus and then out by the mall and the strip of chain restaurants. While we moved, I thought about what Abby had said at the house. *Buster called. He told me what you're doing.* Would she call Ryan and tell him?

Without a doubt.

'Where are we going?' Caitlin asked.

'It's too early. We need to pass some time.'

'Where are we going to do that?'

I cut through the center of town, dangerously close to the police station. I didn't say anything, but I looked over at Caitlin as we approached. Her eyes widened a little. She understood.

'The dog pound?'

'Remember when we used to go there?'

She nodded.

I parked in the back so the car would be out of sight of the street.

We didn't get out right away.

'What?' Caitlin asked.

'You know, I tried to get Frosty back after I brought him here. Your uncle Buster drove me here one day.'

'What happened?'

'He was gone. Somebody had already adopted him. I tried to get their name so I could go get him. I would have paid them for him, but the shelter doesn't give out that information.'

'Oh.'

'It's probably someone in town who has him,' I said, trying to be reassuring. 'Somebody who likes dogs.'

'I don't want to talk about Frosty anymore.'

'Do you want to go in?' I asked. 'They might let us walk one.'

She nodded.

'Did you . . . ? You said Colter was walking a dog when he picked you up at the park that day. So you had a dog where you were?'

She shook her head. 'It wasn't his,' she said. 'It was his mom's. And they put it to sleep after a couple of years. It was old.'

'He started the whole thing with a lie,' I said. 'You see what he —'

'Dad,' she said. She sounded tired. And maybe she was – of me, no doubt. 'What does any of it matter now? You know?'

I didn't say so, but silently I agreed. We got out of the car and went inside.

Caitlin found a midsized mutt, something that looked like a cross between a collie and a poodle, and after getting a few minutes of instruction from a volunteer, we took it for a walk. For a shelter animal, the dog did surprisingly well on a leash. It must have lived in a home where it had received some training at one time. It didn't resist the leash or work against it. Rather, it accepted the tie and walked by Caitlin's side.

While Caitlin talked to the dog, I looked over my shoulder, expecting at any moment to be surrounded by police cars. After about twenty minutes of strolling, we brought the dog back to the shelter. The volunteer smiled at us.

'Well, this looks like a perfect fit,' she said. 'Will we be making an adoption today?'

I looked at Caitlin expectantly. I would have given her whatever she wanted.

But she shook her head. 'No, thanks,' she said. 'I'm just about to move.'

Chapter Fifty-three

We made one more stop before driving to the cemetery. The sun had slipped away, a red band of sky spreading just above the treetops. The air was considerably cooler, and the wind increased. Huge flocks of black birds moved across the sky, migrating.

I drove behind the grocery store to an area near its loading dock. No one was back there after hours, and when I dropped the car into park, Caitlin looked over at me.

'Why are we here?'

'I need to ask you something. I'll only ask one more time. Are you sure you want to do this?'

She didn't blink or hesitate. 'I'm sure.'

'Nothing will be the same if we go there and do this,' I said.

'I know. That's what I want,' she said. And then, after a pause, she added, 'Is anything the same anyway?'

'No,' I said. 'But sometimes there are chances to turn back and sometimes there aren't. I think we're at a point where it's going to be hard to turn back.'

She took a deep breath. It almost looked like she shuddered.

'I'm ready,' she said.

I'd been thinking about the setup of the event all morning, the logistical aspects of making what was supposed to be a trade. All I had to do was bring Caitlin to Colter, let them see each other, and I would be able to extract the information I wanted. The difficult part would be pulling back at the right moment, making sure Caitlin left with me and not with him.

'I want you to get in the backseat,' I said.

'Why?'

'How do I know you won't just run when you see him?' I asked. 'If you're in the back, I can have some measure of —'

'Control?' she said.

'Certainty,' I said. 'Certainty that you won't just run.'

'I won't run away. I promise. Do you believe me? I won't run away. I'll do what you want.'

And I did believe her. Her eyes were clear, her voice level.

'Okay,' I said. 'But I do want you to get in the backseat. And stay down.'

She didn't argue further, and she didn't even bother to get out of the car. Like a little kid, she wormed her body over the front seat and into the back. She landed with a light thud.

'Okay?' she said. 'Happy?'

I made sure the child locks were activated.

I knew Caitlin was behind me. I sensed her. But I felt alone in the dark. Very alone. The wind picked up again, scuffling leaves across the parking lot, and I shivered.

No turning back.

I drove to the cemetery.

Chapter Fifty-four

I thought of the first time I ever drove Caitlin, when she was a newborn and we brought her home from the hospital. I drove slower than slow, sensing disaster at every stoplight, in every other car on the road. New-parent syndrome. I outgrew it, let go of the fears and anxieties, let her grow up, fall down, and make her own mistakes.

At some point, she'd have to be let go again. But not then, not yet.

I reached the narrow road that divided the cemetery from the park and turned. The park was closing. The tennis courts and ball fields were empty and dark, and any day now the grounds crews and workers would begin preparing them for winter, rolling up the nets, covering the dirt infield. I flashed back to that day months ago, back when I walked Frosty here while the weather was still warm and Caitlin was gone, her memory preserved by the headstone in the ground. And I thought of Jasmine, the girl who'd looked so much like Caitlin at the time. The one who *was* Caitlin, as far as I was concerned. She seemed so much younger than the girl in the back of my car. Younger and more carefree, an innocent who could still run and laugh and move with the buoyant happiness of a spirit. Where was that girl tonight?

To my left, the cemetery sat in darkness. I could see the outlines of the heavy monuments and stones, the vigilant angels on top of markers and mausoleums who stood watch through the night, indifferent to the cold and the human drama in my car. As I moved farther down the road, my eyes adjusted to the light and I was able to make out the shape of a car sitting at the back corner of the park. It didn't have its lights on, and in the darkness I couldn't yet see if there was a person inside. It could have been Colter, but just as likely it could have been groping, fumbling teenagers, steaming the windows while their clueless parents ate dinner and watched the news. I pulled behind it, my headlights illuminating its rear and the license plate. It appeared to be empty.

The car looked enormous and old. It was an elderly person's car, an Oldsmobile 88 or something like that, the kind of thing an elderly lady would keep in her garage and drive on special occasions.

'It's him,' Caitlin whispered. 'John.'

'You're staying in the car, remember?' I said. 'Just wait a little while longer. For me.'

She didn't answer, nor did she move.

I stepped out onto the road and gently closed my door. I looked around, scanning the landscape for a figure. A late, straggling jogger went by on the track, huffing in the dark. The band of red in the sky was almost gone above the trees, and a sliver of moon rose to the east.

It took a moment for my eyes to adjust, but in the distance, off in the direction of Caitlin's 'grave', I saw someone. I knew it was Colter before I went over. His thick, squat body and large head made a distinctive shape in the twilight. He stood at the grave with his head bowed, an almost reverent pose, and his hands were folded in front of him. Even though it took me a full minute to walk over to him, my shoes crunching through the leaves, he didn't look up as I approached. But he did speak.

'You were right to do this,' he said, still staring at the ground.

'You mean to come here tonight?'

'That too.' He looked up and gestured toward the stone. It was still there, tipped over and flat on the ground. 'But I meant this. The stone. You were right to do this. To bury the past. This girl doesn't exist anymore. She really is gone. She disappeared that day I picked her up.'

'You destroyed her.'

'No, no. I released her. I freed her from the chains you had put on her – we all had put on her, in this society we live in. It restricts, it binds. I gave Caitlin freedom.'

'By raping her? By locking her in a basement?'

Colter turned toward me, raising his index finger. 'No, no. Never that. Never.'

'How did it happen then? How did you have sex with her?'

'What makes you think I did?'

'She's not a virgin. The doctor checked her out when she came back. She was a virgin when she left our house that day.'

'Was she?'

My fists clenched. I wanted to strike out.

'Don't say those things,' I said.

'But really – do you know that? Do you?'

'I know my daughter.'

'You thought you did. You thought she wouldn't leave. You thought she wouldn't get in the car with a strange

389

man. You thought a lot of things. Wrong things. Why did your brother come looking for her?'

A light mist started to fall, speckling against my face. Caitlin said she thought she'd heard Buster's voice in the house. Buster knew Brooks, who knew Colter . . .

'What are you talking about?' I said.

'Your brother, William. I know that was him at my mom's house, hiding in the dark, right?'

I didn't answer, so Colter went on.

'He came to my house once. He said he knew I liked little girls, and his niece was missing. He'd heard rumors, talk from the lowlifes I associated with. So he showed up on his white horse, Sir Galahad style. He was going to get the girl back, be a hero and save the day.'

'What happened?'

'I told him if he hassled me again, I'd call the police, tell them what I knew about him. Hell, I'd make stuff up if I had to. Or maybe I'd just tell Brooks to call in the debt.' He shrugged, casual as the falling rain. 'Now why did he show up at my door and you didn't? Why the special interest from the uncle and not from the father?'

'We looked. We looked and looked. We never gave up.'

He raised the finger again. 'I'm sure you did. But I made sure Caitlin heard my chat with William. I made sure she knew *only* her uncle came to the house to find her. As far as she was concerned, her parents had given her up for dead. She felt rejected by you. When I told her you weren't looking for her anymore, she felt like she didn't have a family. *I* became her family. Hell, I became her everything. Rejection is a powerful motivator, as I'm sure you know.'

My hands were still in fists and my anger swelled. But I

didn't know where to direct it. This man before me? Brooks? Buster?

For his part, Colter didn't seem to care. He craned his neck, looking behind me.

'Where's the girl? Did you bring her? We had a deal.'

'She's in the car.'

'And she didn't run out here?' Colter lowered his eyes to mine. 'Did you lock her in there? You see, that's the problem. You're holding her back from what she wants.'

'Where would you go with her?' I asked. 'What do you think is going to happen here?'

But Colter didn't answer. Once again, his eyes looked behind me, back toward the road and the car where Caitlin was waiting.

I turned, expecting to see Caitlin coming, but then I saw what Colter saw.

Headlights, coming down the road. Another car approaching mine.

'What did you do?' he asked.

'They're probably just turning around,' I said. But the car stopped right behind mine.

'Is that a cop? Did you screw me?' He started moving back into the dark.

Someone climbed out of the car and looked toward us. I recognized the figure before he said anything. I had run into him out in the cemetery before.

'It's my brother,' I said. 'It's Buster.'

Chapter Fifty-five

I walked over to the cars and approached Buster, leaving Colter behind in the dark. 'What are you doing here?' I asked.

'Looking for you. I drove all over town looking. I figured you might end up here eventually.'

'You're not needed – or wanted. Leave me alone.'

'Where is she? Where's Caitlin?' He looked into the car, squinting in the dark. 'Tom? What did you do? Did you hand her off to him already?'

'She's in there, okay?'

Caitlin must have heard our voices. She leaned closer to the glass, allowing us to see her. But she didn't make a move to come out.

Buster looked horrified. 'Tom, just get in the car and take her home.'

'She's my leverage. She's safe in the car because I can't have her running off before I get what I need.'

'That's cold, Tom. Cold. Jesus – referring to your daughter as leverage.'

'Did you call the police like you called Abby?'

'We're family, Tom. All of us. We protect each other. I did what I thought was right.'

'Family. Why did you do it, Buster? Why? You gave her away, like a piece of meat. Why? You went to that house. She was there. She heard your voice.'

He made a hurried shushing gesture by bringing his finger to his lips. He pointed at the car.

'I don't care,' I said.

'Come on,' he said. 'Over here.'

'No.'

'I want to explain.'

We stepped away from the cars, far enough so Caitlin couldn't hear us.

'What did the police tell you?' Buster asked.

'Enough. That you owed a guy money for drugs. And he knew Colter. So —'

'I didn't *give* Caitlin to anyone. I couldn't. But I did . . . I was messed up. You remember. I owed him money.'

'Colter?'

'Brooks. He was all over me. I was scared. I thought I might just leave town, never come back.'

'You should have.'

He looked hurt, but he went on. 'I talked about Caitlin. I talked about her all the time. She's my niece. You have to understand – I felt like she was more than that. Like she was mine. My kid.' He threw his hands up a little. A hopeless shrug. 'I'm never going to have any of my own. You can feel that way about a niece or nephew. Even if they're not your own, you can feel like they belong to you in some way. There's a bond there that goes beyond blood or family or who gave birth to who. Right?'

'I'll have to take your word for that one.'

'Like me and you, Tom. Am I your brother or your half brother? Does it matter what it's called? Look – okay, so you wanted me to admit that my old man used to get after us and beat us, and I wouldn't before. I was a dick, I know.

393

Well, I'll admit it now, right here. He used to beat us and terrorize us when he drank. And he used to come down on you most of all, probably because you weren't really his kid. You see – I said it, Tom. I said it. You were right about my dad and all of that.'

'Thank you.'

'It's the truth. But something else is the truth, too. I used to protect you, Tom. I used to put my body over yours. I tried to get in between you and him. I know you remember that, too. See, that's what I'm talking about. There's a bond there, one that can't be broken by some circumstances.'

'Go on,' I said. 'What about Colter and Brooks?'

'When she disappeared, I thought of those guys. Maybe I had talked about her too much around them.'

'So you knew Colter?'

'I knew of him at the time. He didn't know me. I thought of going to the police, but what did I know? Really? That I knew a guy who might know a guy who might have taken my niece?'

'You tell them anything you know.'

'Like you told them about me after last night? I know they came to you asking about me. Did you cover for me? Did you protect me?'

'I shouldn't have.'

'Did you tell them about the girl we saw here in the cemetery? That little girl.'

'Why didn't you say anything about this?'

'I had a record. They busted me for being naked by a school. And the drugs. What were they going to do with me?' He shrugged again and walked in a small circle.

394

I looked over to the cemetery and saw Colter's figure in the dark. Listening. Waiting.

Buster came back to me and stood even closer. 'I decided to check it out myself. I asked Brooks about it, if he knew about Colter and the little girls. He said Colter was a creep and a pervert, but he didn't think he had anyone in the house. He'd been in there a few times. He hadn't seen anything, or so he said.'

'Caitlin says she heard your voice in Colter's house.'

Buster shook his head. 'No, no. Never. I didn't know where he lived. Brooks put me off. He said he dealt with unpleasant people, but he didn't know anything about Caitlin. Tom, if I had gone there, if I had been in that house, I would have turned it upside down. I wouldn't have left without Caitlin. Never.'

His words rang true to me. Despite Colter's story, I believed my brother. I believed him.

'Why didn't you tell the police I'm meeting Colter here tonight? You could have stopped all of this.'

'The cops are looking for me now because of what Brooks's girlfriend told them. I can't make contact with them. They want to lock me up. And I wanted to come find you. And help you. After last night, with the fight and everything, I wanted to be the one to help you see this from a different angle. You're not seeing it clearly yet, okay? But you still can. You can just get back in the car and drive her home. That's all you have to do.'

'It's that easy?'

'It really is.'

'What about the rest of our lives?'

'I don't know . . .'

'You see, something happened in that house, in that basement room. Something happened that transformed my daughter and transformed my life. I need to know what it was. If it was able to so profoundly, so completely turn me off the course of my life, I need to know about it. All about it.'

'You can't.'

'Why not?'

'Because ... it's gone. And you weren't there. And whatever it is or was ... it's not really relevant to your life now. It's not going to change the past.'

'What will?' I asked.

And I meant it. What would wipe the past away, clean the slate?

Buster pointed to the car.

'You know what to do.'

I moved to the back of the car and took out my keys.

Chapter Fifty-six

Before I could reach the car, the driver's door came open. Caitlin looked scared, disoriented, in the faint glow from the dome light. She must have slid back over the seat into the front and opened the lock. She came out into the night, looking back and forth between Buster and me.

'Where's John?' she said. 'Is he here?'

I nodded toward the cemetery. 'He's here,' I said, but I put my hand on Caitlin's arm.

'Let me go.'

'We're leaving, Caitlin.'

I held on to her and released the door locks with my fob. I maneuvered her toward the backseat of the car again.

'You promised,' she said.

I pulled the back door open and had her halfway in when Colter came running up.

'Hey!' he said.

'John! John!'

I kept my body between the two of them, felt myself wedged and pressed between their grasping forms. Caitlin cried out for him, a plaintive wailing, and I felt Colter's hot breath on the back of my neck, smelled the onions he had eaten for his dinner.

Then the pressure against my back eased. Colter fell to the ground and Buster stood over him. Then Buster dropped to his knees by Colter's side, his fist going up and down like a piston while Colter squirmed beneath the blows.

'Enough,' I said. 'Enough.'

I let go of Caitlin long enough to grab Buster's arm, to stop his pummeling of Colter. When I had him pulled back and under control, I looked down.

Colter was still there, his face bloodied. Caitlin slipped past me and went to the ground, cradling his face in her hands.

'Oh, John,' she said. 'John, did he hurt you?'

But Colter didn't take his eyes off mine. He even smiled a little, his teeth stained with blood.

'Satisfied?' he said. 'Is it over now?'

Caitlin's eyes were full of tears, and she sniffled in the dark, her hand now resting on Colter's arm.

I bent down a little, wrapped my hand around her wrist, and pulled her up.

'She's coming with me.'

Caitlin gasped a little, but she didn't resist as much as I'd thought she would.

'We had a deal,' Colter said. 'A fucking deal.'

I pulled Caitlin toward the car, not looking back. I knew Buster was behind me, watching the rear, not letting Colter up off the ground.

'Let me go!' she said, pulling against me. But I kept my grip – loose enough not to hurt, tight enough that she couldn't get away. I never should have brought her, I thought. I never should have exposed her to Colter again. It was over. We were going home.

'No,' I said. 'You're coming with me.'

The wailing began again, but this time it was more distant, more sustained.

I looked out to the main road. The blue and red lights strobed, approached the cemetery, and turned in. I looked at Buster, and he shrugged.

'Abby?' I said. 'She called them?'

He shrugged again.

Colter pushed himself to his feet. The police cars were coming toward us, blocking the way for our vehicles. There was only one way out, and he took it. He didn't even look back. He turned and ran into the cemetery, into the darkness, past Caitlin's headstone and into the darkening night.

'John!' she shouted.

Caitlin tugged against me, but I held on.

I wasn't going to let go.

Epilogue

Weeks later, I return to the park with Caitlin.

It's early December. The leaves are all stripped from the trees, and the first frost has already come and gone.

It was Abby who'd called the police that night.

It took her a while to think of it, but she, like Buster, knew me well enough to know the spot I'd pick for a meeting with Colter.

The police arrested John Colter in the cemetery as soon as they arrived. He'd had nowhere to run, and they found him crouched behind a mausoleum. He had slipped in the wet grass and twisted his ankle, making his escape all but impossible. As Ryan had promised, new indictments were handed down against Colter, charging him with the kidnapping and sexual assault of Caitlin. In the wake of his intention to flee the area, his bail was revoked and he remains in custody at the county jail awaiting a trial in the spring.

Whenever I ask Ryan about the possibility of a conviction, he hedges his bets and reminds me that sometimes plea deals have to be struck, especially when eyewitness and forensic evidence remains slim. Caitlin refuses to testify or admit anything, and I try my best to believe that John Colter no longer exists.

The murder of Tracy Fairlawn remains unsolved,

although it is widely suspected she was killed by John Colter. Murder charges may still be forthcoming against him.

Jasmine, the cemetery girl, has never been found. Ryan suspects she's a runaway, and it seems little effort is being expended on tracking her down.

For a while after Colter's arrest, I found myself in trouble with the prosecutor's office. They were displeased with my actions on those nights, and they contemplated pressing charges against me. Obstruction. Witness tampering. Assault. In the end, they did nothing but scare me. When news of the arrest reached the public, popular sentiment turned my way, and the prosecutor's office, facing an election year, decided against continuing their pursuit of the father of a kidnapped and confused child.

My family was not so forgiving. It took less than forty-eight hours for Abby to move out – taking Caitlin with her. They made temporary quarters in dormitory-style housing at Pastor Chris's church. Abby has filed for divorce, which I have no plans to contest, but I see Caitlin just about whenever I want, especially on weekends.

Caitlin is not allowed to have any contact with John Colter while he is in jail. No letters, e-mail, or phone calls. To do so might lengthen his sentence, and as far as we can tell, neither he nor Caitlin has violated those terms. She continues with her therapy – both with Dr Rosenbaum and with Susan Goff – and no doubt receives plenty of unsolicited help from Pastor Chris when she's at the church.

I've brought the situation up only once with her, just a week after John Colter's arrest.

'He ran away in the cemetery,' I said. 'He didn't try to help you.'

'He was scared. The police were after him.'

I should have let it go, but I had to know one more thing.

'So what are you going to do now?' I asked.

She didn't hesitate. 'I'm going to wait for him.'

Buster and I have spoken to each other only once since that night. He, too, faced more heat at the hands of the prosecutor's office in light of his connection to Loren Brooks. But after careful examination and investigation, it was determined that Buster had broken no laws.

He called me one night, out of the blue, the phone ringing late while I was reading in bed. He didn't identify himself when I answered, nor did he ask how I was doing or waste any time with pleasantries. He jumped right in.

'Why did you grab Caitlin and take her away with you that night at the cemetery?' he asked. 'You seemed deter-mined to hand her over.'

I took my time answering. While I thought about it, Buster waited patiently. He didn't push me or hurry me along.

'I didn't plan to give her away,' I finally said. 'In the end, my instincts as a father are stronger than anything else. I could never let my daughter go with a man like that.'

There was another long silence. Then Buster said, 'That's about what I figured.'

He hung up, presumably satisfied.

Caitlin and I often walk in the park. We don't talk about everything that happened there, but I take it as a good sign that she's willing to go back. She may be returning there out of a sense of nostalgia for its associations with John Colter, but whenever that thought enters my head, I chase it away. Instead I choose to believe that this is a step toward the future and not a glance back at the past.

On this particular day, we sit on a bench near the walking and jogging trail. Fewer people pass this time of year, the cold having chased all but the hardiest of exercisers indoors. The tips of my ears and my cheeks tingle. My hands are balled into fists inside my pockets. I notice, for the first time, that Caitlin no longer wears the topaz necklace, her birthstone, the one John Colter gave her while he was holding her. I take it as a small victory, although I don't comment on it.

From where we sit, I can see the cemetery. The spot on the ground where I wrestled with Colter and, beyond that, where Caitlin's headstone once stood. It's gone now, removed in the wake of Colter's arrest.

I'm enjoying the day, enjoying what little time I have with Caitlin even now.

I've almost allowed myself to relax, to believe that our life is returning to some semblance of normal – or what normal will be for us in the future.

And when my guard is sufficiently lowered, Caitlin jumps up from the bench.

It takes me a moment to process the speed of her movement and the direction she's heading in.

She's running toward the cemetery.

Running *away* from me.

I follow, calling her name, my breath huffing. Little puffs come out of my mouth and disappear in the air.

But just as quickly as I start, I understand.

I can't believe what I'm seeing – but I understand.

Caitlin stops in the middle of the park. She goes down on one knee.

There's a dog jumping against her, licking and pawing at her. A very familiar dog.

And when I get there, when I come alongside of them, I watch with the dog's stunned owners, an elderly couple holding an empty leash. They'd apparently adopted Frosty from the shelter and attempted to make him their own, but now they seem to realize he isn't their dog anymore.

And he never was.

Caitlin's face is streaked with tears, but she's smiling as the dog licks them away.

'You're home, Frosty,' she's saying. 'Oh, my Frosty. You're home. You're home.'

Acknowledgements

I have to begin by thanking Ed Gorman. Not only is Ed one of our finest writers; he has been a great friend and supporter of my work. Without Ed, this book wouldn't exist. And Tom Monteleone has believed in my work for many years. He's answered questions, boosted my morale, and advocated on my behalf more times than I can count. For their advice and support, I'm indebted to Will Lavender, John Lescroart, Jonathan Maberry, David Morrell, and Paul Wilson. I'd also like to thank my friends and colleagues in the English department and the Potter College of Arts and Letters at Western Kentucky University, especially Karen Schneider, Tom Hunley, David Lenoir, Mary Ellen Miller, and Dale Rigby. And a special thanks to my students past, present, and future, who teach me a lot about writing whether they realize it or not. For friendship above and beyond the call of duty, I'm grateful to Bob and Carrie Driehaus.

Special thanks to my editor, Danielle Perez, and everyone at New American Library/Penguin. Danielle's ability to ask the right questions at the right times, to gently guide and casually prod while always maintaining her sense of humor, has made this process more enjoyable than I ever thought it would be. And the book is better for her efforts.

And words cannot express the gratitude I owe my amazing agent, Laney Katz Becker, and everyone at Markson

Thoma. Laney has worked tirelessly on my behalf over the past two years, and her faith, wisdom, and patience have made me a better writer. I'm so fortunate to have Laney in my corner.

Finally, I have to thank Molly McCaffrey for ... everything.

If you enjoyed CEMETERY GIRL look out for

THE HIDING PLACE

Twenty-five years ago, the disappearance of four-year-old Justin Manning rocked the small town of Dove Point, Ohio. When his body was found in the woods two months later, the repercussions were felt for years.

Janet Manning has been haunted by the murder since the day she lost sight of her brother in the park. With the twenty-fifth anniversary of Justin's death looming, a detective and a newspaper reporter have begun asking questions, opening old wounds and raising new suspicions.

And a shallow grave holds the deepest secrets . . .

Read an extract now . . .

Prologue

What do you remember from that day, Janet?

Janet remembered the heat. The way it shimmered in waves in the distance, making the edges of the trees, the cars in the parking lot blurry and indistinct. Wherever she stepped, the grass crackled or the dirt puffed. The heat rose from the ground and scorched her feet through the soles of her cheap plastic shoes.

She was seven years old and in charge of her baby brother for the first time ever.

Janet watched Justin. She thought of him as a dumb four-year-old, a silly kid with a bowl of blond hair and a goofy smile. He sat with the other kids in the sandbox, scooping piles of sand into mounds with his hands, then smoothing them over. Back and forth like that. Sand up, sand down. Dumb and pointless. Something little kids would do. She watched him. Carefully.

But no, that wasn't right. That wasn't right at all . . .

Justin wasn't silly. And he didn't smile all the time. He was a quiet kid. A loner. He sat in the sandbox alone that day. And he didn't smile much. Not much at all. No one in her family smiled much, not when she looked back on her childhood . . . or even her life now.

What did she remember from that day? What did she really remember? It was so hard to —

Michael showed up.

She remembered that.

Michael showed up, her seven-year-old playmate, the boy from the neighborhood and school. Their parents were friends. They played together all the time. Her boyfriend, she liked to think and giggle to herself, although they never touched each other. Never hugged or kissed or held hands. They were too young for that, too young for a lot of things.

But Michael showed up wearing denim shorts with a belt like a long rope and sneakers with holes in them. His hair hung in his face, and he brushed it out of his eyes constantly. He lived on the other side of the park. And so Michael called her name, and when he did her heart jumped and she turned away from the sandbox and the swings and the other kids. And she followed Michael wherever he went. Across the playground, over the base-ball diamond, over by the trees. She followed him.

Is that all she did? Run across the playground?

It was enough. She let Justin out of her sight. Dad was at work and Mom was at home, and Mom let them go to the playground alone that day for the first time ever, but it didn't seem like a big deal. The park was near the school and the church and the other kids would be there, other kids they knew and even some parents. And all Mom said on that day when they left the house was, 'Janet, don't let Justin out of your sight. He's a little boy . . .'

But she did. She let Justin out of her sight.

Did she see the man?

Janet can't say anymore. She's seen his face so many times. At the trial. In the newspaper. The mug shot. His face stoic, his eyes round, the whites prominent. His full lips, his black face. Not really a man. Now when she looks at the face, she sees a kid. Seventeen when he was arrested, but tried as an adult. He would have looked like an adult back then, that hot day in the park . . .

But she doesn't know if she saw him.

Other people did. Adults and kids. He was in the park, talking to kids at the sandbox and the swings. He carried Justin, according to some of the witnesses. He paid special attention to her brother, they said. Walked around with him. Talked to him. Lifted him on his shoulders.

For years, Janet thought she saw that, thought she remembered that. The young black man with the frizzy hair and the dirty clothes carrying her brother on his shoulders. Justin's blond head up high, almost as high as the top of the swing set. Justin parading around like a champion. Being tricked by this man. And then being taken away.

But she doesn't really remember that, does she?

She thought there was a dog. A puppy. It ran through the park, and Justin ran after it.

Is that what happened? Is that how Justin got away?

What do you remember from that day, Janet?

She can't be sure anymore. Not after twenty-five years.

She isn't sure she saw the man that day. But she wishes she had. She wishes she knew.

And she really wishes she had kept her eye on Justin, like she was supposed to.

She didn't see the man and she didn't see Justin.

And when it was time to go home, when Janet finally did look around and try to find her brother, he wasn't there. The adults became hysterical and the police arrived and people asked a lot of questions, but none of it mattered.

Justin was gone. Long gone.

I

Janet hid the morning paper from her father. She saw it when she'd come downstairs, and even though she knew it was coming – knew for close to a week that an interview with her brother's murderer would be on the front page – the sight of it, the sight of his face, hit her with the force of a slap. And then she thought of her dad. His anger, his roiling emotions at the mere mention of Dante Rogers. She folded the front page in half, with Rogers's face inside the fold, and slipped it beneath a chair cushion.

Janet heard water running in the bathroom down the hall, then her father's feet on the hard wood. She was breaking her own rule. When she'd moved back in with her father after he'd lost his job, she'd made a silent vow not to be his household servant. She wouldn't become some version of a substitute wife to him – cooking, cleaning, laundry. But on certain days, she made exceptions. She took out eggs, cracked them into a skillet, and watched them sizzle. Summer work hours at the college left her just enough time to do it – and it might take the old man's mind off his troubles.

'Where is it?'

Janet turned. Her father, Bill Manning, filled the entrance to the kitchen. He was still tall – over six feet – but since being laid off he had gained about twenty pounds, mostly in the stomach and the face. He'd been out of work for nearly two years, ever since the recession had hit and his company, Strand Manufacturing, 'went in a different direction', which meant laying off anyone over the age of fifty. Twenty-seven years working in product development and then an unceremonious good-bye.

Janet recognized the foolishness of trying to hide the paper. She pointed to the chair. Bill picked up the paper and sat down. Janet put the eggs in front of him.

'I thought you said you wouldn't wait on me,' he said.

'I felt like it.'

'You felt sorry for me,' he said.

Janet didn't answer, but there was some truth in what her father said. Years ago, he'd lost his son and then his wife. Then came the recent job loss, and Janet moved in to help make sure he didn't lose the house. Her father might be reserved and distant – difficult even – but she never outgrew the desire to protect and help him. And that desire only became stronger as her father grew older. He was sixty-two and starting to look his age.

'Jesus,' he said. He folded the paper, snapping the pages into place with a flick of his wrists, and leaned close to read the story. 'Not even at the top . . .'

Janet knew what the story said. Her brother had disappeared twenty-five years ago that day, and the local paper was running a couple of stories to commemorate the anniversary. The first one detailed the life of Dante Rogers, the man convicted of killing her brother. Paroled three years earlier, slowly adjusting to life back on the outside, working part-time at a church on the east side of Dove Point, Ohio . . .

While her dad read the article and cursed under his

breath, Janet turned to the sink. She ran a rag over some dishes from the night before. 'Today's our day, remember?' she said. 'The reporter is coming over at two. I'm leaving work early —'

The paper rustled and fell to the floor. When Janet turned, her dad was cutting into his eggs, shoveling them toward his mouth with machinelike quickness. He paused long enough to ask a question. 'Do you know what I think of all this?' he asked.

'I can guess.'

He pointed to the floor where the paper rested, the article about Dante Rogers facing up. 'This article – it's like they want me to feel sorry for this guy. It reads like he got some kind of a bum rap because he went to jail for twenty-two years for killing a kid —'

'Did you read the whole story?' Janet asked.

Her dad kept chewing. 'I already lived it.'

Janet leaned back against the counter and folded her arms across her chest. 'He still says he's innocent,' Janet said.

Her father's eyes moved back and forth, giving him the look of a caged animal. His cheeks flushed. 'So?' He looked down at his plate, pushed the remains of the egg around, making a runny yellow smear. He didn't look back up.

'He says —'

'I don't want to hear it,' he said, dropping his fork. 'He just wants sympathy from people. Probably living on welfare.'

Janet took hold of the belt of her robe. She worked it in her hands, fingering it, using it almost like rosary beads.

'If it makes you feel any better, I don't really want to tell my story to the reporter either,' she said.

'I know the story. Rogers killed my boy. That's it.' He pushed away his plate and rose to his feet. The first year after being laid off, her dad dressed just like he did when he went to work – shirt and tie, neatly pressed pants. The past year had seen a change. He no longer dressed first thing in the morning and went days on end without shaving. He stopped reading the classifieds a few months earlier.

'Then I guess it's silly for me to ask if you want to do anything special today?' Janet asked.

'Anything special?'

'For the anniversary of Justin's death.'

'Have I ever before?' he asked. 'Have you?'

Janet shook her head. She hadn't. Every year, she tried to treat the day like any other day. She tried to live her life, work her job, and raise her daughter.

'Then there's your answer, I guess,' he said. 'What time's that reporter coming over?'

'I just said. Two o'clock. So, are you going to talk to her?'

He left his dirty dishes on the table. 'I've got nothing to say to any of them,' he said. 'Nothing at all.'

Ashleigh sent Kevin a text: *Where R U?*

She waited near the swings, the sun high overhead prickling the back of her neck. It was just eight thirty and already hot enough to send sweat trickling down her back. Ashleigh scuffed her sneakers in the dirt and checked her phone.

No response yet.

Where was he?

She watched the little kids scream and play. They ran around like monkeys, their mouths open, their hair flying. They never tired or stopped. Ashleigh felt something swell in her throat, an emotion she couldn't identify. She took a deep breath, like she needed to cry, but swallowed back against it, choking it down. She turned away. She couldn't watch the kids anymore. They looked so vulnerable, so fragile, like little glass creatures.

This is the park, she thought. *This is where it happened.*

Kevin came out of the trees. She recognized his loping gait, his broad shoulders. He wore his work uniform – black pants and a goofy McDonald's smock. He'd decided to grow his Afro out over the summer, and it made him seem even taller. Ashleigh took another deep breath, collected herself before Kevin arrived.

'Hey, girl,' he said.

'Thanks for writing back.'

'I got called in.' He pointed at his shirt. 'I have to be there at ten.'

'That's bullshit.'

Kevin shrugged, casual as could be. 'I have to earn my keep.'

'Let's get going then. These kids bug the shit out of me.'

They didn't talk much. Ashleigh imagined that the parents on the playground – the ones who always came to watch their kids, whether they knew what had happened there twenty-five years ago or not – had noticed the two of them: a tall black boy and a short white girl, walking side by side. She'd known Kevin for three years, ever since the first day of junior high, when they'd sat next to each other in history class. At first she thought he was dumb, maybe even retarded. He was so big, so quiet. Then she noticed the jokes he cracked at the teacher's expense, his voice so low only she could hear.

'What's your plan?' he asked.

They came out into the neighborhood that bordered the park. It was opposite where she lived with her mom and grandfather, and a little nicer too. She supposed it was upper middle class as opposed to simply middle class. Bigger houses, nicer cars. A neighborhood where no one got laid off.

They walked past older homes with nice yards. Retirees lived there, old people who spent their days digging in their gardens and sweeping their walks. If a piece of trash ended up in the yard, they'd probably call the police.

'I don't have one yet,' Ashleigh said.

'You usually have a plan for everything.'

'I don't for this.'

They reached Hamilton Avenue, a major road dotted with strip malls and gas stations.

Kevin said, 'So you're just going to go up to this dude and say, "Hey, what do you know about my dead uncle?"'

'Be quiet.'

Ashleigh looked down the road. She saw the bus.

'If I go with you . . .' Kevin sounded uncertain. 'I'm going to be late for work. I'll get written up.'

'Then don't go,' she said. 'Make hamburgers for strangers. Forget about all those football games I went to with you.'

'Come on, Ash. My dad says if I don't have a job this summer, he's going to kick me out of the house.'

'And remember how I helped you proofread your history term paper? Heck, I proofread all of your papers last year.'

'You're going to throw that back at me?'

'I'll go alone. The guy's probably not dangerous.'

'You know how my dad is,' Kevin said. 'He's old-school. He worked his way through college, so he thinks I need to earn my keep.'

The bus pulled up, air brakes exhaling. The diesel stank, burned Ashleigh's eyes. When the door rattled open, she didn't even look at Kevin. She just climbed on and dropped her coins into the slot, where they rattled like loose teeth. She moved down the aisle and took a seat, staring out the window and watching the traffic go by.

She picked up movement at the front of the bus, something in her peripheral vision.

'Hey,' the bus driver called.

It was Kevin. He ignored the driver and walked right back to Ashleigh's seat.

She looked up into Kevin's face. A cute face, she had to admit. Beautiful eyes. A little puppyish.

'What?' she said, trying to sound mad.

'You really want to do this?' he asked.

'Yes.'

'Come on, goddamn it,' someone yelled from the back of the bus.

'I have one problem,' Kevin said to her.

'What?'

'Can I borrow fifty cents?' he asked, smiling.

She reached into her pocket and handed him the coins.

3

Janet tapped lightly on Ashleigh's door. Nothing. Then she knocked again, using more force.

'Ash?'

The knob gave as she turned. Janet stepped into the darkened room and saw that Ashleigh was already gone, so she pushed the door open all the way. It wasn't unusual for Ashleigh to leave the house early. Not unusual at all. She'd be with Kevin most likely, or sitting at the library thumbing through books and magazines. Kevin. Ashleigh didn't bring him around much anymore, not since they'd moved in with Bill. But the two spent all their time together. Janet tried not to pry, tried not to be a nosy mother, but she wondered sometimes. Did her moody daughter have a boyfriend? That at least was a normal concern for a mother to have, worrying about her daughter's dating life. The other things Janet worried about were a product of her own childhood, and they made her heart flutter . . .

It's okay, she told herself. It's okay to let her out of the house. She's not a child – she's fifteen. She won't get taken and it'll be okay.

Janet reminded herself to breathe. She'd half entertained the notion of taking Ashleigh out to lunch or shopping, something to break the usual routine and mark the importance of the day. But Ashleigh was living her life, just the way Janet wanted her to. Why burden her or anyone else?

Janet turned her attention to the things in the room. She had to give Ashleigh credit for something else – the girl knew how to keep order. No teenage mess in that room. The bed was made, the closet closed. Janet went over and opened the blinds. The light fell across a neat row of photographs on the shelf above Ashleigh's bed. The photos were all familiar. Janet and Ashleigh at a school awards ceremony. A portrait of Janet's mother – high school graduation? – the grandmother Ashleigh never knew. And on the end, facing the light, the last portrait of Justin ever taken, the one that ran in the newspaper and on TV during the summer he disappeared. Janet picked the photo up, ran her hand across the dust-free glass.

Janet had once asked Ashleigh why she kept a portrait of her dead uncle above her bed. The girl just shrugged.

'It's the past,' she said. 'Our past. And isn't the past always with us?'

Janet shivered. Out of the mouths of babes . . .

She went to get dressed for work.

Janet had begun working at Cronin College fourteen years earlier. She'd started in the mailroom just after high school, sorting packages alongside work-study college students from all over the country. Ashleigh was a year old then. Janet didn't think she could work, raise a baby, and attend college, but she took the job at Cronin with an eye toward bigger things. She knew – *knew* – her daughter would go to college someday, and employees of the college received a huge tuition break. Janet even planned on getting a degree herself and had taken classes over the years as she worked her way from the mail processing center to the copy and print center to the chemistry department and finally to her current position working for the dean as office manager, overseeing a staff of five. She loved her job. She loved supporting herself and her daughter with her own work. She even enjoyed knowing that her job and salary helped her dad hold on to her childhood home.

But she didn't love her job the day the story about Dante Rogers ran in the paper.

As soon as Janet walked into the office, she knew everyone had read about it. Nobody said anything – at least not right away. But she could tell by the looks on their faces. Her co-workers smiled at her, but they weren't happy smiles. They were forced, toothless, the heads cocked to the side a little, the lips pressed tight. *Oh, you poor thing*, the smiles said. *The tragedy. You were there that day . . .*

You were supposed to be watching him . . .

In the break room during lunch, Madeline Hamilton, the office's resident busybody, approached Janet, sitting down next to her and casually removing a soggy sandwich from a plastic bag. Madeline had known Janet's mother, had landed the job in the dean's office with Janet's help. Janet knew Madeline's interest wasn't casual, and Janet even found herself happy to see the older woman cozying up next to her. She hoped someone would break the tension, pop the black balloon that seemed to be hovering over her head.

'So,' Madeline said, drawing out the *O*, her tiny mouth formed into a similar, circular shape. Madeline didn't bite into her food. She raised her right hand and fussed with the pile of bright red hair on the top of her head. 'Crazy day for you, huh?'

'Do you want to ask me something about the story?' Janet said.

Madeline took a bite of the sandwich and gestured with her free hand. 'If you need someone to talk to . . .' she said, the free hand floating in the air, a heavy, fleshy butterfly. 'I've always thought of you as family. And I know today's that awful anniversary. Are you going to the cemetery or anything?'

Janet shook her head. She had a Diet Coke and a bag of pretzels in front of her. She'd eaten two pretzels and barely touched the drink. 'They're interviewing me today.'

'Oh, really,' Madeline said. She wiped her mouth and set the food aside, shifting to all-business mode. 'But you read that story? The one today?'

'Yes.'

'Can you believe he's still here in Dove Point? Just living here? Among all of us?'

'Where is he supposed to go?' Janet asked.

'I'd think he'd want to live anywhere but here.'

'His parents are dead. He lived with his aunt . . . back then. But she's dead, too.'

'See,' Madeline said. 'No ties here. He could just pick up and move anywhere.'

'You make it sound so glamorous. He's an ex-con. What's he going to do? Besides, I don't think he's going to hurt anybody.'

'He's already killed two people,' Madeline said. 'First

Justin and then your mother. She'd still be with us if not for the grief.'

Janet didn't disagree. Her mother never recovered from her brother's death. Diabetes-related complications, they'd written on the death certificate nearly eighteen years ago. Janet knew the truth – her mother had died of a broken heart. But Janet just couldn't summon the same anger toward Dante Rogers that everybody else did.

'Don't you feel sorry for him?' Janet asked. 'Even a little? He looks so pathetic, so empty.'

'Sorry for him?' Madeline fanned herself with both hands. She looked like she was choking. 'Sorry? For a killer? He better hope he doesn't come my way or cross my path. I can't be held responsible.'

Janet checked the clock. She needed to get back to her desk. The dean's office didn't rest in the summer, despite the shorter hours. In fact, summer brought more work. Annual reports, budgets, faculty travel arrangements. But she wasn't ready to go back.

'Do you ever wonder?' Janet said. She knew her voice sounded dreamy, distracted. She didn't know what she wanted to say. She didn't know if she should even give voice to her thoughts.

'Wonder what?' Madeline asked.

'The way he maintains his innocence, even after all this time. He has no reason to. He's already done his time.'

'Remember what was lost,' Madeline said. 'Your mother never had the life she wanted because of that man. And neither did you. You've been without a mother for eighteen years because of that man.'

'I'll see you later, Madeline.'

'You call me and tell me how it went when you're finished.'

Janet left without agreeing to make the call.

But Janet didn't go back to work. She took the back stairs down to the parking lot. She stepped out into the hot day, felt the wave of humidity wash over her. The trees just beyond the parking lot were a rich summer green and the traffic on Mason Street just off campus hummed back and forth, the steady rhythm of Dove Point's life. When she needed a break from work, a moment alone or a moment to think, she came to the back of the building. No one else ever went there unless they were coming or going from their cars. Janet knew she could steal a quiet moment.

She noticed the man almost immediately. He stood by a parked car, watching her as she stepped outside. The man was tall and lean like a runner. He looked to be the same age as Janet, and despite the heat, he wore jeans and a long-sleeve button-down shirt. Even though about two hundred feet separated them, Janet could sense the piercing nature of his eyes. Was he a faculty member, perhaps someone newly hired she had never met? She thought of turning away, of simply stepping back inside Wilson Hall and going back to work, but something about the man's posture and the way he held his head looked familiar to her. She had seen this man before – hadn't she? – but not for a long time.

And then he raised his hand and made a waving gesture, beckoning her to him.

He just wanted a decent book to read ...

Not too much to ask, is it? It was in 1935 when Allen Lane, Managing
Director of Bodley Head Publishers, stood on a platform at Exeter railway
station looking for something good to read on his journey back to London.
His choice was limited to popular magazines and poor-quality paperbacks –
the same choice faced every day by the vast majority of readers, few of
whom could afford hardbacks. Lane's disappointment and subsequent anger
at the range of books generally available led him to found a company – and
change the world.

*'We believed in the existence in this country of a vast reading public for intelligent
books at a low price, and staked everything on it'*
Sir Allen Lane, 1902–1970, founder of Penguin Books

The quality paperback had arrived – and not just in bookshops. Lane was
adamant that his Penguins should appear in chain stores and tobacconists,
and should cost no more than a packet of cigarettes.

Reading habits (and cigarette prices) have changed since 1935, but
Penguin still believes in publishing the best books for everybody to
enjoy. We still believe that good design costs no more than bad design,
and we still believe that quality books published passionately and responsibly
make the world a better place.

So wherever you see the little bird – whether it's on a piece of
prize-winning literary fiction or a celebrity autobiography, political tour
de force or historical masterpiece, a serial-killer thriller, reference book,
world classic or a piece of pure escapism – you can bet that it represents
the very best that the genre has to offer.

Whatever you like to read – trust Penguin.

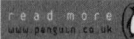